Praise for Fanny Blake

...t, Blake offers a
...amily's enthralling drama'
Sunday Express Magazine

...e friendship comes under the microscope ... a fabulous
page-turner'
Prima

'An easy-to-read, sun-soaked family drama'
Sunday Mirror

'A deliciously witty look at female friendship'
Daily Express

'Full of interesting characters and intriguing twists and turns,
once started you will be completely absorbed in the story.
Highly recommended' Kaye Thorne, *Hot Brands Cool Places*

Fanny Blake was a publisher for many years, editing both fiction and non-fiction before becoming a freelance journalist and writer. She has written various non-fiction titles, acted as a ghost writer for a number of celebrities, and is also Books Editor of *Woman & Home* magazine. To find out more visit www.fannyblake.co.uk or follow her on Twitter @FannyBlake1

Also by Fanny Blake

What Women Want
Women of a Dangerous Age
The Secrets Women Keep
With a Friend Like You
House of Dreams

Novella

Red for Revenge

Our Summer Together

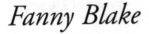

Fanny Blake

First published in Great Britain in 2017 by Orion Books,
an imprint of The Orion Publishing Group Ltd
Carmelite House, 50 Victoria Embankment,
London EC4Y 0DZ

An Hachette UK Company

1 3 5 7 9 10 8 6 4 2

A CIP catalogue record for this book
is available from the British Library.

ISBN 978 1 4091 5992 6

Typeset at The Spartan Press Ltd,
Lymington, Hants

Printed and bound by the CPI Group (UK) Ltd,
Croydon, CRO 4YY

www.orionbooks.co.uk

For Clare A, with love

Caro ran her finger over the page in her sketchbook, following the contours of his face, remembering that moment when she had first picked up her pencil to sketch him. She had already been falling for him then but still refusing to admit it to herself. Too many obstacles stood in their way. She followed the straight line of his nose, the curl of his nostril, the curve of his cheek, the livid trace of his scar, then lay the book down on her bed.

Damir.

She had been sleepwalking through her life when he came into it. Her marriage over, her daughters having left home, she was getting through the days on automatic pilot with little thought for herself or what lay ahead. Meeting him had changed all that. What he had been through humbled her and drew her to him; and he had allowed her to believe in herself again and imagine a future.

They'd had one summer together, just one summer, in which they had lived and loved against the odds.

And now he had gone. He had left without explanation. Was he missing her as much as she was him, she wondered. Or had he forgotten about her already? Could he really want to cut short so soon the adventure they had begun together? Her heart screamed, No. Her head answered, Perhaps. Perhaps she should have expected this. He had once said that he never stayed in one place for too long, that he always moved on. Was he that allergic to commitment? At the time she had not paid proper attention, but now how she wished she had.

Perhaps if she'd challenged him then, things would be different now.

In the kitchen, the dog gave a sharp bark at something. She started then put down her pencil and sketchbook and stood up. Could it be him? Could he have come back, after all?

She went downstairs but there was no one there. She opened the back door and let the dog into the garden. Turning back into the house her gaze landed on the calendar that she had marked during every day of their affair. Longer than she had thought possible. Shorter than she would have liked. She unhooked it from the wall and tore off all the marked pages with a heavy heart. Nothing would be the same now. She screwed them up and put them in the recycling before standing at the door and staring out at the garden that, like the house, was so full of memories. She could almost hear the shouts of the children when they were young, the clink of glasses from parties, the laughter when her family was at its happiest. She had spent many contented years planting and nurturing and soon both it and the house would no longer be hers.

She went back to the bin to retrieve the calendar pages. She smoothed them out on the table, reordering them so March was on top. Six months ago. So much had happened since then. A small, pencilled dot marked the Monday they had met: the Monday when Fate had thrown them together and her life had changed.

I

All Caro wanted was to be at home, preferably stretched out on the sofa in front of a decent film. Instead she was on a crowded train travelling in the right direction with another hour to go. Everywhere there was noise when all she longed for was peace and quiet.

She shifted in her seat, straightened her legs, feeling a sharp reminder of where her grandson, Danny, had rammed his tricycle against her shins. Through the window everything was pitch black. All she could see was her own reflection, her hair unruly. She closed her eyes against the unwanted reminder of time passing and pressed her forehead against the cold glass. Looking after just one small child for a day had exhausted her. Hard to imagine now how she had once looked after two of her own without batting an eyelid. The wheels clattered over the tracks and the carriage swayed from side to side. Lickety split. Lickety split.

She opened her eyes as the motion of the train bounced her head off the glass and back again. Shifting again in her seat to get more comfortable she picked up the paperback that lay face down, broken-backed on the fold-down table in front of her. After a minute or two, she put it down again, unable to concentrate, and took a sip of her gin and tonic. Better.

Perhaps that man was on the train again. She had looked up and down the aisle when she got on but just because she always got in the third carriage didn't mean that he would too. If he was on the train at all. She'd probably never see him again.

He had looked like a man with a story.

3

She took another sip. And what story would that be? God only knew.

She hadn't recognised the language of the newspaper he had with him. He hadn't looked happy as he read it. Did it take one unhappy person to recognise another, she wondered. But she wasn't unhappy, she reminded herself. Not exactly.

The previous week, he had sat beside her, leaning back in his seat, eyes shut, earphones in, grey hoody overlapping the collar of his dark waterproof coat. The music he was listening to leaked from his earphones in tinny bursts. She was on the point of asking him to turn it down when she heard the rattle of the refreshments trolley. This was her favourite part of the journey home: the moment when she began to be her own woman again: just herself, no one's ex-wife, mother or grandmother.

'A gin and tonic, please.' The words were almost out before the attendant had put the brake on the trolley.

As the ice was being shaken into the plastic beaker, Caro had reached down for her bag. Her wallet felt oddly bulky. She unzipped the purse to find no cash just a few of her grandson's Lego bricks. The man beside her was pulling out his earphones and asking for a cup of tea.

She remembered looking at the beaker of ice, the inviting little green plastic bottle of gin and the tin of tonic before picking them up to give back. 'I'm sorry, but I don't seem to have any money. My grandson . . .'

'That's all right, love.' While the attendant finished making her neighbour's tea, Caro rummaged in the bottom of her bag, hoping to find some loose change.

'Let me,' said the man next to her. 'How much?' he asked the attendant. 'Yes. For both.'

Caro couldn't place his accent. East European, maybe?

'That's very kind of you,' she jumped in, 'but I can't let you do that.'

4

'Why not?' He waved her away before counting out the cash. 'There.' He passed the gin and tonic back to her.

'Your lucky night, love.' The attendant had winked and smiled before turning to his next customer.

'Thank you.' She began to mix her drink. 'Best bit of the day.' But her joke was met with a polite smile. She had tried to talk to him, explaining about Danny taking her handbag and emptying her purse, telling him about her family then asking him about his. But he was less forthcoming. All she had elicited from him was that he had been married once, and no, he had no children. At her question, he had shut his eyes, taken a breath. She hadn't imagined it. He hadn't been unpleasant but he apparently did not intend his generosity to be taken as a sign of wanting anything from her. Her usual knack of getting people to open up to her hadn't worked at all. Instead he held back, maintaining his reserve.

Someone was walking down the aisle, grabbing at the seat tops to keep their balance, swaying with the motion of the train. Him! It was as if she'd conjured him out of the ether. He saw her and stopped.

'Hello.' He stood looking down at her. This time she registered how tall he was, his slight belly, his dark unreadable eyes. A man somewhere in his forties, she guessed, younger than her, his hair flecked with grey just above his ears. There were specks of paint on his hands and under his nails.

'Hi. I was hoping I'd see you. I'd like to pay you back for last week.' She gestured for him to sit down. 'The trolley's been past but I'll go to the buffet.'

'There's no need.' He looked as if he was going to walk on.

'But I'd like to. It's the least I can do. Please.'

Looking reluctant, he nonetheless put his rucksack in the overhead rack and sat down. When she returned from the buffet with his cup of tea, he'd moved to the window seat so she could sit beside him.

'You've been with your grandson ... Danny, isn't it ... again?' His smile sparked something in her, surprising her.

For a wild moment, she considered saying, No, I've just spent the afternoon with my Italian lover ... Yeah, right! Only in the wildest of her dreams.

'You remembered,' she said instead, flattered that he had. 'Yes. Every Monday. Danny's a handful at the moment. Terrible threes!' The tantrum he'd thrown as soon as Lauren came through the door that evening, under the pretext of not liking carrots – which he'd liked perfectly well the week before – had been one of his best yet: heels drumming on the ground, fists flailing. 'Attention-seeking, I suppose.' She turned to see if he'd understood. As he poured the capsule of milk and the sugar into his tea, she noticed the shape of his hands, strong and workmanlike, nails cut squarely. He turned to her, his smile revealing an even row of white teeth only marred by the two slightly overlapping in the front.

'You're still working in London, then?' she asked.

'Yes, but we've finished. I'm in Guildford next week.'

'Your English is so good.' Was that patronising? The last thing she wanted to be.

But he looked pleased. 'I learned a little at school, but I spoke it a lot when I lived in Germany.'

'But you're not German?'

He shook his head. 'No. I go from Bosnia to Germany.'

'And then to here,' she prompted him.

'Yes. To Birmingham and then my friend writes to tell me there is work down here. Sometimes I work with him, sometimes on my own. The rent is better out here than in the city and I'm with friends.'

'Bosnia?' She wasn't even sure where exactly it was. Somewhere in the Balkans, near Croatia, she thought.

'Yes, I left in the war.' She could see the shutters had come down again so tried a different tack.

'And you're a painter?'

He held his hands out in front of him and laughed. 'You guessed?! A painter and decorator. I was to be a carpenter but there wasn't enough work. And you?' He nodded towards the leg of her jeans.

When she had dressed that morning, she had thought the splat of Sap Green was so small no one would notice it. 'Different kind of painting. I'm a portrait painter and art teacher.'

'You paint people?'

'I sometimes work from photographs too, but I prefer to paint the person in front of me if I can. It doesn't feel so second-hand, and a painting is so much more than just a moment in front of a camera.' She looked to see if he understood.

'That must be hard.'

'It can be, but I love it. I've met some interesting people and it's fascinating how much you learn from the smallest move-ment.' She almost started to tell him about the family portrait she'd been working on, what she had gathered about the parents' testy relationship while she painted, from their body language as they sat with each other and how it contrasted with the cheery façade they presented to the world, but thought better of it. Why would he be interested in people he had never met? But she was pleased with what she had achieved. Another two sessions, and the painting would be ready.

When silence fell between them, he put in his earphones. Caro took the hint, picked up her book and pretended to read but the noise of his music distracted her so she stared out of the window instead.

As they approached Guildford, he stood up, hauling down his rucksack from the overhead rack. She stuffed her book into her bag.

'My car's in the car park. Can I give you a lift?' Immediately she regretted her offer. He could be anyone.

'So's my van.'

7

Why ever had she assumed he wouldn't have his own transport? She hadn't read him right at all.

He walked with her down the platform. When they reached the exit, he stopped. 'Let me walk you to your car. It's not nice for a woman on her own at this time of night.'

'That's kind of you.' He was right. It was a short walk but one that she never liked doing on her own. Too many TV police dramas had taught her nothing good ever happened in a car park. When they reached her Lexus, she unlocked the door, aware he was waiting for her.

'Thank you for the tea.' He gave a little bow. 'And if you ever need any decorating...' He pulled his wallet from his jeans pocket, took out a business card and presented it to her. Then he bowed again and turned to walk away with an almost imperceptible limp, pulling his hood over his head. She watched as he took a pack of cigarettes from his pocket, flicked one into his mouth and lit it. He tilted his head back and a plume of smoke rose into the air above him.

Caro stuffed the card in her pocket without even looking at it and got into the car. His giving it to her had felt more intimate than a mere business proposition. She dismissed the thought. He was touting for work – that's all – and who could blame him? She switched on the radio and put him right out of her mind.

The landline was ringing as she turned the key in her front door. Ignoring the post on the floor, she dumped her bag on the hall table and rushed into the sitting room. Too late. She sat down and switched on the nearest light. Even after two years she still half-expected to see the Tangerine Twist walls Chris had so loved – 'warm and welcoming,' he'd insist against her objections. Instead she was surrounded by the soft greys and greens she had taken months to choose, at first hesitating over changing anything that was 'his'. But once the colours on the walls had changed, so had the atmosphere in the room. Peace at last. No more of Chris's tutting and ticking about whatever had happened to him that day at the studios or about which programme she wanted to watch on TV. This room had been transformed to her taste and that had made a difference. One day she would get around to doing the rest of the house. She went over to the piano and played a few tentative notes – she really should practise more often. After a few scales and arpeggios, she embarked on her favourite 'Moonlight Sonata', a perfect match for her sombre mood, breaking off when her mobile started ringing from her bag. She reached the hall just as the ringing stopped.

'For God's sake!' She checked the caller ID and saw Amy's name. Caro still missed her younger daughter who had moved back in for a while after college then left home for a second time. Amy had been instrumental in getting Caro through the months immediately after Chris left. Sympathetic but upbeat was her style and, not wanting to show how crushed she really was, Caro had done her best to respond. It was true what they said: fake it to make it. The positive spin she initially faked gradually became a reality.

The cat flap in the kitchen snapped shut as Tigger came in from the garden to greet her. She missed the usual welcome from her dog, Milo, but Amy looked after him most Mondays. Caro bent down to greet the cat as he threw himself on the floor so she could tickle his stomach. He had arrived from nowhere and adopted her just when Chris had packed his bags. Another saviour.

'Just you and me tonight, old thing,' she said. 'I'm going to light us a fire and then we'll have supper. I'll get Milo tomorrow.'

Her mobile started ringing again. This time she was ready.

'Mum, it's Amy!' Her younger daughter sounded out of breath. 'Where have you been?'

'At Lauren's. She wanted me to stay over so she could go back to the office till I reminded her that it's my day in the shop tomorrow.'

There was a sigh of impatience from the other end. Amy never hesitated to show her frustration at her sister's exploitation of her mother's good nature. However, she moved swiftly on to what interested her more. 'That's what I was phoning about. You will be here tomorrow?'

'Tuesday. Aren't I always?'

When it came to arrangements, she and her daughter were at opposite ends of a spectrum. Amy relied on her mobile, arranging everything at the last minute. Caro liked knowing how her week was going to go in advance: it made everything less stressful.

Amy brushed Caro's question aside. 'Patrick's phoned in sick and there's no one to cover in the shop. I've got to start prepping a wedding tomorrow, I've got a funeral on Thursday, and Ellie's only coming in at lunchtime.'

Getting up at dawn to be behind the counter at Bloom wasn't Caro's favourite way of spending a day but she liked helping Amy and having the chance to spend time with her, even when things got fraught. Amy had high standards for her business and was a demanding boss, but she was a much-loved younger daughter too.

Caro pictured herself at the shop. The heating would be turned off in the front section where the flowers were and Amy would park Caro at the table by the door where she would sit, layered up like the Michelin Man, her fingers red with cold, her nose running. On the ground, the one-bar heater she took with her to ward off the chilblains made no discernible impact.

Can't wait. The words, thick with irony, were on the tip of her tongue but instead, she said, 'Don't worry, I'll be there. Don't you want to know how your favourite nephew is?'

'Of course I do. What did you get up to?'

'I took him to toddler yoga.'

There was a snort from the other end of the phone. 'For God's sake. What is Lauren like?'

'The classes would probably do her more good than Danny or

me. She's so stretched at work.' Caro felt a dart of disloyalty. 'I'm so old, I could be everyone's grandmother, but they're all really friendly. The things we have to do! I was hopeless. We had to sit it out in the end.'

'Lauren wouldn't have the patience. She's lucky to have you.'

Was she? Sometimes Caro wondered whether Lauren took in how much she did with Danny. Her work as a criminal lawyer seemed to leave little room for noticing much else.

'And Jason? How's he?' Caro was fond of Amy's hipster boyfriend who, to the family's delight, was proving a calming influence on her volatile daughter.

'Great. He's got some new project that I don't understand but he's happy and we're cool.' What Jason did as a digital business analyst was a mystery to all of them.

After they said goodnight, Caro stood holding the phone, wishing they could have gone on but knowing Amy had Jason to get back to now she had sorted work out for the next day. The girls had been so generous about including her in their lives, doing their best to help her get over their father's abrupt departure. She flashed back to their faces on the day when they found out – anger, grief, resignation. All of those emotions that she knew she had to deal with, as well as her own. Sometimes she even had the unworthy thought that the girls almost needed her to be bereft to justify the hurt and anger that they were feeling. If that had been the case at the beginning, the need had become habit.

Because Chris waited until Lauren and Amy had both left home before making his move, they all understood that he'd been unhappy for years but hadn't wanted to jump ship until the girls could look after themselves. His leaving threw all the good times and the bad into a new light.

'It's like nothing was what it seemed,' confessed Amy as she sobbed in Caro's arms. 'It was all a lie. He didn't love us at all.'

Everything they believed the family was had been overturned.

Then, a year ago, after several short-term girlfriends, Chris had announced he was in love with Georgie Florence, an actress with a bit part in his TV production of *Little Women*. Caro was adjusting rather better than she'd ever thought she would. She straightened her favourite picture, the rural scene that Chris had never let her hang after she'd bought it on holiday in France – 'too amateur,' he pronounced after she'd spent her own money on it. But she loved studying the brushwork, the build-up of the paint to convey the landscape. She adjusted it again. There.

Although she inevitably had her low moments, she had grown to understand them as being part of her recovery process. If anything, she was beginning to think it might be something of a blessing to be living on her own. She suspected Paul, a friendly graphic designer she had met at one of Fran and Simon's dinner parties, was harbouring hopes that their acquaintance might develop into something more, but she was unsure. He had been widowed a year or so ago, and Fran was taking huge pleasure in matchmaking them despite Caro's discomfort about conducting any relationship at all, let alone in the glare of her friend's inquisitive eye.

'Of course you bloody well should meet other men,' Fran had said. 'You've got years ahead of you.'

'Yes, I suppose I should,' Caro agreed. Liar.

To Fran's badly disguised delight Caro had met Paul for a quiet drink but they were both taking their new friendship very slowly indeed – one tiny step at a time. The truth was: the thought of anything more intimate than a walk over the Downs or a meal for two terrified her. It had been too long since she had been with anyone other than Chris.

She stroked the threadbare throw that covered the back of the sofa. Once upon a time Amy had taken it to primary school and used it to nap on during the sleep break. Her nametape was sewn on to one of the corners. Caro felt for it, then rubbed her thumb along it. Yes, it was good that the girls still needed her.

2

Every time Caro came to Bloom, Amy's ingenuity and obvious talent impressed her. That morning, five bicycle wheels were suspended in the window, each one with an explosion of flowers arranged at its hub, ivy trailing towards the floor. Beneath them were bicycle baskets overflowing with early daffodils and tulips. A blackboard advertised the coffee and cakes that could be bought inside – at the back where it was warmer.

She could see Amy moving around, picking flowers from the stands for one of the pre-arranged bouquets that would go under the outdoor awning to tempt people in a hurry. Her auburn curls were scraped back in a ponytail, emphasising a determined chin and eyes that sized people up on first sight. Caro tapped on the window so Amy swung round, alarmed, then smiled when she saw who it was, and unlocked the door to let her in. Inside, the invigorating scent of fresh flowers – hyacinths, freesia, blowsy pink lilies and stocks – was sharp in her nostrils.

The modest corner-shop front was deceptive. Inside was an Aladdin's cave that stretched back in a deep L-shaped room that Amy had divided into two – flowers at the front and coffee and cakes at the back where young mums gathered during the mornings and after school, accessible by a side door. Caro looked around her at the flowers, vases and gift cards. There was a big table with the till at one end and space for laying out the flowers for arrangement at the other.

The two women hugged as Milo ran out from the back, ecstatic to see Caro. She bent down to greet him then straightened up. She raised a hand to Amy's cheek, worried her daughter was looking tired.

'Oh, Mum, I'm so glad you're here.' She dodged her mother's hand, keen to get on.

Caro walked through the brick archway to the café at the back, stopping to consider the paintings by local artists on the wall – some of them hers – and checking if any of them had the red dot marking a sale. She was delighted to see her portrait of a lined Italian *nonna* she had met in Italy had been stickered.

What do you want me to do first?'

As she spoke, a van pulled up outside and hooted twice.

'That's the Dutchman. Bang on time. When he's brought in the flowers, could you condition them and get them in the buckets? Ellie washed a load last night, so they're in the back. Then there's a whole pile of admin... If you can bear to sort that out, I can finish off the displays and make a start on sorting out the wedding flowers.'

After she'd taken and dealt with the delivery from Holland, Caro went to the back of the shop to make them both a tea. She reached for cups and saucers from the collection of mismatched junkshop crockery that Amy loved. As she waited for the kettle to boil, her phone rang.

When she saw it was her mother, her worry-meter started ticking. Though elderly, May was still perfectly able but naturally Caro was her first stop when there was a problem. And there were many. Caro's parents had moved south from Lincolnshire when her father retired so that they would be close to her and their grandchildren. Since her father's death Caro had felt the weight of responsibility for her widowed eighty-three-year-old mother. Not that May needed much – not yet. But Caro was always watching for signs of her deterioration into all the things old age was advertised to bring. She did her best to help when she could but May was not always easy. She came from a generation that had experienced and dealt with the tragedy of world war, to emerge with that stiff upper lip and a determination to get on with life because there was no choice.

'Do you think I need double-glazing? Someone's just quoted me such a good deal.' Her mother never wasted time with small talk.

'How many times have I told you to hang up on those cold callers? They're sharks.' Caro squashed the familiar but unreasonable rush of anxiety and irritation.

'They sent someone to the house yesterday. Such a nice man.'

Caro sighed as May explained. Her mother's marbles were intact but her age and the fact she lived on her own made her a perfect target for savvy salesmen. And sometimes she was lonely so she invited them in. Caro worried what might happen.

'. . . eight thousand pounds.'

'How much?! Tell me you haven't signed anything.'

'No, but he's coming back. I said I needed to think about it.'

By the time she persuaded May that she didn't need double-glazing, Mandy and Sarah had arrived in the café and the smell of coffee was drifting through to the front of the shop. Caro positioned herself at the front counter with the business laptop and some paperwork, the electric bar heater at her feet and Radio 2 in the background. The music occasionally took her back to life before Chris, to university, to her early independence and lack of responsibilities. To freedom. The songs reminded her of particular parties, old boyfriends, of falling in and out of love, the first joint. Those were the days, my friend. She stared out of the door, trying not to worry about May, wondering whether she should be doing something more decisive about her mother's living arrangements. But May liked where she lived, and her friends. Caro hummed to the Stones' 'Get Off of My Cloud', stuffing her fingers in her pockets for warmth where they touched the business card given to her by the stranger on the train. She took it out and looked at it for the first time. A yellow fleur-de-lys was set against a deep blue background with his name and contact details beside it: Damir Davić.

'What's that?' Amy was winding string round the bunch she had been working on.

'Just a card that a man on the train gave me.' Caro put it into her bag.

'A man? On the train? Mum!' Amy tied the knot and snipped off the ends, sweeping the cut stems and bits of string into the bin.

'Nothing like that! He bought me a gin and tonic last week because Danny had swapped my money for Lego. I saw him again and I bought him a tea as payback. That's all.' She couldn't help smiling. Her daughters could be like mother hens when it came to her. 'So don't go leaping to conclusions.'

Amy ignored her. 'He picked you up! Good for you. About time.'

'That's not what happened at all. He bought me a drink and I bought him one back. He even walked me to the car.' Admitting that piece of information was a mistake. The desire of her daughters and friends to find her a suitable partner was coupled with a degree of over-protectiveness that sometimes bordered on the stifling.

'To the car? Jesus, Mum. He could have been anyone.'

'Well, he wasn't. He was travelling home after a day's work in London. That's all.'

'What did he look like?'

'I didn't really notice.' Not true. She remembered the lines of his face and his five o'clock shadow, the scar on his cheek. He would make an intriguing portrait. 'He was younger than me, interesting looking.'

'A younger man. All the more reason to notice, I'd say. Was he hot?'

'I'm not actually looking for another man, thanks very much – however much you all think I need one. Your dad was quite enough for one lifetime. I'm perfectly happy with things the way they are. I know where I am.'

'Methinks the lady doth protest too much.' Amy elbowed her arm.

'Ow!' Caro rubbed the spot, then tapped the keyboard of the laptop so the screen came back to life. 'Stop it! I don't know. Maybe.' Yes, he was.

'All right, I give in. So . . . has anyone replied to your ad yet? I still think a lodger's a good idea. You enjoyed having Helen.'

'But she wasn't exactly a lodger. She filled the gap you left.'

'Aching void, you mean!' Amy teased. 'You've got to admit it was a genius idea of Fran's.'

When Fran had suggested her god-daughter rent a room from Caro while she did a year's apprenticeship at the Heathrow Academy, Caro had hesitated about sharing her home with someone she didn't know. Amy was one thing . . . but a stranger. In the end, she had been persuaded that she would be doing Helen a huge favour when in fact it turned out Helen had been doing one for her. Caro had enjoyed having her around and was sorry when she had moved out. Amy had convinced her to advertise for a lodger. 'Stupid to be rattling around in that big old house when it could be earning you some income.' She was right. The extra money did come in handy. Being self-employed was more hand-to-mouth than she would sometimes like. 'And they'll keep you company.'

'Two so far but they weren't right. One was your age and had blue hair. She was obviously dying to move out of home to somewhere she could have her friends over and party. So nope.'

Amy screwed up her nose. 'Don't be so judgmental.' She had started to pick out lilies and white roses for another bouquet.

'Says you! Anyway I'm not.' In fact, like Amy, she did make up her mind about people quickly, but that was only after years of practice. Or that was how she justified it to herself. 'And the other was an elderly man who wanted to bring his ancient Westie with him so what with Milo' – the dog lifted his head at the mention of his name – 'it was a non-starter. But I haven't given up. I just want to get the right person.'

'You didn't mind me and Lauren having people round.' Amy had reverted to the young woman with blue hair.

'I'm not having her... Someone else will turn up. Anyway, I think I'd like someone a bit older. It might be quite fun. I don't want to be anybody else's mother.'

Amy's raised eyebrows said what she thought of that.

'But that's what happened. Helen was always pouring out her woes about work. As for her love life... I want someone who'll keep their distance.'

'I thought you liked discussing love lives.'

'Only if they're yours or Lauren's. And even then, there's a limit! Talking of which, what about you and Jason?' She remembered their last conversation. 'Cool's a good thing, right?'

'Actually...' There was a pause as Amy put the flowers in a bucket at her feet. 'I've been meaning to tell you. I think we're going to move in together.' She waited for her mother's reaction. 'At least once his flatmate Ben's moved out, some time in the summer.'

'You are? But that's great.' Caro was genuinely pleased. After getting to know him, Jason seemed a decent and thoughtful guy who probably deserved someone less high-maintenance than her daughter but he certainly brought out the best in her. The last time they had been together, she had caught him gazing at Amy as if he couldn't believe his luck.

'It's a way off, but you don't think it's a mistake, do you? Lauren says we should.'

Caro glanced at her daughter who had already moved on to the next arrangement and was picking out neon orange, red and pink gerberas. 'Do *you* think it is?'

'No, of course not.' But Amy sounded unsure. 'Suppose it doesn't work?'

'Why shouldn't it?'

'I do love him, I do, but sometimes . . . oh, I don't know. I don't really understand what he does all day. Digital business analyst! What does that even mean?'

Caro thought of her own marriage, begun in such a whirl of optimism and excitement ending in such shattering disappointment. 'It's not as if you're getting married. Think of it as a trial run.'

'I don't think I believe in marriage any more.' Amy put the new bunch into its own bucket and moved it to the door. Of the two girls, she was the one who had been most upset by Chris's defection. Her disillusionment about marriage had come from that, Caro was sure. Lauren's hurt, on the other hand, had been channelled into a fierce anger towards her father for letting them all down.

'Nobody's saying you should, and anyway, you may change your mind.' Caro moved on, not giving her own feeling of responsibility for Amy's disenchantment time to sink its claws deeper. Could she have tried harder to keep the marriage together? 'Lauren's right. If you don't take a chance, you'll never know.'

'I suppose.' Amy straightened up, her hands full of flowers. She went over to the table and laid them out ready to arrange, leaving Caro to answer the phone if it rang. 'Just shout if there's anything you don't understand or can't deal with.' She turned back to her mother. 'I am excited really. Just nervous. I want it to work more than anything.'

'I know.' Caro stood and watched her for a moment. All she wanted was for both her daughters to be happy. Was that such a big ask? She went back to the laptop and the paper bills entering the amounts on monthly spreadsheets, filing them, not looking up until the phone rang with a customer making an order for a delivery. She took the details, steering the customer's flower choice to cover what she could see Amy had in stock, choosing pale pinks and whites to celebrate the birth of a baby girl, and noting everything down for her daughter. That done, she began to go through the cards on the stands, rearranging them, filling up the empty pockets with more from the drawer, before straightening and dusting the shelves of empty vases for sale. The next phone call came from a bride wanting to discuss her wedding flowers. Caro made an appointment for her in the diary later in the week.

Before returning to the laptop, she looked in her bag, hunting for her lip salve. Encountering the stranger's card again, she took it out from the bottom of her bag, stared at it again, thoughtful, then tucked it safe in her purse.

3

A waiter led Caro into an almost empty dining room full of black-lacquered tables laid with rush mats and chopsticks. Pictures of Mount Fuji and a couple of pagodas in cherry blossom time completed the Japanese vibe. At her table, she ordered a bottle of white wine. Fran was always late but Caro never minded. She had dashed home from Bloom with Milo, changed, and come straight out again so was glad to have a moment or two to sit alone and reflect. She knew what Fran would want to talk about.

Caro had long wrestled with her conscience over her friend's affair and where her loyalties lay. Her friendship with Simon, Fran's husband, went back a long way to when they had all met at some ghastly school quiz evening. The other parents on the team, including Chris and Fran, were hideously competitive so she and Simon had observed from the sidelines, bonding over how slow they were with their answers and their failure to take the whole thing sufficiently seriously. They were responsible for the team's humiliating defeat. She and Fran had gone on to forge the closest of friendships after a joint stint as school governors when they discovered a shared disrespect of authority and sense of humour. But her friendship with Simon was almost as important to her as the one she had with Fran. She had been over the reasons why she hadn't told him Fran was seeing Ewan behind his back hundreds of times. She had been a coward. Saying nothing meant never confronting the situation or involving herself. But if Simon were ever to find out she had known all along, he would see her silence as a betrayal. And he'd be right.

Before Chris had announced their marriage was over, Caro had indulged Fran's affair, believing it was just a flash in the pan. But after his departure, not long after the affair had begun, she felt increasingly angry and impatient with her friend. 'Do you know what you might be doing to a family?' she had asked, raw from her own break-up, exhausted from juggling her own and her daughters' seesawing emotions. 'Look at mine.'

But Fran had dismissed her concerns. 'It's not the same. We're not harming anyone. No one knows apart from you.'

And more than two years on, Caro's knowledge of the affair had become part of her and Fran's friendship. It seemed too late to say anything, and anyway was it her place? So she tolerated it. Was this wrong? Probably. But their friendship was too important to her to risk.

'You look exhausted.' Fran's voice made her turn. 'You OK?'

The first thing Caro saw was the large faux-fur hat that made her friend look as if she'd walked off the set of *War and Peace*. 'Just a day in the shop.'

Fran took off her voluminous check coat and scarf, draping them over the back of her chair so they immediately slid to the floor. 'You don't really enjoy working there, do you?' Fran, a theatrical agent working in a small company, didn't believe that anyone could enjoy working somewhere without central heating, or doing anything that they didn't really love. 'Life's too short,' she'd say. Her positive attack on life was one of the things Caro loved about her. Their careers couldn't be more different, but Fran's was a fund of good stories that Caro could relate to, some of them even about Chris, who Fran occasionally had to wrangle with professionally. That had sometimes made things difficult between the four of them, but unlike Chris, Fran made an effort (not always successful) not to bring the office home with her. She removed her hat and put it on the table before picking up and reorganising her coat on the chair. She looked fabulous, her clothes as bright as her personality. Black was not an option in her wardrobe.

'I like being with Amy and helping her out. The work's not the point. Wine?' Caro poured a glass for her as Fran stuffed her hat into her orange bag.

Fran sat down with a sigh. 'I'm gasping. Cheers! What a day. I've been battling for a part for Jon Flood in *EastEnders* then, when I finally secure it, he only turns it down. It's beneath him! Can you believe it?!' Settled into her seat, Fran returned to her original subject. 'But seriously, you should say no to Amy some-times. Those girls take advantage of you.'

Caro looked at Fran. *And don't you do the same, sometimes?* Hastily she dismissed the thought, springing to her daughters' defence instead. 'No, they don't. I agreed to this arrangement. I like being involved with their lives. I can always say no.' She pulled a face at what they both knew was a lie. 'You'd be the same.'

Fran shook her head, not a hair of her chic crop moving out of place. 'Yes, I admit I drove Will's laptop to Newcastle when he needed it for revision but he had an exam the next day.'

Caro laughed. 'And you paid for him to go to Italy with you last summer. You spoil him.'

'OK. We're both still slaves to our children even though they've left home and are supposedly fending for themselves. But he doesn't really need me or Simon any more, and I get that. I couldn't wait to get away from my parents either. We're doing it for us really, aren't we?'

Caro and Fran were different in many ways, and this was one of them. Despite her occasional complaints, Caro enjoyed being part of her daughters' lives. Her own would be so much emptier if she weren't. Was that the difference between having daughters and sons? She twisted the two semi-eternity rings that Chris had given her when first Lauren and then Amy were born around her finger. She always wore them as a memento of the happiest days of her life. The tiny diamonds flashed in the light. 'Wait till you have grandchildren.'

'Not something that's on the cards, thank God. Will's too busy in London, working hard and playing hard. Who'd have thought he'd end up a City boy?' A note of pride had entered her voice. 'I can't even keep track of the girlfriends.'

'You wait. You'll love them.' A memory from the day before of feeding the ducks with Danny and seeing his happiness at them squabbling over a bit of bread gave Caro a little glow of pleasure.

'Not yet. I'm not ready. Really not. It's way too aging apart from anything else.' Aging was not something Fran would do without a fight. 'What do you think of the hair?'

Caro wasn't sure how it differed from the last time they had met. 'I like it shorter.'

'I had it lightened a bit,' Fran corrected her with an arched, neatly threaded eyebrow. 'Lifts my face, I think.'

'Your face doesn't need lifting.' Caro picked up the menu although she knew exactly what they would order.

'Why don't you try it? Might make all the difference with Paul. Have you seen him again?'

'No.' In fact they had gone to see the latest Matt Damon movie together only a week ago but there was nothing romantic to it. She didn't want to enflame Fran's hopes.

Fran narrowed her eyes and squinted at her. 'Really?'

Caro laughed. 'It's not about to happen, whatever your fevered imagination is telling you. He's a friend.'

Fran looked disappointed. 'Why not? He's a nice man. You could do a lot worse. You should make the effort anyway.'

Caro didn't need reminding that since Chris had left, she had stopped paying the attention Fran thought every woman should give herself, but Fran was determined Caro shouldn't shrivel away unnoticed in life. With Caro's best interests at heart, she was a hard taskmaster – stimulating and irritating – and Caro loved her for her energy and the fact that she cared.

'I mean it. You look great but you could look even better with those curls under control. Why don't you go and see Nina? Say I sent you?'

'Maybe.' The idea of a new hairstyle was vaguely appealing. Caro pushed the offending curls back behind her right ear. 'What are you going to have?'

'The usual. And this is on me by the way.'

Caro couldn't read Fran's expression. There was clearly some kind of agenda she had missed. 'Why don't we just split it?'

'I insist.' Fran raised her glass. 'I need to ask you something.'

Caro braced herself. Of course this meeting wasn't going to be all about how she could improve herself. There was always some drama going on in Fran's life, at home or at work, and Caro didn't have to guess what this might be about. She sipped her wine. 'Just don't ask me to cover for you, that's all. You know how uncomfortable it makes me. Let's get on and order.'

'You don't even know what I'm going to say.' Fran pretended a pout. 'But OK, let's get the food out of the way.'

Once the waiter had taken their order, Fran put both forearms on the table and leant forward, looking intent. 'You're right. It is Ewan.'

'You promised you were going to cool it down.' Not that Caro had ever really believed she would. It was over two years since Fran had met Ewan at the funeral of a mutual friend. He had travelled down from Scotland to be there. Caro had witnessed for herself the instantaneous attraction between the two of them. Simon had been away at one of his alternative health conferences so hadn't been there to discourage his wife from flirting with this stranger. Not so unusual. Fran liked men, and they liked her. Simon condoned her flirtations because they amused him. He liked his wife to enjoy herself and was confident they went no further. But this time, he would have been wrong. The flirtation had developed into a long-distance affair that had gone on for a couple of years with Simon none the wiser.

Not long after that funeral, Fran had called Caro just before she was due to teach her U3A art class. In a hurry, she'd taken the call, aware the waiting pensioners wouldn't appreciate her being late. Of all her pupils, they could be the most demanding, wanting every minute's worth from their hour.

'Ewan's asked me to dinner!' Fran didn't even wait for a hello.

'You're not going?' Caro could see her students through the glass door, looking in her direction.

'Of course I am. It'll be fun. Simon's away next week at another conference in Switzerland. He won't even know.'

'Even so . . .'

'Don't spoil things. Just because Chris never lets you out of his sight . . . Nothing's going to happen, if that's what you're thinking. It's just a night out with someone new who makes me laugh.' Her excitement was infectious.

'So you'll be telling Simon, then?'

'Of course not. He'd only worry.'

Caro allowed herself to be persuaded that nothing would come of it, that it was just a bit of fun. This was easily done since she believed that they had reached a point in their life where little changed. They had chosen their futures and were hurtling along well-maintained tracks towards the final destination. How short-sighted she had been.

She lifted her wine. 'You haven't said anything to him, have you?'

'Not exactly. I do feel guilty about Si and I meant to call it a day but the sex is too amazing. Still! I can't resist.' Her face had lit up. 'He does everything in the bedroom that Simon doesn't. And not just in the bedroom.'

Caro briefly considered her current non-existent sex life and was surprised by a tiny prick of envy that she hadn't felt before. Even in the last years of her and Chris's marriage, the space

26

between them in the emperor-size double bed had felt like a chasm. Maybe a new hair cut was the way to go after all? And Paul?

'He just knows all the right buttons to press. Si doesn't. Simple as that.'

'Can't you tell him?' Listening to Fran talk about Ewan made Caro feel guilty about Simon, too. She wanted Fran to be happy but not at his expense. 'We've talked about this so often. Last time you promised you'd end it.'

'I did try. And then . . . well, you know.'

Had Caro ever felt that sort of magnetic attraction to Chris? Of course she had – once – but so much had happened since, it was hard to remember the feeling. Her loneliness came rolling back towards her.

Fran looked around her then said quietly, 'You should try it, you know, then you'd understand.'

Should she? 'It's not the sex. It's just I hate you cheating on Si. He doesn't deserve it. Anyway, there's no way I'm about to try it, thanks.' Caro grinned, any earlier envy disappearing in a puff. 'Those days have long gone as far as I'm concerned. Getting the kit off, going to all that trouble . . . I haven't got the energy.'

'You'd be surprised. I used to think . . .' Fran stopped as Caro gave her a look. 'Anyway the point is, I haven't seen him for ages. We text and email a lot. And Skype sex . . . You've no idea.'

'No, I haven't.' She tried to roll a mental shutter over the image that Fran had just planted in her mind.

Fran laughed. 'Your face! I'm sure you weren't always this buttoned up.'

Wasn't she? Perhaps that was one of the reasons why Chris had gone looking elsewhere. She didn't like the thought that she might not have been exciting enough in bed for him. At the same time, she questioned whether she had ever felt that real spark that seemed to exist between Fran and Ewan. But what more could she have done?

'Don't look like that! I'm joking. Ewan's a bit more out there than most. That's all. But the point is he's coming down again in a few weeks, after I get back from the States. I think he wants us to make a proper go of things.'

'What?' Caro coughed as her wine went down the wrong way. 'You don't mean you're going to leave Si? You can't.' Them splitting up was unthinkable. Nothing would be the same after that.

They waited while the waiter put down the miso soups, the shared tempura, gyozo dumplings and a sushi board, angling everything till it was just so.

Fran snapped apart her wooden chopsticks with impatience. 'If you'd rather we didn't talk about it . . . I do get that it's difficult for you, but there's no one else I can talk to. No one else who I trust.'

Caro was touched. 'It's OK. I've come to terms with Chris leaving now, and with you having a better sex life than I've ever had. I can take it. My shoulders are broad!' She sighed as if Fran's confidences were a monstrous burden. But her friend had been such a support when Chris moved out – always available, always clear-sighted. Caro had poured out her heart time and again to Fran who had provided meals, poured wine, made endless cups of coffee and listened. No, she would never turn her back on her now. 'Don't do this to Si. He'll be devastated.'

If she wanted to talk, then they would, but Caro would be straight with her, as Fran always had been. That honesty was what gave their friendship that special closeness. 'But what about Si?' she began. Dear Simon: a man who had devoted his life to his family, who adored his wife and asked no questions. 'And anyway, why would Ewan suggest that now?' It made no sense.

'Why not now?' Fran challenged her. 'Neither of us have any kids to think about now they've all left home. We can do anything with our lives. It's the last throw of the dice.'

It might as well have been Chris talking.

'Don't be so melodramatic! Think about all the other things:

your finances; the house. What would happen to that? And where would you live? Would you move to Scotland? What about your job? This is insane.'

'Don't.' Fran put her head in her hands. 'It's so hard. I think about Simon all the time and I really don't know what to do. I love him and I don't want to hurt him, but I love Ewan too. Si's the loveliest most generous man, but he's just . . . well, I know him too well.'

'He doesn't deserve this.' Caro sipped her soup, her hands warmed by the lacquered bowl.

'Don't you think we all need a bit of excitement now and then?' Fran looked up at her, daring her to disagree.

Caro wondered how to reply. It was a long time since she had experienced true excitement. Did she miss it? 'Has Ewan talked about this before?'

Fran shifted in her seat, looking sheepish. 'Not exactly. You see, we always try to live in the present—'

Caro made a face. 'Oh please.'

Fran was undeterred. 'But then . . . last time he did say we must talk about the future.' Her eyes were shining like a child's at the prospect of Christmas. 'But work's got in the way, and now I've got to go to New York to see a few shows, check on how a couple of my clients are doing out there, find out what's coming up and meet up with the people who matter. I'm hoping the transfer of *Wild Horses* will take Marisa Flight with it. I've promised her I'll try to make sure they do. On Broadway . . .' She hummed a snatch of the tune. 'That's what they all want: a Broadway show. Then, when I get back, Ewan and I will get together.'

'Such a glamorous life.'

'You wish.' Fran's eyes glittered with excitement at the thought of the weeks ahead.

But Caro hadn't meant to sound envious. She would enjoy hearing about the shows, the meals, the people Fran met, but it wasn't something she wanted to be a part of herself. She was a homebird and was content to be so.

They picked at their sushi, both of them preoccupied by their thoughts. Fran prodded a piece of plump salmon with a chopstick. 'This is Simon, so kind, so dependable, but dull.' Then she added wasabi and ginger. 'And this is Ewan ... Spicier and irresistible.' She popped it into her mouth. 'Look ... If I stay with Si, I know exactly what my life will be like for the next thirty years.'

'No, you don't,' interrupted Caro. 'Anything might happen.' She grasped wildly for an example. 'Simon might lose his job ...'

'Some chance!' Fran laughed. 'He'll be running that health clinic till he drops down dead, brought to his knees by vitamins and supplements.'

Caro smiled. His single-minded devotion to the clinic that promoted every type of alternative health care imaginable was a joke among his close friends. He took the teasing with a good heart while at the same time retaining his absolute conviction that he and his practitioners were providing an invaluable service to the community.

'But if I go with Ewan, our future's unknown. And that's exciting.'

That word again!

'Think about Ewan's wife.' Caro's heart went out to this woman she had never met. She knew better than anyone what it was like to have your life's expectations and future certainties thrown into the air, leaving you bewildered and bereft.

Fran's eyebrows rose. 'But they haven't slept together for years. They're virtually estranged.'

'And you believe that?' Caro smiled at Fran to take away the sting. 'Be careful—'

'Cynic! Even if you're right, I've got to hear what Ewan has to say.'

Caro looked down at her plate. She might not be as worldly as

Fran but Chris's departure had taught her a thing or two. 'Must you?'

'Yes. Simon needn't know. He'll think I'm with you.'

'Ah.' And finally they had got there. 'No! What did I say when you sat down?' Caro pushed back her chair. 'I'm not being your alibi again. I won't lie to him.' If only she had been as firm at the very beginning. But nothing she could have done would have stopped Fran. She was an adult, capable of making her own decisions and living by them. She was not Caro's responsibility, nor was her marriage to Simon. If Caro had told him what was going on, she would have broken the bonds of her friendship with Fran. She didn't want that. Poor Simon. But at least her lies to him so far had been of omission not commission. Wasn't there a difference? She wasn't so sure any more.

4

Caro had just said goodbye to another potential but unsuitable lodger (too chatty, too inquisitive) when the blue sports coupé that marked her ex-husband's middle-age crisis pulled up outside in a spray of gravel. She stood on the doorstep and watched him get out of the car.

Chris had changed since she had last seen him. Still small and punchy, but his pepper and salt hair had been cut shorter and gelled so it stood messily on end. He looked younger and fitter than he had for ages. A thin grey scarf was draped over the black polo neck that he wore under his jacket. Caro thought of all the shirts she'd ironed, the ties she'd matched with each one for him. Where had the wearer of those gone? And that woman she had once been?

'Come in,' she said, holding open the door. She wished she had dressed up for his visit. Her jeans were tight at the waist and the jumper she had chosen wasn't quite loose enough to disguise the muffin top that resisted all exercise. She felt at a disadvantage already.

'Girls here?' He ran his hand over the hall table. Possessive.

'No.' Caro shut the door. 'Let's go in the sitting room?' The kitchen was her space now and she didn't want it polluted by whatever Chris had to say.

'You've moved the chair.' That was more a reproach than an observation.

'Yes. The hall's better without it. Less cluttered.' In fact the chair that he had given her as a wedding present was in the garage gathering dust.

In the sitting room, he looked around as if checking that everything was as it should be. 'I do like this colour.' He nodded towards the walls before walking over to the mantelpiece where he inspected the cards and couple of invitations that she had tucked into the mirror, lifting up an invitation to Brian's 60th birthday and giving an interested 'hmm' as if he was surprised at their mutual friend's age. Or that Caro had been invited. Or that he hadn't. She didn't ask.

'I'll make coffee.' The perfect excuse to get out of there and regroup.

'That French picture.' He considered it. 'Doesn't look as bad as I thought it would.'

Caro left the room. She was grateful and unsurprised that he didn't offer to help. Already she was counting the minutes until he left. By the time she returned, he was standing at the window, hands clasped behind his back, legs apart, master of all he surveyed. 'Have you pruned the wisteria?'

'Surely you can tell.' But rather than get embroiled in a gardening conversation where she would be given advice she would resent, she said, 'So what's all this about?'

'Shall we sit?'

Chris took what had always been his chair, in the best position by the fire.

The phone broke the tension in the room.

Caro picked up to find herself unexpectedly pleased that Paul had chosen that moment to call. 'Hi!... Yes, I called back but must have missed you. Yes. Yes, seven o'clock for a drink would be perfect...' She had thought she wouldn't meet him if he phoned, but Chris's presence made her reckless. 'Yes, yes. I know... No, I'll see you there... Yes, me too.' She put the phone down, her cheeks burning.

Chris was staring at her as if expecting an explanation. Her reaction had told him the call was from someone who might be more than a friend, but she didn't have to explain anything to him any more. She waited, her left hand clasping her thumb hard; the pain in her knuckle made her focus.

'I'll get straight to the reason for my being here.' He paused and looked at the floor. 'Er ... I've asked Georgie to marry me.'

There was a silence.

She felt suddenly cold, as if someone had thrown open the doors and let the last of the winter in. This was the one thing she had chosen to believe would never happen. But she should have known. She squeezed her thumb harder.

'But you're still married to me.'

So this was the end. She got to her feet and went over to the mantelpiece and put Brian's invitation back where it was before.

Chris's eyes were on her all the time.

'And she's said yes, I take it.' She turned to face him.

His smile was smug. 'Yes.'

Of course she had.

'So no more Chris and Caro,' she said. 'A relief all round, I guess.' But that wasn't what she was feeling at all. She was feeling cast adrift, with panic eating away at her resolve to appear unmoved. 'I didn't think you'd get married again. At least not so soon.'

He looked at her mystified. 'But that's what people in love do.'

That hurt. That had been the reason they got married – he in his navy-blue suit and her in duck-egg green, a calf-length fitted skirt and a fitted jacket with a peplum and little round covered buttons that were a nightmare to do up. They had been in love then, honeymooned on the Greek island of Samos, lay naked on empty beaches, made love in sweat-soaked sheets against the scream of cicadas in the heat of the night. How much had changed.

'Congratulations.' She couldn't think what else to say. The first Mrs Chris Prior had just been tossed on the scrap heap and silenced. A door had just been slammed shut on her life with him – the good times and the bad. She wasn't sure what she was feeling. Shaken? Definitely. Sad? A little. Relieved? Perhaps. Angry? A little of that too, now.

'You're not upset?' He sounded surprised.

'Upset? Of course not. I'm pleased for you both.' She was determined not to let him see how much the news had thrown her. After all this time, she had got used to the status quo. Married but not married. 'When?' Her fingers travelled to the wedding ring she still wore out of habit and out of hope that had been gradually eroded.

'Well that slightly depends on you.'

'Because?' She was ready to drink her coffee now. Let him say it. She wouldn't make it easy for him.

'You know perfectly well.' He was rattled by her refusal to co-operate. 'We need to divorce.'

'Oh, of course.' She spoke as if she had forgotten that detail.

'You're not going to be difficult are you?'

This was her moment. She could screw up his plans by being exactly that. But what was the point?

'For God's sake, Chris. Who do you think I am? We haven't lived together for two years. I'm surprised you haven't asked for one before.' But he had been too busy enjoying himself with different women before and after he left her. The rumours had reached her. Georgie was the first one really to get under his skin.

'There is one other thing.' That awful wheedling tone meant worse was to come.

Caro was only just readjusting herself to the idea of being divorced and what it would actually mean to her. It shouldn't but it would change how she felt about herself. Being married, even if only in name, had nonetheless given her a sense of security that he had just removed like a rug from under her. She had been warned this might happen, been advised to take the divorce into her own hands and drive it through while he still felt guilty about leaving her. 'Don't wait,' Lauren's ex-colleague Daphne who specialized in family law had said. 'Once the guilt wears off, the gloves come off.'

'We'll have to sell Treetops.' His voice broke through her thoughts.

'What?' He can't have meant that. Treetops was her home. He couldn't take that away. 'But you've always said I could stay here. This house means everything to me.'

'I'm sorry, Caro. But unless you can buy me out . . .' He knew that was an impossibility. The little she had managed to stash away with her limited earnings from her painting and teaching would be nowhere near enough. They'd had the house valued just before he left her – she only understood why now: his insurance policy – when it had been worth close to a million. Finding half of anything like that sum was going to be near impossible.

'But I live here. You can't do this.' To her annoyance, her eyes were stinging. She clamped her teeth together and forced the tears away at the same time wanting to run him through with the poker.

'I'm afraid I can. I've spoken to my solicitor.' Of course he had. Chris would have had it all worked out before coming here. He knew exactly what he wanted from her and what he could get.

'Then I must speak to mine.' Would Daphne help her again? Or would Lauren put her on to someone else?

'You have one?' He ran one finger up and down his throat – the tic that always revealed when he'd been thrown off kilter.

'Of course.'

'We'll need to get the house valued again.'

Her heart quailed.

There was the sound of tyres on the gravel outside.

'Are you expecting someone?' He shifted in his seat.

'It's probably Amy. She sometimes pops in on her way home from work.'

A car door slammed, footsteps crunching on the gravel to the door before someone burst into the house. Two familiar thuds meant Amy had kicked off her Doc Martens in the hall. As she came into the room, shaking her hair out of its ponytail, she took off her Puffa jacket.

She gave her father a brief hug. 'Hi, Dad. What are you doing here?'

Caro moved along the sofa to make room for her.

'Don't worry,' said Chris, looking as if he was about to stand up. 'I can't stay. Mum will explain everything.'

Caro tightened her grip on the end of the arm of her chair. 'Oh, I think you should say something yourself, given you've driven all the way here.' She was not going to let him off the hook.

He blushed and sat, poised on the edge of his chair, glaring at Caro while acknowledging his responsibility.

'What are you talking about?' Amy took a peachy-coloured rosebud from her pocket and laid it on the coffee table.

Chris shifted in his seat again and peered round her to get a clear look at his ex-wife and daughter. He gave a short portentous cough. 'Good news, really.'

'Perhaps I should start. We don't want to hold you up,' Caro said, nausea rolling up from her stomach. Married. Did Chris really imagine his discarded family would share his joy without feeling regret, heartache, fury – all the emotions that were bubbling up inside Caro at that moment?

Amy gazed at Caro then at Chris and back again. He could at least have spared a thought for his daughters.

'Dad wants us to get divorced,' Caro said, ignoring Chris's frown and shake of the head.

'About time. But what's brought this on?' Amy took a strand of hair and twirled it round her finger.

Caro envied her level-headedness.

'I'm going to marry Georgie.' Chris wrested back control of the conversation.

They both glared at him.

'Wow!' Amy broke the silence. 'You mean she's going to be my step-mother! That's weird.'

'And . . .' Caro said. She wanted everything in the open.

Chris interrupted. 'I've been explaining to Mum that we may have to sell Treetops.'

Caro glared at him as he hedged round the truth. 'May?'

This time Amy did look dismayed. 'But you can't do that!'

Chris's finger travelled up his neck. 'You must have thought that would happen eventually.'

'The divorce, yes. Although it's a shock. But Treetops...' She couldn't finish the sentence. 'You said you wouldn't. It's Mum's home.'

He shuffled his feet on the carpet. 'Things have changed. Georgie and I can't live in her tiny flat forever.' He glanced at Caro. 'I'm sorry, love.'

In that brief second Caro heard an echo of the Chris that she had once fallen in love with. He must know exactly what was running through her mind but had the grace to look away.

'Let me put it another way, Amy. Mum can buy me out of Treetops but if she can't then we'll have to sell.'

Amy was incensed, her face outraged. 'You can't just come here and demand she sells up without any warning. Next thing, you'll be asking me to sell up Bloom.'

Caro remembered how uncertain she had been when Chris had proposed he invest generously in Amy's business. Some twenty thousand pounds' worth of guilt money. At the time, she had been glad that he was decent enough to support each of the girls in different ways. Lauren's share had gone on a loft extension.

'That won't happen. And I'm not demanding she sells up.' He was the voice of reason, calm, persuasive, his hands still again. 'But I need my share of the capital, I'm afraid. I don't mind how we arrive at this. We're giving her plenty of notice.'

That 'we' again.

'It's a big house for one person...' He stood up again, positioning himself with his back to the fireplace, as he always used to. 'Don't tell me you haven't been thinking of downsizing, Caro?'

'Have you, Mum?'

Caro was concentrating on breathing.

'No,' she said, before standing up to face them. She clasped her hands so neither of them could see them shaking. 'Thanks for coming to tell us the news. We'll pass it on to Lauren, and I'll let you know what I'm going to do.'

'I'm not asking you to do anything immediately – except perhaps get the house ready for a sale. If you could make it look a bit more presentable...'

Caro froze. How dare he?

'We want to get the most we can for it.' He ignored the glares of both women. 'Of course I'll pay my share of any redecorating. The outside needs attention: windows, doors, guttering. I also thought the hall and stairway could do with...' His voice faded in the face of their obvious hostility. Then he recovered himself. 'And the kitchen, and bathrooms.' He was doing what he was good at: deliver the killer blow then try to smooth things over as if he wasn't the bad guy after all. 'Just to maximise the asking price,' he added, as if no criticism was intended.

'If "we" do anything, I'll decide what and when.' Caro had always been in charge of things on the domestic front before and she was damned if she'd let him dictate to her now. 'Anything else, we can discuss later.' She got up and walked towards the hall, making it quite clear she expected him to leave.

Chris looked surprised. But she was not going to show him the devastation she felt. Nor would she beg. Instead, she opened the front door and watched him go in a blast of thick exhaust and a roar of engine.

'Mum, I'm so proud of you.' Amy enveloped her in a hug the moment the blue coupé turned out of the drive. 'You were fantastic.' Then she pulled back, her hands on Caro's shoulders, face to face. 'But you've got to see a lawyer straight away. He can't do this.'

'I'm afraid he can.' Caro felt exhausted. 'I've been incredibly stupid. I should have done something ages ago. Everybody warned me this would happen, but I wouldn't listen. I thought I knew better and I trusted him never to turn me out of here whatever happened between us. That's what he promised.'

'He's a complete bastard. Just because he's with her – he's flexing his muscles, showing off. It's pathetic. I bet she's behind it.'

Caro felt a blaze of affection for her younger daughter. 'He can do what he wants now. He doesn't have to answer to me.' She felt much shakier than she was sounding but somewhere, deep down, a seed of anger had taken root.

'Of course he does.' Amy led the way into the kitchen, by force of habit going straight to the cupboard where the biscuits were kept. She helped herself from the tin. 'He can't just dictate to you. Treetops is *our* house! You can't sell it.'

Caro smiled. 'But you've got your own homes now. You'll be moving in with Jason soon. You don't need this one any more.'

Amy was nibbling off a layer of chocolate Bourbon before eating the filling. She stopped. 'Yes, we do. We like knowing it's here.'

Caro laughed. Perhaps she could try to get what she'd need otherwise her own future suddenly looked very different. If she didn't have Treetops, where on earth would she go? This was where she had brought up her family: the house meant everything to her. Neither did she want her daughters to see her as their responsibility. They had done enough for her. But how on earth would she find that kind of money? No building society or bank in their right mind would lend to a sixty-one-year-old self-employed single woman with an irregular and, some would say, limited income. Nonetheless she would try all those she knew. Then, if she drew the blank she feared, she would have to ask her mother for help: a long shot but she would have to be her last resort.

'Let's look on the bright side,' she said, despite the beat of loneliness that was thumping inside her. 'He's not throwing me out into the street tonight. I've got time to plan.'

'I'll call Lauren on the way back to the shop and tell her. She's bound to have tons of advice for you or she'll know someone.' In the hall, Amy sat on the bottom of the stairs as she laced up her Doc Martens. 'Seriously, Mum. What will you do?'

If only Caro had an answer. Instead, she said the first thing that came into her head. 'In the first place, I think I'll take his suggestion and smarten the place up! If he's paying, I'm going to go to town.'

'And what about a lodger now? Will you bother?'

'I'm not sure. Maybe something short term. The last woman who answered the ad seemed OK until she wiped her finger along the mantelpiece and inspected it for dust! I mean – no!'

Amy laughed. 'Someone will turn up.'

'Maybe there's no point, if we're going to be selling.' Where would she go?

'Don't think like that. You might end up not selling for ages so you might as well enjoy a bit of company and extra cash until you do.'

Caro gave her daughter a level look. 'When will you two understand that I quite like my own company?' She needed her daughters to believe that, whatever the truth. She had taken a long time to realise that what she was lacking was not someone to do things with – she had plenty of those – it was someone with whom to do nothing at all.

'Really?' Amy was unconvinced.

As soon her daughter left, Caro sat down at her desk with a sheet of paper, intending to list the options open to her. She drew a large heart on the paper and wrote 'Paul?' underneath it. Then she drew a stick woman with frizzy hair and a pair of wellies walking a dejected-looking stick dog. Underneath that she wrote: 'Me?' Then she drew an arrow between the two and labelled it: 'Start afresh?'

What on earth would she wear to meet him that evening?

5

The next day Caro arrived at Lauren's just as her daughter was leaving for work. She always found it hard to believe that this expensively black-suited young woman was her daughter. She and Amy could have come out of two different gene pools. Lauren was taller than both her parents, a pretty girl but her brow was always furrowed with anxiety. Ambitious in her chosen career as a criminal lawyer, as a mother and as a wife, too, everything had to be done the right way. Mike would have left a couple of hours earlier so he could be home before Lauren to take over Danny from Caro. Theirs was a life of constant boxing and coxing that Caro didn't envy.

'Come in, come in.' Lauren sounded rushed.

Caro squeezed past, yanking Milo in with her.

'God, Mum. He stinks!' Lauren waved her hand in front of her nose. 'Did you have to bring him too?' She didn't wait for Caro's reply. 'He can go in the basement but don't let him upstairs. I'm so sorry about Dad. Amy called me. You OK?' She obviously wasn't encouraging a long reply.

'I'm getting used to the idea.' Caro struggled to get her coat off without letting go of Milo's lead. She wasn't 'OK' at all, having spent the night going over and over possible solutions to her predicament.

'Daphne said this would happen but I'll call her today to see if she can help. We've got people coming for supper tonight. God knows how I'm going to get back in time.' She sailed on, barely acknowledging Caro's thanks.

'Would you like me to lay the table? Do anything else?'

'Would you? You're a star. There'll be eight of us. You know where everything is. Danny!' She had a hand on the banister and shouted towards the open door to the living room. 'Mummy's leaving now.' She turned back to Caro. 'He's watching CBeebies. Thank God for them! I don't suppose you could make the watercress soup, could you? Yours is always better than mine and I just didn't have time.' She barely waited to hear Caro's agreement but squatted down to kiss Danny who had come to say goodbye. 'Bye bye, favourite boy! Now be good for Granny and I'll be back very soon.'

Danny peeled himself out of her arms and ran to fling his arms round Milo's neck.

'Mum, don't let Milo lick him. I don't want him to catch anything.'

This was exactly why Caro only brought Milo with her when she had to. Eventually Lauren departed in a further flurry of last-minute instructions and kisses and thanks. As she raced off down the road to the bus, the house seemed to heave a huge sigh of relief before shaking itself down and beginning to relax. Everything Lauren did was done in the heat of the moment. She was someone who flourished with too much on her plate, sometimes at the expense of others. In her haste to get things done, she sometimes spoke without thinking. Caro knew that any call to Daphne would only confirm what she already knew. Before doing anything, Caro made herself a large cup of coffee and gave Danny a drink.

'So, no yoga today. Milo can't do it. Shall we go to the playground?'

Danny laughed. 'And can we read *Winnie the Pooh*?'

They had started reading it the previous Monday so she was thrilled he liked and remembered it. The rest of the day whizzed by. By the time Mike came through the door, the table was laid, the soup made, Danny was fed and bathed having been on a walk to the park with Caro and Milo. They had swung on the swings, been on the roundabout, and Caro had watched Danny race around the playhouse while she stood stamping her feet and rubbing her hands on the sidelines.

She started at the sound of the front door shutting. A shout. She and Danny were curled up together on the sofa in the basement reading *Winnie the Pooh*. She turned round to see Mike in the doorway, suited and booted from the hospital. 'Hi, Caro. You must be done in.'

She sat upright. 'Not quite, but we have been pretty busy. We even made brownies for your guests, didn't we, Danny?'

'Mmm.' He was engrossed in a picture of Pooh and Tigger in Hundred Acre Wood.

'Sounds good. Just let me change and then I'll relieve you of this little monster.'

'Daddeee!' Danny leapt from the sofa and ran to his father who swung him up into the air. They went upstairs together, leaving Caro to gather up her things, checking the contents of her bag, finding Milo's lead and putting on her boots and jacket. When they came back down, she was ready to go.

At Waterloo, she climbed into her usual carriage to give herself the shortest walk to the car park at the other end. She made herself comfortable at a table seat, tucking Milo under the table as best she could. As always, she wondered how she'd survived all those years of looking after two children. They had even considered adding a third to the mix but a series of miscarriages then Chris's change of heart had put paid to that. Was that when he had his first affair, she wondered. She hadn't thought of that at the time, too wrapped up in her own disappointment, but looking back it seemed possible. After a bit of shifting and shunting, Milo settled at her feet. She unfolded her newspaper and began the sudoku.

She hardly noticed him standing beside her. Only when he said, 'Hello, again,' did she look up.

'Hello,' she said, surprised by the pleasure she felt on seeing him. 'It's you.' Could she be more obvious?

'Can I?' He nodded towards the seat opposite her.

'Of course. Unless you mind dogs.' She pointed out Milo who raised his head and banged his tail once on the floor.

'Not at all.' He slid into the seat and gave Milo a pat.

Close up, she noticed white paint in his hair, making it look greyer than last time. 'I thought you finished last week.'

'Just some last touches. It's done now.'

Despite his smile, Caro thought she once again detected a sadness and wondered what caused it. An idea struck her. 'Have you got more work lined up?'

He looked interested. 'Some. But something else always comes along.'

'I'm looking for someone to do some painting for me. I may be selling...' She broke off as the enormity of the prospect swept over her combined with embarrassment. 'But I'd need a quote, of course.'

'I could come round and look at the job.' He pulled up the sleeves of his sweatshirt, revealing more paint spatters on his arms. 'One evening this week?'

'Perfect. Wednesday?'

He nodded as she took her diary from her bag and tore out the last page before writing down her address. 'You never told me where you live.'

He took the paper and put it in his wallet. 'You didn't ask. But I have to move next week anyway. The landlord's converting the house into flats. He doesn't mind throwing us out.'

'But that's awful.' She tried to imagine what it must be like to be at the whim of other people. How lucky she was to have Treetops. And then she remembered her own position. She had a very good idea of what he must be feeling after all. But was he as scared as she was when she imagined a future without the home whose every last creak and detail was ingrained in her?

'I'm used to it. I never stay in one place for too long.'

'I'm exactly the opposite. I've lived in the same house for about thirty years. I can't imagine being anywhere else. Wouldn't you rather put down roots, call somewhere home?'

He shook his head. 'I don't want to become too attached. Nothing lasts. For me, it's better to keep moving.'

She couldn't imagine such a nomadic life for herself. 'Where will you go?'

He shrugged. 'I don't know. Something will come along.'

'I hope so. The same thing's happened to me. My husband . . .' She noticed him glance at her ring. She covered it with her other hand. 'We're getting divorced and I may have to find somewhere else to live too. But I've got to smarten the place up before we put it on the market.'

He looked at her, appraising her, his eyes understanding. 'You're upset. I'm sorry.'

Was it that obvious?

'Don't be. We split up a couple of years ago but I don't want to lose my home.' Why was she confiding in this man again? There was something about the way he listened, inclining his head slightly, his eyes on hers, his attention absolute. He wasn't dismissing her as someone older with nothing interesting to say. She had a vivid mental recall of the frizzy-haired stick woman she had drawn being beaten over the head by a more glamorous one armed with a high heeled shoe – Fran. She couldn't help a smile.

Slightly to her relief, the rattle of the trolley stopped her from going into any more detail. This time they bought their own drinks. When they had them on the table in front of them, they returned to the conversation.

'So where *will* you go?' she asked again, keen to steer the conversation away from herself.

'There are lots of places, but the timing . . . I may stay with friends till I find a place.' He stirred the sugar into his tea.

'Or . . .' She stopped herself. This was ridiculous. Her family

46

would think she'd gone mad. But why not? She knew him better than any of the random strangers who answered her advertisement. And he'd already told her he never stayed anywhere for long.

The dark eyebrows lifted in question. 'Or what?'

The harsh strip lighting emphasised his poker-straight nose, a thin trail of white scar tissue running down his angular cheek – planes and shadows. A face that she'd love to paint.

'This may sound a little crazy, but I'm looking for a temporary lodger.' She put the emphasis on 'temporary'. *Steady, Caro. Is this wise?* She could hear Fran's voice.

'What do you mean?' He looked genuinely puzzled.

'I've a room in my house that I'm renting. It's quite big,' she added, in case he got the wrong idea. 'Four bedrooms. You'd be quite private.'

'But you don't know me.' His hands were quite still on either side of his beaker of tea.

'I know you as well as anybody who's answered my ad.' *Are you quite mad? Stop this at once.* Chris's voice joined Fran's. That was enough to encourage her. She enjoyed the idea of his shock when he found out. 'Well, maybe it's crazy. But if you don't find somewhere, you'll see the house on Wednesday. If you don't like the idea, we'll say no more.'

'And if you change your mind?'

'I'll say so. I may get others answering the ad. My daughters like the idea of me having someone for company, although I really don't need it.'

'Do you always do what they want?'

'Not always. But it makes for an easier life sometimes. They've got quite protective since my husband moved out. One of them moved back for a while then and someone else moved in after that. I'm used to having someone there, but we've always led quite separate lives.'

What on earth was she doing?

47

The memory of her conversation with Fran ran through her mind – 'But Simon is so safe . . . and Ewan offers something else . . .' – followed by the memory of Paul adjusting the position of his watch on his wrist so he could glance at it when he thought she wasn't looking.

'Let me think about it.' He lifted his tea and stared at her over its rim. Those dark eyes, impossible to read.

What was he thinking? Probably that this was a mad plan dreamed up by some lonely old woman. And perhaps that's all it was. She wouldn't mention it again unless he brought it up on Wednesday. Assuming he even turned up. Besides, someone else suitable was bound to answer the ad before then.

On Wednesday morning, Caro got to the college in good time and went round setting up the easels ready for her morning class. First to arrive at nine thirty as always were Janey, Clare, Susan and Liz: four women of a certain age who had taken up art late in life and came for the pleasure of learning to draw and paint. They had been regulars for about three years now. Then came Johnny, the sixty-something-year-old who she suspected, despite his real talent, came with another motive in mind. But, as far as she knew, none of the ladies had yet fallen for his charms, although she had noticed Liz ducking out to have a cigarette with him. He was followed by Mike, a resting actor, then the two art students, Tess and Pete, who were supplementing the work they did at college. Occasionally there were drop-ins, but not today.

The model agency had sent Anthony, a middle-aged man who Caro had used before. Once the students were all behind their easels, he stripped off his robe and got on with his series of poses. He knew exactly what he was doing – a half-hour pose to let them work their way into the session, then a series of short ones from one minute moving to five at most before finally giving them three half hour poses: sitting, lying, and lying again. Caro went round the class, making sure everyone had everything they needed and helping if they had any questions.

Caro liked working with Anthony because he understood how to make the poses interesting for them. He twisted his body, turning to look over his shoulder, jumping and holding the landing position, crooking an arm or a leg. The room was quiet as her students concentrated, exclaiming with frustration when they got something wrong, stepping back to consider an angle, a line. Caro walked among them, encouraging, suggesting, praising, but always careful never to dictate what they did. She remembered her own teachers and tried to give the best parts of them to her students so they would develop their own style and take their painting to another level.

This was one of her favourite classes. Drawing from life made her students look at the person in front of them properly. Every time the model moved, there was something new to work on: tone, skin, the structure of the body. She enjoyed nothing more than seeing how her students improved and gained confidence in these classes.

They stopped at lunchtime. Caro left the group chatting and comparing notes while she excused herself to phone her mother. After May had told her about the cakes she was making for a charity tombola, it was Caro's turn. She described Chris's visit and explained why he wanted a divorce. The waves of disapproval coming down the line were almost audible.

'You're better off without him,' was the eventual considered verdict.

'I thought I might come and see you this evening. I could take a look at the double-glazing literature, if you like.' The question of borrowing money was too delicate to broach over the phone. And anyway it was too soon – she hadn't yet exhausted the other avenues.

'I'll be at the library, I'm afraid. We're going to hear a writer talk about their book. I told you about the one I was reading set in the Arctic – I've got to finish the wretched thing this afternoon because afterwards we're going to the Chinese next door for supper to discuss it. I don't suppose I will, though.'

Sometimes she thought her mother had a better social life than her.

When she returned to the room, her morning students had all left. Caro opened her sandwiches and sat by the radiator, remembering. She and Chris had met when she was starting out in set design and he was a lowly production assistant. He had been 'locking out', busy keeping people off the set, and he tried to stop her getting to where she was meant to be, not believing she was one of the crew. She couldn't help smiling at the memory. She had been taken with his determination to get to the top, doing whatever lowly job was asked of him. They got married in their thirties, and how happy they had been to begin with. When the girls were little. Chris had been busy with his career, focused and ambitious, while she had abandoned the unpredictable and demanding world of set design to look after first Lauren, then Amy. But he had been happy for her to lead the life she wanted. That's what love was, wasn't it? Allowing one's partner the freedom to be the person they were. But that was just at the beginning.

She laid down her sandwich and picked up a piece of charcoal for an instant sketch of a cramped room filled with children's clobber. It only took her a moment. Their first home.

She took another bite of sandwich. Then she sketched Treetops – a house full of big rooms, and with bicycles and a playhouse in the garden. She finished it off with a chimney on the top with a curl of smoke coming out of it.

The family home. Happy days.

Once the girls were old enough, she had started going into the school to help in the art classes, and loved it whether she was helping stick pasta onto sugar paper or encouraging the sixth formers. Chris could never get his head round the fact that she actively wanted to be around her children while they grew up and not compromise the experience by going back into set design once they went to school. As she started to develop her love of portraiture, building up her teaching work and painting around the children's school hours, he started to express his true feelings.

'It's not exactly a proper job, is it?' 'Are you going to go back to work?' 'I carry all the financial burden in this family.' Subtle at first, then increasingly heavy-handed, his comments became unbearable. She fought back, pointing out the cost of the child-care, commuting and that she was bringing in some money of her own. His acceptance was grudging at best.

She found herself escaping to her studio space when she could. The space was Caro's room of her own that she rented for next to nothing in a converted factory on the outskirts of town where she could have the occasional moment of peace and quiet while she focused exclusively on whatever she was drawing or painting.

'Penny for them.' Alan, the first of her afternoon class came in, dropping his rucksack and taking off his cycling helmet before choosing an easel to work at.

Caro screwed up her sketches and tossed them in the bin. 'Just daydreaming when I should be getting ready for this afternoon's class.'

At that moment, the afternoon model arrived: a generously proportioned middle-aged woman. Caro showed her where she could change and the afternoon took off from there.

That evening, she and Milo settled together in the kitchen as she made herself some quick pasta sauce. This was the room she had always loved most: the hub of family life. The girls used to sit round the table doing homework, playing board games, squabbling over nothing, planning what to wear, where to go. Gone were the children's drawings that used to decorate the walls, the noticeboard overflowing with announcements and stuff to remember, the row of terrible clay models that Lauren had made during her pottery phase. The boxes Caro transformed into ridiculously complicated stage sets for their puppets and toys. The only remaining reminder of childhood was the clock made out of plywood, coloured Fimo shapes marking every quarter hour, and a battery that she always forgot to replace. It had said seven thirty for weeks. But it wasn't the stuff that was important, it was the memories. She missed those years so badly, had thought she would never forget a detail of them but all she could conjure up now was an indistinct rosy blur with incidents that could have happened during almost any year.

She tore the basil leaves, inhaling their peppery scent, and threw them in the mixer with garlic, pine nuts, pecorino and olive oil. Once they were whizzed up and ready, she put the kettle on, pulled the spotty teapot from the shelf and a mug from the cupboard. Tigger strolled in, tail high. Just the three of them.

She went through into the living room and sat at the piano. She ran her fingers over the keys, tentative at first. She had grown rusty over the years despite her repeated resolve to practise more. A book of Christmas carols was open on the stand, where it had been since December. She played a short burst of 'In the Bleak Midwinter' and stopped. Too lowering. She flicked through her book of Beethoven sonatas but she wasn't in the mood. Instead she twirled round on the stool and checked her phone for the first time since lunchtime. Three missed calls. One from Paul. Did that show a worrying keenness after their last pleasant but unremarkable drink together. Or was she flattered? And one from a number she didn't recognise. A possible lodger? She hoped so. If she was honest, the girls were right. She did sometimes miss having someone else in the house. First she'd return Paul's call, then she'd try the other, see what they had to say.

6

By the end of the following week, Damir had given Caro a price for the work, and Chris had finally approved it after insisting she got a couple of comparative quotes. She went along with his request for a quiet life while knowing it was the sensible thing to do. As days passed, she began to feel more positive about the divorce. At least they finally all knew where they stood and, if nothing else, she was forced to think about what she wanted out of the next years of her life. She considered moving to the country or having a town flat, but so far remaining at Treetops always won out. The idea of leaving all her memories behind was still too much.

Raising the money she would need to buy Chris out was proving as difficult as she had anticipated but she refused to abandon hope. The mortgage broker recommended by Simon had been sympathetic but unhelpful.

'I don't think we're going to be able to find anything for you, Mrs Prior.' He steepled his fingers, tapping the tips together, wrinkling his nose as if he could smell something nasty. 'Without a regular income or the promise of a lump sum, it's unlikely you'll have any luck, but I will ask for you.' He put his pad and paper in the drawer of his desk and pushed it shut with a bang signalling the end of the meeting.

Her bank had been no better. A young man who looked as if he was just out of school dealt with her in the most peremptory way, calling in someone more senior to confirm what he was saying. She was not creditworthy. She left disheartened but determined not to give up. Perhaps the mortgage broker was wrong, and there were always the insurance companies.

A job postponed meant Damir was able to fit in the work for her around another bigger job. Nothing more had been said about him moving in. But neither had she found a lodger. The last call she received was from someone who then didn't turn up to see the room at the appointed time. Since then, she'd had no more interest. She liked his presence in the house and didn't mind him coming and going provided the work was done. He was discreet, worked hard, seemed to know when not to disturb her. She had begun to look forward to the moment when his van pulled up outside the house. She had even started, almost unconsciously, to make more of an effort to look presentable at all times just in case he turned up. Once she caught herself watching him as he worked, studying his profile, the way he moved. If she were younger, would she make a pass – if she could remember how – and would he respond if she did? What would he be like in bed, she wondered, then reprimanded herself for even asking the question. She wasn't a young woman any more.

After a couple of days of him stripping the stairwell, she had come in from a walk to find him on his mobile in the hall. He raised a hand in greeting but went on talking in his own language. As she removed Milo's lead and sat on the bottom of the stairs to take off her shoes, he ended his call. 'Damn you!'

'Problem?' she asked.

'It's nothing.' He pocketed his phone. 'Kamil's OK, he's moving in with his girlfriend. Esad and I found rooms but now the landlord says he has only one room after all. That we can share.' He pulled a face that showed exactly what he thought of that idea. 'So we must look again.' He shrugged.

'Take the day off,' she suggested. 'I won't mind.' She didn't want to embarrass them both by offering him a room again. Besides the longer he took with the job, the longer she had before the house could go on the market and she had to make some decisions.

'Maybe. We see.' He shook his van keys. 'For now, I'm going to get lining paper. I'll sort out what to do later. Not your problem.'

At least the idea of moving and having the rooms decorated had pushed her towards doing what should have been done a long time ago: clearing some of the clutter. Once the two rooms were cleared, she hoped the house would stop feeling quite so much like home and leaving – if she had to – would be less of a wrench. But after thirty precious years, a good part of Caro's heart had detached and buried itself in the infrastructure. It hurt to think of leaving it.

She started on the girls' rooms. Amy's was a jumble of clothes, books, posters, shoes that she had put off doing anything about since she had left home. Caro couldn't face it and shut the door. She spent the rest of the morning beginning the clear-out of Lauren's more ordered room.

Both girls had always been too busy to do the job themselves. Amy employed delaying tactics: 'I will. Just not this week. I'm soo busy.' Whereas Lauren would brush her off with a weary, 'Honestly, Mum, I haven't got time. There's nothing there I want, I'm sure. Just chuck it all.'

During her I'm-going-to-be-an-actress phase she had persuaded Chris to put up a mirror surrounded by light bulbs. She would spend hours in front of it, experimenting with different make-up. The mirror was still stuck with teen postcards and photos. Post-it notes that helped her with her last lot of revision had unstuck from the walls and been saved by Caro in a bowl. The make-up scattered on the table top was tarnished and claggy, and should all have been thrown out years ago. Keeping the girls' rooms in aspic, unwilling to accept that part of her life as a mother and her marriage were over, had kept Caro going. She used to enjoy coming in, turning things over, remembering. Nostalgia had been a comfort. But those days were over. She clicked on Lauren's tape-recorder and listened to her daughter reciting some abstruse legal nicety that she'd had to commit to heart. Lauren used to record her revision then listen back to it whenever she could. She had never gone anywhere without the recorder and earphones. That focus and determination had been part of her make-up since she was born.

Caro couldn't bring herself to bin Lauren's teenage years just like that. Instead she boxed up the things that seemed most amusing or of sentimental value, dividing the rest between bags marked for charity, recycling and rubbish.

As she worked, she thought about Damir's situation, wondering whether to mention the idea of him taking a room again after all. Perhaps he was waiting for her to bring it up first. What harm? She went down the corridor and stood at the top of the stairs where he was back stripping the walls, steam rising from the steamer. 'Can we have a word?'

His eyes were dark, searching. 'Sure.' He followed her on to the landing, rubbing his hands on his overalls.

They stood in the corridor, her leaning against the banister, the smell of his sweat catching in her nostrils.

'Is it something wrong?'

'Not at all. I've been thinking.' She hesitated. Was she about to make a terrible mistake?

He stared at her, the right side of his face lit from the light on the hall, the left in shadow. 'Yes?' He was impatient to get on.

'This house really is too big for one person. You can see that, and you don't have anywhere to live.' She gestured along the corridor. 'Are you sure you don't want to move in? Just for as long as it takes you to find somewhere, I mean.' She must be clear this was only a temporary arrangement, nothing more. 'You'll pay rent. The girls have moved out,' she explained. 'I'm emptying their rooms at long last. You could take Lauren's at the end of the corridor down there.' As far away from her room as it was possible to be. Offering him the spare room next to hers, the one she had pinned as the lodger's, seemed wrong. Too close. 'It's got its own shower.' In the silence that followed, she regretted saying anything. Heat rose from her chest, up her neck and cheeks so that they were burning. Sweat pricked her forehead. 'Actually, perhaps it's a daft idea. It's probably not even very convenient for you.' She shook her head, pulled at the sides of her T-shirt. 'Let's forget it. I shouldn't have brought it up again. I'm so sorry.' Mortified, she turned away and headed back to Lauren's room.

'Actually, I think maybe it's a good idea.' His voice travelled after her.

She turned round to see him leaning with both arms on the balustrade. 'You do? The room does need decorating though.'

'I can do that for you.'

He was going to say yes. She smiled at him.

He returned the smile. 'Perhaps it helps us both. No?'

'Just for a while. Until you find somewhere of your own.'

'Yes. I would like that. When shall I move here?'

'As soon as you've painted the room.'

'What do you mean you've bagged everything up! What if you've thrown something away that I want?'

'But it's all there for you to go through in the garage. You said get rid of it all!'

'I didn't mean get rid of it! That's where it all lived. I liked knowing it was there.'

Caro had to smile at her daughter's outrage. 'I *have* been asking you to sort it out for the last two years.' Her requests, like Lauren's deferrals, had become a habit between them. They both understood that neither really expected the other to do anything and so it had gone on. Until now, when change was in the air. 'Anyway, I've done it now. If you want, you can go through them before I get rid of them. Or you can always take them home with you.'

'We'll come over. I should have helped you but I'm just so

busy at the moment.' Lauren was already calming down. Of course there was nothing she really wanted. She had taken all that mattered years ago.

'I'm trying to detach myself from Treetops by emptying it of memories. Then selling won't be so hard.' Caro wanted her to understand.

'Do you think you will?'

'I can't see how I'm going to raise the money. I've drawn a blank everywhere I've tried so far. I'm still waiting to hear from the mortgage broker but I'm not holding out much hope. The only alternative is to go to an insurance company but an equity release scheme, even if I could get one, would make a difference to what I can leave to you two.'

'That doesn't matter.'

Caro could tell Lauren was putting on a brave face. Besides, she was quite clear what she thought. 'That's sweet of you but it matters to me. So I think I'm going to have to ask Mum if she can help.'

'Have you talked to her?'

'Not yet. But I will when I next see her. I don't want to do it over the phone.' In fact, she had delayed asking for help in the ludicrous hope that something miraculous might happen. She didn't want to worry her mother until she absolutely had to.

'I'm sorry. I didn't think. But you can't let Dad and Georgie make you lose Treetops.' Lauren had the determined look on her face that she'd got from her father. 'Have you spoken to Daphne yet? I told her to expect your call.'

'Yes, last week.' Lauren's ex-colleague had been knowledgeable but unhelpful. 'She told me exactly what you thought she'd say. Chris has had sound advice from his lawyer. There's not a lot I can do.'

Lauren gave an exasperated sigh. 'Bastard!'

'Lauren, don't!'

'Well, he is. This is your house. No, it's *our* house. Our *home*. If only he hadn't met that woman.'

'But he did. So if we're forced to sell, we might as well do it successfully. That's why I'm doing it up a bit. Speculate to accumulate and all that, and spending Dad's money while I'm at it. And, you'll be pleased to know I've found a lodger.'

'Really? Who?'

Before Caro had a chance to reply, there was a yell from upstairs.

'God! Mike, can you deal with him?' Lauren gave a long sigh. 'Sorry, but Danny's so difficult these days. Haven't you found?'

'He's probably tired.' Caro had seen the tantrums he occasionally threw with Mike and Lauren but he hadn't given her a moment's trouble. Perhaps she was more lenient with him than his parents – the pleasure of being a grandparent. But perhaps it was simply because she wasn't one of his parents and he didn't need to play her up for attention.

'You'll need more money than a lodger'll bring in if you're going to buy Dad out.' She looked thoughtful. 'You're not putting them in my room are you?'

Caro felt herself heating up under Lauren's gaze.

'Oh, Mum! What's wrong with Amy's? Or the spare room? Didn't Helen have that?'

'Yours is bigger and it's at the other end of the corridor to me.'

But Lauren wasn't listening any more. Mike had appeared at the doorway with a tear-stained Danny in his arms. 'Only Mum will do, I'm afraid.'

Lauren reached out her arms and took her son, kissing his forehead. 'Oh Danny boy, what shall we do with you?'

'I wanna story.'

'Just one and then the light's going off.' She turned to Caro. 'I'm sorry, Mum. I'd better go up with him. Mike'll take you to the station.'

Mike took the car key from the key rack.

Caro was glad Lauren's mind had been diverted from the lodger although she would have to tell her eventually. When she did, she might be less forgiving. Lauren liked things done the proper way and she wouldn't see Damir, or indeed any man, as being a suitable lodger for her mother. She would imagine all sorts of gruesome scenarios from simple trickery to blackmail, rape and even murder, her imagination stoked by the cases she came across daily at work. The only suitable person in her eyes would be a like-minded woman of a similar age. A companion! Caro kissed Danny goodnight a second time and watched Lauren go upstairs with him before following Mike out to the car.

Sunday lunch. At one end of the table Jason was pulling faces at Danny that sent him into shrieks of laughter while Amy tried to tell Lauren and Caro about the flat she was moving into with him. But Lauren's attention was on her son, an indulgent smile on her face, and Caro was beginning to gather up the plates.

'I'll do that.' Mike took them from her.

'Let me help.' Jason collected up the vegetable dishes and followed him out.

'Is he going to propose?' Lauren asked in a stage whisper.

'Lauren, honestly! No! It's not like that. Let's get the moving in together over first.' Amy grabbed the gravy jug. 'I'll get the pudding.'

'What did I say?' Lauren seemed completely taken aback.

'You can be a bit direct sometimes,' Caro said. 'She's nervous.'

'That's daft. He adores her.'

Jason came in at that second, holding a pile of plates. 'You're talking about me?' Above his gingery beard, his face flushed.

'I'm sorry.' Lauren concentrated on picking a couple of scraps of roast beef off Danny's lap. 'I shouldn't . . .'

'Don't be.' He put the plates on the table and sat down. 'You're right. I do. It's just a question of persuading her.'

'Persuading who?' Amy came in carrying her lemon meringue

pie, triumphant. The girls always took turns at bringing puddings when Caro gave them lunch.

'You.' He stood up and kissed her cheek.

'Oh, stop it!' She dodged his embrace, laughing. 'I'll drop this.'

'See?' he said, looking despondent and stuffing his hands in his jeans pocket. 'I've a hard road ahead.'

They all laughed, even Amy. 'Don't be daft. I've agreed to live with you. Count yourself lucky.' She looked down at the table to hide her embarrassment.

Jason shrugged and raised his eyebrows, then turned and pulled a face at Danny. 'What can you do?'

'Where's Granny?' said Amy as she dished up.

Neat change of subject, thought Caro. 'She couldn't come. Local whist drive. I'm going to take Danny over to see her next week.' She would have liked May to be there. She knew how much it meant to her mother to be included, and how much, even if her deafness made it difficult, she loved being at a table with them all. But her mother had her own life too and wasn't over-dependent on the rest of them. She had achieved a pretty good balance so far, despite causing Caro the odd alarm. She looked at her daughters. Her mother was setting a good example.

After lunch Amy and Jason left to see a football match with friends while the others went for a walk. Caro realised that she still hadn't told them who her new lodger was, and Damir was bringing his things over that evening. She told herself that she was making far more of their reactions than need be. She'd say something when they got back from their walk.

Damir had redecorated Lauren's room, painting over the old bubble-gum pink in an inoffensive off-white and Caro had replaced the flowery curtains with wooden blinds. She went to inspect them. The room smelt of paint and she pushed open the window. Lauren would have to be told. Untying the blind cord, she sent it rattling down, cutting off the light. These days who was mothering whom? Slowly she hoisted the blind back up and the room came back into focus. Too bad, my daughters, she thought. You will have to trust my judgment.

She spent a happy couple of minutes rattling the blind up and down, told herself she was being childish and went to check on the towel situation.

The others had just come back from their walk when they heard a car outside followed by the ring of the doorbell.

'I'll get it,' Caro said, leaving Lauren and Mike to take off Danny's outdoor shoes and coat in the kitchen while she went to open the front door.

'Is this a bad time?' Damir looked back at his blue van, a ladder on its roof, parked by the four-by-four. 'I can go away, come back later.'

She had been expecting him much later but held open the door. 'No, no. Come in. My daughter's here with her family but you can bring in whatever you've got and we can take it up.'

'If you're sure . . .'

'Yes, yes. I'd like you to meet them.' Better to get it over with.

As he went to get his bags from the back of his van, Danny came out and pulled at Caro's hand. She swept him up into her arms and kissed his cheek. 'You little monkey. Where do you think you're going?' She turned to Damir. 'So this is the grandson you've heard about.'

Damir gave Danny a serious look then winked. He took his hand to shake it. 'Pleased to meet you. I'm Damir.'

Danny stared back, stilled for a moment. He pulled his hand away and snuggled his head into Caro's neck, then began to wriggle so hard she had to put him down.

'Go on then. Go in and find Milo.'

As Danny headed into the house, Lauren appeared. 'Hallo.' She smiled at Damir, then looked at her mother, puzzled. 'You didn't say you were having workmen today, Mum.'

Caro was aware of Damir beside her, undecided whether to unload his stuff from his van or not.

'I'm not. This is Damir, my new lodger. He's just brought some of his things over.'

'I'm sorry to have come too early,' he said. 'But I can come back.'

Lauren's eyes widened. '*He's* your lodger?'

Caro heard alarm bells ringing. 'He's been redecorating for me too. Damir, this is Lauren, my oldest daughter.'

Damir came to the doorway, his arm outstretched. 'I'm pleased to meet you. Your mother's told me about you. She's been very kind to help me out.'

Lauren gaped slightly but she remembered herself in time, swallowed, and shook his hand. 'Typical Mum! She always helps when she can. How long are you staying?' she asked, her voice slightly out of register.

'I'm not sure yet. I have to find somewhere else to live.'

'You'd better come in then.' She stood to one side so he could pass. 'We should go, Mum. You've obviously got things to do.'

'Don't go yet.' This was exactly the sort of reaction Caro had feared. 'I'll just show Damir his room and then we can have tea. I've made that Smarties cake for Danny.'

'And I have to go and meet friends,' said Damir, obviously aware his presence was causing tension between mother and daughter. 'I will only be a moment.'

'Well then, that's sorted. Lauren, can you put the kettle on while I just help Damir to his room?' Caro was as business-like as she knew how, ignoring her daughter's frown.

Moments later, Damir's bags were in Lauren's old bedroom and his van was turning out of the driveway. Caro, Lauren and Mike were sitting at the kitchen table as Danny covered himself in cake.

'I thought you'd choose someone more your own age.' Lauren picked at her piece of cake. 'A woman.'

'So did I. But no one quite right answered my ad.'

'And he did?'

'Not exactly. I met him a few times on the train—'

Lauren's eyebrows shot up.

'Good for you.' Mike looked at Caro with a new respect, and she held back a smile.

'It's nothing like that. I felt sorry for him when I found out that he had nowhere to go. Look...' She offered the plate of scones to Mike. 'He's helped me out, so it's the least I can do.'

'He's not *helping* you, Mum. You're paying him to work on the house.' Lauren was indignant.

'Lauren, steady on.' Mike helped himself to jam. 'You don't really know...'

'I don't like the idea of anyone taking advantage of Mum. That's all.'

'He's not. It was my idea. This is only a temporary thing until he finds another place.'

'But he's got my bedroom! I can't believe you've given it to him.' So that was it.

'Don't worry, he won't be here for long,' Caro said, covering her daughter's hand with her own.

'He'd better not be.'

'Lauren!' Mike frowned at her, warning her she had gone too far. 'Don't you think you're over-reacting? You wanted Caro to have a lodger and she's perfectly capable of choosing the right one herself. You don't have to live with them.'

'I don't like the idea of Mum being alone in the house with him though. We don't know him. Anything could happen.'

Now Caro had to laugh too. 'Don't you trust me?'

Lauren managed a smile. 'You know that's not what I meant.'

'I do. But I don't think you need to worry. He's been working here for a couple of weeks and nothing's happened yet.'

'Unless you get lucky.' Mike winked again, and dodged his wife's punch to his arm.

7

Caro was lying in the bath, soaking off the effects of a day in Bloom. She had spent ages soothing a customer complaining that the flowers she had bought four days earlier had died and insisting on a free replacement bunch. In the end, Caro had given in. Amy's good will had been less forthcoming. 'How am I meant to make a profit if you give the flowers away?'

'I'm only keeping up your reputation for customer service.' Caro had emptied the bucket in the sink. 'Don't take it out on me.'

She stirred the bath water with her hand, letting the scent of geranium oil rise up in the steam. Amy had apologised. No hard feelings. Caro liked the way her daughter dealt with her staff. It wasn't just her who received an appropriate apology or was thoughtfully shown how to do things Amy's way. Amy treated everyone fairly. Caro slid herself under the water until everything but her head and toes was submerged when suddenly she heard the door handle turn and the door opened. Like a whale surfacing from the deep, she sloshed into a sitting position, an arm across her breasts, a hand over her pubic hair. The curls that emerged from her biscuit-print shower cap hung limply round her overheated face.

Damir stood there. 'I'm sorry.' They stared at each other, impossible to know who was most horrified, before he began to back out.

'That's OK.' She tried to sound as if having people walk in on her in the bath was nothing unusual, disguising the unwelcome awareness of how lived in and altered by childbearing her body was. 'Worse for you, I expect.' She attempted a laugh.

'No, no.' The door was shutting behind him. Caro heard him going downstairs, as if he couldn't get out of the building fast enough. She lay back in the bath again, mortified. This was the last way she would have chosen to be seen. After a moment, she lifted her leg into the air and smiled. Still, it wouldn't kill him.

She didn't see him again that evening. However, two days later when she went to the bathroom, she was surprised and touched to find a small bolt on the inside of the door. Even so, she thought, being a landlady is not as easy as I'd imagined. If it's not me skirting around him. It's him skirting around me. He was nothing like Amy or Helen but made her conscious of what she did in a way she never had been before. Treetops felt quite different.

Breakfast was part of their deal but he was not his best first thing, eating quickly and silently before one or other of them left the house. In the evenings, he waited until she had made her meal before going into the kitchen to make something for himself. Their initially relaxed relationship had become awkward. The house had changed too. The smell of aftershave lingered in the upstairs landing. His shoes crowded the front porch where he took them off. His coat hung beside hers on the rack in the hall. The door to Lauren's room remained firmly shut.

However, he was a considerate tenant. She had to give him that. He always knocked before he came into a room since the bathroom incident. He had repaired several things around the house without mentioning them: the leaking washer on the kitchen sink that she had been meaning to repair for months; the section of skirting board in the sitting room where Chris, in a fury, had once kicked a hole in it. He rehung the picture that had been leaning against the wall waiting for her to replace the broken cord; he replaced the bunch of dying daffs on the kitchen table with blood red tulips. He was trying. She should too. After all, she reminded herself, he wouldn't be there for long.

'Why don't you come and watch the news?' she said one evening.

His eyes flicked to hers. His were questioning, wary. 'Are you sure?'

'Of course.'

They sat, side by side, watching footage of the Syrian war with streams of exhausted, bewildered refugees forced to leave their homes and walk miles with the little they possessed to some form of safety. Then shots of an abandoned city, shelled to smithereens, the few upstanding walls of houses riddled with bullet marks. There was a sudden burst of gunfire and Caro, who had been watching appalled and upset, was startled by Damir's intake of breath as he shifted position abruptly. His hand was shaking as he wiped it across his brow.

'Are you OK?' Caro turned down the volume as he sat back again, ashen-faced, sweat running down his temple.

'I'm sorry. I couldn't help . . . that's what it was like for us too. Gunfire . . . the smell of gunpowder in the streets . . . the screaming, shouting and crying.'

She switched off the TV and looked at him. 'What happened to you?' She paused. His eyes were shut as he made a concerted effort to calm his breathing. 'You don't have to tell me, of course. Only if you want to.'

He looked at her, eyes distant in a face shaped by shadows, his fingers twisted together.

'The war. That's what happened. That's what happened to all of us. You can't imagine.'

No, she couldn't. She could not even come close. His life had been so different to hers or anyone's she knew. Two people from backgrounds that were poles apart, who had taken such wildly contrasting journeys to reach this point. Did that mean the gulf between them was too wide to bridge? Should she not even try? More than anything she wanted to reach out to him, to understand what had made him the man he was, to know the suffering he had been through, to help him.

'We were driven from our homes like animals.' His face contorted with the memory, though his voice remained steady. 'Homes that had become prisons with no running water, no electricity, little food. The streets were too dangerous.' He paused. 'My father went to get bread one day and was gunned down by a sniper.'

Caro gasped. 'Killed?'

He bent his head. 'At least he was spared worse. Many friends were taken to Luka camp, an old warehouse in Brčko, the town where I come from, where the Serbs tortured and killed them. They only came out on the trucks that were piled high with dead bodies.'

'But how did you . . . ?'

He gave a little shake of his head as if clearing it of the memories. 'My brother and I joined the army to fight on the front line against the Serbs. It was all we could do. We had to.'

She had read about the war, seen the TV reports. Of course. They all had. But she hadn't understood the complexities of what went on. To be as up close as this was another matter, close to a human being who *knew* about that war. Whose blood had been shed. Whose family had been destroyed. She took a deep breath. 'You don't have to go on.'

He was looking past her to a point over her shoulder. His eyes were shadowed, his thin lips bracketed by deep lines. 'Not everyone was so unlucky. There were many refugees who left Bosnia. Some have returned to rebuild their lives, others stayed away.'

'Like you?'

He shook his head. 'I've visited. But it's not the same for me any more. I don't like meeting old friends who became enemies overnight. Can you imagine what it's like to have a neighbour or a close friend who one day turns and spits at you in the street, calls you names, picks a fight, holds a gun to your head? Then years later you meet them again ... I find it hard to behave as if the war never happened. It did. And I can't forget.' He stood up. 'I've said enough. You don't want to hear more. I just look at the TV and see that nothing's changed. The world has not learned.'

But Caro did want to hear more. Not of the war itself, but of him – his story. Her decision to help him had been the right one. That was the very least she could do for someone who had suffered so much. Even after so long, trauma still lay hidden, waiting to ambush its victims.

She looked up at him and gathered her courage. 'I probably can't help but I'm here if you ever want to talk.'

There was a silence – he bowed his head. 'Thank you.' And he left the room.

He didn't open up to her in the following days. Instead, they went back to skirting round each other, unsure how to be. Occasionally he joined her to watch TV again when she made sure she wasn't watching the news. If anything, it was as if giving so much of himself away had shut him down, taking him away to a place she could never go with him.

The prospect of seeing Paul again came as something of a relief.

She made an effort getting ready for him, trying on several outfits but none of them quite right. With each one, she could imagine Chris voicing his opinion. *'Not too much cleavage, Caro, doesn't suit you.' 'Do you really think you've got the legs for that?' 'Would that be better if it was a bit looser/shorter/longer?'* She was annoyed that she couldn't shake that voice off. No wonder her confidence had gone walkabout. Finally she plumped for a slightly fitted dress in teal blue with a tie neck, like something from the sixties. *'Bit* Mad Men, *isn't it?'* This time she shut her ears to him, recalling instead how he'd looked the last time she'd seen him – how things had changed. Being with Georgie had given him the impetus to spruce himself up. She should take a leaf out of his book and kickstart herself out of her rut. But looks shouldn't matter so much, should they? Wasn't she past the age when they were the first thing anyone thought about? It was what went on inside that counted. Staring into the mirror, she made up her mind to book an appointment at the hairdresser.

As she went downstairs to wait for the cab, Damir emerged from his room and walked along the corridor towards her. He stopped at the top of the stairs to let her go down first.

'Going out?' he said. 'You look good in that colour.'

She was stopped in her tracks, self-conscious, unused to receiving a compliment that didn't have a nip to it.

'Your perfume reminds me of something.' He paused as if remembering. 'I like that too.'

She turned to smile at him. Their eyes met just for a second before she looked away, embarrassed by the unexpected connection she found there. 'It's pomegranate and . . .' She stopped. He wouldn't want the detail.

'Yes?' He returned her smile before she carried on down the stairs, taken aback by what had just happened. But what *had* just happened? *Nothing*, she said to herself as she took her coat from the stand. As she was struggling to get her arm down the inside out sleeve, he took the back of the coat and helped her on with it. 'There.' For a second, his hand rested on her back, she could feel its solidity, its warmth. He stepped away from her, inclined his head. 'Have a good evening.'

'Thanks. I'll do my very best.' She still felt the pressure of his hand on her back.

He frowned, not understanding the irony. His English didn't run that far. She didn't stop to explain but went into the porch to wait for the cab to pull up outside the gate.

She had accepted the invitation to Paul's for supper without giving it much thought. But now, as the cab approached his flat, she was suddenly nervous. They had eaten out, gone to the cinema, met for drinks, but this was different. Being on his turf for the first time definitely changed the agenda. She remembered Fran's words. There were many men worse than Paul. If she were ever going to find a partner, she would have to take the plunge sometime. Perhaps it didn't matter who with. Rediscovering physical intimacy inside a relationship might not be as bad as she feared. She remembered the strength in Damir's touch. Felt it.

She hadn't done anything like this since before she met Chris although she hadn't forgotten those evenings spent by the phone, hoping it would ring, the nervousness that once meant she managed to flick all twenty cigarettes out of a precious packet of Gold Leaf onto the cinema floor. How was she meant to behave now she was sixty-plus? Was dating different? She didn't feel different inside.

Paul buzzed her in, greeting her with a kiss on the cheek. 'Come in. I'm so glad you said yes.' He was taller than her, what was left of his hair was shaved short and his eyes were kind behind his dark-framed glasses. He was sporting gold corduroy trousers (a pet hate of Caro's) and a green jumper that silhouetted a modest paunch.

Caro looked around her. Waxed floorboards, modern white furnishings. At one end of the room were a Scandi-looking dining table and chairs – all edges and angles. At the other end, a sofa and chair; a fireplace with a coal-effect gas fire. Modern prints on the white walls. There was nothing comfortable or homely about the room at all. She paused in front of a garish geometric effort.

'That came from Denise's mother and I haven't the heart to get rid of it,' he said, returning with two glasses of wine. Caro immediately thought of all the things that Chris had loved that she had shunted out of sight immediately after he left: the green and orange rug they had bought on that long weekend in Morocco; the golf clubs in the back porch; the hall chair. The list went on.

The mention of Denise had made her uneasy. Competition with a dead woman who had achieved sanctity in her family's eyes would be hard to win. Her eyes travelled to a pair of framed photos. The only personal touch in the room. 'Your kids?'

'Yes.' Funny how much pride could be fitted into that short word. 'Pip and Gerry. That was taken on our last family holiday all together. France.'

Caro picked up the frame and gazed at the two beaming faces: Pip squinting into the sun; Gerry doing a double thumbs up, his eyes hidden behind his aviator sunglasses. In the background a woman was lying back in a deckchair, her arm bent across her face, covering her eyes.

'And that's Denise?'

'Mmm.' His eyes were half shut as he remembered. 'She was remarkable, never complained. Even towards the end.' He seemed to make a huge effort to pull himself back from wherever the thoughts of his wife had taken him. 'We'll never forget her, of course, but life must go on.'

'It's hard though,' she said. Was that what this evening was about? Was he making the same reluctant effort as her? 'You're expected to carry on so quickly these days. Everyone's so sympathetic and kind to start with but no one can keep that up forever. So you have to carry on as if you've got over it when inside you're still in pieces.'

'That's right.' His shoulders relaxed as he sat down. 'You really do understand. I knew you would.'

Encouraged, Caro carried on. 'Well, divorce is like that too. But you were lucky to have Denise.' Oh God, what was she saying? He looked grief-stricken. She blundered on, trying to make things better. 'I mean, some marriages just aren't meant to be. I believed mine was forever. I was ready to compromise as much as it took. Even in the bad times, I never thought about giving up on it. It didn't cross my mind that Chris would either.'

'But why?' He seemed perplexed.

'The children,' she said quickly. 'That's why you stay. Nothing matters more. You have to put them first, however miserable you are.' She raised her glass and let the chilled wine trickle down her throat. 'That's what Chris did too.'

'But can't separating be seen as putting them first too? Imagine what it must be like living with unhappy, arguing parents.'

'Maybe.' Caro didn't have to imagine but she was cross that he had effectively sided with Chris.

'Supper and a change of subject,' he said, seeing she was offended. He left the room, as uncomfortable talking about Chris as she was about Denise. When he returned, he was carrying two plates of something steaming and meaty smelling. 'Lamb tagine,' he announced as he walked to the dining table. 'Come and eat.'

'Wow! I'm impressed. It smells amazing!' And it was. As was the lemon syllabub they had for pudding and the two cheeses they had to round off. Chris could no more have produced a meal like that than fly to the moon. *Stop comparing*, she lectured herself. *You're starting again. From scratch.*

'When Denise died, I decided to teach myself to cook,' Paul explained when she complimented him. 'I find it really relaxing and, on the odd occasion when it works, very satisfying.'

'Well it worked tonight.' She was feeling warm and slightly fuzzy having drunk too much too fast as she tried to force herself to relax.

He took her hand. 'I'm glad,' he said. 'I wanted to make you feel at home.'

She stared at her hand lying in his, immobile. He placed his other hand over it, hiding it from view, cocooned.

No!

She wasn't ready for this yet. She quickly pulled her hand away and excused herself. In the state-of-the-art bathroom, she laid her cheek against the marble tiled wall, feeling the cool against her cheek, and gave herself a good talking-to. She shouldn't have come if she wasn't prepared to see this through. They both knew the game they were playing. *Come on, Caro. You can do this.* She squeezed out some of his toothpaste and rubbed it round her mouth with one finger then ran the cold water until it was icy, cupped her hands and sluiced it round her mouth. She got her lipstick out of her bag and quickly applied it, followed by a dab of powder to her nose, a squirt of perfume, then she stood and stared at herself. What must he see?

Her face still looked good, if a little soft at the edges. Her hair was wild. Separation from Chris had at least meant she had lost some weight. She took a deep breath. She was as ready as she ever would be.

8

Back in the sitting room, Paul had changed the music to something slower, softer. He was lying back on the sofa and turned his head when she came back in. 'Something else to drink?'

'I don't think I should,' she said although a bit more Dutch courage wouldn't go amiss. 'Well, perhaps a small one.'

He got up, poured the wine and brought it to her, and suddenly – she wasn't sure how it happened – they were kissing. How peculiar it was to be kissing someone who didn't have Chris's lips, whose nose was bigger, who didn't do the things Chris did and that she was used to. She winced as he nipped her lip. Paul's hands were quite different, less confident, more tentative. They moved as if he was scared to touch her, as if he thought she might recoil or break into pieces. All these thoughts flashed through her head, stopping her from letting go. But having got this far she wanted to see where it would take them. Unbidden, her mind went to Damir. Paul was less obviously fit than him, less solid and considerably more awkward. She forced herself back to the immediate present. She definitely felt a frisson of sexual desire. So her libido hadn't entirely given up the ghost after all.

He murmured something about the bedroom and she agreed, holding his hand as they made the short journey across the corridor. Now they were sprawled on his bed, fumbling, missing, laughing, wishing the lights were out as her dress was removed then his shirt. These were self-conscious fumblings that reminded her of her teenage years; that race to the inevitable finishing line.

She tried to get over her inhibitions but the more she was aware of them, the more she was aware of what they were doing.

She couldn't help thinking that rediscovering sex at this time in her life after years of drought was oddly like discovering it for the first time. She had been in a hurry then and lost her virginity to a boy from school: something that had to be got through before they could start to enjoy themselves. Like then, once they'd got that hurdle out of the way, it would all get easier – unless middle age and the menopause had robbed her of everything. She hadn't thought she cared about the lack of sex in her life but now she found that, after all, she did want to achieve the kind of pleasure that she had allowed herself to forget.

After a few minutes Paul excused himself and went into the ensuite. She heard the loo flush then the sound of cupboards opening and shutting. Surely he wasn't looking for condoms? At their age. Or should she be insulted by a slur on her sexual hygiene? Caro straightened her slip then, thinking that looked too reserved... inched it up again – she should try. She let her gaze travel round the room. At least this one had some character. The walls were as white as everywhere else in the flat but the shelves were rammed with books with every now and then a gap for the odd vase or photo frame. A tartan dressing gown hung on the back of the door. The king-size bed had a dark blue and green throw at its foot that they'd rumpled up with the duvet. She yanked it back into the right position. Now what?

She consulted the many romantic films she'd sat through. She couldn't remember anyone sitting on the end of a bed, straightening a throw, waiting. They took the next step... She stood up and removed her slip, wriggled out of her tights – not sexy even back in her twenties – and left them abandoned on the floor. Quickly, before he came back, she climbed into his bed, pulling the duvet up round her neck, breathing in the smell of detergent mixed with the smell of Paul. As she was trying to make herself look halfway desirable – one or two arms out in the open? A glimpse of bra? Hair tousled or combed? Lipstick? – she noticed another photo of Denise on the bedside table. She was saying something to whoever was taking the picture, while the man behind her was laughing. She seemed to be looking straight out of the photo at Caro. *He's mine!* Caro turned away. If this was going to be a night of passion, however lukewarm, she would have to ignore the opposition, channel herself into a state of abandon. She took a deep breath.

By the time Paul returned, she was feeling less and less like a femme fatale. She rolled onto her side and held the duvet open to him, sucking in her stomach until it was almost flat. 'I thought you were never coming back.' A little laugh. The invitation could not have been more obvious.

But instead of leaping in with her, he sat on the edge of the bed. Feeling both ridiculous and redundant, she covered herself up. His hands twisted together in his lap and he looked miserable.

'What's the matter?' Caro felt pretty sorry for herself. Being rebuffed, however little it really mattered in the scheme of things, was humiliating.

'Nothing. It all feels . . .'

'I thought this was what you wanted.' How could she have misread the signs so badly?

'It was. I do.' The fingers of his right hand twisted the wedding ring that he still wore on his ring finger.

'Well, come on then.' She raised the corner of the duvet again, less generously than last time, giving him a brief glimpse of her bra, her breasts. Was this seductive at all?

But he picked up the photo nearest him. His knuckles were white as he grasped it. 'I thought I was ready,' he said. 'But I'm not. I do want you, Caro, but I can't with Denise watching.'

'But that's easy. We can turn the photos round,' Caro suggested, reaching out for the other one.

'No! Leave it!' He barked the order as if she was about to commit a crime.

She snatched her hand back under the duvet.

'I'm sorry. Perhaps it's too soon after all.' He bent forward over his knees and put his head in his hands.

'Perhaps it is,' she said, wishing she was anywhere but in his bed, and wondering when the best moment would be to get out of it, and how. 'You're sure you don't want to even . . . ?' She tried to sound as inviting as she could.

He shook his head. 'It feels all wrong. I can't.'

Feeling an absolute idiot for having presumed too much, Caro reached for her slip but it was just out of her reach. Dragging the duvet with her to protect her modesty – something she was all too conscious of since the change of mood – she hooked it between finger and thumb, and pulled it back into the bed. She didn't feel like parading herself almost naked round his bedroom now. Paul didn't look up as she pulled the slip on. 'Excuse me,' she said, as frosty as she could be.

He emerged from his trance, and looked at her as if startled to find her there at all. 'Yes, of course. I'm sorry.'

'Paul, if you say you're sorry once more . . .'

'I'm sorry . . .' He made a face and left the room.

Alone she got out of the bed, grabbed her dress and wriggled into it, before picking up her tights and pulling them on. She left the bed unmade and stalked into the hall.

'Caro, I . . .'

'It's fine, Paul. I completely understand. Let's not mention it again.' She reached for her coat on the stand.

'Will you have a coffee before you go?'

Only if I can throw it over you. But the thought remained in her head. 'I've had enough for one evening. I think it's better if I just call a cab.'

'Good night out, love?' The driver half-turned his head. She saw him wink in the mirror.

'I've had better.' She got out her phone and started texting

78

Fran who had been due back from the States only days earlier. The driver turned his music back up and hummed along.

You back?

Yesterday. Had a blast. What's up?

Paul was a disaster.

Immediately a text pinged back. *On sofa in front of TV with S. What happened?*

Caro smiled to herself. *Too long to text. But wanted to warn you it's a non starter.*

Oh no! Well at least you're out and about. Glass half full.

One way of looking at it! Half empty.

Caro settled back in the seat of the cab, reliving the evening. Although she had always been adamant that she didn't need a man after Chris, now she wondered. She had forgotten what it was to feel desired. And Paul had desired her for some of the evening. But had that part of her really withered up and died? Apart from self-consciousness and rustiness, she dug around inside herself to see what else she had felt before it all went wrong. There had definitely been that flutter she thought she would never feel again, and she had enjoyed that. Those buttons she thought had jammed ages ago were still working after all. All she needed was the right man to press them harder. Perhaps Fran was right.

She was pondering this state of affairs, clutching on to her seatbelt as the minicab screeched round the corner into their road. 'Can you slow down a bit?' she shouted over the music. 'We're nearly there. You're going to miss...'

There was a squeal of brakes and a thump. The car swerved onto the carefully manicured grass verge belonging to her neighbour. The driver switched off the engine, and stared out of the window at the road. 'Fuck!'

'What was that? Have you hit something?'

'Some bloody animal! Just ran straight out. I didn't see it till it was too late.' He banged the steering wheel with his fist. 'If it's damaged the car...'

'Probably a fox,' she said, pulling back in her seat, away from his violence. 'Is it OK?'

'I'd better have a look.' He grunted as he hauled his bulk out of the front seat, leaving the car door open. Caro pulled her coat tighter against the cold as she watched him. First he went to the front of the car, bending over, touching the bumper, shaking his head. Then he walked a little way down the road out of the beam of the headlights and stopped by a dark shape in the shadow of a tree. He touched it with his foot then gave up and shuffled back to the car.

'Is it a fox?' Caro asked as he got in.

'Nah! Some bastard cat. Dead.' He switched on the engine.

'You can't just leave it there. It belongs to someone. We should at least move it to the verge.' She would hate it if someone left Tigger to be run over repeatedly. She opened her door.

He sighed and turned off the engine. 'All right, all right. Let me see what I've got.' He got out again and shone his phone torch into the boot and pulled out a moth-eaten blanket. 'Best I can do.'

As they crossed the tarmac, her feet pinched and painful, she cursed her choice of shoes and her vanity. Paul hadn't even noticed them. She caught the driver up as he eased the animal onto the blanket with his foot. Although she didn't want to, she couldn't stop herself peering at the cat stretched out in a dark smear of blood. Perhaps she knew its owner. She shone her phone torch on to the animal to see if she recognised it. She gasped. The bushy tail, the ginger coat, the single white front paw only belonged to one cat around here: Tigger. She looked again, swaying on her heels. But it couldn't possibly be him. Tigger had been dodging the cars on this road for years. She took a reluctant step forwards.

'You all right, love?'

'I think it might be my cat.' She swallowed. Not Tigger. This was not how he should end his days. She hadn't been driving the car but the coincidence of her being a passenger made her feel in some way responsible. If only she had told the driver to slow down sooner.

The driver stared at the pile of fur at his feet. 'You sure?'

'One hundred per cent.' There was no mistaking that face and the white bib that went from under his chin across his right leg. 'Oh, Tigger. No, no, no . . .' She squatted down and touched his paw, half-expecting him to roll over with a purr. There was no response. She looked up at the driver. 'I asked you to slow down. This didn't have to happen.'

'It wouldn't have mattered how fast I was going. He nipped out from between the cars. Didn't stand a chance. But I'm sorry.' He shifted from foot to foot, keen to make his escape. 'What do you want to do with him?'

They were only a few yards away from Treetops. 'Could you bring him to the house?' she asked. 'Just down here.' She was ashamed that she couldn't bring herself to carry her dear old friend on his final journey home. Chris had always looked after anything that made her squeamish. 'Come to the side door of the garage and we can put him in there overnight.' Burying him now was out of the question. Tigger would spend his last night in his bed, not chucked in a wheelbarrow or on the floor. She switched on the light.

'Where do you want him?' The driver was getting impatient, wasting valuable cabbing time as he carried Tigger in a sling he'd made with the blanket, the cat's tail hanging limp and lifeless out of the back.

'Hang on a minute.' Caro rearranged Tigger's sheepskin so it was flat in the basket. 'Here.'

Tigger slid from the blanket, leaving a trail of blood behind. His injuries were hidden underneath his body. He lay on his side, his legs stretched out in front of him, just as he would in life. Caro rubbed his nose. 'Poor old boy.' Her eyes were stinging with unshed tears.

'Anything else, love?'

'No. Nothing else. Thanks for bringing him in.' She was as keen for him to leave as he was, now.

'Well, I won't charge you, love. That's the least I can do.'

Caro had a sudden urge to burst into laughter or tears, she wasn't sure which. 'Thanks.' She wasn't going to argue.

He shut the door behind him and his footsteps crunched across the gravel. Caro heard the latch of the gate drop into place. A few minutes later, she heard the car turn then roar off into the distance and she was left alone.

By contrast, the silence surrounding her was complete. There was no wind, no birdsong, not even the bark of a distant dog. As she gazed down at Tigger, tears ran down her cheeks at last. He had been an extraordinary, exceptional animal to her. All through her separation from Chris, Tigger had been there, a reliable companion and comfort. He had adopted her just when she needed him. He had never failed to welcome Caro when she came in, or to keep her company in front of the TV, lying heavy on her lap. Occasionally he'd even come upstairs during the night to sleep on Chris's empty pillow.

Sometimes she worried about becoming a sad old cat woman – and so what if she did? Tigger had given her companionship when she needed it.

She folded the bloodied blanket over his body, then she switched off the light. 'Night night, old boy.' Her voice caught in her throat.

It wasn't until she got to the house that she realised just how sore her feet were. When she eased off her shoes she wiggled her toes as Milo pottered out onto the gravel for a late night pee. 'It's Birkenstocks and Crocs from now on, nothing else,' she told him. He wagged his tail in response to her voice.

As she went in, she missed the sound of the cat flap snapping open and shut as usual. She wondered how long it would take for Milo to notice Tigger was gone. In the kitchen, feeling the tiles cold but soothing under her feet, she picked up the cat bowl, emptied out the few remaining dried biscuits and put it in the dishwasher. After a minute, she opened the machine up again, removed the plate and chucked it in the bin. If Tigger wasn't going to eat from it, no other animal would either.

The house was silent. Damir must be in bed or out. This had been one nightmare evening. Feeling more alone than she had for years, she poured herself a brandy, pulled out a kitchen chair, put her head in her hands and sobbed.

9

The next morning, the spring sun filtered through the curtains. Turning her head, Caro considered the unoccupied space beside her in the bed, the pillow undented by anyone else's head. At moments like these, she missed the presence of Chris – even now – while at the same time relishing the quiet calm his absence had restored in her life. She lay for a moment, letting the voices on the radio wash over her, listening to bits of news that interested her, just like any morning. After a while, she got up and padded into the bathroom and began her morning routine. As she brushed her hair, her eye was caught by her solitary toothbrush in its mug and a wave of misery rose up into her chest.

The death of Tigger represented the end of everything else in her life. The end of her marriage. The end of Treetops. The demise of her sex life. What else was left?

Your family, came the answer. At least she had them.

Downstairs, she was greeted by the smell of toast and coffee. Damir had made breakfast, enough for both of them. He looked up as she came in. 'Did you have a good evening?'

'Not really. Everything went wrong.'

'Maybe next time it will be better. I hope so.' He passed her a piece of toast and slid across the butter and marmalade before pouring her a coffee.

'Thanks. Me too.' How lovely it was to be looked after even in these little ways. It had been so long. She wanted to take his hand and thank him but he'd probably run a mile. Instead she told him about Tigger. 'So this morning I've got to bury him. We've got a bit at the end of the garden where all the pets are buried – even Amy's goldfish. I need to get this done before Lauren brings Danny over. He's spending the weekend here while she and Mike go away.' Oh God, she was going to cry. For a moment, she struggled and then gave in. Wiping the tears on her cheeks, she said, 'Sorry.'

'It's strange,' he said. 'How animals can make you feel the deepest grief sometimes.'

She shot him a look, but he gave nothing more away.

'Let me help you. I can dig, perhaps?' He pushed his chair back.

'But aren't you working?'

'This is important. I liked that cat. I can work late today to make up.'

Caro was touched by his offer, glad he would be helping her with such a miserable and lonely task.

Despite the sun, the air outside was still crisp. She pulled on her wellies and an old anorak that one of the girls had left behind before getting two spades from the garden shed. The two of them walked up to the spot where there was a group of battered crosses made of twigs bound together with string by the kids, gravestones made of floor tiles. There they all were, the pets that had brought so much pleasure to the family. Caro pointed to a space next to a cloud of snowdrops where Tigger wouldn't be far from the other pets. 'There's room there.'

Milo barked at a squirrel that raced up the apple tree.

They dug together, Caro trying to keep up with the rhythm Damir soon established. It was hard work, and she was glad of his muscle. 'You've done this before,' she said.

He stopped and leant on his spade. 'When I was first taken to the front line, I was expecting to be given a gun so that I could fight. Instead I was given a spade and told to start digging a trench. Compared to that, this is easy.'

'But they gave you a gun in the end?' She hated the idea of this gentlest of men killing anything.

'We didn't have enough weapons so we had to share what we had. I took from someone leaving their shift and then, when I finished mine, I handed it back again. Our army had very little. We had to capture what we could from the Serbs.' He shook his head at the memory, then went back to digging.

'Let me. I can finish this now. You've done enough.'

He raised his hand. 'No, no. You shouldn't do this alone. We'll finish it together.'

Caro carried Tigger to his grave. The body was so stiff it didn't feel like her cat any more. How death changes everything. Her mind drifted to the last time she had seen her father lying in the hospital mortuary, looking as if he was carved from stone. So still. Only hours earlier he had been her dad but once his spirit left him, there was nothing of him there. All that remained was a shell. She had leant forward and given him a last sad kiss on his forehead. Her mother had hung back, unwilling to touch him.

Damir's cough brought her back to the present.

Tree roots prevented the hole from being any bigger so they had to lay Tigger propped at an angle, his legs pointing heavenwards. They stood on either side of the grave, looked up at the same time to catch each other's eye and burst out laughing. For a moment Caro thought she couldn't stop but then pulled herself together. Damir turned away to fill in the hole. He stamped down the earth while Caro picked a few snowdrops and laid them on top. They stood side by side, heads bowed, Damir taking his lead from Caro. How much she would miss the cat's presence around the house. The tears wouldn't stop. *Please, please.* Chris would always say a few words over the pets' graves but then the weeping girls expected that. Beside her, Damir stood silent. Thinking how much he must have lost made her shy away from being so sentimental. He must think her over-reaction was absurd. She pulled a grubby tissue from her pocket and blew her nose.

He was standing so close they were almost touching. She felt his arm move beside her then the weight of it across her shoulders, his hand gripping the top of her arm. She almost froze mid nose-blow before acknowledging human contact was exactly what she needed at that moment. He had sensed that. She needed someone who cared, who understood what she was feeling. He didn't say a word, didn't move, just kept gazing at the grave, the lower part of his face hidden by his scarf. His coat smelled of paint and white spirit. When he looked at her, she was surprised to see tears in his eyes, too. Something fluttered in her stomach and she caught her breath.

He cleared his throat and was about to say something when . . .

'Mum! What *are* you doing?' Marching towards them was Lauren, her puzzled expression half-hidden by her scarf, with Danny running beside her.

Damir's arm fell to his side and Caro stepped away from him, feeling his absence.

'Tigger was . . .' Caro stopped, aware that Danny was gazing at her, all ears. 'Tigger died last night.' *Tell you later*, she mouthed over Danny's head.

'Oh no.' Lauren lifted Danny up and kissed his forehead, shielding him.

'Your mother was upset, so I help her,' Damir explained. 'Now I must get to work.' He gave his little bow and went round the side of the house to his van, leaving Caro to wonder what would have happened if Lauren hadn't turned up when she did. But, no. The idea that something might was out of the question. He was just being kind.

'I'm sure she's fine,' Lauren called after him. 'We'll look after her. Mum, honestly! He's your lodger!'

'Don't be silly. It wasn't anything.' Caro felt herself heating up. Wasn't it?

'That's not how it looked from where I was.' Lauren gave her a beady look as if expecting her mother to confess all.

'Take my word for it.' Caro shut the conversation down. 'Danny, you go on in. I've put a biscuit and a drink for you on the kitchen table.' He didn't need to be told twice. As soon as he had disappeared inside at a run, she turned to Lauren. 'I know you're only looking out for me but it's a long time since Dad left, and I can stand up for myself now. Promise. Damir's a good lodger, he's done a lot round the house and he was just helping me bury Tigger who was run over last night.'

As she described the accident, Lauren's hand flew to her mouth. 'I can't believe you were in the taxi. That's terrible.'

But Caro hadn't finished. 'I was more upset than I thought I would be. When he saw me crying he put his arm round me. A friendly hug that anyone with a heart would have given. That was it, whatever you thought you saw.'

Had she wanted it to be more? What had Damir been about to say? There had been some sort of a connection in that look they shared, she was certain. She had seen that deep sadness behind his eyes again and longed to know more of what had caused it.

'Poor old Tigger.' Lauren slid her arm through her mother's and guided her back to the house. 'Poor *you*. Where had you been?'

'Just out with a friend.' Let Lauren assume she was with one of her women friends, as usual. She wasn't ready to share the debacle of the previous evening with anyone, least of all her own daughter. She didn't expect Lauren to be sufficiently interested to ask.

'I'm sorry I jumped to conclusions but I don't want anyone taking advantage of you, that's all.' She kissed Caro's cheek. 'I'll apologise when I next see him.'

Lauren's lawyer radar was always on high alert. Her job meant that she saw the criminal in everyone. In her eyes, the most plausible person was capable of being the most untrustworthy. 'I'll tell him you didn't mean it.' Caro bent over in the porch to remove her wellies. 'Tea?'

They were only a mouthful into a ginger biscuit when Lauren started talking about the summer. 'Have you made plans yet?'

'I've barely thought beyond this spring. Isn't that what we're meant to be these days – mindful? Being aware of the present and not looking to the future.'

Lauren laughed. 'If I only thought about now, I'd never get anything done. So Mike and I were wondering if you'd like to come to Italy with us. We thought we'd rent a house somewhere and we'd make sure you'd have your own room—'

'Thanks!'

Lauren laughed. 'You know what I mean.'

'That sounds lovely. I was vaguely wondering about going back to the Alps and Fran and Simon have talked about me joining them in Cornwall. Let me see what their plans are.'

Lauren looked astonished. 'I thought you said you hadn't thought about summer.'

'I just meant I hadn't got anything fixed.'

To her surprise, a tiny streak of rebellion had flared into life. A year earlier, Caro would have agreed like a shot, glad to be needed and glad to spend more time with them as a family. However, she had been on holiday with Mike and Lauren before and knew how tense it could get. They both took several days to relax out of work mode and then all too soon they were thinking about what was waiting for them when they got back. She thought back to the chilly cottage in the grounds of a substantial manse on the Scottish borders, those tiny damp rooms hung about with their drying clothes, Danny refusing to go to bed, the TV being on the blink as the rain sluiced down outside, pieces missing from the jigsaw. Of course Italy would not be like that.

Caro loved her daughters and she adored her grandson but she was beginning to see that she needed to carve out her own path through the rest of her life before it was too late. She should stop saying yes to everything either of them suggested without thinking but stop to consider what she wanted to do too. Being a spare part on their family holiday wouldn't necessarily be the best thing for any of them. It was kind of them to include her but much as she enjoyed being with them, they needed time together as a family – without worrying about work and without her.

'Wouldn't the three of you rather be on your own?'

She got up to take the mugs to the dishwasher and remove herself from the focus of Lauren's gaze. Her daughter was used to things panning out the way she wanted them to. That you-can't-be-serious look crossed with the but-I-need-you look was extremely hard to refuse.

'Would Mike's mum go with you?'

There was a snort from the other side of the kitchen. 'Oh please. Helen's still working every hour God sends. She talks about retirement but she's so driven, I don't see it. She's not like you.'

'What's that supposed to mean?' Caro was insulted by being thought of as someone with nothing important to do.

'Just that you *don't* work every hour God sends, and you have the school holidays off.'

If, like Helen, she had been the British CEO for a global confectionary, food and pet-food brand, she would probably still have been working her arse off too. But Chris would never have tolerated marriage to such a high-flyer. He might have made noises about her going back to set designing but her taking up painting and its teaching, working round the girls' school times, had its benefits. Working locally meant she could always be home when he got back from a day at the studio, be mother to his kids, make a nest for the family. Lauren was the one like Helen, nose to the grindstone every day, working early, working late. Criminals didn't wait while mothers looked after their children. Caro only understood the basics of Lauren's job as a criminal lawyer, but she did understand it meant Lauren had little time for anything else and had to rely on other people to look after her family. Mike seemed happy with the arrangements, but then he was used to a mother who was never there. Helen provided a role model that Lauren aspired to whereas she, Caro, had been nothing of the sort.

'I never wanted to be like Helen, or you, or Amy. I've chosen my own way of dealing with the demands made on me. Besides, I do work in the holidays.' Although to Lauren, painting hardly counted as work.

'Amy?' Lauren spluttered. 'We're nothing alike.'

Caro immediately leapt to her younger daughter's defence. 'She might not be in your world, but she works incredibly hard.'

'It's hardly the same.'

'Don't ever say that to her.' Sometimes Lauren was impossible. But pursuing the subject would only end in a row so Caro backed off and looked around. 'Where's Danny got to?'

Immediately distracted, Lauren got up. 'I think he went into the living room. Danny!'

He came running in, beaming and clutching a DVD. 'Found it! Can we watch?'

Smiling, Caro took it, already knowing what it was. And sure enough – *Peter Pan*. The two of them had watched it together at least twice, Danny riveted by the children's adventures in Neverland and on board the *Jolly Roger*. She had loved the story as a child herself and liked nothing better than having Danny curled up tight beside her as they clapped as loud as they could to save Tinkerbell's life. 'Good plan,' she said. 'Though let's take Milo out first and then I'll make us some popcorn and we can settle down.'

'Yeees!' Danny jumped up and down. 'Popcorn.'

'You spoil him, Mum.' Lauren stood up, an indulgent but-I-don't-really-care smile on her face. 'I'd better go. Come here, monkey.' She scooped up her son and gave him a kiss. 'Now you be good and Daddy'll be back to get you tomorrow.'

She put him down and turned to Caro. 'You know I didn't mean what I said about Amy. The shop's fantastic and she's doing a brilliant job. It's good Dad helped her with the money to set it up. At least he's done that as well as our loft extension.' She looked around her. 'Have you decided what to do about this place yet?'

'I'm going to stay here if I can. I'm not ready to leave yet but the money's the problem. I've tried everything I can think of. Mum's my last hope, and I can't believe that she can lay her hands on the sort of amount I need.'

'Really? Do you think she'll help?'

Caro thought of May, left reasonably well off by her father, coping on her own. She tried to be there for her as much as she could, but she should do more. 'I've no idea. But if I don't ask...'

Lauren's eyes widened. 'Does anyone we know have access to that sort of cash?'

Caro shook her head. 'I doubt it.'

'And if she can't?'

'I'll have to agree to sell.' As she spoke, Caro felt the cool breeze of an unknown future blow through her.

Lauren looked thoughtful. 'Amy's doing the right thing moving in with Jason, don't you think?'

'Yes. I'm happy for her. Both of you off my hands at last.' She grinned.

'Mum!' Lauren pretended indignation.

'I'm only teasing.'

But the cool breeze had sharpened into a cold wind. *You are going to be free,* Caro told herself. *Free.* And what would she do with that new freedom? The question was both exhilarating and daunting.

10

After she'd got Danny to sleep, bribed by the promise of going to see her mother in the morning, Caro poured herself a glass of red wine and sat at the kitchen table, determined to sort out her bills. It was no good pretending to herself: she was struggling to keep on top of things. Chris contributed something to the running costs of Treetops but not enough. Asking him to up the amount was out of the question because it would only give him further ammunition for selling the place. Although she loved the work she did, it simply wasn't sufficiently lucrative and she was going to have to face up to it. She pulled the pile of envelopes towards her, opened her laptop and clicked through to her online bank account. Not empty but not as full as she would like. In the morning she would set about getting some more commercial portrait work – she would ginger up her agent who had been quiet for ages and advertise in the local paper to drum up some word-of-mouth custom.

She was exhausted but not quite ready for bed. Looking after Danny gave her such pleasure but it was the sense of responsibility that came with him that was draining too. She never thought of all the terrible things that could happen to her girls when bringing them up. Perhaps being younger had protected her. But now she was aware of all the risks, from stranger danger to E-numbers, allergies and accidents. Danny could be such good company, inquisitive and funny, that she sometimes felt she was letting him down by being over-cautious.

Her phone was on silent but the lit screen told her Chris was on the line. Reluctantly she took the call.

'We're just wondering if you've come to a decision about Treetops yet.' His tone was pleasant but firm but his insistence irritated her. As did the inclusion of Georgie.

'Everything's in hand. The place is beginning to look much better.' That's all he needed to know. A bit of her was still hoping that his and Georgie's plans would change, that Georgie would see the light before it was too late and hitch her wagon to a man closer to her own age.

'We need to get someone round to look at the place.'

'Not yet. Not till it's ready.' Her delaying tactics were so obvious.

There was the sound of a key turning in the lock. 'Hello,' Damir called.

'Must go,' she said. 'Someone's here. We'll talk about this another time,' and cut Chris off before he could say any more. She wondered what Damir would think when he saw her drinking alone then asked herself why it mattered. She could do whatever she wanted in her own home without looking for anyone's approval or disapproval – least of all her lodger's. And that's all he was. 'I'm in the kitchen.' She was still curious to know what he had been about to tell her when Lauren had appeared.

'Danny in bed?' he asked, standing in the doorway. A dash of black paint decorated his cheek.

She felt the pull of him, like a magnet drawing her in, but she sat tight where she was. This was surely all in her mind, not his. Unlike her, he could have his pick of anyone. He had done nothing to indicate he felt the same. 'Yes. He's exhausted after running after Milo on the Down. He could barely stay awake when we were watching TV.'

He crossed the room and pulled out a chair with a sigh. 'Can I join you? Or you're busy.' He glanced in the direction of the paperwork.

'I'm glad to have an excuse to stop,' she said, hastily shoving everything into a pile as he pulled out a chair. 'You must be tired too.'

'It's OK. I'm used to hard work.' His fingers drummed a tattoo on the table.

'I'm so sorry about Lauren.' Caro broke the silence. 'She asked me to apologise. She jumped to conclusions.' She gave an embarrassed laugh.

He shrugged. 'That's fine. I don't mind.' He dug in his pocket and held something out to her. 'I made this for Danny.'

She took it and turned it in her fingers. The wooden dinosaur was carved in recognisable detail. 'You made it?'

He nodded. 'All boys like dinosaurs.'

'But it's a perfect Stegosaurus. He'll love it. Thank you. Would you like a drink?'

He hesitated, looking at the glass in her hand. Of course, he was Muslim.

'I'm sorry. I didn't think . . . stupid of me.' She put the glass down. 'A cup of tea?'

'Actually I would like a small one.' He held out his hands to the warmth of the Aga while Caro got him a glass. 'Some Muslims do drink.' He reached for the glass. 'But wait, I have brought you something, too.' He got up and went out to the hall. When he returned he was holding a brown paper bag that he put on the table. 'For you.'

'Really?' She was touched. Soap, she guessed. Or a scented candle. She pulled the bag towards her. His expression was indecipherable. Amused, perhaps? Unsure?

She reached inside and took out a wooden box. She didn't know what wood it was, but the grain was beautiful, the corners perfectly aligned, the lid a perfect fit. Its beauty lay in the simplicity of the design, the only decoration being a carved fleur-de-lys on the lid.

'It's a thank you. I made it, too.'

'It's exquisite.' She lifted the lid. 'And so beautifully made.'

'I wanted to give you something special from me. The flower is from the Bosnian coat of arms.'

She held his gaze. What was he saying? That they were friends? A thank you? She put it on the table. 'I love it. Thank you.'

After she'd poured his wine, she ran her hand over the empty dent in Tigger's chair cushion. 'I'm sorry I was so upset this morning. I hope I didn't embarrass you.'

'No. I was sad, too.' After a moment he added, 'Death is always sad. Burials remind me of other deaths.'

'Even a cat's?' she asked, trying to lighten the moment.

'Even a cat's.' He pushed his glass away from him. 'Grief can be set off by anything. This made me think of another funeral a long time ago.'

'Can you tell me?' Her heart was racing.

He stared at his hands for a long time, turning his glass on the table. 'My sister's little daughter, Anita.'

'Oh no.' His niece. For a moment everything stopped. Caro could imagine nothing worse than the death of a child in the family. How would anyone get over that? All words were inadequate. 'I'm so sorry,' she managed.

He turned towards her, his pain all too visible. 'She was three, just like Danny.'

Caro caught her breath, reminded of her grandson sleeping safe upstairs. Instinctively her gaze flicked to the baby monitor Lauren had insisted she put on. She would check on him in a minute.

'She was playing outside the house when a shell exploded. My sister was blown to the ground and when she looked round, Anita had gone. Just her shoe was on the grass, and her doll. She had been buried under earth and rubble.' A look of deep sadness crossed his face.

Caro found herself kneeling on the floor beside him. All she could offer was the same contact he had offered her in sympathy. She reached out a hand and took his. 'I'm so sorry. So sorry.'

She felt his grip tighten – firm and warm – and they stayed there, not speaking, until the sound of the doorbell broke the moment.

Still feeling the weight of his hand in hers, its rough skin and calloused palm, Caro went to the front door, assuming it must be Amy. But instead of her daughter, Fran was standing there. Her mascara was smudged, her red lipstick faded, her hair dishevelled. Her coat hung open and her hat was in her hand. This was not the Fran the world was used to. Something was obviously wrong.

'I'm sorry, I had to come. There's no one else I can talk to.' She brushed past Caro into the house.

'What's happened?' Caro followed her back in, wishing she could wind the clock back five minutes and not answer the door at all. But Fran was her friend. Despite her sympathy for Damir, he would have to wait.

'Ewan.' Fran went straight to the living room and threw herself on to the sofa. Caro noticed, out of the corner of her eye, Damir slip out of the kitchen and up the stairs. If only she could go with him and comfort him. 'Wine?'

Fran straightened her skirt as her orange suede heels thudded to the floor and looked around. 'You're not busy?'

'You're only stopping me paying the bills. So you're doing me a favour.' She left the room to return with two glasses of wine. Having handed one to Fran and put hers down, she took a log and put it in the fire. 'Ewan, I take it.'

'He said he was going to be in town unexpectedly on business but he wouldn't be able to see me after all.' Her voice went up a notch at the hurt. 'But he's always here on business – that's exactly when we do meet. We still haven't properly talked about what we're going to do. My American trip got in the way. So I couldn't wait...'

'Oh, Fran.' With a sinking feeling, Caro realised that whatever happened with Ewan was not going to be easy.

'In the end he agreed to meet for a drink at St Pancras before he got his train back home. Well, anything's better than nothing. Right? So I turned up, only five minutes late, and for the first time ever, he wasn't there. I just assumed he was delayed.'

Caro could picture her sitting uncomfortable, alone, in the dimly lit, high-ceilinged bar, her gaze roaming between the various doorways, checking her watch every now and then. Fran was a woman who liked making an entrance, not one who hung around waiting.

'And then...' Her voice rose again, indignant. 'And then, after half an hour... *half an hour*...' She paused in between each word to give Caro a proper sense of the insult. 'He texts to say he's not going to make it after all. He's sorry.' She paused again so Caro could share the outrage. 'And when I call him, he doesn't pick up.'

'So what did you do?' Caro wondered what Ewan was up to. Why hadn't he contacted Fran sooner?

'I left. What else could I do? I got the Tube to Waterloo and came back here.'

'Where does Simon think you are? Won't he be worried?'

'I told him I was having a drink with Ginny and Josh after work – he'll never check – but that I'd be back for late supper. Which I will be.' She looked at her watch. 'Oh God, no, I won't. How can it be this time already?'

'Phone him?'

'Yes, yes. In just a minute. But first I want to know what you think happened. Just quickly. Why didn't Ewan turn up?' She sounded completely bewildered.

'I can't think. He probably *was* caught up with a colleague.' Caro said what Fran obviously wanted to hear. As far as she knew, he had never let her down before, and if he really was going to suggest she leave Simon... there couldn't be another explanation.

'On a Saturday night? I don't think so.' She made it quite clear what she thought of that idea.

'Why not? Plenty of people work on Saturdays – if someone had come to town specially to meet him... things run on. You know that. Deals can be delicate things and if he'd walked away at the wrong moment...'

'But I'd come specially to meet him. To talk.'

A sense of horrible foreboding stole over Caro. 'I'm sure he'll have a perfectly good explanation.'

But it was obvious both were deluding themselves.

Fran looked at her, big smudged eyes over the rim of her glass. 'You think?'

'Of course. Now for God's sake call Simon.'

Fran pulled a white iPhone from her bag, scanned it for messages and put it back. 'Wrong phone.'

'Do it. Now.' Caro was impatient. Her heart was with Simon, patiently waiting at home.

'I'm not calling him on the phone Ewan and I use. He'll wonder where I'm calling from. Wait a minute.' She rummaged in the depths of the holdall. 'Here.' This time she produced a black iPhone and quickly located the number. It must have rung for at least a nano-second.

'Yes, it's me. I'm really sorry I'm so late. We ran late and then I bumped into Caro on the way back. I'm at hers now... Yes, I know I should've... but you know what she's...' Her voice tailed away to a whisper, presumably to suggest that Caro was in some sort of crisis that she couldn't expand on at that second.

Caro pulled a finger and thumb across her lips to signal she didn't want to be used as an excuse although aware she must have been many more times than even she knew. Fran's shamelessness was one of the things she loved about her. When she wasn't in its firing line.

'Anyway, we're just having a quick drink, and then I'll be right back. Have you? Sounds delicious. Won't be long.' She blew a kiss down the phone and ended the call. 'Fish pie! That's the last thing I feel like eating. So you don't think there's anything to worry about?'

'Fran! Stop asking me. How would I know?'

Fran held her glass out for a top-up. 'It's just that I'm worried that I've got it all wrong. That I've misunderstood something.' She sat up straight. 'No, no. Of course I haven't.'

Caro watched a variety of expressions chase across her friend's features, chief among them fear. 'And Simon? I know I keep reminding you, but what about him?'

'Don't. Just don't. I can't bear to think about it.'

There was the sound of footsteps coming downstairs. She sat up. 'Who's that? You didn't say anyone else was here.'

'Only my lodger.' Caro got up to shut the living-room door so they wouldn't be interrupted. Fran was looking curious. 'It all happened while you were in the States and I haven't seen you.'

'A lodger! Are you really that hard up? You only had to say – I can lend you something.'

'No, no. The girls wanted me to have company, so I thought I'd go along with it, and Chris is being difficult – understatement of the year. He asked me for a divorce. He's getting married.'

'Not to that Georgie woman?'

Caro nodded, not trusting herself to speak.

'Why didn't you say something sooner? I'm so sorry. Are you OK?'

'I suppose it had to come eventually. I accepted it was over years ago but this seems so final at last. He wants his share of Treetops.'

'He's going to move back in?!'

'Hardly.' Caro laughed at the idea of the three of them co-habiting. 'What a thought. Either I buy him out or we sell it.'

'You can't!' Fran was horrified. 'This is where you belong. This is you. Where will you go?'

There was a tap at the door before it opened and Damir put his head round. 'I'm going to see friends, and won't be back tonight.' He nodded at both women.

Caro felt herself blushing. 'Thanks.' She was glad to know she could lock up without wondering whether he was coming back. 'Have a good time.'

Fran was gaping at the now empty doorway then at Caro. '*He's* your lodger! Where did you find him?'

Caro leant her face on her hands to cover the colour in her cheeks. 'Quick version. I met him on the train. I was looking for a lodger. He was looking for somewhere temporary to live. He's been doing some decorating for me.' As she explained, she realised how improbable it all sounded. Fran's eyes were wide and then a grin spread across her face as her imagination went into overdrive. 'No. Nothing like that. It's only going to be for a few weeks and in fact I think the arrangement quite suits us both.'

'I bet it does.' Why was Fran so relentlessly single-minded sometimes?

'You know I don't mean like that!'

'But he's not bad looking.' There was a definite twinkle in her eyes.

'So?' Caro refused to rise to the bait.

'And he's young.'

'Too young for me.'

Fran's smile widened. 'Only teasing. Don't be so touchy. Talking of your love life – not that we were, of course – how's Paul? You haven't told me what happened that night.'

'Nothing really. Just a misunderstanding.' She refused to respond to Fran's grin. 'He's nice enough but I'm not absolutely sure we're right for each other.' She wasn't ready to confess to making such a fool of herself. Not even to Fran.

'Not right? He's affable and he's solvent. He's perfect for you.'

'No,' Caro was firm. 'He's the one *you* think is perfect for me. It's not necessarily the same from where I'm sitting.'

'Then get over here and share my seat!'

Caro couldn't help but laugh. 'Get back to your husband and stop causing trouble, woman.'

Fran looked at her watch again. 'Yes, I should. He'll have laid the table, candles and wine, managing to make even fish pie romantic.'

'You can't leave him, Fran. And you can't go on treating him like this. He doesn't deserve it.'

'Perhaps what I feel about him is something like what you feel about Paul.'

Caro was incensed. 'Don't be ridiculous. I haven't been married to Paul for decades. He's just putting his toe back in the dating pool after his wife's death, unlike Simon who's loved you for years, and you've had William.'

'But it's all about chemistry, isn't it?' Fran twisted her wedding ring round her finger.

'But marriage is more than just chemistry,' Caro insisted. 'What about the friendship, the support, the . . .' She tailed off as she considered the failure of her own marriage.

'All those things are the bricks, but chemistry's the mortar that holds them all together.'

'You really believe that?'

'You've just forgotten because it's been so long. Trust me, when you find that spark again, you'll change your tune.' Fran gave her a knowing look as she stood up to go. 'If I hurry, I'll be home by nine thirty.'

Left alone, Caro picked up the box Damir had given her, running her finger along the grain, feeling its smoothness, and over the fleur-de-lys. He must feel something for her to make this, even if no more than friendship. She knew, oh she knew so well, what Fran had been talking about. Facing someone glumly over the breakfast table. The excuses not to go to bed together. The flare-ups of irritation. She remembered the first time Chris had turned away from her, then the swift mechanical sex that seemed to satisfy him but never her. Those were the markers of the spark having left a marriage.

But she would never have left, however bad things were between them. Of course, there had been the odd flicker of lust for other men but she had made sure that those flickers never went further. When she felt miserable and at sea in her marriage, she had concentrated on her family and friends. The marriage vows were hard to keep, but not impossible, and she had tried, *she had tried*...

Her parents had stayed together in what from the outside looked like a loveless marriage. She had done her best not to replicate it but perhaps Chris was right to have seen the signals and acted on them...

Before she went to bed, Caro slipped out into the garden. It was cold and smelt of damp earth after that evening's drizzle. She made her way to Tigger's grave and stood in front of it for a long time before returning indoors.

II

Danny raced ahead up the paved garden path that ran between two gravel squares. In the centre of each a small olive
tree was pruned to look like a lollipop, a drooping yellow ribbon
tied around the top of their trunks, surrounded by a circular box
hedge. He waited for Caro in the porch of the bungalow, his
finger on the bell, waiting for her to give him the OK to press
it. In his other hand was the wooden dinosaur that Damir had
given to him before they left.

'I have something for a good boy.' Damir had put his hand in
his jacket pocket.

Danny stared at him, eyes wide, uncertain.

'Here.' Damir held out something in his hand.

Danny didn't move.

'You like dinosaurs? I made one for you.'

The boy stretched out his hand, his mouth widening into a
grin as he nodded. 'Thank you,' he whispered at Caro's prompt.

Damir squatted to be on the boy's level. 'I can make him a
friend, if you like.'

Danny nodded his agreement. Since then he had refused to
be parted from the Stegosaurus and insisted on bringing it with
them.

Net curtains swagged across the two bay windows on either
side of the front door, so that no one could see in. All that was
visible on the window ledge were two pastel-coloured china
shepherd boys from May's collection and a lattice-work porcelain
bowl full of wax fruit.

At Caro's nod, Danny pressed the bell. The chimes rang in three descending notes and then there was silence. Danny tipped his face up to Caro, his gappy grin and freckles making her want to scoop him up in a huge hug. 'Is she out?'

'No, no. She's expecting us. It just takes her a little bit of time to get to the door.'

'Why?'

'She's got a bad hip . . .' She tapped her own. 'So she can't walk very fast.' As she spoke there was the rattle of a chain then the sound of two bolts being slid back before a key turned and the door was pulled open.

'Welcome to Fort Knox,' whispered Caro.

Danny looked puzzled. 'Is that in *Batman*?'

'What did you say?' said her mother at the same time.

'Nothing. I was talking to Danny. Hello, Mum.' She leant forward to kiss her, the familiar smell of loose powder and her mother's signature tea-rose scent in her nostrils. 'How are you?'

'Not so bad.' She hated to admit to there being anything wrong. Always dressed well 'just in case I'm run over by a bus', she was smart in a narrow camel skirt, a tucked-in pussy-bow blouse and a pale green cardigan. Her thinning hair was dyed an improbable russet red. The comfortable elasticated pumps on her feet were her only concession to age. She stood back to let them in, wincing as she reached forward to tousle Danny's hair. 'Hello, Danny.'

He hung on to Caro's legs and peered out from behind them, wide-eyed.

'Don't be shy. You remember me.' May reached out to touch the dinosaur. 'Who's this?'

'He's a Stegosaurus.' Said with pride.

'Fancy knowing that.' She looked up at Caro, then back at Danny. 'Lucky you.'

Danny beamed back at her. She took Danny's hand as they

walked in then waited while Caro removed her cardigan and his jacket and hung them on the coat hooks.

'Come in, come in.' May leant on her cane as she led the way to the living room. Every available surface was covered in knick-knacks: china figures, animals, bowls, souvenirs from holidays, family photographs. May's long-suffering cleaner kept it all immaculate. No self-respecting speck of dust had a chance there. By the French windows leading into the garden – her mother's pride and joy – was a table bearing two square cut glass decanters, one of medium sherry, the other of brandy: favourite tipples at the beginning and end of an evening. A strong smell of something floral with chemical overtones hung over everything, originating in a diffuser, half-hidden behind the TV.

'How are you?' asked May.

'How long have you got?' said Caro, sitting down so Danny could climb onto the chintz sofa and her lap. She gave him a book from her bag.

'It can't be that bad, darling.' May lowered herself into her leather La-Z-Boy chair (that Caro had found second hand) with a groan. 'Oof! This wretched hip.'

'I don't know why you don't see someone about it.' Caro leant forward towards the tray that May had all ready for their visit. She began pouring the tea, wondering how many times they would have this conversation before one of them was carted off in a coffin.

'I don't want anyone messing around with me in hospital unless they have to. There are more germs in there than there are out here. Shall we play Snakes and Ladders after tea, Danny?'

He nodded, and took a homemade flapjack from the plate.

'Why don't you get the board ready when you've had your drink?' She pressed her chair's control pad so her feet were lifted into the air. Danny watched, amazed. 'That's better. So... tell me what you've been doing.'

As Caro began the edited highlights of the past week, Danny

ventured from her side to explore the box of books, board games and Dinky toys May kept on the bottom bookshelf. The tiny cars were part of Caro's father's collection, left after he dropped dead from a massive coronary in the queue in Nationwide. Still in their boxes, they were only brought out when Danny came.

'And then he didn't even turn up,' Caro said, having told Fran's story, confident that her mother had no one she could tell who would be interested. 'I don't know whether that's good or bad.'

May was laughing. 'Serves her right. Women should never do the chasing.' She punctuated her opinion by tapping her stick on the floor.

'Times have changed. Women do now.'

'Big mistake if you ask me.' May closed her eyes for a second: her way of signalling the subject was closed.

'Mum.' Caro stopped, hesitating to bring up the subject of money.

'Yes, dear . . . You are keeping an eye on Danny?'

'Yes, don't worry. Actually, there is something I want to talk to you about.'

'Danny, don't touch those. That's a good boy. Caro, can you stop him?'

Distracted by the photos on the side table, Danny picked out a silver-framed one of a young man in a tightly done-up suit and tie, his hat at a rakish angle and brought it over to Caro. 'My daddy,' he said.

Caro laughed. 'No, that's *my* daddy.' Indeed, this was her father as she had never known him. When she was born, his star was in the descendant and he had become a workhorse, slaving away to keep up appearances and provide for his family.

'That was taken before we were married,' said May. 'He must have been home on leave.' She looked as if she was about to say something else, then stopped herself. 'The Bridge club came here on Tuesday.'

'Mum? Can we . . .'

But May was keen to share her news. 'Mrs Dee was a wonder, helping me with the supper. If only you could have been here.' Caro only then noticed the four card tables folded and propped up behind the door.

'Sorry, but I was working. You know I'm hopeless at cards.' Losing at all those wet holiday games of Racing Demon, Old Maid and Rummy had ruined so many family holidays for her.

'I thought you were going to do less.'

'I don't know where you got that from. But if I'm not teaching, I help out Amy and Lauren during the week. And I like to keep at least one day for my own painting if I can during term-time. I can do more in the holidays.'

'I know.' She picked a couple of crumbs off her skirt. 'But you might have enjoyed it. Patricia and I make a good partnership. Have you got the box, Danny? Caro, can you help him?'

Caro went over to the box where Danny had been side-tracked into a game involving his dinosaur and a Matchbox Bus. Inside it were the few games that had been saved since Caro was a child. She suggested playing the Peter Rabbit race game, once her favourite of all with its tiny metallic figures, but Danny rebuffed her idea and pulled out the disintegrating box of Ludo, spilling the coloured counters onto the carpet. Underneath lay the Snakes and Ladders.

May won the first three games without making any concessions to Danny at all. She ignored Caro's signals to let him win once, even after he had caught her cheating. 'You've moved four but you threw three,' he pointed out to Caro's delight as May deliberately moved over the tail-end of a snake.

'Nonsense,' said May as she went on to win again.

Afterwards, Danny watched cartoons on Caro's iPad. While he was glued to the screen, she finished off telling May about Tigger's death, mentioning Damir without thinking. May's eyes had been closed as she fought off sleep, but they popped open at the mention of his name, as alert as ever. It wasn't just Caro's friends who were keen to see her happily partnered with someone new.

'*Who's* this man who helped you?' She pressed the control pad and sat herself up straighter.

'Didn't I tell you that I've got a lodger?' Caro knew she deliberately hadn't. 'He's very nice. He's Bosnian,' she explained, unnecessarily.

'Just the two of you in the house?' Her mother's raised eyebrow was comment enough.

'For heaven's sake, Mum. It's all above board. He needed somewhere to live and I wanted to help him out. You'd have done the same.'

Her mother was looking thoughtful as if there might be more to the arrangement than Caro was telling her. But Caro had convinced herself by now that any connection between her and Damir was merely a figment of her imagination. They had comforted one another, nothing more. And yet, as she sweltered in the dry heat of her mother's bungalow, she found herself looking forward to seeing him again.

'I have been out with someone else though, you'll be glad to hear.' Why was she even sharing this? Nothing more was likely to happen in that department.

Immediately May perked up. 'Really? Who?'

'You'd like him.' And that was exactly the problem. Paul was kind, deferential, keen to please – and May would love all that. *And at your age, have you any right to expect more?* asked her inner voice. *Yes, absolutely, you have*, came Fran's.

'It doesn't matter whether I like him or not. Do you?'

'It's not that I don't like him but he hasn't got over his wife's death.' There was no way she was going to share their disastrous last meeting, though the more she thought about it, the funnier she was beginning to find it. Getting into his bed had been such a stupid thing to do. She deserved his rejection.

'Second-hand men – they come with such baggage.'

'How would you know?!' Caro couldn't help laughing at the strength of her mother's feeling. She sometimes wondered if her mother believed that it was Caro's inattention that had allowed Chris to slip between her fingers like a well-pitched cricket ball. She would never convince her that there was nothing she could have done to prevent him leaving, nor that she enjoyed her life as it was now with its limited demands and her involvement with Lauren and Amy. Didn't she? Chris hadn't wanted that for himself but had seen a new life and grabbed it.

'Well, I don't of course. But I hear about other people.' May cleared her throat. 'Was there something you were going to ask me?'

'Yes.' Caro took her mother through Chris's last visit. 'So, as you know, he wants a divorce so he can marry Georgie. But what I didn't tell you was that we're going to have to sell Treetops unless I can buy him out.'

'Oh no!' There was a flash of anger in May's eyes. 'And you want me to help you?'

'I feel terrible even asking, but I've got to. I've tried everything I can think of. Treetops is still everything to me and the girls. I'm not ready to leave it. I don't know where I'd go.'

'It's big for one person.' May ruminated as she looked around at her own modest home.

'I know, and I will move out one day, but at the moment I can make a bit of extra money by renting out a room, maybe two and, if I can, I'd like to find a way of not doing everything the way Chris wants to. I've done that since we got married.' Caro heard herself adopting that defensive tone she only used with her mother, falling back into a childhood habit that had never gone away.

'I've always thought of the money your dad left me as a cushion in case I need care one day.' There was that flash of fear in May's eyes again as she made herself more comfortable.

'But I'd look after you. You know that.' Although they both

knew that living together, they would drive each other round the bend.

'But you don't earn all that much. Besides, I'd drive you round the bend.' This time May smiled, acknowledging that they knew each other better than either of them cared to admit.

'Oh, Mum.' Caro got up and kissed her mother's forehead. May held out her hand, bony and veined, dusted with age spots, and Caro took it. In one of those most precious of moments, they understood one another completely.

'Let's be realistic,' said May. 'How much do you need?'

This was the moment Caro had dreaded. 'Maybe as much as half a million.'

May gasped and shook her head. 'That's a lot.'

'I know it's a big ask, but I need to try. Even if you could find some of it.' But, even then, how would she find the rest?

Her mother recovered her composure. 'Let me talk to Jack and see if there's anything I can do to help.'

Jack was one of the partners in her husband's old firm. He had respected the older man and done what he could to help May manage her modest legacy in the most effective way. If anyone could come up with a financial solution to Caro's problem, he would.

The common stairway up to Amy's flat needed a good clean. Dust had collected in the corners, the chilly blue walls were smeared with dark streaks from where furniture, prams and bikes had been carted up and down. Behind the open front door was a pile of mail addressed to people who no longer lived there and some unwanted circulars.

'Come on up!' Amy's voice ricocheted down towards them. 'Danny! Are you there? I've got something for you.' No aunt loved a nephew more, and her love manifested itself in funny little gifts that didn't amount to spoiling, not exactly, but ensured her love was returned.

Danny charged ahead so that when Caro arrived at the open front door, she could hear his and Amy's voices over the music that was playing in the front room. She went into the large open space where Amy lived and ate. Although Amy had yet to acquire much in the way of belongings, the place was a mess. Caro wondered whether she would change when she was under Jason's roof.

The two of them were on their hands and knees having already begun a brand new game of Pickasticks.

'That one moved!' Danny shrieked in delight so Amy put her stick on the reject pile.

'OK, you do it then. No cheating.'

'Shall I make tea?' Caro didn't wait for an answer because she knew that was what was expected. She crossed to the cluttered work surface running along the far side of the room and put on the kettle. 'We can't be too long because Mike's coming to pick up Danny.'

'Oh, OK.' Amy stood up. 'If I get you the bricks, can you build me a house, Dan?'

Danny nodded, always happy to please her.

Once he was settled in a corner, Amy and Caro sat at the round table where a pile of bills and business papers had been shunted to one side. Amy's books were mostly in piles waiting to be boxed and her pictures were leaning against the wall.

'Don't say anything,' Amy said, seeing her mother glance at them. 'I've just been so busy.'

Caro accepted the mug of tea, an exclusive brand of mixed herbs guaranteed to promote the drinker's well being. It tasted like clippings from a hay field soaked in warm water, but she drank it without complaint. 'No Jason?'

'He's working today. They're developing something that's so top secret and urgent he can't even tell me so he's staying at his own place this weekend. That's why it was a good time for you and Danny to come over.'

'And?' Caro knew there was something else behind the invitation.

'OK.' Amy hesitated, her eyes fixed on her mother as if trying to read her likely reaction to what she was about to say. 'We're worried about you.' She lifted her hair and flicked it back over the shoulders.

'There's no need to be.' Caro didn't want to justify herself to her daughters, who seemed to think her incapable of looking after herself. She thought of her own mother's determination to remain independent – that's just how she wanted to be too. And she thought of her own attitude to May – not so far from her own daughters' attitude to her. Time for a rethink.

'But, Mum, what are you going to do about Treetops? Where are you going to live?'

'Don't worry, not with either of you.' Caro tried to joke her way out of the conversation. 'I haven't decided exactly what I'll do yet. If I can, I'm going to stay at Treetops so I've had to ask Mum if she can help me. I'm also hoping something will happen to make Dad change his mind.'

'That's hardly likely now Georgie's up the duff, is it?'

Caro froze then instinctively glanced at Danny. Her face must have betrayed her ignorance and shock. Amy looked horrified, as if she would bite the words back if she could.

'Didn't you know? Mum, I'm so sorry. I thought he'd have said.'

'No, he hasn't.' Her own voice seemed to be coming from a long way away. At the same time, the tiny ball of anger that had been set spinning since Chris came to visit was gathering momentum, turning, expanding.

'He called me to tell me and he said he would.'

'I'm sure he did.' This was so typical of Chris. He'd probably called her once and that was enough, even when she didn't pick up. If he'd called her on her mobile, she would have seen, but there was no record of his call.

A baby... a wild uprush of bitterness took her by surprise. Chris would soon have a new family, new priorities. Whereas she would be left with nothing but the tatters of the life they had once made together. But what tatters they were, she reminded herself – two wonderful daughters, the families they would make. She couldn't and wouldn't wish them away.

The bitterness grew less sharp as it changed into sadness.

'Mum? Are you OK?'

She shook her head. Her daughters had bright new lives to be getting on with but hers seemed full of dark corners. Maybe, just maybe, Chris was right not to have told her, sensing that she sailed near breaking point sometimes.

A baby.

'Mum? Are you OK?' Amy asked again, reaching under the table to rest her hand on Caro's knee.

'I'm fine,' Caro reassured her, gripping her hand tightly. 'It's just a shock. I should have seen this coming.' What other way was there for Chris to be sure of keeping Georgie? What else would make him feel young and virile again?

'I feel terrible.' Amy's face screwed up in concern. 'I shouldn't have said anything.'

'Of course you should. You weren't to know, and I had to find out some time. How do you and Lauren feel?' Whatever she was feeling – jealousy? A little. Anger? That too. Regret? Perhaps. And a little unspecified fear – the girls' feelings were much more important than her own. She didn't want them to suffer any more than they already had because of their parents.

Amy shrugged. 'I mind for you, but at the same time I guess he has to do whatever's best for him.' Always the one to live and let live. 'I quite like the idea of a new baby in the family.'

'And Lauren?' But Caro could imagine the answer.

'Furious. She called him "a dirty old goat"! Hates the idea that Danny is going to be older than his aunt.'

'I hadn't even thought of that.'

'But, Mum, we want you to be happy too.'

'I am.' She looked at Amy's anxious face. 'Honestly. I quite like my independence now I've got used to it.' If she said it often enough, would it become the truth? 'Perhaps now Dad has made these decisions, I should start making some too.' Caro took a sip of her tea, grimacing at the taste, determined that she was not going to let Chris and his brand new life ruin hers. At least she had reached an age where there was no possibility of her starting another family. She didn't envy him that. No, she was more than happy with the one she already had.

12

Caro was in the kitchen, her mind only half on Radio 4 in the background. Steam rose from the pan of vegetable soup that she had just thrown together for lunch. In front of her a sketch pad where she was jotting down thoughts for how to increase her commissions, her pencil occasionally straying to doodle or sketch something that flashed into her mind. Advertising herself was something she found hard, much preferring to rely on personal recommendations, but they were like buses, coming all together after a successful portrait, or with a long gap in between. She needed them to become more regular.

Outside, the sun was bright, but not quite warm enough to sit out in for a long time. Not quite. There was a knock at the door before Damir came in. The top half of his overall was unbuttoned and knotted around his waist, his T-shirt uncreased. Running down almost the length of his left arm was a deep uneven scar, finger-tip wide. He noticed her looking at it and turned so it was no longer visible, a sign he didn't want to be questioned. It was as if a bolt of electricity had shot through the room. Was he aware of it too?

'Something to drink?' she said in an attempt to appear perfectly normal.

'I'll do it,' he said, pausing for a moment to look at her. 'One for you?'

She could feel herself melting under his gaze. This was crazy. She was a woman over sixty with a teenage crush on a man who could never be interested in her. They were too different in too many ways. What was she even thinking? This must be a last hormonal burst before they disappeared forever. She coughed, sat straighter. 'Thanks. I'll have a coffee.'

'Paul called by,' he said. Something in his voice alerted her.

'What?' She couldn't have heard him properly.

'Paul. He came when you were out yesterday.' He turned from the coffee machine to look at her. 'You left something at his flat.'

She rewound through the disastrous evening as fast as she could. She didn't remember missing anything but watched as Damir put his hand in his pocket and pulled out the bracelet she'd been wearing that night: something she rarely wore. 'Oh that! Chris gave it to me years ago, I hadn't even noticed it was missing.'

'He's your friend?' He sounded suspicious. 'He said he was sorry to miss you and would call you.'

'I suppose he is.' Although after what had happened between them, she wasn't so sure.

'Ah. I see.' He nodded, as if he understood everything now. He sat opposite her at the table, pulled a knife from his pocket and a piece of wood and began whittling at it, taking care that the shavings fell on the table. 'Another dinosaur for Danny.'

She longed to scream *No. You've got it wrong. It's not like that.* Instead she said, 'Don't move.'

The light through the window fell on his face so the sides of his nose seemed perfectly flat, the curl of his nostril distinct. His lips relaxed, slightly open, sensual. His brow furrowed as he concentrated on what he was doing.

He looked up from his carving. 'What?' He sounded annoyed at being interrupted.

'Don't move.' The pencil was already in her hand and moving over the fresh page as, with a few clean strokes, she began to capture his likeness. She stopped. 'May I?'

He shrugged. 'Why not?'

For the next half hour or so, they continued in silence, each concentrating on their own craft. Caro drew a series of preliminary studies, moving her chair slightly so she could capture him from different angles. Having her pencil move over the paper, following the line of his jaw, his cheekbones, the lines that told of a life lived, that scar, was like caressing his face as she learned every one of his features.

'Where are your family?' she asked. 'Did they come here with you?'

'I have no family.'

There was that empty look in his eyes again, as if he was numbing some terrible pain.

'No one at all?' Everyone had someone somewhere, surely.

He shook his head. 'Soon after the war began, my mother, my sister and my girlfriend – we were going to be married – were all rounded up with many other women and taken to one of the rape camps. There was nothing I could do to help them. Nothing.' His fist was clenched so tight, his knuckles stood out white. 'I don't know what happened to them but I have heard what happened there. I can only hope they didn't suffer for long.' His voice choked.

'Rape camps?' Caro's shock was palpable.

'That's what we called them. The women were kept like prisoners by the Serbian soldiers, tortured and raped. Some of them escaped, some of them bribed their way out but many of them never came back.' He registered Caro's horror fighting with her disbelief. How had she been so blinkered to what was going on in the world? She had probably been worrying about where Lauren was going to go to school, why Amy's grades were so poor, untouched by the plight of those so far from her own little world. He shrugged. 'That's what it was like.'

'You mean . . .'

'We never saw them again.' He pulled a piece of sandpaper from his pocket and started rubbing away at the wood. Subject closed. Too painful to continue.

Nothing Caro could say would be adequate. She started drawing again, trying not to imagine what it would be like to lose all your family. She thought of Lauren and Amy, her mother and father. Each of them difficult in their own way, as she no doubt was in hers, but she loved them and they her. Each of them had a place in the others' hearts. What would it be like to lose all that? Her pencil moved almost unbidden, turning round the curves of his ear, capturing the slant of his brow.

Eventually he stopped sanding and placed a small Tyrannosaurus rex on the table. 'There!'

Without putting down her pencil, she picked the dinosaur up, turning it in her hand. 'He'll love it. Thank you.' Without thinking, she reached out and took his hand, placing it on the table. That electricity again. He must feel it. He must. She made herself let it go, aware of his eyes on her. 'Can I draw your hand?'

He inclined his head. 'Yes. But I haven't long.'

She pulled out her phone. 'I'll just do some quick sketches, but if I photograph it, I can finish something in more detail.'

He sat patiently as she lost herself in her work, studying the hand that had held a gun, that had shot other soldiers, that laboured every day. She registered the small scar between his first two knuckles, the veins on the back of his hand, the strength in his fingers, the squared-off nails, the slight curve of the middle finger to the left.

'So you'll see him again?'

She was jolted out of her concentration. 'Who?'

'Paul.'

'I don't know. Maybe.' She started shading to accentuate the bones leading to his calloused knuckles when the landline rang. 'Hang on.' She got up to answer it.

He got up too, sweeping up the wood shavings with his hand and putting them in the bin. 'I must go.'

She put the phone to her ear. 'Hello? Mum? Yes, of course

I've got time. Hang on one minute.' She put her hand over the mouthpiece. 'I've kept you too long, I'm sorry.'

He shook his head. 'No. I liked watching you work.' And then the door shut behind him. The room felt empty without him.

'Who was that?' Her mother was ever curious.

'Just the lodger. He's made Danny another dinosaur.' Caro tried to slow her racing heart and focus on this new conversation.

'I'm not calling about finances, although I've spoken to Jack and he's looking into it.' May paused and Caro heard her taking a drink. 'Do you know ... I phoned him this morning and he said I'd already asked him yesterday. I'd completely forgotten.'

Caro covered up her immediate concern with a laugh. 'I've done that. It's just that you've got information overload. Too much in the brain to remember it all. That's all.'

'Hope you're right. Aging is no fun, you know.'

'Actually I do. Only too well.' Caro moved the phone to her other hand so she could ladle some soup into a bowl. 'So what did you call about, then?'

'Oh yes, of course.' She gave a flustered laugh. 'My laptop's stopped working. The screen's just blank. I've switched it on and off, so it's not that. What do you think it is?'

Caro sighed. 'I haven't a clue. May be your hard drive? You'll have to take it to be repaired. Isn't Amy coming to see you this weekend with Jason? She could do it for you.'

'Yes they are. Maybe he could take a look at it? It must be getting serious.' May loved the intricacies of her granddaughters' love lives.

'It'd better be. She's moving in with him in the next couple of months. You'll like him.'

Only the day before, Jason had come to see her, making her promise to keep his visit secret. After a day at Bloom, she had been putting the key in the lock of Treetops when someone stepped up behind her and said, 'Caro!' almost making her jump out of her skin. She screamed, dropped the key, and turned to find Jason standing behind her.

'My God, you scared the living daylights out of me. What on earth are you doing here?' She looked round for Amy then bent to get the key, regaining her composure.

'I'm sorry.' He put a hand on her back. 'I didn't mean to frighten you. Can we talk?'

'Of course. Come in.' She picked up the key and let them in. 'Amy's not with you is she? Of course she's not. I've just left her at the shop.' Now she had a chance to look at him, she could see that under the thatch of ginger hair and hipster beard, he was more than usually pale. In the kitchen they sat down and she poured them both a small glass of wine. 'Long day,' she said by way of explanation. 'Shoot.'

Jason shifted on his chair, looking the most awkward she had ever seen him. He took a sip of wine, obviously getting up the nerve to say something.

'Whatever it is, I won't bite,' she said, trying to put him at ease, beginning to guess why he had come.

Jason breathed in then said, 'I want to ask Amy to marry me. Would you mind?' All the words ran together into one long breath. Then he took another sip as his shoulders lowered. He stared at the rip in the knee of his black jeans.

Caro felt as if she'd just been wrapped in a blanket of the softest cashmere. She couldn't stop the tears as she jumped out of her seat and flung her arms round him. 'Of course I don't mind. And you really didn't need to ask. She's not mine to give away. But it's lovely that you did.' She felt his arms come up as he hugged her in return, his beard brushing her cheek.

When they separated, he was welling up too. 'I'm not sure when I'll ask her, but I will. She says she doesn't believe in marriage but I don't believe her. I've just got to be sure I pick the right moment. I don't know when that will be but I wanted to be sure you'd be OK with it.'

Caro sat down again. 'Amy's her own person. She's the one you need to ask. Not us.'

'Not even Chris?'

She saw the anxiety cross his face.

'I don't think you need to. This is the twenty-first century. But he'd better not know you've asked me.'

'He won't.' His relief was obvious. 'No one will. Thank you. And you won't say anything, will you?'

Remembering the conversation gave her a rush of pleasure. No one could be more pleased than her that both her daughters had found partners who made them happy. She only hoped Amy said yes, whenever the time came, or the poor boy would be shattered. Her pleasure was shot through with the realisation that this really did mean she was on her own now. The only one of her family with no one to go home to. Immediately she thought of Damir. But he would not be here for much longer, either. She hadn't asked him about how his house hunt was going because she didn't want to hear the answer. She hoped that he had put it off to stay at Treetops for a bit longer. She longed to find out whether they really were on the brink of something more. Or had she let her imagination run away? But supposing they were, even a fragile start to a relationship between them could lead to something wonderful or it might as easily lead to disaster.

She put the Tyrannosaurus rex on the side where she would remember to take it with her next time she was Danny-sitting. Beside it was a note from Chris in which he agreed to the decorating costs. Chris. She had almost successfully blocked him and Georgie from her mind since hearing their news. The two working days with Lauren and Amy had been busy and without much chance to chat. However, thinking about him now brought a blast of anger. Why should she be the one to lose out because he wanted to move on? It was time for her to stop coasting and to take control of her own life again. It was true that Amy wasn't theirs to give away. But it was just as true that she wasn't his to command either. She really didn't have to honour and obey him any more. Though breaking the habit was harder than she'd imagined.

She had stewed over the situation for long enough. What she needed to do was talk to him face to face without an audience: no Georgie, no daughters; just the two of them. She wanted to see his face as he told her about the baby. Somehow it was bound to put the final seal on the end of their relationship and she would wish him well. Perhaps this would mark the start of a newly civilised relationship with him. As importantly she needed more time if she was to have any hope at all of raising the money she needed to buy him out. If she could just persuade him to give her longer to get used to the idea and to plan for herself.

Discussing anything over the phone was not an option – they always ended up rowing if they tried to discuss anything that way, and then the phone would be slammed down by one of them (usually him) and nothing achieved. However, she didn't have that problem with his assistant who managed his diary.

She picked up the phone and dialled his office number.

Caro picked up a copy of *The Times* and began to read but her eyes slid across the print, taking in nothing. Instead she listened to the receptionist's conversation about her booze-filled weekend and the scrapes she and her friends had got into: 'Eight double shots and then . . .'

'Caro!' A woman's voice startled her.

'Georgie! How nice to see you.' Georgie's loose top gave nothing away. Caro sat up straighter, folding her arms across her own stomach, pleased she had taken the plunge and visited Fran's Nina at last. Her hair had been bobbed in line with her jaw and expertly layered so the curls, still wild, looked as if they were meant to be where they fell. The cut and colour had taken years off her – and never had she needed that more than now: Fran had been right. She felt good. 'I gather congratulations are due.'

Georgie didn't look the slightest bit awkward, given the situation, but looked directly at Caro. 'Thanks. It's a bit of a surprise.'

'Really?' But Caro didn't want to engage in a conversation about the pregnancy. She was not ready to be friends with the woman who had snared her husband. Not that she had ever thought she would be.

'Are you here for Chris?' Her hand moved to her stomach.

'Yes, we've got a few things to talk about.' Caro looked away.

'I'm sure.' Georgie's smile didn't waver but tightened slightly.

'Not many.' Caro remained as nonchalant as she could be. 'Just a couple of points we need to sort out.'

'Girls!' Chris emerged from a door beside the reception, his expression one of alarm and forced pleasure at seeing the two women together. He inclined his head in surprised approval of Caro's new hair.

Caro bridled at his patronising approach. Girls, indeed. The old Chris would never have used the word.

'I didn't know you were coming in,' he said to Georgie.

She crossed to him and gave him an unnecessarily territorial kiss, glancing over at Caro as if checking she had seen. She had. 'I've got to sort something out with accounts. I know you two need to chat, so I'll get on with it. I'll see you later, darling. Bye, Caro.' She wiggled her fingers in farewell, the light bouncing off her blood-red nails.

'Indeed.' Chris let his hand trail down her arm, before he remembered Caro was watching and unlaced his fingers from Georgie's. 'I thought we'd go to Chez Justin, just round the corner. All right with you, Caro?'

'Of course.' *Just don't tell me how much work you have on.*

'I've got a lot on at the moment so I'll have to be quick.' His eyes followed Georgie as she sashayed down the corridor, giving the hip swing all she had.

'Fine by me.' *Don't rise to anything*, she told herself. *Otherwise you won't achieve what you want.*

'How are Amy and Lauren?'

'Amy's going to move in with Jason in the summer, but you know that of course. Otherwise she's just really busy with Bloom. Lauren's fine, working hard. Nothing new.'

'And Danny? I haven't seen him for a while.'

'He's great. Growing up fast. Mad about dinosaurs at the moment.' As she caught him up on their grandson's progress, they fell back into the easy way they once had together, sharing the same interests. As soon as they walked through the door of the restaurant and sat down, the tension between them ramped up again, both of them knowing that what came next would be personal. Caro was regretting her decision to come at all.

When they were sitting opposite each other, a white tablecloth and gleaming place settings between them, she had a chance to look at him properly. She had to admit that whatever his new life involved was doing him good. This time he wore a white T-shirt under his navy jacket: not a look Caro had ever seen him in before. More of the Georgie effect. And blue suede shoes, neatly stitched, that must have cost the earth. She waited until they'd ordered. When he plumped for two salad starters, she swiftly revised her choice from pasta, sticking to two starters even when the waiter pointed out how insubstantial they would be. They'd be good for her.

'Water all right with you?' He picked up the blue bottle.

She could tell by his tone that Chris was expecting her to say no. She curbed her longing for a steadying glass of something cold, white and very expensive. 'Perfect. If we haven't got long, then let me say what I've come for.'

He nodded in agreement. Despite his superficial congeniality, his eyes gave nothing away. 'You should know that I've instructed my solicitors to start the ball rolling. So you'll hear from them soon. It's all going to be very straightforward.'

She hesitated, swallowing the ball of nausea in her throat. This meeting was definitely one of her worst ideas. 'I'm sure it will be. After all, I'm hardly going to put up a fight.'

He visibly relaxed as he put the bottle of water at the edge of the table, about to say something.

Caro wouldn't give him the chance. She wanted to wrest back control of their meeting. 'About Treetops. I'm still trying to raise the funds to buy you out.'

That surprised him. 'Really? How are you going to do that?'

'Leave that to me.' She wouldn't let him throw cold water on her plans. 'But I need you to give me a little more time. I need time to plan.'

He looked disbelieving. 'Did the girls tell you Georgie was pregnant?'

'Of course. But you should have told me first. I could have paved the way for you telling them.'

'They're not twelve any more.' His gaze fixed on her in a way that made her uneasy.

'They may not be twelve, but it's hard for them to accept you're marrying someone virtually their age.'

'I think you should give them more credit. They're young women who know what goes on in the world.' He forked a piece of artichoke and a few pomegranate seeds into his mouth. 'But I'm afraid the pregnancy makes a difference. We need to get a move on.' He gave a short bark of laughter at his own joke.

'I can't raise the money that fast. You know that.' Caro didn't want her desperation to show but they both heard it in those last three words. 'After everything we've been through together.' Enough!

'I can't promise anything. I'm sorry.' For a second, he almost looked as if he meant it. 'Georgie's mother's thrilled about her first grandchild.'

The change of subject took Caro by surprise. A second extended family. He had been such an absentee father when the girls were little, Caro wondered if Georgie knew what to expect.

'She's a great woman,' Chris went on. 'We all get on tremend-ously well. Is that all you wanted to say? We could have done this over the phone.'

How strange it was that thirty years of intimacy could dis-integrate so easily into nothing. All that intensity of feeling, that shared experience, had come to mean so little. Caro wondered if he ever thought about the years when the girls were young, when the two of them dreamed and talked about little else. He could not possibly have forgotten but he must have somehow shunted it all away to the recesses of his mind. He didn't need those memories any more, whereas she still thrived on them. They were part of her in a way they seemed not to be of him any more.

'What are you thinking?' He finished his water and put the glass by his empty plate.

'About us,' she admitted. 'About how we got to this and where everything we've been through together has gone.'

Chris held both hands up, palms towards her. 'Whoa! Don't go all emotional on me. We've been there. Of course we share the girls and Danny. That'll never change – and I wouldn't want it to. But I've moved on. And you must too.'

Oh God, he thought she wanted them to return to the way things were, that she had come to win him back. 'Oh, I am,' she lied. 'I've been seeing someone, too.'

'Really?' He could at least have kept his surprise better hidden.

'Yes. I met him at Fran's.'

'Always knew that woman would be good for something.' His professional links with Fran, who was like a tiger when acting on behalf of her actor clients, meant their personal relationship was only superficially civil. He had caved in to her demands for them more than once.

At that moment, staring at this man who once meant so much to her, Caro realised that she had finally to let go at last. Moving away and hooking up with a younger woman may have improved Chris on the outside, but on the inside, he had become someone she didn't recognise any more. If nothing else, this meeting had finally driven the last nail into the coffin of their marriage. She wouldn't initiate another. She had to accept that Chris had another life and his emotional ties with her and with Treetops were broken forever. Accepting was not the same as knowing. Accepting was harder. She had known their marriage was over for a long time and she had learned to live with that knowledge, but she hadn't fully let go. That was the next big step. Complete closure at last. However hard it might be, she must look to the future, not rely on the past. She had to stand on her two feet at last without relying on anyone else to help her.

'Coffee?' He wiped his mouth with a napkin, dropping it onto his plate.

'No, thanks. I've got an appointment on the other side of town.' If she left now she could get the three o'clock train home.

Chris didn't even ask who her appointment was with. He really wasn't interested in her or what she did with her life any more. Instead he asked for the bill. It was enough for him to know that she had recovered sufficiently from the break-up not to cause him any trouble. All he wanted from her was his share of the equity from the house, however he got it. The realisation gave her an unexpected detachment from the situation. The penny had finally dropped. What mattered from now on was what she chose to do. She had to start looking forward, not back.

13

At home, she changed swiftly into her dog-walking clothes, relying on the walk to lift her spirits. On her way downstairs, Damir came through the front door. He was in his overalls, undone to the navel so the small Bosnian flag on his navy blue T-shirt was visible.

He looked up at her, pushing a hand through his hair so it stood on end. 'We finished early today.'

'I'm just taking Milo out,' she said at exactly the same time.

'Can I come with you? There's something we should talk about.'

Surprised by his question, she hesitated over her reply. But she liked the idea of company on the all-too familiar walk. What harm could come from that?

'If I change quickly.' He nodded down at his overalls. 'May I?'

'Of course. Why not?' She took the dog lead from the bottom of the banister.

He waited until she reached the hallway, then bounded up the stairs two at a time. 'Won't be long.'

She went to the porch, yanked on her wellies and jacket, realising as she did that she felt better already. She looked down at her left hand, thinking of her meeting with Chris. She twisted her wedding ring round her finger, then in a moment of decision, pulled it off and put it in her jeans pocket. Over.

A couple of minutes later, Damir was back, wearing jeans and heavy boots with a thick shirt. 'Let me get my jacket.' He tugged it out from under her good one, took a beanie from the pocket and pulled it on. There was something almost too intimate seeing his face without its usual framing of hair. So very different from Paul. Caro looked away as he unravelled a scarf from the other pocket and wrapped it round his neck. 'Ready,' he said.

'I think I'll take you somewhere special just a short drive away. We should have enough time.' She unlocked the car, let Milo leap into the back and waited for him to climb in.

'Where are we going?'

'It's a local landmark that I bet you've never been to.'

A few minutes later she was pulling into the car park of St Martha-on-the-Hill.

Damir got out and looked around at the oak trees surrounding them. The smell of damp new bracken scented the air. He took the ball launcher from her, stepped away with Milo, the dog wild with excitement now he was out of the car. Damir raised the launcher behind him and threw the ball up the hill as hard as he could. Delighted, Milo chased off after it between the trees, bringing it back for a repeat performance. He lay, his tail thumping on the ground, his eyes fixed on the ball, his body thrumming in anticipation of the throw.

'You're going to regret that. He'll never leave you alone now.' Caro walked ahead towards the sandy path that led up through the trees as the ball zoomed past her right ear with Milo in hot pursuit. Damir caught her up and fell into step with her. He walked close beside her, their arms almost touching. The trees thinned out, hinting at a view beyond but nothing would be given away until they reached the church at the top. They passed a large seat cut from a tree trunk.

'This is beautiful. I love walking through woods.'

'Isn't it? I thought you might enjoy it. I often come here to think.'

'It's very peaceful.'

'What did you want to say?' She longed for and dreaded his reply.

He kicked his feet in the sand. 'About staying at Treetops. Esad is going back to Bosnia for the summer, taking his father who wants to see his town again. When he comes back, we will find somewhere to live together. So I want to ask if I can stay on till then?'

'Oh.' Surprised, but pleased that he'd be there for longer. 'Of course you can.'

'Thank you. You're kind.' He threw the ball as far ahead up the path as he could, Milo racing after it.

They both lapsed into silence as they continued up the path.

Caro was the first to speak. 'What happened to you after the war?'

He looked surprised by the question but didn't hesitate to answer it. 'I went to Germany. But not because the war was over. I was badly injured in the fighting.'

'The scar on your arm?'

He nodded. 'Shrapnel. I couldn't fight after that. My family were dead or disappeared. My friends had escaped, or were fighting or were dead, too. I couldn't return to Brčko. There was nothing for me there. My life there was over.' He paused, stood still with his eyes shut and took a deep breath. Caro waited beside him for a few seconds, unsure what to do, then he came to. 'I'm sorry. Sometimes remembering is hard.'

'Then let's not talk about it.' Caro put her hand on his arm and he jumped. She let it rest there for a couple of seconds. When he looked down, she removed it. 'I don't want to make it difficult for you.'

'You've been kind to me so I want to tell you. You've cared enough to ask about these things that other people avoid. They change the subject because they think I don't want to talk about the past or because they can't bear to hear. It's too hard for them.'

'But does it help to talk? If not, I'd understand.'

'Sometimes yes, but sometimes It's difficult. It depends who I talk to. But it's important the world knows what happened. Karadžić and his kind have been tried and found guilty of war crimes in the Hague but there can be no reckoning for all those who suffered so much and those who died so horribly.' His face was a portrait of inexpressible sadness. 'I like talking to you.'

'Tell me then. Tell me as we walk.' Talking could be much easier side by side, with no chance of eye contact.

As they walked in step, Damir began to speak. 'The Serbs wanted our city of Brčko because it lay between two pieces of Serbian territory. Although we had heard about the threat of war, we didn't really believe anything would happen. I was in my house when I heard the very first explosion. They blew up the bridge over the river, cutting us off from Croatia. That was the first thing they did. I ran with my friend down to the town square to see what had happened. There had been people on that bridge and pieces of them were scattered into the surrounding gardens and streets. After that hundreds of Muslim citizens were driven out but hundreds more were caught. If they weren't killed in their doorways or in the street, they were held in prison camps. At Luka prison camp in our town, they made people lie with their heads on the rubbish so when they were shot, their blood drained into it, before their bodies were thrown into the river. The stories of torture were so terrible that for many, death must have been a relief.'

Caro was silent, shocked. This was so far removed from anything she knew, nothing she could say seemed adequate.

'The town was turned inside out. Friends and neighbours became the deadliest enemies.'

'And you? What happened to you?'

'I joined the army. I stayed to fight until I was too badly injured to go on. I left at the end of 1993. Family friends had gone to Germany so I went to join them. I got out on one of the UN aid convoys but it was dangerous. We feared ambush or even being turned around and sent back. But I got out to Croatia with my money inside my boots.' He grinned. 'I walked and caught buses and trains up to Austria and then to Germany. To Munich.'

'You found your friends?'

'Yes, and I was given refugee status too. But I've talked enough.'

'No, I want to know,' she protested. 'It's just . . . I've just never met anyone who's been through anything like that.'

They reached the little gate in the churchyard wall, flanked by two large yew trees. On the other side, the view opened up around them, in its centre the tiny church of St Martha's, its door wide open in welcome. She watched as Damir took in their surroundings, his eyes widening. Turning to the right, they stood looking towards the South Downs. The view extended for miles to Winterfold Forest, Chanctonbury Ring and the Devil's Punchbowl. Caro stood beside him pointing out the local landmarks while Milo sniffed around the gravestones.

Damir pulled off his beanie and spread out his arms, turning in a full circle. 'It's very different here. Especially on a day like today when it's so beautiful and nature is coming alive again. What happened is in the past and can't be undone. Instead, we have to try to enjoy our new freedom. But it's not always so easy.' He turned to look at the Victorian church, its stubby square tower silhouetted against a blue sky where a few puffs of cloud moved across it.

They walked through the graveyard, stopping at one or two of the stones, reading the names, remembering the dead. Caro imagined he must be thinking of all those people he had once known and loved. Whenever she came up here, she always found a peace that eluded her anywhere else.

'This is a very special place.' He broke the silence between them.

'You can feel it too? Wait till you go inside. Hang on while I tie up Milo.'

With Milo secured to the leg of a bench that backed against the church wall, they went through the double arched door into the church. She heard Damir's intake of breath beside her as she stared up at the timbered vaulted ceiling. She could feel the heat of his hand close to hers. Neither of them moved. Caro was barely breathing, this time certain she wasn't imagining the return of the tension between them.

She made herself walk away from him, down the aisle towards the simple rood screen and the altar beyond where she gave herself a strict talking to. If she was going to have a relationship it would be with someone like Paul, not a younger man with a modest income and a terrible past she would never be able to understand fully. She felt him come up behind her, standing close by her shoulder.

'That window's beautiful. What is it?' His breath on her cheek was light as a feather.

'I think it's Jesus with St Martha and someone else. Martha was the sister of Lazarus who Jesus brought back from the dead.' She was gabbling. All she could think about was this sudden but almost overwhelming desire to be touched: something she hadn't felt for years. At least not like this. She tipped her head to his, as his eyes fixed on her face. They stood motionless, then he turned back to the door and the moment had gone.

She had been right all along. Whatever she felt, he did not share. She put her hand in her pocket and felt her wedding ring.

'Perhaps we should go now.' He was at the door.

'Yes, we should.' Of course Damir wouldn't be attracted to a woman like her: a woman of her age. At least she hadn't embarrassed them both by throwing herself at him. What had she been thinking? But of course she hadn't been thinking anything at all. She had let down her guard and her instinct had taken over. He had made the right decision to walk away when he did. For both of them.

Caro and Damir kept their distance as they walked to the car, she walking behind him while he concentrated on Milo and the ball. Eventually he stopped to wait for her, and she began to tell him more about the church and its position on the Pilgrim's Way to Canterbury until it was almost as if nothing had happened between them in the church. Almost. Caro was annoyed that she had allowed herself to imagine things that were never going to happen, even to want them to happen. Keen to smooth things over, she moved the conversation on to her family, which soon led into Chris and their divorce, the detail of which she had spared him.

'But you have someone else now, of course.' This was said not as a question but as a statement.

She thought of Paul: nice, safe Paul who was trapped in his past, trying to free himself too. 'Not exactly,' she answered. 'It didn't go terribly well the last time I saw him.'

'I think he'd like to see you. He came for that.'

Had Damir's voice taken on a harder edge or was she imagining it? Either way, she wanted to reassure him – and her. 'My friends would like me to find someone – especially Fran who you met the other day.' Was she saying too much? 'But I've got my daughters, Danny, my friends and my painting. They're enough for me.' There. She was pleased with the way she had delivered the message loud and clear.

'But you're a beautiful woman. You should have someone.'

She caught her breath. *Beautiful!* Not even in the good times had Chris ever called her that.

'Oh, I'm way too old to be beautiful.' She batted the compliment away. 'Those days are long gone.'

'I don't think so.' He seemed surprised by her denial. 'Perhaps you should make Paul happy.'

'Paul's a friend. Nothing more than that.'

He winked. 'I see.'

Was he teasing her? But he gave no sign as he went ahead again, tossing the ball for the tireless Milo. He looked so solid from behind: tall, broad-shouldered, the suggestion of a limp. After a moment or two he stopped, turned round, waiting for her again. He didn't seem to think he'd said anything remarkable.

When she caught him up, she turned the tables. 'And you? You must have a girlfriend here?'

He shook his head. 'At the moment, no one,' he said. 'There have been women in my life and maybe there will be again. But I haven't stayed with anyone for a long time now. Not committed, you say . . . ?' He paused, thoughtful. 'It's not good to shut yourself down. It's easier but it's not good.' His voice was quieter as if he was talking to himself. 'I've lost too much in my life. I don't want to lose any more.'

Coming up behind them was a group of hikers who must have been on the Pilgrim's Way. They all reached the car park together, their chatter changing the atmosphere and stopping Caro from asking more.

When they reached home, Damir excused himself and went straight to his room. As Caro pottered around downstairs, she imagined him in Lauren's old room, wondering what he was doing, what he was thinking. Something had shifted between them in the church. Something infinitesimal, but there. However, the way he had left so abruptly must mean that if he had noticed he wanted to ignore it. His subsequent compliment was just to put things right between them. Their age difference was deterrent enough.

I am much older than he is, she told herself. Then repeated: *older, older, older . . .*

She must be at least fifteen years older than him. With her sixty-second birthday looming, she was becoming sensitive about her age, whatever anyone said about it being only a number. Even when she dressed up, it was increasingly hard to hide the fact she was some way past her sell-by-date. But her body had been good to her. It had given her two wonderful daughters and never caused her any significant health problems – she touched the wood of the piano lid. Bits of her had sagged, and dimpled, and creaked and expanded like the bodies of almost every other woman she knew – even Fran who took so much care of herself.

Once the menopause was over, everything began to head south as the waist widened. Nature was much kinder to men.

She acknowledged that one of the reasons she held back from a new relationship was down to the embarrassment that she was certain would arise from any physical intimacy. All that short hand she and Chris once shared would mean nothing to anyone else. She would have to start again, find new ways, establish new habits. And look what had happened with Paul. She had briefly overcome her inhibitions only to be rejected. As time had passed, she had convinced herself that if a younger woman had been lying under the duvet, Paul wouldn't have hesitated. The problem hadn't been his but hers. Had her libido run out on her when Chris did, or was it just this self-consciousness holding her back?

She took the book of collected Beethoven sonatas from the top of the piano, turned to the 'Pathétique' and began to play. Her playing was clumsy but still satisfying enough. The sonatas usually calmed her, taking her to places that didn't demand thought, just concentration on what she was doing as the music flooded her head. But this time they weren't the answer. She crashed both fists onto the keyboard.

Milo sat up and barked at the noise.

Putting the Beethoven to one side, her fingers started marking out the Scott Joplin rag that her piano teacher had made her play again and again. It had become a staple in the rather limited repertoire that she still knew off by heart. She had played it to the girls when they were growing up and they still got her to play it at family gatherings. But she was rusty now, missing some of the notes and stumbling over the cadencing. Nonetheless the piece lifted her spirits as it always did.

She didn't hear the door open but was aware that Damir had come into the room. She didn't stop playing – why should she? – but she became self-conscious and her fingers became less agile as she segued from 'The Entertainer' into 'The Maple Leaf Rag', jumbling the notes until the music was almost unrecognisable. Eventually she stopped, laughing at herself while Damir clapped.

'Usually, I'm much better than that.' She played a couple of scales and arpeggios to steady her hands.

'I need to say something to you.' He didn't move, but she could tell he was watching her.

She swung round on the piano stool to face him. 'Fire away.' Perhaps he had changed his mind about staying. He would be relieved to move out after that moment in the church. The smile she had pinned to her face was in danger of slipping. A twinge of sadness went with the unwelcome realisation that she would miss his company. More than anything at that moment, she wanted him to touch her. Just once. *Stop it.*

'You're moving out after all?' She stood up and went to the French windows, away from him, so she could stare out without him seeing her expression.

He cleared his throat. 'No, not that. Not that at all.'

She was aware of him crossing the room towards her then, before she had time to turn, his hand was on her shoulder, gently pulling her round. Her heart thumped against her ribs. Surely he could hear it, but he gave no sign. They stood as close as they had in the church. Her stomach was somersaulting. She hadn't felt like this for as long as she could remember. But this time he didn't turn away and neither did she. His head dipped towards hers and before she could say anything he was kissing her.

After the first moments of disbelief and resistance, she found herself responding. She was weightless, ageless, giddy with desire. Only when they parted, slightly breathless, did all those reservations come whirling back into play. She must be hallucinating. But her hands were clasped in his, and he was gazing at her.

'You can't...' But she couldn't go on, realising she didn't know what she wanted to say. She wanted to object – she should – but the words wouldn't come.

'But I have.' A smile creased his features as he looked at her.

'I wanted to kiss you in the church but that was wrong. When we got back here, I thought perhaps I had made a mistake, that you wouldn't want that.'

She squeezed his hands. 'I did.'

He extricated his right hand and stroked the hair back from her eyes before running a finger down her cheek and along her jaw until it stopped on the point of her chin. 'I know. But I needed to know about Paul too.'

So he did have doubts about what he was doing.

'And what did you decide?' She was feeling as nervous as a teenager on a first date, longing and yet not longing for him to kiss her again.

'That if I didn't say anything, I might be sorry. And that if I was wrong about you, it was going to make things difficult for us.'

'You weren't wrong.' She almost whispered the words.

'I know that.' He led her to the sofa, pulled her down beside him and kissed her again. This time, she didn't hesitate. This was what it was to feel desired. All her nerve endings that might as well have been cauterised years ago were coming back to life. It was as if she was being lit up inside.

14

They broke apart at the ring of the doorbell, followed by the sound of the front door opening.

'Mum! Mum, where are you?' Amy's voice rang through the house, followed by the sound of her walking into the kitchen.

Caro slid out from under Damir so that she was standing. She straightened her clothes and ran her hands through her hair. Her face was burning.

'You look beautiful,' he said in a whisper, as he got to his feet, grabbing the remote control and flicking on the TV. 'You go to her. We've been watching TV. That's all.'

'This early?! She's not going to believe that. Coming,' she called. Could Amy hear the wobble in her voice? She ran a hand over her chin, feeling the sting from his stubble. The enormity of what she had just done hit her. What would the girls say if they knew? She remembered Lauren's over-reaction to finding them standing with his arm round her, realising how little she wanted a repeat of that. Caro took a deep breath and went into the kitchen, hoping Damir would sneak upstairs when he could.

'I've put the kettle on. Do you want a tea?' Amy looked at her mother and frowned. 'Are you OK? You look ... I don't know ... feverish.'

'Yes, of course. Why wouldn't I be?'

'No reason. But you've gone kind of pink. Maybe you're coming down with something.'

Caro raised her hands to her cheeks, willing the colour to fade. 'I went to see Dad and when I got back I went on a long walk with Milo to clear my head.' She could barely get the words out. She didn't want to lie to her daughter, but what choice was there? *I've just been making out with the lodger* was not a line that would necessarily be well received or go unquestioned. 'I was so knackered after that, I lay on the sofa and went to sleep. I only woke up when you came in.' Too many excuses. Change the subject. 'Anyway, to what do I owe this particular honour?'

'You know I hate it when you're sarcastic.' Amy screwed up her face and stuck out her tongue.

'I'm joking, darling. And I don't much like that face.' As she picked out two mugs and separated two teabags, Caro thought she heard the front door close. She closed her eyes with relief, felt her shoulders relax. A few minutes later, they were sitting on either side of the fireplace, Milo on the rug between them. Amy was talking but Caro was only half listening. Before he left, Damir had plumped the cushions so there was no tell-tale sign of any kind of activity. She remembered Dorothy Parker's hurly burly of the chaise longue as opposed to the deep peace of the marriage bed and smiled. But the hurly burly couldn't go any further. Amy had brought with her a sharp blast of reality. Damir was unsuitable in every way. He was too young. They were too different. It could never work between them.

'Mu-um! Have you heard anything I've said?'

'You want me at the shop another day this week?'

'Not at the shop.' If she'd been much younger, she would have stamped to show her frustration. 'I'm asking if you'll help me with the wedding flowers on Friday. Ellie's got to do the other one and it would be brilliant if you could step in.'

Caro spoke carefully, softly. It was time. 'Isn't there someone else you could ask?'

Amy's eyes were wide with amazement. 'What?' She twirled the ends of her hair round a finger, pulling so the curl straightened out. 'But why?'

'I love being there on Mondays. And I'm really glad to help

when I can.' Caro immediately found herself having to justify her words despite them both knowing that Amy asked her for two reasons. 'But sometimes more's too much.'

'What are you doing on Friday, then?' Amy's disbelief that her mother might have something more important to do made Caro more determined to stand her ground. Just this once.

'I'm going to an exhibition at the Tate.' The idea came from nowhere but once she'd had it, she liked it. That's exactly what she would do. 'Then I'll be coming back to paint.'

'Can't you go another time?'

'No. I'm going with a friend. We've made plans.'

'Who?'

Oh, for heaven's sake. Then it came to her. She would ask Paul and put things right between them. She didn't want him to harbour any expectations or any awkwardness to hang over them if they met again at Fran's. They would be friends again, just as she'd described him to Damir. This would put things back on an even keel and perhaps deter her from embarking on something close to madness. But that kiss with Damir. Just the memory was enough to make her nerve ends tingle.

'No one you know. I'm sorry but it's all arranged.' Another lie. 'I help you whenever I can, but this once, you're going to have to find someone else.'

'In that case, I'd better go and do just that.' Amy was cramming her feet back into her Doc Martens. 'I can't believe you won't rearrange for this. It's so important to me. I suppose I could ask Sandy, but she's not as good as you.'

Caro was perfectly aware that there was a small pool of friends Amy could draw on if need be. The first port of call happened to be her because Caro always said yes. Amy had to learn she couldn't always rely on her.

Saying 'no' felt good, she realised. Better than good. This was the next small step in taking back the reins of her life, and she was not going to be made to feel guilty.

The rain poured from the flat grey sky as if it was emptying itself for good. Raindrops bounced off the pavement and spat back from the slate-coloured spread of the Thames. Once they reached the end of the Jubilee bridge, Paul and Caro joined the others sheltering beneath it. Eventually the rain eased off enough for them to make a dash to the Tate.

Paul had been surprised by her invitation but then accepted, agreeing when she explained that she'd like to cement their friendship. Immediately after she had asked him to go with her, Caro regretted it, wondering what Damir would say if he knew. But he wasn't going to find out, she argued to herself. And even if he did, he had no say over what she did. He wasn't going to be around long enough for that. He had told her when they first met that he never stuck around. She refused to let herself feel disloyal to him. If anything, they might be about to have a fling that wouldn't last – that was all. *Could Paul really be a friend and Damir her lover?* The question flashed across her brain as they entered the Tate's vast turbine hall.

Leaving their wet coats in the cloakroom, Paul and Caro went upstairs to the galleries. As they wandered through the large airy rooms, stopping whenever a painting especially caught their eye, they moved in and out of each other's orbit, pointing out the artists they particularly liked to one another. Caro hovered in front of a Kandinsky, wanting Paul to enjoy its energy and colour as much as she did but he moved her on towards the more figurative work of an Edward Hopper.

After a while, the two of them exited into the main landing, where the escalators spewed out more people onto the same floor and took others away, children shouting and running about among them.

'Coffee?' asked Paul.

Caro nodded. 'I could kill for one.'

They took the lift up to the members' room where Paul insisted she sat down while he queued. With Chris, it was always the other way round. She found a table by the window that gave on to the river and stared out at the rain. From here, the city skyscrapers were easily visible, tall red cranes rearing up between the Cheesegrater and the Walkie-Talkie while to the west of them the monolithic dome of St Paul's was cast against the skyline. She turned to see how Paul was getting on. He was the tallest man in the queue, quite distinguished looking with his square-rimmed specs. He raised his hand and smiled at her when he saw her looking. She raised hers back.

A couple joined the end of the queue, laughing at something the man had just said. The woman must have been in her fifties, stylish in black trousers, a biker jacket and a red scarf. She threw her head back and laughed again before saying something that made the man laugh in return. Caro found herself envying their easy banter, their relaxed togetherness.

She looked again and gasped. *Please, no.*

The man had stepped out from behind the rest of the queue as he kissed his companion. Their arms went round each other as they faced forwards, easy in each other's company like long-term lovers. Caro could see him quite clearly now. She wasn't mistaken. Although she had only met him once before, as well as seeing him in a couple of photos Fran had showed her on her phone, there was no doubt in her mind. Same dark wavy hair, same sharp chin, same weasel smile, same neat physique. Ewan. Ewan who was living in Scotland, enduring a miserable marriage. This relationship looked anything but miserable. Ewan, who was going to extricate himself so that he could be with Fran. This didn't look anything like a relationship that was about to implode. She watched the couple deliberating over the food, his thumb tucked into her back jeans pocket, her hand on his shoulder. Her hair fell across her face as she pointed at something. As they moved towards her, Caro turned her chair so she was facing the window. She didn't want to risk being recognised. Fran believed he was on the point of suggesting she leave Simon . . . Caro slowed her thoughts, remembering his recent no-show . . . that was only her interpretation. This woman was an obvious explanation.

The chair on the other side of the table scraped the floor as Paul pulled it back to sit down. She hadn't even noticed him put down the tray with the coffees and a sizeable piece of carrot cake with two forks.

'Thought we needed this,' he said. 'I'll eat it if you don't want.'

'You're kidding! Of course I do.' She speared the cake through the thick icing and pulled off a piece.

Just at that moment Ewan and his companion passed them looking around for somewhere to sit. Caro turned away, hiding her face as she ate. To Caro's relief they chose a table on the other side of the room.

'You OK?' Paul sounded anxious as if he might have done something to offend. 'Did you want something else?'

'No, no. Just thought that was someone I knew. It's nothing.' But it was something. It was very definitely something.

'Go over,' he said, looking around. 'I don't mind if you want to say hello.'

'Maybe on our way out,' she said. 'Not now.'

'I thought we might grab something for lunch and then go to a matinee. Or is that too much for one day?'

'Can we do that?'

'We can do what we want! Otherwise we can get the train home. I just want to make up to you for last time.'

'There's no need. Let's forget that happened. And yes, let's see if there's something on we'd both like.'

He beamed with pleasure and pulled out his phone to start looking for what matinees were on. In the end they plumped on a play at the National, just along the South Bank.

Coffees finished and arrangements made, they stood up to leave. As they headed to the exit, Caro saw Ewan and his friend bent head to head, studying one of the gallery leaflets. Fran was all she could think of. She would not condone Fran's relationship with him but equally she could not tolerate her friend being hurt. Just as she reached their table, Ewan straightened up smiling at something his companion had just said. Caro could smell her perfume, musky and seductive. Then he looked straight at Caro.

'Hello, Ewan.' The words were out before she'd even thought them.

She was pleased to see the uncertainty on his face. 'Hello.' He clearly half-recognised but couldn't place her.

'You probably don't remember me,' she went on, wind filling her sails. 'I'm a friend of Fran's.' His eyes widened and she thought he paled a little.

'Aren't you going to introduce us?' The woman touched his arm.

Caro recognised a slight Scottish burr in her voice.

'I don't think . . .' he began.

'It's Caro.' She paused then added, 'Fran's friend.' His eyes registered understanding and alarm, pleading with her not to say any more. Her work here was done. 'I just wanted to say hello.' She turned to a somewhat bemused-looking Paul. 'We must go.'

As they left, she heard the woman ask, 'Who *was* that? Who's Fran?'

If only she could have stuck around to hear Ewan struggle with his answer. She shouldn't have said anything but she hadn't been able to help herself. An inner demon had taken over. If she could protect Fran, she would. It was enough to know that she had put the cat among the pigeons. The next question was whether to tell Fran and, if she did, how.

'That'll be his assistant, Suzy.' Fran reacted to Caro's story without a shadow of doubt. She turned her wine glass on the table, before picking it up then putting it down again.

'Really? They looked very friendly.' Caro hesitated before saying any more. Fran should know what Ewan was doing behind her back, that things might not be quite as she thought. She hoped that telling Fran what she'd seen would give her friend the upper hand, and, much more importantly, make her see sense.

'Of course they are.' Another turn of the glass. 'They've worked together for years. Odd he didn't mention he was down over the weekend though.' And another. 'We're meeting next week – at last.'

'I know,' Caro said with feeling. She had just refused to be Fran's alibi again.

'Don't give me that look!' Fran pushed the bowl of olives across her kitchen table. 'I know what you're thinking. But I'll sort it all out once and for all.'

'I wish you would. But maybe you should be ready to hear something you don't want to.'

Fran's face changed. 'For God's sake! Suzy's his assistant! I've told you.'

'How many people thread their finger through their assistant's belt loop and let their assistant put their arm round them?' Caro wasn't enjoying this at all but, as Fran's closest friend, she felt bound to tell her. 'I'm sorry, Fran, but there was more to it than that.'

'They really did that?' Fran's voice wavered for the first time. 'He wouldn't cheat on me. Not now.'

'But if he's cheated on his wife, mightn't he cheat on you?'

Two spots of colour appeared on Fran's cheeks as she brushed a hand across her eyes. 'You don't know him. He wouldn't. I don't know why you're so insistent. You're meant to be my friend.'

Her calling their friendship into doubt shamed Caro. Especially when Fran had been such a friend to her. 'I *am* your friend. I'm being honest with you. Isn't that what friends are for too?' Fran's stare was fixed on the table, not showing what she was thinking. 'I don't know him, that's true, but I do know what I saw.'

'And you had to rush back and tell me.'

'That's not what I did at all. That's not fair.' Fran had it all wrong. 'I wasn't sure whether I should say something but I'm only thinking of you. I'm sorry you're upset but you'd be furious if you found out that I knew and hadn't told you.'

'You shouldn't have spoken to him.'

'I know. I wish I hadn't, I did it without thinking. Well, I was. I was thinking of you. But look, he can explain and you can laugh about your idiot friend who made such a stupid mistake.' But she hadn't made a mistake, she was certain.

'OK. That's what we'll do.' Fran got up and went over to the oven to take out the salmon tray bake. 'I get that you were only thinking of me but you've just made everything worse.'

'But why?' Caro insisted. 'If it's all above board, there's no big deal. And if it's not, then you should know.'

Fran was concentrating on getting the fish to the table as the door opened.

'Ladies!' Simon came in, holding a bunch of cellophane-wrapped flowers. 'Glad to see you've started without me.' He kissed his wife on the side of her head and gave her the flowers. 'Happy anniversary.'

'Oh God, it's not! I completely forgot. I'm so sorry. Work's been crazy – they're casting a new musical in the St James theatre and I've been trying to get Daisy Markham in there.' The excuse reeled off her tongue as she unwrapped the yellow, pink and orange flowers that were curled in tight round balls. 'Ranunculus – my favourite. You are wonderful.' She kissed him.

Simon almost managed to hide his disappointment. 'Never mind. Good to be the one who's remembered for once.' He took a glass from the cupboard and helped himself to wine, topping up their glasses. 'Twenty-six years since we braved the doors of Finsbury Reg. What's for supper?'

'Is it really?' Fran touched his arm. 'I can never remember exactly. You are good.'

'Yeah, I know.' Simon grinned as he made himself comfortable at the table.

Supper was swift. The three of them did their best to fill the silences but there was so much that couldn't be said, each of them distracted by their own problems. Fran with Ewan. Caro with thoughts of Damir. Even Simon didn't seem to be able to muster his usual good cheer.

As soon as they finished their meal, he excused himself. 'I want to watch last night's *Match of the Day* and you being here gives me the perfect opportunity.'

'Glad to be of service.' Caro raised her glass at him, and a shiver of relief and remorse ran through her as he left the room.

As soon as he'd gone Fran rounded on her. 'Whatever you think, I don't want you to say another word. I don't expect you to understand, but if you're ever in the same boat, in love with someone – however unlikely that might be at the moment – then perhaps you will.' She stacked the plates and took them over to the dishwasher.

'You're right, I don't understand, and every time we talk about it we go round and round in circles. I don't understand why you want to throw over all this...' Caro gestured round their kitchen, '...for someone you barely know.' But what she was beginning to understand better was the strength of feeling Fran had for Ewan. Since that kiss, Damir was constantly in her mind. What she wanted to do more than anything was confide in Fran, to ask her advice about him. Nothing more had happened between them. What did that mean? Had he changed his mind, just as Paul had? What should she do? 'I was only thinking of you.'

Fran's back was to her as she bent to load the plates. Her distress was visible in every movement. 'Go home, Caro.' She was so choked up that Caro barely made out the words. She went over to her friend and put her hand on her shoulder.

'I'm sorry. I hope I'm wrong and you sort it out.'

Fran shook her head. 'Just go.'

They had argued before but this was the first time Caro had

been asked to leave. 'I'll call you tomorrow. We're not going to fall out over this. We've been friends for too long.'

Fran looked up, her eyes welling with tears. 'So can I say I'm at yours next week after all? Please.'

Caro hesitated then caved in. How could she refuse after this? 'OK.'

Fran's look of gratitude persuaded her that she had made the right decision, even though it went against what she believed in.

'But just this once,' she said. 'Never again.'

15

Milo gave Caro a hero's welcome as she hung up her coat. The TV was on in the living room. Since the day of their walk, she and Damir had barely crossed paths. She didn't know how she was meant to be so tried to avoid him. If she wasn't going out in the mornings, she got up after she heard him leave and in the evening he came back late and usually went straight upstairs. In truth, she was glad. She didn't want to know that he'd changed his mind, seen sense, that her excitement was transitory at best. Torn between the longing and the deep apprehension that had haunted her ever since their kiss, she went to the kitchen and made herself a cup of tea. She needed to wind down before she went to bed.

When she walked into the living room, she found Damir asleep in front of the TV. As she entered, his eyes opened. He pushed himself upright. 'Hello.'

Immediately she felt that dart of desire again. 'Long day?' She pushed it away.

'The same as every day.'

There was a silence as they considered each other. A lazy smile spread across his face, lighting up his eyes. She felt herself smiling back, as any doubts deserted her.

'I've missed you,' he said.

'And I've kept missing you too. But you leave so early and get back so late.'

'That's not what I mean.'

'Oh?' She looked at the floor, straightening a corner of a rug with her foot.

'I thought you were avoiding me.'

'Why would I?' So he had noticed. She sat down.

He rubbed a hand over his stubble, his expression becoming serious. 'Perhaps it would be better if I leave before the end of the summer after all.'

Her heart tumbled but she steadied herself, trying not to over-react. 'All right. I have been avoiding you.'

Again that smile did for her. 'Why?'

'Because . . .' She found herself smiling back. 'Don't go.' A sense of excitement took her by surprise.

'I should. I like it here very much but if it's difficult for you . . .'

'But you don't need to.' She didn't want him to go. She liked him being there and wanted to know more about him. But who was she trying to fool? She wanted more than that. She wanted him. He made her feel alive again, open to possibility. Things might change with him around. 'Wait till the summer's over and Esad is back.'

She stood up at the same time he did. Face to face, they said nothing but looked unblinking into each other's eyes. She could see the flecks of different browns in his irises; the dark pools of his pupils. Were they really the windows to his soul? But she couldn't see through to see what was there. She felt as shy as a young girl, but was thrilling with anticipation too. He raised his hand to her face, running his finger over her cheekbone, her jaw, as if imprinting them in his memory. Her hand was on his chest. She could feel his heart beating as he bent his head and she raised hers to him. It was as if she was melting.

'Come upstairs with me,' she heard herself whisper, frightened he might refuse. Whatever happened next would be a moment of truth for both of them. Someone shouted something on the TV. A shriek of brakes. But neither of them turned to look.

He took her hand and led her out of the room and up the

stairs. The lights, the TV, Milo – they could all wait until later. Anticipation and longing were thrumming through her, their beat obliterating everything else. He hesitated at the top of the stairs, uncertain whether to turn towards her room or his.

'It's OK,' she said, reaching the top step to kiss his cheek, breathing in the smell of him. She passed him and led the way to her room. He stood in the doorway as she went in to turn on the bedside light. The tension between them hummed. Nothing mattered except for this moment.

He watched as she stood at the end of the bed facing him. His eyes never left her as she removed her clothes down to her bra and pants. She stopped there, too shy to let him see her completely naked. But he was removing his shirt, his bare arms and torso as strong and muscled as she had imagined. He slipped off his shoes and pulled off his socks. Then the belt of his trousers dropped on the floor, the buckle clicking on the bed leg, and he unzipped his jeans, letting them drop to the ground before he stepped out of them.

'Come here,' he said, shutting the door behind him as he stepped further into the room. Without the light from the landing, the room was more intimate, the dimness welcome. Caro took the couple of steps that separated them. Before she had time to think about what she was doing, his arms were round her, undoing her bra, letting it fall to the floor as their bodies pressed together. His mouth was on hers, soft but insistent, then moving over her neck while his hands touched her until she thought she couldn't bear any more.

They moved to the bed without speaking, neither letting the other go. Caro barely noticed the chill of the sheets as Damir lifted the duvet and they slipped underneath with only one shared idea in mind.

Afterwards, lying in bed, on what was once Chris's side – the side she never normally visited – Caro could hardly believe what had just happened, nor that she felt quite so good as a result. It was as if Damir had wakened a part of her that had been dormant for years. He had been gentle and loving, always thinking of her. Caro stretched her arms behind her then folded them to cradle her head, as she lay there, eyes closed, her mind untethered by pleasure.

She could hear Damir downstairs, clattering in the kitchen, turning off the TV and the lights, letting Milo into the garden for a last pee. Eventually, he reappeared with two cups of tea that he put on the bedside tables before climbing in beside her.

'That was good? No?' He lay on his side, propped up on an elbow. He traced a finger from her chin, down her neck and between her breasts.

'Very,' she said, allowing herself to sink back under his weight as he started the whole thing all over again.

The next morning, she was stirred into life with a new sense of surprise and joy. She turned her head to see Damir, still asleep on the pillow beside her. To be able to watch someone like this was a gift. Her gaze lingered on the scar on his cheek, the curves of his ear and the mouth relaxed in sleep. She ran her finger along the scar on his arm, barely touching it.

He murmured something and reached out for her, his eyes barely opening.

Later, leaning against the pillows, cups of tea beside them, they began to talk. He told her of his childhood and of the happy times doing the usual boyish things, and of his boyish ambition.

'Brčko was a beautiful city. My father was a carpenter. We weren't rich but we had a good life. I wanted to be a premiership football player,' he confessed with a laugh. 'And when I wasn't playing football, I swam in the Sava, the river than runs by the city. I fished from its banks with my father, and when I was older I sat there with girls watching the fireflies over the water at night. I learned how to be a carpenter in my father's workshop.' He sounded wistful. 'We thought everything was possible then.'

In return she told him about the limitations of the family in which she had grown up, how much she would have liked to have had a brother or sister, the restrictions of being an only child, the escape from her lonely childhood that she had found through her art. 'Even at school, I knew that's what I wanted to be. An artist.'

'And you are,' he said, gesturing at the portrait of her daughters on the wall by the bed, the reclining woman over the mantelpiece, conveyed in a few brief strokes of charcoal.

'I did that so quickly, but somehow it captures her exactly the way I wanted it to.'

'I like it.' And then his hand moved down her body and she gave herself to him again.

After that night, their relationship intensified quickly. There was no more avoiding each other. Although they had only been together so briefly at the same time it felt as if it had been forever and they abandoned themselves to the change in their relationship. Caro had forgotten what it was to feel like this: light-headed, looser, on fire. Her thoughts of Damir took precedence over everything else, making it impossible to concentrate. She wanted to shout from the rooftops, announce to everyone that she had found happiness again, but at the same time, she wanted to hug their relationship to herself, keep it secret, away from comment. Besides, she was aware that what had lasted for only a few days might fizzle out as quickly as it had begun. There were no guarantees. This was a mad middle-aged fling. That's all. It didn't deserve to be raked over by her family. The rest of her life should continue as usual so it could catch her when she fell – as she almost inevitably would.

Am I being a fool, she asked herself? *Not if you know what you are doing* was the answer. He said he never stayed in one place for long. So how long would he stay with her. Weeks? She couldn't bear to think it would be over so quickly. Months?

Snatching up a pencil, she turned the pages showing six months on the kitchen calendar. *That's how long it will be.* She made a small almost indistinguishable dot at the beginning on the day in March when they first met and at the end, six months later, when the summer would be over. No one would notice them without looking closely, but she knew they were there and what they meant. Each day, each week, each month would be precious from now on. *When it finishes I will be ready, I will understand,* and she composed her features into the expression she knew she must adopt when that happened. But this was madness. How could she believe that one week would necessarily turn into months? She went back and rubbed out the final dots, chastened. Because she could dream. That's why. She tapped the pencil against her teeth and marked the dots in again.

Paul had phoned to ask her to a concert but she made an excuse not to go. Although they had promised each other a friendship, she wasn't sure Damir would understand. She didn't want to risk upsetting what they had found together and, besides, she wanted to spend all her spare time with him. She took her art classes as usual, getting through them on autopilot. She spent time in her studio, re-energised as she phoned her agent to remind her she was looking for more commissions, placed another ad in the local paper and agreed to paint a portrait of the outgoing mayor. She babysat Danny one evening and worked in Bloom for an extra morning. Saying 'yes' or 'no' was unimportant to her now. She had to carry on in a way so that no one would suspect anything in her life had changed.

The only person she was tempted to tell was Fran, who called, apologetic but single-minded, to remind her that Simon thought they were spending the following Wednesday evening together. She was going to meet Ewan at last. He had shrugged off her questions raised by Caro bumping into him: Suzy was a colleague who shared an interest in visiting the London galleries, that's all; he wanted to see her. Caro said nothing. She had said enough.

As much as Fran needed her, she wanted to confide in Fran, too. They had always told each other everything and her friend would be over the moon to know the barriers round Caro's safe little world were breaking down. But, this week, Fran was so wrapped up in her own drama, Caro decided to wait.

That day, she had her students concentrate on single parts of the body – a hand, a foot, an ear or part of the face. Their model was an elderly woman who was happy to sit as still as requested. There were only a few of them there this week. The early quick sketches were more successful than the longer attempts. The detail required defeated most of her students apart from Susan who completed a creditable hand, detailing the ropes of veins that strung across the bones, the arthritic knuckles, the slim wedding band. Eventually, satisfied but exhausted, Caro said her goodbyes and went home.

She opened her email that evening. The first in the inbox was from her mother whose laptop had come back to life once the charger had been switched on at the wall. A simple problem that Jason had solved to May's embarrassment. She had embraced new technology with nervy enthusiasm. Caro tried to discourage her from online banking and shopping, worried she'd get into some terrible financial tangle. Now she realised how patronising she was being. May had shown she was quite capable, if cautious. All Caro was doing was treating her in the same way she disliked her daughters treating her – as if she was incompetent, incapable of looking after herself. She vowed that she would be more generous in the future.

Dear Caro
I'm writing this because I know you're at work. First, I've
seen Jack who needs to go through the figures before knowing
how much I can safely lend you. But I suspect it won't be
nearly as much as you need.

Her chances of saving Treetops were receding. The last building society she had visited had gently explained that she really wasn't the kind of business they could accommodate. Yet she was reluctant to give up hope. She read on.

I'm going to Tenerife for a long weekend with Patricia next week. To her timeshare. Could I stay with you on Thursday night when we can discuss further, and perhaps you could drive me to Gatwick in the morning? Or I can get a taxi.

Gatwick. Caro felt an overwhelming desire to jet away from home herself, where she wouldn't have to worry about the opinions of her friends and family when they found out about Damir and her. Being observed, even if only out of well-meaning concern, could be like being in a prison. She had only been abroad once with Amy since Chris had left. They had stayed in a friend's chalet in the French Alps where they walked, ate well and were surrounded by the natural beauty of the mountains. Back then, she had been paralysed with grief then indecision. But now, she was stronger, braver.

She rapped out a quick reply expressing her thanks and agreement, then wasted an hour or so googling holiday destinations and reading reports on them, remembering how she'd enjoyed her time with Amy in the Alps. Eventually Milo wandered in to remind her that a walk was overdue.

When the night of Fran and Ewan's meeting finally arrived, Caro and Damir were having supper together when the doorbell rang. She had dimmed the lights and lit candles: instant atmosphere for their scrambled eggs and the *apfelstrudel* that he had been taught to make by his mother. She had been telling him about her own mother's imminent visit and how she envied her jetting away to the sun.

'Don't answer it,' he said, catching her hand to pull her back.

'But they'll have seen the lights on. If I don't, they'll think something's wrong.'

'Or that we're busy.' He winked.

'Exactly. That's what I'm terrified of.' There was another more forceful knock. 'Listen to that! What if it's Amy? I must go.' Perhaps Jason had plucked up his courage and proposed at last. Perhaps they were both here to break the news.

Damir released her hand, inclining his head to one side with a small smile. 'Go, then.'

Caro hesitated, almost overwhelmed by the desire to kiss him. At the third knock, she tore herself away because if she didn't, she would be lost.

As she crossed the hall, the knock sounded again, even more urgent than before. She unbolted the door and flung it open to find Simon standing there.

'I need to see Fran,' he said, grabbing her arm. 'I didn't want to interrupt you both but she's not answering her phone.'

'She's not here.' There was no point pretending. This was the situation she had dreaded, that Fran always swore would never happen.

'Not here?' He seemed to deflate in front of her eyes. As he stepped inside she saw his eyes were red-rimmed and tired. He must have found out. But how? Fran had always been so careful.

'Come and sit down. What's wrong?' She led him into the living room, preparing herself for his answer. Simon had a huge heart, but not even he would be generous enough to understand why she had helped Fran keep her secret for so long.

'It's Will.' Simon stopped and leant forward, elbows on knees, head in hands.

Caro closed her eyes, breathing deeply. 'What's happened?'

'But where's Fran?' He looked up at her, bewildered, pale with anxiety. 'She said she'd be here.'

'She's been and gone.' The lie was the best Caro could do. If she said Fran was delayed, Simon would want to wait for her and, in the end, Caro would have to tell him the truth. 'What's happened to Will?'

'Where to? Where's she gone?'

'She just said she was meeting a friend. She didn't say where.' This was awful. Caro hated herself more with each lie. Simon didn't deserve this. 'What's happened?'

'He's in hospital.'

'No! Why?' Caro went to sit beside him, put her arm round him. She dreaded whatever he was going to say next. Not Will. Not lovely Will who had inherited his mother's exuberance and charm and had his whole life ahead of him.

'A car knocked him off his bike.'

Caro covered her mouth with a hand. 'Oh no.' She had known Will since he was born, watched him growing up and turn into the fine young man he was now. 'Is he badly hurt?'

'He's in hospital. UCH. Sarah, the current girlfriend' – he couldn't help a wry smile – 'called to say he's OK but was being kept in overnight. They think he's broken his wrist and leg – he was waiting to be X-rayed then – and has bashed his head badly. They're checking him for concussion, and maybe worse. At least he was wearing a helmet. We should be with him so I thought I could pick Fran up and we'd go straight there.'

'You've tried her phone?' She couldn't admit to Simon that Fran was somewhere in London herself.

'Yes, I told you. She's not answering.' Panic made him impatient. 'I'll just have to go without her.' He held up his car keys.

'You're not driving,' Caro said. 'Not like this. You having an accident won't help anyone. The train will be much quicker anyway. I'll take you to the station.'

'No, I couldn't ask you . . .'

'You didn't ask. I'm offering and it's the least I can do. You need to get to Will in one piece.' She took the car key from the hall table and gave it to him. 'You go and get in the car while I get my bag.'

Minutes later they were on their way, Caro having given Damir the briefest of explanations. As she drove towards the centre of town she could feel Simon willing her to drive faster.

After a few moments, he finally spoke. 'I'm not an idiot, Caro.' His change of tone made Caro glance sideways. Simon was staring straight ahead, his right hand moving up and down his seatbelt.

'What do you mean?'

'You must both think I'm stupid.'

'Sorry?' She had imagined all sorts of versions of this situation, but not this.

'Fran's been having an affair.'

'She has?' She did her best to sound shocked. She turned into the one-way system that would take them to the station.

'Caro, don't.' He turned his face to the side window. 'Don't insult me by pretending you don't know. I know it's been going on for ages. So do you.'

'I'm sorry.' If only she could explain.

'There's nothing to apologise for. I don't blame you. I might have done the same in your position. I know better than anyone how persuasive she can be.' How could he be so controlled? In his position, Caro would be raging. The scenes she and Chris made still filled her with shame: things had been thrown, voices raised, insults and blame hurled at each other. There had been nothing like this deadly calm. 'As long as it didn't threaten what we have, I was prepared to put up with it. I may not be everything she needs but I would rather share her than lose her.'

Caro gripped the wheel as she turned into the station forecourt and found a drop-off space outside the main building.

'My guess is, she's with him.' He didn't sound bitter, just disappointed.

When Caro had discovered Chris's affair, she had been uncontainable. Her trust and love had been breached for ever. That Chris had no interest in repairing the damage made her devastation worse. Simon's self-control was the more awful to her

161

because she had experienced some of the pain he must be hiding. Her breath caught as she remembered what Fran might be about to do after this evening. She couldn't bear to think of the effect it would have. Should she suggest that she called Fran? She might be more likely to pick up a call from her.

'No. It's OK. I've left a message. She'll get back to me when she picks it up. She always does. I'm just going to run for the train.' He glanced at his watch. 'Four minutes.'

'I don't know what to say.'

There was a click as he opened the passenger door and swung his legs out. He looked back over his shoulder at her. 'There's lots we could talk about. But not now. The sooner I get to the hospital the better.'

'I hope Will's OK.'

'I'll call you.' He ducked his head as he got out, and raised a hand in farewell before running into the booking office. Caro sat for a moment, listening to her breathing as she tried to calm herself down. That Simon had known about Fran's affair all along made her feel so ashamed. She rested her head on the steering wheel then leant over, opened the glove box and got out the tin of butterscotch that she kept there for long journeys, now squidgy and sugary with age. She pressed a piece on to the roof of her mouth and waited for its comforting sweetness. Every justification she'd made to herself for not telling him seemed so flimsy now.

Her ringtone startled her. She took her bag from the back seat and pulled out her phone. Fran. She took the call, her anger returning. 'Have you called Simon? He came to the house looking for you.'

'Why? What did you tell him?'

'About you and Ewan? Nothing, of course. I didn't need to.'

'What do you mean?' Real anxiety had entered her voice.

'Fran, he'd worked it out for himself ages ago.'

'He can't have!'

Caro wished she was with her, able to give her some sympathy, and not at the end of the phone. 'He told me himself. But there's something else, something more important...'

This time there was an audible sniff. 'Oh Caro, I've made such a mess of things. I was so wrong about Ewan. And you were right.'

But this wasn't the time. 'Fran, listen to me. Will's in hospital and Si's been trying to get hold of you to tell you.'

'Oh my God, why? What's happened?' Ewan was forgotten immediately.

'He's in UCH. He was knocked off his bike but his girlfriend called Si. It sounded as if he's OK but pretty bashed about. Simon wanted you to be there.'

'What shall I do?' Fran sounded lost.

'Call Simon. Tell him you've spoken to me and you're on your way. Get a cab to UCH as quickly as you can. Si's getting on a train now, so you'll get there first. Sort out Will before anything else. And then...' She drew a deep breath. 'Well... then go somewhere or come home and talk to Si. Straighten this mess out.'

An hour later, when Caro was back home, Fran called to say that Will was being kept in overnight 'just in case'. He had been lucky: two breaks, bruised ribs and a crack on the head that was sore, but he'd recover. As Fran said, 'It could have been so much worse.' She and Simon were coming home, then returning first thing in the morning to bring Will home with them when he was discharged.

'And then, when I've got him settled, can I pop over?'

'Of course.' That would be another precious evening with Damir interrupted – when those months on the calendar seemed so short, so quickly vanishing. Fran gave a half-sob. Caro swallowed. 'Of course you can.'

16

That evening, Damir and Caro held hands across the table. 'You want me to go away again?' Although he was smiling, she could tell he was hurt.

'Oh God, of course I don't want you to.' She tightened her grip on his hand. 'Never that. Just not be around while the family is here.'

'Because you are embarrassed or ashamed?' He withdrew his hand.

'No! Neither of those. I just want to keep us secret for a bit longer. To have you to myself. Is that stupid?' She had spent ages thinking about what they should do. As soon as they told her family, the pressures of the outside world would crowd in on them and this gorgeous bubble of unreality would burst. She didn't want to hear her family's opinions, at least not until she knew what she felt herself. The last thing she wanted to do was to think about the future. She would rather they indulged themselves in the pleasures of the present without worrying about what might happen. If this was only going to be a summer fling – then she wanted it to be the best one they could make of it.

'Your friends and your family, they make it difficult.' He frowned, the corners of his mouth turning down in disappointment.

'And my mother's going to be here for a night next week,' she added.

'How will we ever see each other?'

'They all go home in the end,' she pointed out, worried he

was beginning to feel the whole thing was too difficult. 'Then we're alone.'

'That's what I want. To be alone with you. But many evenings, I have to hide or be hidden away like a secret.' She was glad to see a smile as he said this. 'It's not good. And soon Esad will be back and I'll move.'

'You know you don't have to.' She stopped herself from saying more, not wanting to insist. But she thought of all the things that could happen if he were out of her sight – even before those special six months she had allowed them were up.

'Let's make a deal,' she said in a rush.

He looked puzzled. 'A deal?'

She felt an absurd and tender smile on her lips. 'Why don't we go away? Together. Get away from them all.'

His brow furrowed. 'But I have work.'

'Just for a few days, a week maybe. I know somewhere we could go.' The idea had come to her the previous night as she lay sleepless, staring at the ceiling in the dark, listening to him murmur, restless beside her. Some nights his sleep was troubled. She didn't ask what he dreamed of, didn't want to make him relive any nightmares connected with the war unless he volunteered them. Going away was the only way they would be alone. If he didn't like her suggestion ... then she'd know where she stood.

'Really?' His face brightened.

'Well, if you think it's a good idea.' And nobody need know they had gone together. She would say she was recharging her batteries alone in a place she loved. 'When the term's over and if you can take leave.'

'But where will we go?'

'A friend of mine has a small chalet in France. Her family uses it for skiing and as extra income in the winter but she often lets friends use it when the weather warms up. Amy and I went there for a week last year. It was heaven. What's wrong?'

'How do we get there?'

'We fly to Geneva. It shouldn't be too expensive.' Would he be able to afford it? Should she offer to pay for him or would that be taken the wrong way? Her face must have given her thoughts away.

'That's OK,' he said. 'I have some savings. Wait.'

He disappeared from the room to return carrying a black tin box. He lifted out a passport. She took it and turned to the page where a younger version of him stared out at her, his face set. 'You look so young.' she said.

'But old enough to be married.' He took it back and laid it beside the box. 'I told you I was married once. A long time ago.'

Of course he had, when they first met. He had mentioned a marriage that he'd dismissed so easily that she hadn't even thought to ask about it again. Besides, he'd made it plain there was nothing he wanted to say. She had forgotten the detail, her interest pricked by his life before and after it. 'You did.' She hesitated. 'What happened?'

'I was a young man then with problems that made things difficult between us. I had seen too much in the war, lost too much, and couldn't forget. How could I?' He paused. 'I believed I loved her but I couldn't talk to her about what I'd been through. I couldn't talk to anyone. I didn't know how and I didn't think they'd understand. So I kept it all inside me. I was difficult to live with, always angry – I see that now – and we fought all the time. I couldn't be the person she wanted me to be. I made her unhappy although she tried for as long as she could. She believed she could put me back together again but no one can do that for another person. It has to come from inside and with time. We were so young: she didn't understand and I couldn't explain. In the end, she couldn't live like that any more and left me. I don't blame her.'

His suffering went so much deeper than the impact of war. Bullets and mortars were not the only weapons to wound him. He had lost everything. And worse, it had happened to him twice. First his family and his fiancée. Then his wife. No wonder he kept on the move, fearful of it happening again. 'Where is she now?' It wasn't too late to talk to him about her.

'I have no idea. She moved to Hamburg with the boyfriend she had before she met me.'

'You're still married?' As if it made a difference.

He laughed as if the idea was ludicrous. 'No, no. We divorced. I haven't heard from her since then.' Down came that shutter that said the subject was closed, the shutter she was learning to accept. He took a roll of notes out of the box. 'You see. I have my savings so we can go together.'

Inside the box, she glimpsed other similar rolls each secured with an elastic band, a couple of letters and a photo. 'Wouldn't that all be safer in a bank?'

'If I'm paid cash, it's better to keep the money out of the bank.' He put the passport and cash back in and shut the lid. 'I keep it with me.'

'But if you'd said, I could have put it in the safe.' Something Chris had insisted on after they had been burgled. They lost his grandmother's rings, some other less valuable jewellery, his precious camera and other bits and pieces. He wouldn't let anything like that happen again.

'It's safe in my room.' He lifted it up to take back upstairs.

'But if we're going away . . . Let me.' She went to the cupboard containing the safe, tapped in the code and opened it. 'If something happened to it here, I'd feel dreadful.'

'Then OK. The only photo I have of my mother's here.' He got it out and passed it to her: a tiny faded black and white picture of a young woman, whose face she could barely make out, surrounded by two small children. 'With me and my sister.'

She handed it back to him and he allowed her to lock the box away. In her eyes, the fact that he entrusted the box to her was imbued with significance.

167

'Then I'll ask Alice if the chalet's free,' she said, lightening the mood. 'You never know, we might be lucky.'

Already she could imagine them in the modest wooden chalet, the sun on the mountains, snow in the far distance, the air clean and clear. They would be alone and free from everything except the things he carried in his head.

Fran arrived only minutes after Damir had gone upstairs. She looked as if the life had been drained out of her, shadows like bruises under her tired eyes, her cheeks without the usual blusher. She glanced at herself in the hall mirror as she went past and groaned. 'Oh God!' She rubbed her cheeks to redden them, took a lipstick from her bag and glossed her lips. Last was her hair. 'If you think this is bad, you should see Si! We were up all night.'

'How's Will?'

'He's fine, thank God. Out of the woods. He was bloody lucky. He's safe at home already with us running around after his every whim. Si's there now.'

'And you?' Caro hardly dared ask.

'Wine?' Fran magicked a bottle from her bag and held it out to Caro. 'I think we'll need it. I've made such an unholy mess of everything.'

Within minutes they were sitting together on the sofa, Caro on the left and Fran on the right just as they usually sat, a couple of generous glasses poured and the bottle on the coffee table. This was going to be a long session. Milo stretched out on the mat in front of the fireplace. Occasionally he punctuated their conversation with a groan as he changed position.

'I got it all wrong.' Fran's eyes were glassy as she cleared her throat, sat a little straighter and took a sip of her wine. 'It wasn't what I thought at all. I met Ewan at the hotel but instead of going straight to his room as usual. Usually, we ... OK, OK ...' She read Caro's expression. 'So he rushed us into the restaurant. Even so, I didn't suspect a thing. I thought we were going to be discussing the future. Which of course it turned out that we were. We were chatting – at least when I look back I was doing most of it. I was nervous, excited, talking about anything and nothing, avoiding getting on to the subject. By then I was hoping he wouldn't say what I was expecting him to. I'd decided that if we could just carry on the same way, no one would get hurt. I didn't let him get a word in edgeways.'

Caro adjusted the cushions behind her and leant back. She wanted to hear what had happened but her mind kept wandering upstairs to Damir. She had to force herself to concentrate on what Fran was saying.

'Eventually he stopped me. I thought he looked a bit un-comfortable but I just assumed he was building up to the big question . . . He lifted his hand.' She lifted hers in the same way, palm towards Caro, fingers straight, then dropped it in her lap. 'God, I feel so stupid.'

'Go on.'

'I really thought he was about to ask me to leave Simon. I really did.' She rolled her eyes to the ceiling. 'How stupid was I? He looked so serious, and we hadn't even ordered. I was on tenterhooks. Then he began talking. He didn't look at me and talked so quietly I had to ask him to repeat himself. He had to look at me then.' She shook her head as if unable to believe that this had really happened.

'And? What did he say?'

'Basically that our "arrangement" was way past its sell-by date – "arrangement"! What a bastard. Two fucking years. Literally.' She gave a short laugh. 'But, you know what, I still didn't clock that anything was wrong. I really thought he meant he was going to leave his wife for me.'

'Did you really believe that?'

Fran took a deep shuddering breath and didn't reply.

'So what *did* he say?'

Fran shook her head. 'He went on about how much I meant

169

to him, what good times we had, how he'd never forget the Paris weekend. I told you about that.'

'Yep.' They seemed to have stayed in their hotel room, making love and ordering room service for two days. At the time Caro hadn't seen the point in going all the way there just to have your meals ordered and delivered in French. Everything else they could have done for half the price in the local Premier Inn. But that was not the point, she now realised. 'Go on. Stick to the story.'

'So there was I, feeling so sympathetic, touched that it all meant so much to him and that he was so nervous. Then I put my hand on his knee and he jumped away as if I'd scalded him. That's when I realised something was very wrong so I asked him what he was trying to say. I thought I might as well try and help the poor sod. I wish I hadn't now. So the long and the short of it was you were right. He's met someone else and he's going to leave his wife for her. There.'

Caro bit her lip, suddenly glad she had confronted Ewan after all.

'He actually said that he had once thought we might make a go of things together but now he'd met her he'd changed his mind. There. So he'd leave his wife for her but not for me. Bastard!' She took a swig of her wine.

'But when did he meet her?' Caro remembered that blonde hair, that abandon, that leather jacket!

'Six months ago! At some conference.'

'But I don't understand. Why didn't he say something sooner? Why carry on stringing you along?'

'He didn't want to say anything "until he was sure".' She drew the apostrophes in the air.

'But if he was having an affair with her . . .'

They looked at each other: Fran, wary and stricken; Caro, alight with her own secrets.

'You'd think. Anyway, it doesn't matter. I've been dumped. Just like that. You probably think it serves me right and it probably does.'

Caro looked at her friend's anguished face. 'Oh Fran, why did you do it?'

Fran stared past her. 'Because I needed to.'

They sat silent for a moment.

'I want you to be happy,' Caro said.

But Fran didn't reply.

The affair with Ewan had at least given her that and perhaps even propped up her marriage at the same time. If Simon couldn't give her everything she needed, then maybe it had helped it that she'd found that side of things elsewhere. Caro was beginning to understand in a way she hadn't before.

'And Simon?' she hardly dared ask.

Fran's eyes welled with tears again. 'As you know, he's known all along. He decided not to say anything as long as it didn't affect things between us, and he hoped that one day I'd see sense. He still loves me.' This time no amount of throat-clearing and changing position would stop the tears. 'He really does. Even now, after all this. What I hate about myself is that I've hurt him when he didn't deserve it.'

Caro passed her the box of tissues from the coffee table.

Fran blew her nose loudly. 'I've taken him for granted and that's the worst thing you can do to someone, isn't it?'

Caro nodded. 'I think it probably is.' Was that what she'd done to Chris? But with a family, work, everyday life, she had let him slip to the bottom of the list of demands. And his reaction had been like Fran's. What you can't get at home, you look for elsewhere. *Hang on!* A voice sounded in her head. *Don't blame yourself any more – it takes two to make and to break a marriage.* But Fran was still talking.

'After we were certain Will was going to be all right, we came home. We talked and talked and talked. I can't remember the last time we've done that.' She shrugged. 'We aired everything.

I hope it's not too late to sort it all out. We might try Relate or some kind of counselling...' She made a face. 'I know I've always pooh-poohed people who pay to talk but maybe, just maybe, I'm wrong there too and it'll help us.' She raised her glass.

Caro chinked hers with Fran's. Maybe, this was a first step on a path with no obvious end... but it was at least a first step.

'Maybe Ewan's even done us a favour.' Fran stood up and walked around the room, stopping in front of the photo of Caro and the girls. 'Maybe we can make it work after all. People do.'

'You're not sure?' There was something in Fran's voice that made Caro wonder.

'I don't know. God, I'm going to miss Ewan so much.'

'No, you're not. You're going to miss the sex. But you can do something about that!' She raised her glass.

Fran looked doubtful. 'Mmm. That'll need some work but we'll give it a shot. Talking to Si last night made me remember what I loved about him in the first place. He's so considerate and kind. And now we get in from work exhausted and then just sit in front of the TV, together but not talking. Content enough but relying on habit. But...' She came back to the sofa. 'We're going to try and change things. What about you and Paul?'

'Stop it!' Caro warned. 'Not since the Tate. After that supper at his place, we've decided to be friends.'

'What happened?'

And so Caro told her the whole story at last, which had Fran practically on the floor with laughter. Without Ewan, their friendship was already reverting to what it once was: easy, un-encumbered, open. Was this the moment tell Fran about Damir? But still she hesitated, wanting to hunker down over her secret, cherish it for a little longer.

'Still got the lodger though?' It was as if Fran could read Caro's thoughts. 'Why don't you get him down, I'd like to meet him properly.'

'Fran!'

Fran looked all innocent. 'What?'

'Stop trying to pair me off all the time. I'm happy as I am.' If Fran could be trusted not to say anything, she would tell her everything. But as good as Fran was with her own secrets she couldn't be relied on to be equally discreet with other people's.

'Well something's obviously doing you good. You look great. And it's not just the new haircut, which is stunning.'

'Must be,' said Caro, running a hand over her bob. 'I should have taken your advice ages ago.'

17

Her mother dumped her overnight bag in the hall. The sound it made echoed the thud in Caro's heart as she welcomed her. Everything with Damir had moved so fast in such a short time that she hated any interruptions to their time together. All she wanted was to have the best time for as long as it lasted. The intensity of passion had taken her by surprise, as had the fact that it seemed to be mutual. She already felt bound to him in a way she could never have predicted. But, as she hugged her mother, she reminded herself May was only staying for one night and then, once she had left for Gatwick, she and Damir would have Treetops to themselves again. In the meantime she would throw herself into making her mother welcome.

'Let me take it upstairs.' Caro picked up the bag. 'What have you got in here? Bricks?'

'Everything I need for a couple of nights. Kindle, curlers, you know.' May peered about her. 'The place is looking so much better.'

'Isn't it? He's done a great job.' It was true. Damir's workmanship was of a high standard, and the hall and stairway were much improved by changing the yellow walls she and Chris had chosen in sunnier times to a heathery off-white. Not exciting but it opened up the space and made it look much bigger.

'Is he here?' May held the banister as she went upstairs.

'I'm not sure.' Caro followed her mother, knowing full well Damir had gone out to spend an evening with friends and wouldn't be back till late. She was counting the hours till they could be together. She did everything expected of her out of habit – her classes, looking after Danny, working in Bloom, preliminary sketches of the mayor – but her prime focus was always on getting home as soon as she could. When they were apart, she relived what they had last done together, remembered what they talked about. He had taught her things in bed she had never dreamed of and encouraged her to do things she thought she would never do again. He had brought pleasure back into her life that outweighed her disbelief that a man like him would really desire her. But desire her he did, judging by the things he whispered to her as she fell asleep wrapped in his arms and when she woke surprised to see him there. He didn't seem to see the woman she saw in the mirror who was past her best. He treated her with the tenderness she had forgotten she longed for. He made her laugh, and he made her cry. He gave her more pleasure than she had thought possible. She hoped she did the same for him.

Her mother's arrival brought a taste of the real world with her, reminding Caro what might happen if her relationship with Damir went public. Lauren had already expressed her fears over him taking advantage of Caro, May would be worse. Caro might be over sixty, but May still wanted the best for her only child. Was that how Caro would continue to feel about her own daughters as they grew older? Her family might have her best interests at heart but that was exactly what would make them doubt Damir. What they saw as a perfect partner for Caro was someone similar in age and background – someone they would feel immediately comfortable with. Someone like Paul. But no one can legislate for who they fall in love with. And that was what was happening. Caro finally admitted to herself that she was falling in love with Damir.

Caro wasn't ready for the weight of her mother's anxiety when she found out. She didn't want to hear that she was making a mistake, being used, being made a fool of. Maybe she was. But she didn't care. Being made to feel as good as she did was worth whatever happened to them in the future. She didn't want to think any further ahead than the next day.

May was turning the door handle of Lauren's old room when Caro caught up with her. 'You're not in there, Mum. That's Dam... That's the lodger's room.'

May turned to go through the door that Caro was holding open into Amy's old room. 'I thought you'd be more comfortable in here.'

'*Very* nice. A huge improvement.' May sat on the end of the bed and looked around her.

Gone were the pony posters, the boy bands, the shelves full of children's books and everything Judy Blume had ever written, the empty laundry basket and the discarded clothes all over the floor, the make-up scattered over every surface. Caro had taken up the carpet so Damir could sand and paint the floor a pale grey, slightly lighter than the shade she chose for the walls. The curtains and rugs were in complementary shades of blue. The bed linen was crisp white with blue ikat cushions scattered on top. All obvious traces of Amy had disappeared and, although sad about that, she also felt it was the right thing. *Should have done it ages ago*, she told herself. But she had been a different woman then.

'I'll go and make supper while you sort yourself out,' she said. 'There's no hurry.'

In the kitchen, she measured out the rice for a risotto. Which pub would Damir be in now? Would he be watching football with friends? She chopped an onion, almost enjoying the tears that came into her eyes. She could pretend she wasn't crying from love. He wouldn't be back until late. What sort of late? She fried the onion. *Grow up*, she scolded herself. *Stop thinking about him... and who he might be with.*

'What are we having?' May had changed into more comfortable grey trousers and a jumper. Her hive of red hair seemed to have been toned down a fraction. Caro could smell her familiar perfume from where she stood.

'Mushroom risotto.'

Her mother pursed her lips. 'Oh. That sounds nice.' It was quite clear that it didn't.

Caro reminded herself this was only for one night and took a breath. 'Mum! Last time you were here, you said you liked it.'

'Did I?' May thought for a second. 'But I'm on this new diet now. I'm surprised you haven't noticed.' She looked down at her body that looked no different from when Caro had last seen her. 'An omelette and salad will do me fine. I don't want you to go to any trouble.'

'This isn't trouble. I'm making it anyway now. But if you're sure.'

May passed her the frying pan. 'I'm sure.'

They sat with their different meals, facing each other. May looked around the kitchen, taking in the space, the clean lines of the kitchen Caro and Chris had been so pleased with when they eventually had it put in ten years earlier. 'This will last us out,' he'd said. And it had. Ironic, Caro couldn't help thinking. May turned from the long shelf of cookery books to Danny's latest painting attached with magnets to the fridge.

'This really is a lovely house.'

'Which is why I don't want to lose it, unless I have to.' A knot formed in Caro's stomach as she realised what her mother was leading up to.

'I've talked to Jack.'

Her mother's expression told Caro all she needed to know. 'And it's a no.'

May put down her knife and fork, mirroring Caro who had lost all desire to eat. 'I'm afraid he's confirmed there's nothing like enough there to give you the kind of lump sum you'll need.'

'I thought that's what he'd say.' Caro's disappointment was crushing, despite having been told that in all probability this was what would happen. 'I might not need quite as much as that.'

'He thinks I should hold enough back to look after myself.

Not put that burden on you.' She sounded apologetic, as if she didn't really deserve such care. 'He's right of course.'

'But...' Caro was about to suggest that May move into Treetops with her when something held her back. That was the obvious answer but as much as she loved her mother, their living together would be wrong for each of them at this stage in their lives. Such a move would be thoroughly selfish on her part and would deny them both their independence: something that May had been so keen to protect for herself; something Caro was just learning to enjoy. Was it right to deprive them both of that? When May could no longer look after herself, Caro would step in and help in whichever way she could. She would do whatever she could for her mother but now was not the time.

May clearly understood the thoughts running through her daughter's mind. 'I've been investigating assisted care homes and although there is one that might suit me one day, that day's not here yet. I really don't want you to have any responsibility for me. Financial or otherwise. I know what you'll say, but we don't know what will happen and I want to be self-sufficient for as long as I can. Having said that, there is *some* money we could free up for you – and I know Dad would want that – but you'll have to make up the considerable shortfall. I'm sorry.' She reached out a hand for Caro's.

Knowing her mother was making the right decision for them both, Caro clasped her hand. She ran a finger over the back of it, tracing the pattern of the bones. 'Thank you.'

Her dream of keeping Treetops was receding, just as Chris had known it would, and the feeling that gave her was heartbreaking.

That night after May had finally gone to bed, Caro was getting ready for hers. She heard a car, footsteps on the gravel and the key turning in the front door that then quietly opened and closed. Her pulse quickened. She longed to go and greet him but her mother had the auditory system of a bat. Caro could imagine May in her room, ears twitching, trying to work out the significance of the unfamiliar sounds.

Damir must be making his usual cup of tea before coming upstairs. She waited, listening too, then, sure enough, she heard him make his way along the corridor to his room. His door opened and closed. It was all she could do to stop herself from going to him.

Instead, she climbed into bed, read a little before turning off the light and drifting into sleep. Some time later, the click of the latch on her door woke her. She sat bolt upright, glancing at the clock – 3:45 – and stared at the door as it opened inwards.

'Mum?'

'Are you awake?' Damir shut the door and tiptoed across the room to her. Within a second, his dressing gown was on the floor and he was in bed with her.

'I am now.' She felt him press up against her. 'But you can't be in here! Mum'll hear you!'

'She won't hear this,' he whispered as he ran his hand over her rib cage up to her breasts. 'Shhh.'

Like dandelion seeds on a breeze, her objections were blown away.

Later, stifling their laughter like naughty school children, Damir disentangled himself from the duvet. 'I don't want you to, but you must go.' All Caro's anxieties about being discovered were returning but she pulled him down on her, losing herself in a long kiss before pulling the duvet over both their heads. She could hardly believe she was behaving like this.

'OK. Then I'll see you tomorrow,' he whispered. At last they surfaced, the first intimations of dawn in the sky outside, a lemony light rising from the horizon into a clear sky.

He planted a kiss on her forehead. Their fingers touched then separated.

After he had left, so quietly that even she didn't hear him, Caro lay awake staring at the ceiling.

She thought of the calendar downstairs, each day marked with a tiny pencilled dot that only she would notice. More than three months had passed since they first met.

The next day, Damir left as Caro and her mother were getting up. To Caro's relief, May said nothing about having heard footsteps in the corridor at night. Nothing in her behaviour when she wished him a brisk good morning suggested that she had heard anything untoward. She didn't see the wink he gave Caro from behind her back. Her case was sitting in the hall waiting for her departure. A taxi was ordered.

'If I didn't have work today, you know I'd take you myself, but I've got an appointment to see a woman who I hope's going to commission me to do a portrait of her baby for her husband's birthday. She saw the picture of a pair of sisters I did last year and the mother gave her my number.' Word of mouth recommendations were what she liked best but she found babies hard, their tiny faces changing all the time.

'Isn't it time you were thinking about doing less?' May picked at her fresh fruit salad, with an eye on the fresh bread and butter Caro helped herself to.

'Don't be daft! I love my work and the people I meet. You know I've always enjoyed trying to capture that something about a person that makes them them. Remember when I painted you?' They laughed at that. May had been unable to sit still for more than a minute until Caro got so frustrated, she finally lost her temper: not the way to get the best from your sitter. May kept the resulting painting for as long as was maternally kind, then it disappeared and was never mentioned again. 'As for my classes, I love seeing my students go from nervous beginners into painters who are confident and fearless. That's fun. And I love spending a day with Danny and one with Amy. I like being busy but it's flexible too so perfect for me. I've no plans to stop.' She spread a particularly generous slab of butter onto the bread. May had given up her work as a pharmacist when she had Caro so knew little about the pleasure that could be derived from colleagues and helping students achieve what they wanted. Not that that stopped her from having an opinion.

'At least it's something to do.'

'More than that.' Caro reacted too quickly, before she saw her mother was teasing. 'I've made friends. And I think the work's important.'

Before they could go any further, there was the beep of a horn outside.

'That's your cab.' Caro didn't actually sigh with relief but felt as though she might have.

With May packed off to Tenerife, Caro took Milo for a quick constitutional before getting ready to visit her next potential client. As she walked and he bounded off into the trees down the edge of Merrow Down, hunting rabbits and squirrels, she reflected on how she had meant what she said to May. Teaching offered her one kind of fulfilment, but painting for a living offered her another. And the unsaid: Damir – for the moment at least – another.

Back home, she changed ready for her meeting but a glance at her watch told her she just had time to confirm the details of their holiday. She opened her laptop to check the times of their flights to Geneva, called Alice to double check that the caretaker of the chalet was expecting them and to confirm the route from the airport. Not long before the two of them would be there.

But she had to put her excitement on hold as her professional self took over. Her portfolio of photographed portraits on the back seat of the car, she set her satnav and headed off for the address she had been given just outside Wonersh, alive to the possibility of a new commission.

18

Since arriving in the Alps, Caro and Damir had spent the time in a buzz of happiness. They had explored the small Alpine town of Les Gets, taken the red 'bubble' lift up the far side of the valley and walked the tracks round the beginners' ski slopes that were dressed in their finest summer livery of bright grass and wild flowers. They had driven up to Les Crètes de Zorre where they walked along the mountain ridge with swallowtail butterflies dancing in the air around them. At Lac Montriond, they squeezed into the car park by the little pool then walked along the jade-green water's edge, the cliffs rising high above them. Gradually they left the crowds behind them as they walked through the woods and up towards the waterfall. The evenings had disappeared in dimly lit restaurants, eating substantial mountain food and drinking rough French red wine.

Being with Damir made her see the place with fresh eyes. For the first time in ages, she felt truly happy. She had never expected at her age to fall in love again. But this was really happening. Was what she had thought might be a brief fling at the most turning into something more serious from his side too? Damir's comment about always being on the move had stayed with her. Why would she be the one to make him change? All she knew was that she didn't want their time here to end.

Every day, they watched the bright-coloured crescent sails of the paragliders floating over the tops of the mountains, swooping and turning until they landed in a field on the edge of the village.

'Imagine,' she had said as they walked past, holding hands,

watching those paragliders rolling up their sails on the grass. 'That must be the closest you can ever get to being a bird. I bet it's incredible.' And had thought nothing more of it.

'Come,' said Damir, the next day on the terrace. 'I have a surprise for you.'

'Can't we do nothing for a bit?' She put down her book and stretched out her legs in the sun, looking over the village, listening to the sounds of construction echoing along the valley before them. 'Go to the lake for a swim later, maybe?'

'No, we have something to do. A surprise.' He held out her bag and rattled the front door keys until she gave in.

They drove down the hill from the chalet into the village where he parked.

'Why drive when we could have walked?'

'You'll see.' He was already familiar with streets and alleys leading off the main street. He led her past the chickens already roasting outside the *boucherie/charcuterie*, past her favourite *patisserie*, the souvenir shop and into the square where the market took place every week. The village was already busy with summer tourists. Caro lingered at a soft-toy stall to look for a present for Danny. But Damir was impatient, pressing on to the dark wooden chalet that was the Adventure Sports Centre.

'What are we doing here?' Caro looked at the photos in the window of people canyoning, white water rafting, mountaineering and all the other extreme sports that she thanked God she would never have to do. There were at least some perks of growing old. The need to prove herself had gone – not that it had ever been that evident.

'We're going to *parapente*.' He pointed triumphantly at a picture of three paragliders twirling in the sky; another, a close-up of someone giving a thumbs up. At her, it seemed!

She stared at him in horror. 'You *are* joking?'

He grinned. 'No. We're going to fly like birds. I thought you wanted to.'

'I didn't mean we should do it. Watching them's one thing . . . Imagining.'

'Exactly. And doing's another.' He held open the door of the shop.

'I'm not going in.' But she took a step after him all the same, not wanting to spoil his pleasure. If he wanted to, that was one thing. She didn't have to join in.

'Be brave. I've booked us. Come on.'

'But I . . .' Before she had time to object on the grounds of fear, age, unsuitability of clothing, anything at all, a youngish Frenchman was shaking her hand. '*Bonjour, madame*. I'm Gilles, your instructor. It's the perfect day for a tandem flight.' He was one of those muscled young action men who filled the bars in the evening after a day of testing themselves against the mountains. He was tall, tanned with sun-bleached hair, the right extreme-sports kit to look as if he meant business and a pair of dark glasses so black, there wasn't a hint of his eyes behind.

Had her face already given away how alarmed she felt? 'There's been a mistake. This is for younger people. Not us.'

He gave a Gallic shrug, a down turn of the lips. When he removed his glasses, his eyes were cornflower blue. 'But you are not old. I flew with an eighty-three-year-old woman only last week. It's quite safe.'

The day before, she had envied the paragliders their freedom, the grace with which they rode the thermals, the thrill of flying. Now middle-aged anxiety had ambushed her with its fierce grip.

'Flying like a bird,' Damir whispered in her ear. 'This is your one chance.'

Something in her gave a little. 'It's too dangerous.' But her voice was less unsure.

Gilles shook his head. 'We make it as safe as it can be.'

She found herself walking between the two of them in the direction of the car. Gilles was behind her, burdened with a huge back bag that contained the sail; it reminded her of a body bag.

'Trying something new is good. It's an adventure.' Damir opened the car door so she could get in the back seat. Gilles stuffed all his equipment into the boot and slipped into the front seat ready to navigate. He seemed uber-confident, but could she really trust him with her life? Visions of bodies raining from the sky, smashing into buildings tormented her.

'I'll just watch you,' she said.

Damir winked at her in the rear view mirror. 'Come on.'

By the time they had driven through the nearby village of Morzine and up a winding mountain road, she had almost convinced herself that she should have a go. After all, what had she to lose... She'd had a good life, and this might mean going out on a high. Better than being doolally in an old folks' home. If Fran were there she would tell her to get on and face her fears. If Chris were there, he'd counsel caution – or would he now?

They pulled up on the right of the road and crossed to a large open grassy space. She stood back as Gilles unrolled his blood-red sail on the mountainside. He laid everything out just so, checking the equipment. In the distance below them she could just see Morzine shrunk to a jumble of tiny sloping rooftops before the land rose again into pinewoods on the village's other side. Caro's stomach lurched. She shouldn't even be considering this. *Oh go on*, Fran's voice again. *Get out of your comfort zone and do something different for once. Take a risk.*

Damir was beside her, his arm round her shoulder. 'I'll go first so you can see. Then your turn.' He kissed her temple. 'I'll see you at the bottom.'

She nodded, trying not to show how scared she was, and let him go. She watched Gilles strap them both into the harness. She took out her phone and took a few souvenir snaps. Should she stop them before something terrible happened? But before she had a chance to move, there was a shout of farewell and the two men were running down the slope, Damir's hand out, his thumb up. The sail rose, bright against the cobalt sky, and their feet left the ground. She hadn't even said goodbye.

After a moment, she was back in the car, wishing she could race down to the landing spot that Gilles had pointed out but instead she took the bends with caution, a short queue of cars building up behind her. In Morzine, she joined a knot of people in the field that was the landing spot behind l'Hotel Aubergade, all squinting into the sky, their hands shading their eyes as they waited for a member of their party, cameras at the ready. 'There she is,' went up a cry. 'There's Mum.'

She looked up and above the lemon yellow sail coming towards them she spotted the brilliant red one, translucent in the sunshine, the tiny figures of Damir and Gilles silhouetted against the sky. Her pulse pounded. If anything happened to them . . . but there was nothing she could do. Beside her, the family had gathered around a woman who was landing in front of them, strapped between her instructor's legs, as Damir was. Her face was radiant as they greeted her, clapping as they came to a halt.

Where was Damir? The red sail swung round over the rooftops for a final turn. She could see Gilles' arms up, his hands pulling against something as he steered them in. Were they coming too close to the roofs? Would they overshoot the field? Her heart was in her mouth as she watched, at the same time taking what photos she could. And then they had landed, the two of them running forward, the sail trailing on the ground behind them. She ran towards them, enjoying the elated expression on Damir's face. His eyes were shining, just like those of the woman who had landed before him.

'My God, that was amazing. You *have* to do it. You'll never be sorry.'

Carried away by his excitement, she heard herself agreeing. Before she knew it they had driven back up the mountain, the sail was laid out on the ground behind her and she was strapped with Gilles into the harness.

'Ready?' Gilles gestured at the harness. 'I'll make sure you're safe. I've done this many times.'

She felt Damir's hand between her shoulder blades, giving her the gentlest of pushes. This was his treat.

All at once, saying no seemed churlish and feeble. If not now, when? *Go on*, said Fran. *Take a risk.* She took a step forward, hearing Damir clap twice, excited for her. Her heart was racing, its beat insistent. Before she could voice the objections that were crowding her head, she was running down the slope as the sail lifted up behind them. And, with a jerk, it was above them, her feet had left the ground and they were flying. Underneath them, a pine forest spread out like a blanket and then they had passed over it and were sailing free, with nothing to cushion their fall of thousands of feet. Her heart felt as though it was going to explode from her chest. There was no way to get out of this now. No way anyone could rescue her. Oh God! They were so high.

There was a sharp tug on the harness. Had it broken?

'What are you doing?' Was this it?

'Just changing our direction,' said Gilles, quite calm. 'I pull on the straps. Relax.'

'Don't.' Her voice came out as shrill as a whistle. Nothing could save them now.

'Look over there.' His arm pointed to the left. 'That's where the beginners learning on their own start. And there's the...' He embarked on a guide of the sights that took her eye away from the distance to the ground below them and directed it outwards until she had almost forgotten the precariousness of their flight. He must have reassured plenty of middle-aged women trembling with panic between his thighs. The thought amused her. And as it did, she realised she had relaxed and was actually enjoying – yes, enjoying – the bird's eye view of the ground below. The feeling of freedom and escape was thrilling. Finally she had achieved it. She swung her feet out in front of her, first one then the other as Gilles manoeuvred the sail so they moved in a wide loop above the Lego-like town with its tiny cars and vans moving between bite-sized buildings and people scurrying ant-like through the streets.

As quickly as they had begun, they were heading towards the landing field at the back of the hotel where she could see another couple of sails being packed away on the ground, and there was Damir, standing, waving, grinning, his phone recording her flight. As the ground rushed up towards them, she remembered what Gilles had said about running forward when they landed, that no one he'd flown with in tandem –had fallen over. Her feet touched the ground, she tried to run but the tug from the sail unbalanced her, pulling her backwards. Together they crashed to the ground, Gilles cushioning her fall. She heard his gasp as her body landed on his, winding him. Damir ran towards them laughing and helped them both up.

'Well?' he said, holding her upright while Gilles unclipped the harness and freed himself then bent over to regain his breath.

'Amazing!' Caro was breathless. Adrenalin was giving her the sort of buzz she had only experienced after giving birth. 'Truly amazing.' Her smile felt as if it might split her face in two. After that, she felt brave enough to tackle anything.

'If you want to stay here, I can go back to Les Gets with Klaus.' Gilles looked up from packing the sail and nodded towards another instructor.

Fifteen minutes later, having said goodbye, they were sitting on the terrace of the l'Hotel Aubergade having ordered lunch. In front of them, other paragliders landed at intervals while beyond them the ski lift carried mountain bikers and hikers up to the top of the mountain.

'That was one of the most incredible things I've ever done,' she said, raising her *citron pressé*. 'I'd never have done it without you.'

He grinned. 'It was the same for me.'

She felt so grateful. Somehow he had seen inside her head . . . seen her need to do something that would prove herself. Why?

If it weren't for him, she would never have stepped out of her comfortable rut. Her horizons would have remained as limited as they had been for years. She would never have felt this sense of being able to do anything she had thought beyond her reach until now. For the first time since Chris left, she really did see that her life could be different but only if she recognised and embraced the opportunities that came her way. 'I wish we could stay for longer.'

He lifted his finger to his lips. 'Shh. We have two more days. And we'll make memories that we won't forget.'

The following day, Caro woke to the sound of rain. Not possible. She went into the living room and pulled back the curtains. Gone were the brilliant blues and greens, replaced by thick cloud obscuring the other side of the valley and rain lashing the streets, bouncing off their terrace. Alice had warned her about the summer storms that could last on and off for days but this was the first time she had seen anything as bad as this. Thunder rumbled from the direction of Mont Blanc.

Caro made two mugs of tea and went straight back to bed where they talked, made love and laughed and made love again. It was almost lunchtime when they got up, by which time the cloud was lifting and the rain had eased off enough for them to go out. Damir pulled out the chalet's guidebook.

'Up the cable car and walk the path to Mont Chery for lunch and back?' he suggested.

'Not the cable car.' The idea of inching her way up the mountainside, in a cabin suspended on a cable that looked barely strong enough to support it, frightened the life out of her. The little red 'bubble' lift that travelled up and down the other side of the valley was nothing like as intimidating.

'Why not? You went on the other one with no problem.'

'That was bad enough. But they don't frighten me in the same way. I know it's irrational but I can't explain. Why don't we drive?'

He studied her, astonished. 'Is this the woman who braved the skies yesterday saying she's scared?'

'Damn right I am.' But put like that... She swallowed. 'Not exactly.' She remembered her resolutions from the day before.

'Well, then.' He bent to put on his walking shoes. 'Let's go.'

19

In the cable car, Caro sat rigid, facing the mountain, her grip tightening on the seat every time they rattled past a pylon, convinced they would be unhitched from the cable at any moment. Damir faced out towards the valley and gave her a running commentary on what he could see, trying to take her mind off the journey. When the doors slid open at the first station she bolted on to the safety of terra firma as if the car was on fire. She dodged the mountain bikers removing the bikes from the sides of the cars, and headed out of the hangar to the mountain where, above them, the clouds were moving, the sun a yellowy haze behind them reminding a sodden world of its existence.

Caro bent over, her hands on her knees. 'I hated that.'

'But you did it.'

When she straightened up, he was grinning at her, pulling up the zip of his anorak. 'Yes, I did, didn't I?' Another first chalked up.

They walked past the empty terrace of the restaurant and found the wide path marked to Mont Caly that took them through the woods. Raindrops gleamed in the grass and dripped from the pine trees while the path was pitted with puddles. They held hands as they walked. She couldn't help thinking how lucky she was to have found him. Thank God his war spared him.

'I wish you hadn't had to go through the war.' Caro squeezed his hand. 'No one should have to live with that.'

He turned to her. 'But it wasn't all bad, you know. We'd laugh too. Once one of the guys heard there was a swarm of bees in a

191

tree nearby. We thought we could put it in a hive on his father's farm and sell the honey. He said, "One of you climb the tree and when I signal, hit the branch hard and the bees will fall into the box." So my friend climbs the tree, hits the branch, the bees fall and the other guy catches them – but not all of them. Bees are flying all round him.' Damir was laughing. 'The guy in the tree stays there where he's safe, but the other two of us run away and the guy who caught the bees runs after us, shouting, "Come back. Where are you going?" We shout back, "Away from you and the bees!"' He sighed, threw his head back with his eyes closed. 'It was very funny.'

But Caro was laughing too, infected by Damir's pleasure in his own story. More often his stories were of the terrible hardships he and his compatriots had endured for those four years of fighting. Ashamed of her ignorance, she had watched Angelina Jolie's film *In the Land of Blood and Honey* one Saturday when he was out at work and was horrified. She started googling the Bosnian war, trying to find out more for herself and hoping to be given some sort of key to understanding the reasons why he and his countrymen had suffered and what had happened. She was even making her way through one of the many books about the war by veteran war reporters. She was appalled by the war's brutality and complexity, and by the fact that, as far as she could understand, NATO, and even more importantly to her, Britain, remained neutral and refused to step in to stop the fighting – whatever their reason.

She had heard about the relentless shooting, the appalling war crimes, the deaths of close friends and family, the privations, homes and livelihoods destroyed, the biting freezing cold in winter. Thank God he had taken away a few memories that he could laugh about mixed in with the horror.

As they emerged from the wood into a grassy meadow, with views to their left over the valley, the rain began to fall again. They ran up the steps into Les Chevrelles, a chalet-style restaurant just off the path, and took shelter inside, the rain rattling against the roof.

By the time they had finished lunch the rain was still falling. Their anoraks weren't enough to stop the rain finding its way through the side of their hoods, down the sides of their faces and necks, and through the sleeves. Heads down, drenched, they trudged along the trail, back the way they had come, moving as fast as they could. They exchanged greetings with a few equally sodden people going in the opposite direction. Occasionally a mountain biker rode past, splashing through the puddles. The trees drooped under the weight of water.

When they arrived back at the lift, a few miserable souls huddled in the shelter of the eaves while Damir and Caro went straight into the station. Her keenness to be out of the rain meant Caro almost forgot her fear of the cable car until they were seated and it was rocking over the junction and swinging out into the open, battered by the rain. Within minutes, the inside of the windows had steamed up, sealing them in a world of their own. Damir eased his foot between hers.

'I'm glad we came here.' With his hood tied tightly round his face, he looked like an Arctic explorer.

'Me too.' She leant forward and took both his hands. He would never understand how much he had done for her. She felt truly alive again.

The cabin jerked to a standstill. Caro straightened up immediately, wiping a patch clear on the window. 'We've stopped.' She shrank back against the seat. 'Why?'

'Maybe an accident and they're sorting it out.' His face grew serious as he realised how frightened she was. He loosened his hood and pushed it back. 'Nothing's going to happen.'

'How can you be so sure?' She gripped the edge of the seat as the cabin swung gently on the cable. Her stomach lurched.

'Remember yesterday,' he said, leaning forward. 'Remember how you felt.'

She tried to conjure up the woman who had stood in the sunshine the previous day, confident, inspired, capable of anything. Her resolution had deserted her. 'What if they forget we're here and we're stuck here all night?'

He took out his phone. 'They won't. If they do, I'll call the police but it's too soon.' He looked into her eyes so she couldn't look away. 'Did I tell you about the old house I stayed in with a family who took me in? They had a child and took pity on me. There was no bathroom so I had to wash in a bath for the baby. And there were lots of mouses. I tried to catch them but they were too quick.'

'Mice.' She smiled as he looked puzzled. 'Mice not mouses.' The cabin jerked and then stopped again. 'It's getting dark. They've forgotten us.' She tried to ward off her panic, breathing deeply. In. Out.

He shook his head. 'It's not getting dark. Be patient.'

She tried to control her fear as the car swayed above the treetops. 'What happened to your friends? Do you keep in touch?'

'I've told you.' His voice was soft. 'Many were killed. But you don't want to hear about them now.'

'I do. I want to know about you, about your life.' She was greedy to hear as much as she could about what had happened to him and made him into the man he was now.

His eyebrows lifted as his head tilted to one side. He looked at her long and hard, understanding. 'Very well. We have time.' He paused. 'Some of my friends and their families escaped and took refugee status in Germany, America, Australia and other places, but many of us stayed to fight.' His eyes narrowed and he rubbed both his thighs as if bracing himself for the memory. 'We fought for our country, for our houses and families. But not all of us made it. I've told you about the snipers, the tanks, the shelling that killed so many innocent people, the camps. At night, all you could hear was firing. All night long, sometimes. The hospitals had nothing. There was little food, no electricity to keep us warm in the freezing winters. It was very hard. But my brother . . . he died, too.'

Forgetting their situation, Caro relinquished her grip of the seat with one hand to hold his. 'I shouldn't have asked. I'm sorry.'

'It's OK – it's a long time ago now. Eldin was brave but impatient. Always impatient. He refused to wait for the team to de-activate some landmines. We went alone. The Serbs started to shoot at us. Eldin shouted at me to stay down as he hid behind a tree trunk. After a few minutes, the shooting stopped and I called to him that we should go back to safety. But he didn't answer.'

As she became caught up in his story, Caro forgot where they were and her gut-churning fear lessened. Outside, the rain kept on falling as the light continued to fade.

'I crawled to him. He was lying on his face, quite still. I turned him over and there was a big hole in his head. He'd been shot.'

'Oh my God.'

'You wanted to know, and this is what it was like. I took his gun but I had to escape without him. Of course, none of the others wanted to go back for him. Too dangerous. So we had to leave him there.'

At that moment, the cabin jerked forward and stopped again. Caro gripped his hand, ashamed. How trivial her fear over their predicament was compared to what he had experienced. She was scared by her imagination but what he was telling her was real. She took a breath. 'So what happened?'

'It's funny. When the shooting starts it's not how it is in films. People aren't always heroes. You just try to survive. You don't care about others.'

'You left him there?' she repeated. His brother.

'I had to. Lying there in the mud.'

She had never seen him look so desolate.

The cabin swung sideways in a fiercer gust of wind.

'I'm sorry,' she said. 'I shouldn't have made you tell me. I don't know . . .'

'It's OK. You were frightened. I don't mind. None of it ever goes away. But after so many years, there is a distance. It gets a little easier. I can talk to you in a way I haven't been able to talk before.'

Another jerk and the car began to move. 'Thank God.' Caro let out a deep breath. 'I was selfish and I'm really sorry.'

He smiled though the sadness remained in his eyes. 'It's hard to control what fear makes you do, whatever the fear is for. My guess is that we won't be coming on here again?'

She hesitated, the woman of yesterday returning to her. 'Perhaps when the sun shines and we're back on the ground.'

But the next day the weather was not much better. Instead of staying put they drove down from the mountains and out of the rainclouds to Annecy where the sun was shining. They strolled hand in hand round the old town, along the flower-lined canals and narrow streets crowded with shops, restaurants and bars. After lunch, they took a boat trip on the lake in the sunshine. From the deck, they stared into the gardens of the lakeside homes, watched people messing about in all kinds of boats, swimmers splashing beside the designated beaches, water birds ignoring all of them. Meanwhile the coloured sails of paragliders floated down from a nearby mountain.

'I can't believe we did that.' Caro looked up at them. 'Look how high they are. The girls will be astonished when I tell them.'

'You're going to tell them about us at last?' He looked pleased. 'Good.'

'You want me to?'

'Of course.' He sounded as though she had asked a ridiculous question. 'I want to go on seeing you. You don't feel the same?'

'I do. Oh, I do.' She rested her head on his shoulder. If nothing else, this week had confirmed that this affair was something she wanted to continue. Those marked months on her kitchen calendar nagged away at her. But would bringing their relationship into the open and sharing it with her family cement or change it in ways they couldn't foresee? Would they make him want to move on after all? But she wanted to be honest with them and confess she hadn't really been holidaying on her own.

For their last night, they went out to eat at Le Vieux Chêne. The restaurant wasn't busy so they had a corner to themselves where they leant across to talk quietly to each other.

'Now what? What will we do when we get home?' She wanted to hear him say they'd be together again.

'I'll move into my flat. Esad will be back and he'll want to find somewhere fast.' He must have seen the sadness that she wanted to hide. 'It's time. And maybe that will make things easier for you.' He took her hand and kissed the tips of her fingers.

'I don't want you to go.'

'But I must. We can't go on like this.'

'Can't we?' But in her heart she knew he was right.

'We will still see each other.' He squeezed her hand.

Despite his reassurance, she was scared his moving out would mark the beginning of his inevitable withdrawal from her. *No*, she argued with herself. *Have more confidence.* If their relationship was going to last for longer than a summer, they would have to engage with the world together. Separating would give them a distance and independence that would show them what they truly felt about each other. She turned at the sound of stifled laughter from the table two along. The two young women stopped staring in their direction and turned their attention to the couple who were returning from having a smoke outside. Were they laughing about an older woman with a younger man? Surely not. That was just her own self-consciousness making her imagine what wasn't there. What other people thought didn't matter. That was what she must remember. What mattered was their happiness.

They lingered there, making each course last, prolonging the evening for as long as they could. The last to leave, they stepped out into the silent street. The flags and the flowers in the boxes along the side of the road were the only things moving in the night breeze. The sky had cleared at last to reveal myriad stars pinned in the darkness above them.

'Come on.' He took her hand as they cut between the restaurant where they'd stuffed themselves on tartiflette and fondue earlier in the week and the souvenir shop. They crossed the main road and began the walk up the hill between the chalet buildings until they came to their own.

Caro felt a lightness as she pushed the key into the lock for the last time. The place would never be the same for her again now she had spent this week here. For the first time that day, she took her phone from her bag. She hadn't wanted any reminders of the world they had escaped but now she needed to start easing herself back there by checking if anyone had tried to contact her. She waited for it to come to life, staring at the ski poster on the opposite wall. Above the stylised face of a smiling young woman with gleaming teeth, clutching her skis with hands in Fair Isle gloves, were the words *une symphonie neige et soleil*.

One buzz after another alerted her to a number of texts. Wearily, she tapped into them.

A photo of Danny pulling a silly face from Lauren. Save.

Another of him beaming from behind a massive ice-cream. Save.

From Fran: *When are you back?* Delete.

From Paul: *Getting tickets for Summer Exhibition. Would you come?* A hesitation then: leave.

From Amy: *Help! Need cover on Friday. Can you help out? Just this once. Promise.* Delete.

From Amy (two hours later): *I guess that's a no then?!* Delete.

From Lauren: *Something exciting to tell you. I'll be at the airport. Tomorrow at 3.40 p.m. Yes?* How could she reply? I'd rather you didn't. I've been having the affair of my lifetime and I'm still not ready for you to know. I don't want to hear your reaction.' She could still hear Lauren's disbelief and embarrassment when she learned her father had hooked up with Georgie. '*Young enough to be his daughter.*' Her daughter's distrust of strangers was another hurdle. But apart from being a disruption of the status quo, surely her and Chris's new relationships should be a relief and a pleasure to their daughters. They all needed to move forward together.

She texted: *That would be great. Dying to hear your news. See you then.* What else could she say?

'Everything OK?' Damir came over, holding two cups of tea. 'Shall we go up?'

'Everything's fine except that Lauren wants to pick me up at the airport.'

'That's kind.'

She glanced at the date on the mobile phone, remembered her kitchen calendar for the second time. Less than two months left.

'Except she doesn't know we're here together and finding out in Arrivals might not be the best way to break the news.' Caro pictured that astonished stare that Lauren had perfected when something didn't quite fit with her expectations. 'Neither of the girls were comfortable about Chris having a new partner. I'd like to make this as easy for them as possible.'

He raised an eyebrow. 'Aren't they adults now? They should understand that you have your own life.'

'I know but it's not that simple.' Though it should be, she said to herself. Was it her fault that it wasn't?

'Let's think about them tomorrow.' Damir clearly didn't think it was something worth worrying about. He winked. 'I have other plans for now.'

'Really?' she said, all innocent. 'Perhaps I'd better come up and see what they are.'

'Perhaps you had.'

*

On their last morning, Caro woke early, her mind full of her daughters. Damir was right, they were adults and should be able to accept him in her life. Even if it took time. And if Lauren found out at the airport... so be it. She got up and opened the shutter so a thin slice of morning sunlight cut through the darkness of the room. Damir stirred in the bed, moaning a little in his sleep. He rolled over, turning his face away from the light, but not waking. Through the break in the shutters, the mountain on the other side of the valley was visible, the dark green of the pine trees, the brilliant grass-green of the slopes.

As her eyes got used to the light, she sat in the only chair, moving their clothes so they hung over its back. She slipped on the cotton dressing gown that she had packed as an afterthought and tiptoed out into the living room where she opened the door and stepped onto the terrace. The air was still chilly but the sun was rising into a clear sky that was already losing the lemony haze of dawn and deepening into a clear cobalt blue. Beneath her, the village was entirely still. The noise from builders at work had yet to start. But they wouldn't be long. She could hear the faint chime of cowbells from the opposite side of the valley. A car roared down the main road that divided the town. It wouldn't be long before the village woke up to a new day.

Shivering, she pulled her gown around her and went back inside. Perhaps she should go back to bed. But she wouldn't sleep and she didn't want to wake him, not yet. She wanted to enjoy this moment of peace and the anticipation of the day ahead. Tears stung her eyes. Magic always had to end. And this had been magical beyond her dreams. She dreaded leaving behind the peace and joy and pleasure they had shared here. Equally, she worried that when they returned home to real life, they might feel differently about each other. Was this really just a brief encounter that couldn't last?

She went back to sit in the bedroom to watch over him. Damir hadn't moved. She pulled open the shutter a little more. The soft light fell across the bed, emphasising the contours of his body. His lower half was tangled in the sheet with his left leg bent so only his right foot showed at the bottom. She wanted to run her finger along its arch, bumping over his toes. From where she sat, she could barely see the hair that covered his chest. Instead she concentrated on his back, the curve of his spine, the shadow that cut across him, the skin that she knew almost every square centimetre of, the rise and fall of his ribs. She wished she had time to sketch him but he would soon wake and the mood would change. This was perfect. At peace. To see someone at their most vulnerable like this was a privilege given only by those who love and trust the one they are with.

She took her phone from the top of the chest of drawers. She couldn't resist. What she couldn't sketch now, she could draw later from a photograph. She swiped the screen into camera mode and took several shots, the phone clicking as she went, capturing the line of his neck and shoulders, his back, the jut of his hip before it disappeared beneath the sheet, the top of his buttocks. He murmured something and as he rolled onto his back, the sheet fell off him. She stayed quite still then, when he didn't move, took several more. When she got to his face, she hesitated. Was it wrong to capture him like this without his say-so?

At that moment, his eyes snapped open. For a second, a murderous intent flashed in his eyes, followed by confusion as if he didn't remember where he was, then his expression cleared and he smiled at her.

'What are you doing?'

'I want to draw you, properly this time. You looked so peaceful, I thought I'd take some photographs to work from.'

'Not now.' He propped himself up on an elbow and reached a hand out to her. 'Come back to bed.'

She didn't need to be asked twice.

20

They stood at the airport carousel, enduring an apparently interminable wait for their luggage. Around them, the other passengers from their flight were positioning themselves, ready to push to the front when their cases appeared. Despite the discomfort, Caro felt oddly detached from the scene, thinking back to France and wishing they could have stayed for longer. At the same time she was longing to see her family again. Excited but nervous, she thought of Lauren, waiting on the other side of the Arrivals door. In a few minutes, she and Damir would be an item to be discussed, congratulated and talked about. She turned to him suddenly wishing they could get on another flight out of there before they had to tangle with what waited for them.

He was staring in the direction of the luggage hatch, his eyes had that same faraway quality she had seen when he was talking about his past. In his mind, he was somewhere else altogether. She slipped her arm into his, pulling him to her.

He snapped out of his trance, turning to her. 'This isn't right.'

'What? What do you mean?'

'I mean I shouldn't be with you when you meet Lauren.'

'But why not? She'll have to know sometime.' During the flight, Caro had built herself up for this, was even looking forward to everything being in the open. Their secret time together had run its course. She was resolved to go out there, proud to have Damir at her side. Lauren's opinion didn't matter, however much Caro would prefer her blessing. In the end, she would get used to the idea of her mother having an unexpected new life of her own, just as she had eventually, grudgingly, accepted Georgie.

'Not in an airport, surrounded by other people. And if Danny's there? It will be difficult for all of us.'

'But they've got to know sometime. Danny will only make it easier. A distraction.'

'Not now.' He was quite firm.

'But what do you want to do?' Caro couldn't believe this change of heart. Was this the beginning of what she dreaded – even earlier than her calendar had it?

'I'm thinking of you and her,' he said just before he pushed through the people between them and the carousel. A few seconds later he re-emerged with her case and put it front of her. 'There! Now – you go through and I'll follow later. We can tell her together at Treetops. Won't that be better?'

Thrown by this last minute change of plan, Caro nodded. 'Maybe. But we decided . . .' Despite understanding that he only had her worries at heart, she was fuming that he hadn't even discussed it with her.

'That way, we'll have a little while longer together – just you and me.' He kissed her. 'No one else. Go on. I'll see you later.' He pecked her cheek. 'Go.'

Unless she wanted to make a scene she had to do as he said.

Passing through the last opportunity to buy duty free goods, she paused. She would go back and insist they walk into Arrivals together after all. She should be true to herself and to Damir and trust her family to accept him. But when she turned, she couldn't see him. She went back to their carousel where two more flights were being unloaded. She scoured the crowd for him but he had disappeared. Like it or not, she had to leave without him.

Outside, to left and right behind the barrier, was the usual array of drivers holding up signs scrawled with their passengers' names, waiting families and friends. Caro scanned the faces but couldn't see Lauren. All at once there was a flurry at the end of the exit route.

'Mum! We're over here!'

Danny shot out from between the legs of the crowd and ran towards her. She let go of her case and bent down to hug him, her love for him overwhelming her.

'We've seen aeroplanes,' he said, almost hitting her on the nose with a model plane that he swooped in front of her face.

'And eaten chocolate,' she said with a smile, smelling it on his breath.

When he grinned, his teeth were smeared brown. 'I'm having another one when we go home.'

'Danny! Let Gran stand up,' Lauren's voice ripped through the crowded terminal.

Caro got to her feet.

'Hello, Mum.' She kissed both Caro's cheeks. 'Let me take your bag. Good time?'

Caro put a hand on her case. 'It's not heavy. Anyway I've decided that if I can't carry my own case, I shouldn't be travelling at all!' She smiled to show she wasn't entirely serious.

'OK.' Lauren looked surprised by this new self-reliance. 'Let's go and find the car then.'

'But I can't pick it up if you're sitting on it, Danny.'

The little boy was sitting astride the case grinning, waiting for a lift.

'Danny! Off you get.' Lauren's voice had risen again, but she was looking towards the Exit signs. 'Mum! Look. Isn't that Damir?'

'Where?' Caro's insides went into freefall. Perhaps he had changed his mind and was going to join them after all.

'Over there. He went out the other way.'

Through the other travellers, Caro could just see the back of Damir's head, the maroon sweater that he had tied around his shoulders, his large rucksack on his back. He was moving quickly, heading towards the Trains sign. 'Where? I can't see him.' Liar.

'I was so sure it was him. Has he been away too?'

Caro felt a familiar burning sensation rising up from her chest, over her neck and cheeks. She couldn't lie to her daughter but bent down to hold Danny's hand so Lauren wouldn't notice.

But Lauren had already sailed on to the next subject. 'I wanted to meet you because I've got something really exciting to tell you. Mike would have come but he's playing cricket.'

Caro felt faintly apprehensive. Lauren's ideas, while exciting from her point of view, could be often less appealing to those she involved in them. 'It's terribly out of your way.'

'Not on a Saturday. Anyway I couldn't wait and besides Danny's dying to tell you about his kitten, aren't you?'

The child's face lit up as he remembered, nodding. 'He's black. And we've called him Soot.'

Caro laughed. 'That's a great name.'

'It's because...' But the women interrupted him at once.

'Wait till we're in the car.' Caro was suddenly bone-tired. She wished she were on the station platform waiting for a train, alone with Damir.

Lauren tapped her son on the head. 'Don't say yet, Danny-boy. That's a surprise for Granny.'

He looked crestfallen. 'In the car?'

'We'll wait till we get to Treetops. I've bought us a cake for tea. And Amy's coming over too.'

'Why? What have you two got planned?' asked Caro, her alarm growing. Perhaps Damir had been right to travel separately after all.

'Wait and see. It's a surprise, isn't it, Danny?'

The child's spirits lifted at the mention of the surprise. 'Yes. A secret.' His eyes grew wide with pleasure at the idea.

Caro followed Lauren through the crowded terminal, pulling her case, which, despite her protestations, felt like a ball and chain dragging behind her. Her other hand was gripped by Danny's as he pulled her along behind him.

Eventually they reached the car park that always reminded Caro of the nether regions of hell, because of its dirt, darkness and its urine-stinking corners. They found the car and piled in. Danny was asleep in the back seat before they had even left the airport perimeter. Caro rested her head against the window and closed her eyes, longing for the mountains, the snow-capped peaks of Mont Blanc and its neighbours in the distance, the lush summer landscape that she'd left behind. Damir.

'Good time?' Lauren's voice broke into her thoughts. 'I don't think you said who you went with.'

'Mmm.' How could she begin to describe how good? 'Yes. You know I love it there.'

'What did you do?'

'Nothing much. Just walked, explored, read a couple of books, ate out . . . but simply . . . and recharged the old batteries.' *And I flew! I flew! And I had the best sex of my life.* But she couldn't tell Lauren that yet, if ever. 'I even had a go at paragliding.'

She thought Lauren was going to drive off the road. 'You didn't! Who with?'

Lauren knew perfectly well that the old Caro would never have the nerve to do such a thing alone.

'You're strapped to the instructor. Quite a good-looking French guy, as it happens.' Not exactly a lie. She stared out of the window at the countryside rushing past, and recalled the feel of the cool mountain air, the sensation of flying, of the empowerment when it was all over. She must hang on to that feeling, never forget it.

'Lucky you. See him again?' Her daughter was joking, certain there was no chance of that.

I was with Damir, she longed to shout. In fact the most wonderful man I've met for some time. A man who's made me realise just how different my life could be; that I must grasp my freedom and do something with it, not just coast. How she wanted to confess, but remembered Damir's words. Yes, it would be better to break the news at home. 'No.'

'But who encouraged you to do something like that? It doesn't sound like you at all. And there are terrible accidents.'

'I thought you'd be impressed.' Caro was disappointed.

'But anything could have happened. You've got to be careful at your age. We want you in one piece for a lot longer.'

Caro stiffened. 'Age has nothing to do with it. The instructor had someone of eighty-three do it the week before me. I was absolutely petrified but it turned out to be one of the most fantastic things I've done for years. When I landed, I felt incredible.'

'Well, I'm glad you had a good time.' Lauren's lack of interest in her achievement was disappointing. Then, after a beat, unable to resist, she said, 'I bumped into Fran on her way to lunch in Covent Garden. She mentioned you'd been seeing a friend of hers. Paul.'

'Are you sure? You must have misunderstood.' Why would Fran say such a thing? Then she remembered Lauren's ability to worm information out of people. You had to be careful.

'Seeing's not the right word. He's a nice man, a friend.' Nice. The word was almost an insult. Try passionate, fascinating, loving, mysterious, thoughtful, exciting – none of those were words she could use easily for Paul. 'Now, tell me what you've come all this way to say.'

'No, no. You're going to have to wait till we're at home. I want Amy to be there too.'

Caro had to be content with that. For the rest of the journey, she quizzed Lauren about what she and Danny had been up to while she was away. Lauren told her about her work, the abduction case she was working on where a ten-year-old girl had been found chained in a large drainage pipe after three days. 'We should see the bastard go down for years.'

'I don't know how you can bear to work on such terrible cases.'

Caro could imagine the child's terror, the parents' desperation to find her.

'You develop a thick skin, I guess. People like him should be behind bars, and if I can help put them there...' Lauren concentrated on entering a roundabout. 'I suppose it's about making the world a better place. We all do our little bit, and this is mine.'

Caro applauded Lauren's sentiment but wished it made her less distrustful of others. She couldn't help noticing how tightly her daughter was gripping the wheel as she spoke.

'What about Mike? Is there another strike planned?'

'We're waiting to hear. But what else can the junior doctors do but down tools so their voices are heard? The government contract's appalling. It's not about money but patient safety – so many people don't understand that.'

Mike's feelings as a junior doctor and the demands being made took up the conversation for the rest of the way home. Suddenly the holiday seemed like a very insignificant thing and a long way away. When they finally turned into the driveway, Amy's van was parked beside Damir's. Caro took a deep breath.

Lauren took charge immediately – her father's daughter. While Caro took her case upstairs, checking quickly to see whether Damir had beaten them to it – but there was no sign of him. Her daughters made tea and took everything out to the terrace where they could sit in the afternoon sun. By the time Caro returned downstairs, she was ready for whatever it was Lauren was going to say.

Sitting at the table, she looked around her garden. The borders were doing better than she had ever hoped they would. Deep almost terracotta lupins stood tall beside the lemony hollyhocks and her favourite Echinacea. At the back, the star jasmine was in flower over the front wall of the potting shed. They had come home to a perfect English summer afternoon.

'So?' she began. 'Tell me. What's this all about?'

Amy looked up from pouring the tea. Earth was ingrained in the wrinkles of her hands, under her nails. 'Lauren insisted. It's her thing.'

They both turned to Lauren who was sitting with her hands crossed over her stomach just like a ... and suddenly Caro twigged ... pregnant woman. Instead of being so preoccupied with herself, she should have noticed that telltale glow.

'Haven't you guessed?' Lauren asked, moving one hand over the loose shirt covering her belly, from top to bottom. Suddenly the bump was just visible.

'You're not?' gasped Amy. 'Again!'

Lauren was nodding, looking pleased with herself but there was something else there too. She reached out to hold Danny's hand, who snatched it away so he could get on with the Lego he'd dug out of the toy box in the sitting room. 'I am. We wanted a brother or sister for Danny but ... we're having twins!' She waited for the others to react.

Caro and Amy exchanged a look of amazement. 'Twins!' they repeated at once.

'That's fantastic, darling. Congratulations.' Caro got up to hug her, feeling the tension in her shoulders. Lauren reached up to grip her mother's arm.

'Wow! Amazing! But what about your job?' Amy asked.

'How will you cope?' added Caro at the same time.

'God knows. We were stunned when we found out but it's happening and that's all there is to it. Not what we planned, obviously, but we've made another plan.' She looked up at Caro who felt a flicker of anxiety. She was obviously going to play some part in it. 'You're pleased for us, aren't you?'

Caro let go of her daughter and sat down. Brave face. 'Of course. It's just a bit of a shock. No one's had twins in the family before.'

At that moment, the front gate opened and clattered shut. Damir. Danny ran round the corner of the house like a watchdog minus the bark. 'Dinosaur man,' he shouted, running back. Caro's heart skipped a beat.

'I think that means it's Damir,' said Amy.

'Oh.' Caro tried to give the impression that his coming and going had little relevance to her. She didn't even look over her shoulder. Damir must have gone straight inside and upstairs. Perhaps, now they were all together, she should tell them when he came down. But she didn't want to trump Lauren's news.

Lauren sat straighter and lifted her mug. Caro recognised that face. Ever since she was a little girl, Lauren liked to communicate the ideas that she was excited about as soon as she could. This moment was what she had been waiting for so not the time to derail her. Caro reached for a piece of the lemon drizzle that Lauren had brought with her, then put it down. She wasn't going to be able to swallow a mouthful.

'Don't worry about him.' Lauren tapped her teaspoon on the table. 'This is important. Mike and I have had an idea. Well, more than an idea...'

Caro and Amy waited.

'We're going to sell the house...'

'But you've only just had the loft extension.'

Caro smiled. Amy was always practical when it came to hard cash.

'I know, but even so it won't be big enough for us now. Besides, we've found the most amazing house near Richmond. Quite near the river. It's everything we've ever dreamed of. And not a bad commute for both of us.'

'Isn't that rather expensive?' said Caro carefully. 'And who's going to look after the babies?'

'That's the point. It's more than we can really afford but...' Lauren turned to Caro, her eyes shining.

Caro braced herself for whatever was coming.

'It's got a darling little flat in the basement that's perfect for one person. And a bit of the garden has been sectioned off to go with it. You'd love it, Mum.'

'Really?' The pieces were falling into place to form a picture that Caro wasn't sure she cared for at all.

'What?!' Amy had always been critical of her sister's ambition to scale the social heights. 'A live-in nanny? How impossibly grand.'

Lauren gave a look that in any other world would have cast her sister into outer darkness. 'I think *you*'d be thinking along those lines if you were about to have three children under five and a full-time job. But better than that. Wait till I've finished.' She took a deep breath and Caro's hand at the same time. 'It's obvious you can't live here any more, Mum. At least not now Dad's divorcing you.'

Put that way Caro felt no better than a piece of old scrap. 'It's quite mutual in fact. We're divorcing each other.' She'd never thought she'd say that, and barely heard Amy's curious, 'What are you trying to say?'

'Well, Dad wants his share of the equity in Treetops. Mum's obviously not going to be able to find the money so they're going to have to sell. We've all known that from the get-go. It's great that you tried, Mum, but you must have known too.' She put down the spoon and laid her hands flat on the table, about to make a momentous point. 'This flat is absolutely perfect for her – and a sweet little garden.'

'What a brilliant idea.' Amy beamed, enthusiastic.

'And she'll be able to see so much more of the kids.' Lauren had moved into full throttle now.

'You are clever. But what about Bloom? Mum won't be able to do so much in the shop if she comes and lives with you.'

'I know, but I haven't finished. I've thought of a way you can afford another fulltime staff member.'

'You have? How?'

'Girls! I am here!' Caro was aware she had to be extremely

careful what she said. Her daughters were on the point of deciding her future without even consulting her. She had to intervene but in the most diplomatic way. 'Of course it sounds lovely, but I'll have to see it before making a decision.'

'Mum, you'll love it,' Lauren spoke as if the decision was already made. 'I've got the estate agent's brochure in the car. I'll get it.'

'And my teaching?'

'But you can teach anywhere, can't you?' Lauren dismissed the thought. 'Or you could concentrate on your own painting. You'll love that.' Lauren had the whole thing worked out.

'That's something I'll have to think about.'

'But you said you were tired of teaching,' Lauren reminded her.

Had she? Perhaps once or twice after a long trying day. 'Haven't you ever said you were tired of your job?' Caro was driven to point out. 'Some weeks are better or worse than others. You know that as well as I do.'

'You mean you don't want to move?'

Here we go.

'Not at all. I just want to be sure it's the right thing to do at this stage.'

Her daughters exchanged a puzzled glance. 'But of course it's the right step.' Amy handed a slice of cake to Danny who mashed a handful in his fist with some blue and yellow bricks and dashed inside the house.

'Danny, that's disgusting. Come back.'

'Oh, leave him,' said Caro, grateful for the momentary distraction. 'I don't expect he'll do much harm.'

'Where else do you want to live?' asked Amy. 'I know we'd all love you to stay here, and it'll be so weird if you're not. But this is a great solution for you.' A note of doubt had crept into her voice. 'Isn't it?'

'But I may be able to buy Dad out.' She stopped. She had to let go of that dream. 'Or I might buy a place of my own.'

'Mum!' Lauren had adopted her no-nonsense, be-realistic glare. 'Get real. And even if you could, you can't rattle round here on your own for the rest of your life. Even if you filled it with lodgers. But if you sell, you can put your capital in with ours to buy this house in Richmond . . . And this would be a place of your own. Don't you see?'

So that was it. Both Caro and Amy stared at Lauren who looked down and picked at a fingernail. But Caro had heard the note of desperation in her daughter's voice. As Lauren looked up, their eyes met, and Caro could see panic there. What was really going through her daughter's mind? Maybe this was an answer. But was it the one she wanted for herself? If she moved, and she was beginning to accept she would have to, she wanted her independence. She didn't relish the thought of Lauren and Mike knowing her every move, noticing every visitor. Whatever happened with Damir in the future, life hadn't given up on her after all. Nor her on it. What should she do?

'It's a no brainer,' Lauren went on, seeing her hesitate. 'You can give some to Amy for Bloom and then the rest . . . Yes, what is it, darling?'

Danny was running towards his mother, brandishing a phone. 'Look! Daddy's willy!'

Caro went cold. That was her phone, covered in cake crumbs. Danny must have been rootling through her bag again, taken it out and somehow opened the pictures she had taken that morning of Damir before he woke up. Pictures of his body from every angle, of every part of his body – so she could draw him; so she could remember. Why hadn't she taken Fran's advice and put in a passcode when she got the phone?

'I think that's mine. Could you give it to me, please?' She put her hand out but Danny was already on the other side of the table and handing the evidence over to Lauren.

21

'Look!' Danny was chortling with delight as he jabbed at the phone with a finger. 'Daddy's willy, willy willy.'

'Shh! What are you talking about? Give that to me.' Frustrated by the conversation being truncated, Lauren snatched the phone, startling him. His eyes welled with tears as she looked at the screen. 'Who is this?' She scrolled sideways, her eyes widening a little more each time. 'Mum?' Her shock made the word almost inaudible. 'Is this your phone?'

'What is it? Let me see.' Amy reached across the table.

Caro came to life and grabbed the phone before Lauren passed it on. 'Yes, it's mine.' There was no point trying to deny it. 'Thank you.'

'Who is it?' Lauren's face was stricken. 'Danny, go inside and find your dinosaurs.' He knew that tone was not to be argued with and dashed inside. 'What's he doing on your phone? Danny shouldn't have seen that.'

'Then you should teach him not to take things from other people's handbags.' And she should have learned to keep hers out of reach.

'What are you talking about?' Amy reached out but Caro held her phone to her chest.

'Mum's got a lover.' Lauren choked out the words.

Amy grinned. 'No! Good for you, Mum. You've kept him quiet. Can I see?'

Caro tightened her grip. 'No, of course not.'

'I can't believe it.' Lauren's disbelief was insulting and infuriating.

'That's enough.' Caro finally snapped. 'It's really none of your business but yes, I've got a lover.' And so it came into the open at last. 'I don't know why it's so hard believe. Wasn't that what you wanted?' She looked from one to the other, not expecting a reply. 'I took the pictures so that I can paint him. The light was so beautiful.'

'The light!' Lauren's outrage was almost comic but Caro wasn't in the mood for laughing. This was nothing less than she had expected. If only her daughter could be slower to judge, a quality that no doubt was an asset in her career but not always when dealing with those outside it. However, at least the previous conversation about the house had been temporarily forgotten. For now Caro was grateful for that very small mercy while furious at having allowed herself to be caught out like this.

'Who is he? Let me look. Is he gorgeous?' Amy put her hand on Caro's arm in a gesture of solidarity. 'Please.'

Never had Caro felt so much love for one daughter over the other. 'You don't need to see. They're private.'

'Just one? I think it's great news. You should be pleased for her, Lauren. Come on, Mum.'

Lauren said nothing, just pursed her lips while Caro shook her head, and slipped the phone into her pocket.

Amy looked disappointed. 'Well at least tell us who he is. You can't keep him to yourself now. How long have you been seeing him?'

'Did you meet him in France?' Lauren was relaxing a little.

'No.' Caro clasped her hands tightly under the table. 'Actually, you know him. He's a lovely man . . .'

'We know him?' Lauren was obviously rewinding through the photos, trying to remember an identifying feature.

Caro nodded. 'Yes.' She swallowed. 'It's Damir.'

Lauren's eyes widened in disbelief. 'So it *was* him at the airport.'

Caro nodded. 'Yes.' She pictured him walking away from her through the crowd.

'You lied to me.'

'No, Lauren, I didn't.' Caro had to stand up for herself or there'd be no coming back. 'I just didn't tell you the whole story. I was waiting for the right moment. The Arrivals hall didn't seem the ideal place to tell you we'd been away together, so he suggested we split up and told you later, together. If you hadn't been so set on telling me about the house...'

Lauren just stared at her. 'He told you not to tell me?!'

'It wasn't like that.' How could she twist her words like that? The lawyer in her never went away.

'Damir!' Amy sounded puzzled. 'You're having an affair with *him*?' She began to laugh. 'Oh, Mum. That's hilarious.'

'I don't see why.' Caro bristled.

'But isn't he much younger than you?' Lauren sounded as if this was a bad thing.

'What if he is?' Caro had had enough. 'Why's it all right for Dad to have an affair with someone at least twenty years younger than him, but not me? And anyway, he's not that much younger than me. There's only about fifteen years between us.' A whole childhood apart, but at this age it meant so little.

Lauren's face showed her disbelief.

'Calm down.' Amy weighed in, as she frequently did. 'I can see how hard it must have been to tell us. Can't you?' She appealed to her sister.

'No.' Lauren didn't want to give an inch although she did sound less certain.

'I was going to tell you both when we got back although...' Caro hesitated. 'I was worried that you might be like this.'

'Like what? I don't understand why you haven't said anything before.'

Caro couldn't explain how much she had enjoyed the secrecy, when no one judged them and pleasure was everything.

'Mum, he could be anyone,' Lauren went on, reasonable, lawyerlike. 'We don't know anything about him.'

'You said that when he moved in but *I* know about him,' said Caro, trying to take control of the conversation. 'And I like what I know. That should be enough for you. I thought I understood you, Lauren, but I'm really disappointed. I didn't expect you to be particularly pleased, but I did expect a little understanding. I know it's a shock. It has been to me, too. Things have happened so quickly, but I love him.' She was as surprised as her two daughters to hear herself say those last three words out loud.

'You can't do,' Lauren's voice was cold. 'What's happened to you, Mum? I don't feel as if I know you any more. Sex – I get that. But love – you must have forgotten what that really means. No wonder Dad left.'

'Lauren!' Amy pushed back her chair, scraping it against the flagstones. 'That's completely out of order and you know it.'

Caro looked at her oldest daughter, shocked by her cruelty. 'One day, I'll forgive you for that. I know you're angry, but that was uncalled for.'

Lauren had the grace to look away.

'I think you'd better go now.' Caro stood up, conscious that Damir might appear at any minute, which would only make matters worse. If Lauren started cross-questioning him in this mood, matters would only get worse. 'We'll talk more another time when you've calmed down and I've had time to think about your idea and what I'd like to do.'

Both girls were staring at her: Amy concerned, and Lauren pale, her eyes filming with tears. Her family meeting had gone spinning off track.

'Mum, no.' Amy was pleading. 'Let's sort this out now.'

Caro clenched her fists until she felt her nails digging into her palms. 'There's nothing to sort out. A little time for us all to digest this will be a good thing.'

'I'm sorry...' At last Lauren seemed to realise she had gone far too far. 'I really am. It's just...'

'Not now.' Caro stood up and started putting the tea things on the tray to make it clear their afternoon together was over. 'Thank you for coming to get me.'

'But Mike and I do need...'

'Lauren, leave it. Can't you see how upset Mum is?' Amy looked furious with her.

'OK. But I'll call you tomorrow.' A hand on the bump of her stomach, she went inside to round up Danny. They could hear his objections as his game was interrupted, and then they were gone. Without them, the atmosphere lost some of its charge.

'You too, Amy,' Caro said as she took the tray inside.

'Are you sure you'll be all right?' Amy followed her in.

Caro kissed her cheek. 'I'll be absolutely fine. I've got a lot to think about, and I'll do that best on my own.'

'I don't mind about Damir.' Amy put her arm round her mother's shoulders and squeezed. 'If you're happy, then I'm happy for you. And Lauren'll come round.' She didn't sound certain. 'You know how she's always hated change and how she doesn't trust anyone until they've proved themselves. But do think hard about the house. I thought it was a great idea when she first said it but you'll end up as an unpaid nanny. She won't mean to, but with twins...' She bent down to put her boots back on.

'What? When I could be working in Bloom?!' Caro laughed and to her relief Amy joined in.

'Maybe, I do take a few liberties but I only wanted to help after Dad left.'

'I know you did, Lauren did too, and I appreciate it.'

'I'll ease off a bit. Promise. I think I can almost afford to take on another member of staff now.' She stood up and kissed Caro on the cheek. 'I'll call you later and make sure you're OK. Jason's out again tonight.'

'Everything OK?' He was taking his time asking the question.

Weeks had gone by since he'd spoken to Caro. She hoped the delay didn't mean he was having second thoughts.

'Fine. We haven't seen much of each other recently, we're both so busy. He's always moaning that I stay too late at the shop, but I don't have a choice. If I want the business to work, I've got to put the hours in. So he has a go at me, then says he understands but sometimes I wonder. Anyway it'll be different when we're living together. His flatmate's moving out at last to start his new job in London.'

'Excited?' Caro held open the front door.

Amy beamed at her, but Caro didn't miss the moment of doubt that crossed her face. 'Yes, of course. Provided he stops going on about my working hours. Anyway, he's often late too, as I keep pointing out. But... we're going to go away when everything calms down a bit. It'll be Christmas at this rate.' She pulled a face.

Perhaps he did have everything planned, after all. Caro was relieved though the signs of tension between them made her uneasy. The last thing she wanted was for Amy to be let down.

Alone again, she sat in the kitchen, absorbing everything that had just happened. Surely Lauren wouldn't still expect Caro to live with them after what she had just said. She transferred the offending photos from her phone to her laptop so the same mistake would never be made again, dwelling on them as she did. Longing. Lauren's words came back to her. Was that why Chris had left – because she had forgotten what love was? But if she had, so had he. Its rediscovery must have been as momentous for him as it was for her.

She reached for the calendar and a pencil, marking off each day they'd been away with a dot. Time was nearly up but perhaps these dots were irrelevant now. She longed for Damir's loving touch after such an unforeseen homecoming. He must have gone out again to give her some time alone with her family. Considerate of him, but she couldn't help wishing he hadn't. She picked up her phone and went back outside, scrolling through the remaining holiday photos – the mountains, the wild flowers, the chalets, the town they had enjoyed so much. Having just spent a week she wouldn't easily forget, if ever – what now? Her return to real life couldn't have been more difficult.

She walked along the edge of the border, looking to see what had grown in her absence, pulling out the odd weed. She didn't want to think about her daughters. She wanted to think about how her life had changed. With great emotion edging into her heart, everything seemed different. Take that away and in the cold glare of reality, she had behaved less than well to the man she professed to love – she shouldn't have kept him hidden, despite their mutual enjoyment at being in the bubble. But she should be able to secure a life for herself without compromising her relationship with her daughters. She stopped to dead head a rose. She did not, could not, regret her marriage to Chris, except for one thing: if it had left her timid and unable to see the truth then she had been damaged indeed.

Back her thoughts turned to Lauren and Amy. There was a time when she would have consulted Chris about how best to handle their daughters. Not now. She must work out what to do on her own. The compass had been reset.

Fran joked that her garden was a wildlife sanctuary. Gardening was not a skill that came naturally to either her or Simon. Plants tumbled over one another to get to the light. Those that in other people's gardens would be called weeds – bright blue comfrey, delicate yellow poppies, buttercups and foxgloves – were allowed to flower in glorious profusion here. However, there was room at the end of a winding brick path for a small secluded patio. From her seat there, Caro could just see Simon pottering about in the kitchen, wearing an apron sporting the naked body of a finely honed young man.

'If only,' said Fran when she saw Caro glance at it on the way through.

Simon flicked a tea towel at her. 'Get out there and put the world to rights. I'll bring you supper before I go out.'

'Thank you, darling.' Fran blew him a kiss.

'Everything all right?' Caro hardly dared ask as they sat down.

Fran swithered her hand in the air. 'Getting better. We've taken the big step of seeing someone, so every Thursday night we pay through the nose to talk to them.'

'And?'

'It does seem to help.' She passed Caro a glass of wine. 'We're talking about stuff we never would have otherwise. Some of it's a bit close to the bone but . . . well, it's making me think and we do seem to be getting back on track.'

'And Ewan? Dare I ask?' The flintiness of the wine made Caro cough. 'Do you talk about him?'

Fran looked sheepish, twisting the hem of her top in her fingers. 'Not really. Not yet. He called me though. He wants to meet up.'

'And you said no.' Caro was firm.

'Sort of.' Fran's eyes appealed for her friend's understanding. 'But it was hard.'

'Fran, don't. Please.' Surely she wouldn't contemplate seeing him again after all she'd been through.

Fran's fingers stopped moving as she looked Caro in the eye. 'Of course I'm not going to see him. I couldn't do that to Si, especially not now we're coming out of the woods.'

Caro detected the longing in her voice. Her own feelings for Damir made her more able to imagine what Fran was going through. Then she remembered what she had seen.

'I've moved on. I really have. It was only a silly what-if mid-life moment. Promise. Let's change the subject. You sounded so upset when you phoned. Did something happen in France?'

'Not exactly. More when I got back. I've got so much to tell you. I don't even know where to start.' Though this was the conversation she'd been dying to have, a little bit of her couldn't face going over it again. That afternoon had been enough. Then Damir had texted her to say he was with friends so she could spend time with her family – her family who she had sent away – so she came to see Fran. For the first time, she wished he weren't always quite so thoughtful.

'We've got all night.' Fran gestured towards the bottle of wine and glasses. 'Simon's going out to watch the football. Come on, spill the beans.' She leant forward, eager to hear the latest.

Caro took a deep breath and began. As she went back over the situation with Chris, she felt such relief at being able to share it all with Fran. Shutting herself away with Damir, she had forgotten how much she missed her friend. The one thing she could rely on was a candid opinion – and that wasn't long in coming.

'He's always been such an unreasonable bastard.' Fran rested a foot on the low table between them. 'He's been perfectly happy with you living in the house until it doesn't suit him any more. He should be thinking of you too.'

Caro flinched at Fran's easy dismissal of Chris. Then she remembered all she had been through because of him, how she had done her best to accommodate him and make him seem to do no wrong in the girls' eyes – often at her own expense. 'It's no good. I can't find the money. I suppose I always knew this would happen but I was hoping for a miracle. I'm going to have to move.' Saying it made it real at last and, to her surprise, she didn't feel overwhelmed with sadness or the fear of the future that she had expected.

'But that's exciting. A new start.' Fran's eyes were shining at the thought.

At that moment, Simon came out bearing two plates of chicken stir-fry. 'Here you are. I won't join you because I'm going to wolf mine and then go and meet the lads.'

Fran patted him on the bum. 'Get back to the kitchen where you belong.'

He caught her hand. 'Enough of that. You're cooking tomorrow.'

Caro couldn't remember when she had last seen them so relaxed together.

Once Simon was back inside, they returned to the subject of Chris and Treetops and Caro told her about Lauren's plan. Fran was suitably appalled. 'She can't make you move in with them! Do you even want to?'

'Hand on heart? No. And I'm not sure it's the right answer for them either. But I'm sure something else is going on. Lauren was even more strung out than usual.'

Fran shrugged. 'Twins and a demanding career. Not my kind of cocktail. But what about you? There's something different...' She narrowed her eyes and peered at Caro. 'What aren't you telling me?'

Caro felt a smile spreading across her face as she felt the lightness of being that always came when she thought of him. 'I've met someone.'

'What?!' The stir-fry on Fran's fork fell back into the plate. 'I turn my back on you for a few weeks and look what happens – you're in danger of getting a life.'

'You think?' She told Fran everything there was to tell from the moment of meeting Damir on the train, to his becoming her lover. Fran punctuated the story by laughing, looks of sympathy and astonishment and pouring glasses of wine.

'I can't believe you kept it so quiet for so long. I thought we told each other everything.'

'We do, but you were so wrapped up in Ewan and what was going on. And I was trying to get used to the whole idea myself. It was the last thing I expected. I thought I was well past my sell-by date.'

Fran mouthed. 'I'm sorry.' Then said, 'I've been a selfish cow, haven't I? But is it serious?'

'I didn't want to say anything until I was sure. As for Paul. I told you. It's definitely not going to happen now. I told you what happened. Nice guy but chemistry? Zero.' She couldn't help smiling at the memory. 'We've agreed to be friends. Not that I've seen him for ages.'

'Friends without benefits,' said Fran wryly. 'He's a nice guy. I'm kind of sorry it didn't work out.'

'One more thing.'

'There's more?' She emptied the bottle into their glasses.

Caro took a sip before embarking on the story of Danny's discovery of the photos.

Fran couldn't hide how amusing she found it. 'You've got to see the funny side. Well, at least they know. Would you ever have got round to telling them?'

'Yes, I wanted to but first I wanted to be sure that it meant something to him too.' His words – *I never stay in one place for long* – reverberated round her brain yet again. 'And we were going to tell them together.' She laughed at Fran's look of deep scepticism. 'We really were.'

'You can thank Danny for doing it for you.' Fran reached out a hand. 'Well, aren't you going to show me a photo? Remind me what he looks like.'

Caro took another mouthful of her supper. 'Si's a great cook,' she mumbled with her mouth full.

'Don't be so maddening. Show me!'

'I've only got one. The others are on my computer under lock and password. For my eyes only.' Ignoring Fran's show of disappointment, she pulled her phone out of her bag, noticing a missed call from Damir. Perhaps he was back at Treetops, waiting for her. She longed to return the call but instead found the photo she'd taken of him on the last day at the bar by the square in Les

224

Gets. She passed the phone over, watching as Fran scrutinised him.

'Looks gorgeous. The place, I mean.' She enlarged the image with her fingers. 'And he's not bad either. I'd forgotten.'

'Hands off.' Caro took the phone back from her, and looked at him for a moment. 'He's moving out.'

'But why?'

'Because he's promised his friend. Because he doesn't want to commit himself to me. He's not sure about us. I don't know.' Caro felt herself tearing apart as she ran through the possibilities. 'What shall I do?'

'You've got so much going on. If I were you I'd write everything down and list all the pros and cons under each one – that's what paying to talk has taught me! But seeing everything laid out does help simplify things. Then you'll have to decide where Damir fits in. Is he more than a "fling"?' She said the word Lauren had used deliberately, bracketing it with quotation marks in the air.

Caro thought of her calendar, so carefully marked off. 'I hope so,' she said, cautious about committing Damir to anything or making herself look irredeemably foolish. Now they were back home, things would be different once he had moved out. 'I thought he was to begin with, but now I'm not so sure.'

'In which case, you'd better sort that out, and the rest will come from there.'

'That simple?'

As they talked, the night grew cooler round them, the shadows lengthened and the lights in the neighbours' houses went on one by one. Eventually, when they could barely see each other, they gathered everything up and went indoors.

'So you think come out and be proud?' Caro asked as she piled the plates into the dishwasher.

'Yes.' Fran had the decisiveness born from more than half a bottle of wine. 'If people are shocked or don't like it, so bloody what? They'll get over it in the end and move on. And you're absolutely not going to live with Lauren. I won't let you. Even if I have to lie across her doorway so you can't get in.'

Caro couldn't help laughing at the image. 'I've got to live somewhere.'

'Not there. That's all I'm saying. You're not old enough for a granny flat. Even if Damir goes up in a puff of smoke, you've got a few good years in you yet.'

'I hope so.' It was good to hear Fran confirming the decision Caro had reached that evening. A granny flat smacked too much of life's departure lounge. Being with Damir was showing her that she had to grasp her new freedom and live life to the full while she could – without hurting anyone else in the process.

'There must be plenty of places on the market. The right one's out there somewhere.'

Caro smiled at Fran's typical determination that solved all problems. 'We're not asking much then.'

'Think positive.'

22

The blue van was loaded. Caro and Damir stood, an arm around each other, and looked at it. They held each other carefully, gingerly – there was still ground to make up between them since she'd told him about the pictures of him being found on her phone. His anger over her carelessness masked his humiliation. 'How do you think I'll feel when I meet them again?'

She'd tried to calm him but he had left the house still angry. Since then, they had been building bridges.

'One last cup of coffee?' Caro said. 'Anything? I don't want you to go.'

'Nor I but if I don't, I'll let Esad down. We're renting this place together so I must be there for him.'

'But you arranged that before we . . .' She didn't need to go on. 'You will come back?' She hoped he didn't hear the catch in her voice that sounded so needy. That was not the woman she wanted to be. Besides, him moving out was the right thing, she told herself for the umpteenth time. Independence from one another would give them both a chance to discover the real strength of their feelings. Not rush things.

'Of course.' His arm tightened around her. 'And you will come to me too. Esad has already asked you to come over so he can cook for you.'

Even within the week they had been back, Damir's friends had made her welcome. Even if not all her family could easily accept him, he had decided it was time to introduce her to his world. He had taken her to a small terraced house in a road on the edge of town that Caro had often driven past. The tiny front garden was a patch of weeds and cracked concrete with two motorbikes chained to a metal post. Not certain what to expect, she was bowled over by the warmth and friendship that greeted her in inverse proportion to the unprepossessing exterior.

'Welcome,' boomed Kemal, a large man with eyes that flashed with good humour, and he enveloped her in an expansive hug. 'Come in. A friend of Damir's is friend of mine. My wife, Maria . . .' He stood back to let his diminutive wife emerge from the kitchen, a tea towel over her shoulder, apron round her waist. She smiled and shook Caro's hand. 'Her English not so good,' Kemal explained.

Once he had shown the two of them into the modest front room, neat and tidy with everything in its place, Kemal went into the kitchen, leaving them with other friends Hasan and his wife, Amela. They immediately welcomed Caro into the group without question or judgment. The rest of the evening was a blur of acceptance, warmth, good wholesome food and laughter. In the company of his friends, Damir was relaxed, and for the first time Caro heard his rich baritone that joined in with the after-dinner singing.

'Caro. You can sing the chorus,' boomed Kemal. 'Like this.'

And, laughing when she got muddled, she did.

His friends had made her feel as if she were one of them. She was ashamed of her own family's treatment of Damir by comparison. Her relationship with Lauren and Mike had not improved. Lauren's words still stung. As bad, she had texted to say they wouldn't need her the following Monday because Mike's sister and family were in town and taking him out. Even though she didn't really think this was a deliberate slight, Caro felt a needle of hurt.

'She'll come round, Mum.' Amy had tried to console her during her day in Bloom. 'You know what she's like. It's not Damir, it's just that you've put a spoke in her plans.'

She was brought back to the present as Damir kissed the side of her head. She leant into him, relishing their closeness, reminding herself that all the difficulties were worth it.

'Let's go inside for just a few minutes.' He whispered the words into her ear. 'A last goodbye – and coffee.' They walked together into the kitchen.

Her kitchen table had never been put to such use. For a nervous second, she worried its legs wouldn't hold them both but then it ceased to be a concern. She allowed herself a smile at the thought of Chris's and the girls' reactions if they knew what was going on in the kitchen instead of the usual family meals, homework and games. A few months ago, she would never have believed it herself. She wiggled until some particularly persistent toast crumbs were dislodged from her right buttock then put a hand on either side of his face and drew him to her. They kissed again, long and hard, before he eased himself from on top of her and began to get dressed. She lay watching him, enjoying the intimacy of the moment. She was jolted out of her post-coital daze by the snap of the letterbox and the sound of the post dropping on to the mat. She pulled herself into a sitting position and, feeling suddenly self-conscious, crossed her arms across her breasts.

'Don't,' said Damir, taking one of her hands. 'You don't need to do that. You're beautiful, remember.'

Caro still found it hard to believe that a man who could have his pick of much younger women would choose her. But he had and he was transforming the way she felt about herself. She dropped her arms, slid off the table and stood in front of him as she put her clothes back on. The embarrassment she had felt on being naked at the start of their affair was retreating, and that felt good.

As she dressed, her elbow nudged the calendar off the wall. Damir bent to pick it up and stared at the picture of the Irish cliffs of Moher. 'Incredible place.' To Caro's alarm, he looked closer. 'What's this? Why do you mark all these days with a spot?'

As they drew nearer to the date of his moving out, Caro had been less discreet with her dots. 'Oh, it's nothing.'

He gave her an indulgent smile. 'You know you can tell me. What does it mean?'

'It's just silly.' Should she tell him? But hadn't she learned that more trouble came from not being honest?

He was looking curious, expectant.

'Well, OK ... You told me you didn't ever commit so I marked off six months of the calendar, to see if we would last that long together. I wanted us to but I didn't know.'

He was looking at her as if she had lost the plot.

'I know it's odd ...'

'You've been counting the days together?' He sounded incredulous as he put his finger on that day's dot. 'And here we are.'

'I didn't want it to end.' She couldn't tell what he was thinking, never having seen him look so serious.

He turned the page of the calendar and hung it up again before draining his coffee. 'There. A new page.'

'Tell me what you're thinking.' She tried to keep the plea out of her voice.

'That this is the right thing for us,' he said. 'If I go, I can prove what you mean to me. You have doubts—' He looked at the calendar, tapped it.

She began to protest but he stopped her. 'I see them in your eyes – but I can show you and your family how wrong you are.'

The ring of the landline halted the conversation. Caro picked up the phone.

'Mum! Can I call you back? I've got someone here ... Yes, it will be within the next half hour ... Yes, definitely ... Bye.' She turned to Damir. 'I'm sorry but I'm going to have to call her. I haven't seen her since we've been back and I need to tell her about us before one of the girls do.'

'They'll all get used to it in the end.' He gave a half-smile and got up to leave. 'We'll talk later.'

Although she had always known he would move out – that was after all part of their agreement – Caro felt as if something momentous was in process that she didn't completely understand. She was being carried along on a tide of emotion she had never experienced before. How had she fallen so deeply in love that the consequences seemed less and less important to her?

Standing in the drive, her hand raised in farewell, she was alone again. Her impulse was to run after the van, ask him to stay, but that would be wrong. Most important was to hold on to her newfound independence. She must stand on her own two feet. She tried conjuring up the feelings that she'd experienced after paragliding. This was the new Caro. Empowered. The last thing she wanted was to go back to the old one who had relied on Chris to complete her and had been lost without him. She was going to move forward, forging a new life in which Damir would play an important part – but she was not going to be defined by him. Her dignity and self-respect would come first. She would remember he was a man of his word and trust him. This was far from over. She turned back to the house. Shower – mother – dog walk. Take things one step at a time.

Caro's mother sat on the edge of her seat, her cup angled so the tea was dangerously close to the lip. Outside, rain beat against the diamond-paned windows, sluicing across May's patio, crushing her pot plants, bouncing off the garden furniture. 'Your lodger! Caro, really. I did wonder if something was going on.'

'No, you didn't.' Caro teased her. 'You hadn't a clue.' Then she remembered what had happened after they had gone to bed on the night that May had stayed at Treetops. Maybe her mother had suspected something. 'But I wanted to tell you before you heard it from the girls. It hasn't gone down well with Lauren.

She's convinced he's got some ulterior motive. Or that I've lost my marbles.'

'But I don't think you've lost your marbles. Not necessarily.' A curious look played on May's face.

'But really the point is that she's worried her plan for buying the house she's set her heart on may fall through. She wanted me to sell Treetops and go in with them to buy a bigger house with a granny flat for me.' She made a face that showed how much she disliked the idea.

'What's wrong with living in a granny flat?' May sounded thoughtful. 'Wouldn't it be a solution to everything for you?

'No! It's too soon for that. And you do know she's pregnant again?'

'She called me. Twins!' May was admiring. 'But she didn't mention the house or this new man in your life.'

'She'll have her hands full.' Caro ignored the mention of Damir. 'Of course I want to help as much as I can but I don't want to be tied there every day. Is that selfish? I already spend a day a week with Danny and, at the moment, that's enough. I need to give time to my painting and my teaching. Both of the girls have been so supportive since Chris left but I feel as though it's time for me to let go and live a little. And it's time for them to let go of me too. Do you understand?'

May smiled at her daughter. 'I think I do. I probably didn't help as much as I could have when Lauren and Amy were small but I felt the same. It's not that you don't love your grandchildren, it's just that you have to think of yourself too.'

'Of course. I love Danny to bits. And I'm sure I'll love the twins every bit as much but I don't want Lauren to rely on me to bail her out when things get tough. She's got to stand on her own feet too.' She was surprised to hear herself talking to her mother like this. But realising May was being appreciative not critical made her open up. Perhaps she should have confided in her years ago.

'If you hadn't met this man...'

'It's not because of him, but because of what he's shown me I can do. I don't feel like the same woman that Chris left any more.'

'I'm curious. I'd like to meet him.'

'You would?' This was the last thing Caro had expected.

'Why not? If he's having such a seismic effect on my family, I want to know what he's like.' A quick smile crossed her face. 'Good-looking, is he?' May leant forward again, eyes bright, interested. 'Well?'

'I suppose so. Well, I think so.' She tried to find words to describe him but they slipped away from her. 'He's got dark hair, straight nose, medium build.'

May shook her head. 'That makes him sound like a police photofit not a person.'

Caro got out her phone and found the photo she had shown Fran. May took the phone from her and stared at it for a while, before looking up at her daughter.

'Sad eyes, but it's a kind face. Make the most of him.'

Caro was stunned, unable to read her mother's expression. 'But I thought you'd...'

'I'd what?'

'I thought you'd be like Lauren. Worried about me.'

'I learned a long time ago that you could look after yourself.' May pinched a pleat of her skirt between her finger and thumb and ran them up and down it. Her wedding ring and sapphire engagement ring slipped up and down between her knuckles. Her hands, like the rest of her, were diminishing, the skin loose and age-spotted, the knuckles baggy, the nails neat.

'He's been through so much. He doesn't have a family of his own any more.' And she began to tell May what she knew of Damir's past, watching her mother's face register shock and sympathy.

'Those poor people,' she finally said. 'We've been so lucky in this country over the last eighty odd years. Peace in our time. Poor man.' The saddest of smiles crept over May's thin lips. 'I was young once too, you know. I do understand.'

'I'm hardly young,' Caro protested, pointing at her face with one finger. Then she registered what her mother had just said. 'What do you mean?'

'I know what being in love feels like.'

'Of course. You had Dad.' Although the marked lack of overt affection between her parents as they ran their lives along parallel lines, each fulfilling the role they had, was what Caro remembered most.

'I don't mean your father.'

Caro sat straight as if a blast of cold air had just blown through the room. 'Who then?'

Her mother was staring into the middle distance. 'Oh, I had a little run out with someone else when you were in your teens. I can still remember how good it felt.'

'But who was he? Why haven't you told me before?'

'Why would I have told you?' A smile hovered on May's lips. 'He was a lawyer. Bill Price. We met him and his wife at the golf club.'

Caro sat quite still, shocked by what she was hearing but intrigued. 'What happened?'

'We usually met when your dad was playing golf. That was the only time I had to myself, except when they were both working and you were at school. Once or twice he came to the house, but that was too risky. So sometimes we drove to the Downs or to country pubs. He was such a sweet man – very attentive, funny, and he knew so much. Nothing like your father.' Her lips tightened as if she had decided not to be disloyal about the man she had been married to for more than forty years.

'Weren't you . . .' Caro wasn't sure how to ask what she was dying to know but it just burst out of her. 'Do you mean it was a "proper" affair?'

'Oh yes. But we had to be so careful.' May looked out at the rain-swept patio. 'I remember once under an oak tree – we were all alone on a beautiful summer's day – then we heard someone coming and had to roll under a bush so they wouldn't see us.' She laughed.

Caro stared at her mother. This was a side to her that she had no idea existed. But why not? She should have asked her more about her life instead of being so wrapped up in her own.

'And what about Dad? Did he ever know?' This was a part of her parents' lives that she had never glimpsed, not even suspected. She had only thought of them as her parents, not as individuals with their own needs and desires. How could she have got to her age without having developed more empathy or curiosity about them? She had no excuse. But it was not too late.

May stopped stroking the pleat in her skirt and twisted her fingers together. 'Yes, he found out. I was careless. I left a poem Bill had written for me on my dressing table. It was only five or six lines... He was always doing little things to make me feel I mattered, that he cared. Your dad never did anything like that.' She wasn't being accusatory, just matter-of-fact. 'But I forgot to put it away in my special box. That day, we'd had such a wonderful afternoon while your father was at work. I was on cloud nine, giddy with love.' She shut her eyes for the memory. 'I felt guilty, of course, but I couldn't resist Bill – we had such fun together. Such fun.'

Remembering her short-tempered, buttoned-up father, Caro could imagine that was something in short supply in her parents' marriage. The yearning in her mother's voice, as if telling her daughter at last had unlocked something in her, made Caro want to reach out and hug her, but she also wanted to hear more. 'What happened?' she asked instead.

'What do you think?' May's eyes filled with tears but she cleared her throat, pulled a cotton handkerchief from her sleeve and blew her nose. 'He read it out loud. His scorn made it sound like something else altogether. He asked me who had written it, holding it between his finger and thumb as if it was something dirty. I had to tell him. "Bill!?" he said, as if he was about to laugh. I don't know whether he was shocked, upset or both. Then he tore it into pieces and threw it in the wastepaper basket.'

Caro pictured the poem falling like confetti. 'Oh, Mum.' This time she did get up and put her arms round May.

'It's a long time ago now. It almost feels as if it didn't happen, but it did. I still remember that devastating grief, knowing Bill and I could never meet again. Not even a goodbye. And I didn't want to leave – I had you two girls. Dad would never have let you go with me.'

'But the divorce courts…'

May shook her head. 'I didn't want to wreck your lives, and divorce can do that to children. You've been lucky in the sense that your girls were older. Besides, it turned out that Bill was a coward in the end too. He didn't want to leave his wife for me, and in those days we didn't have the independence that married women have today. Times were different. I had no money of my own to support myself, no job, so I stayed and gradually we buried what had happened. Yes, it made a difference. Of course it did. Your father became more distant although he never forgot his responsibilities. He never let us down, I will say that. And Bill moved away soon afterwards. I've no idea whether they had words. And I've no idea what happened to him, but I didn't forget him. He may be dead by now.'

Caro wondered why she and her mother had never talked about their marriages in such depth before. Her relationship with her own daughters seemed so much closer although occasionally she wondered whether that was necessarily such a good thing. Did being close sometimes cause more upset than need be? The two of them had grown apart once she left home, seeing each other but always skirting round anything too personal that might embarrass either of them. Even her separation from Chris had been dealt with in the crispest of terms. If only they had grown closer instead of more distant over the years. However, it wasn't too late to make amends.

'So you see,' said May, breaking the silence, 'I understand more than you think.'

And now Caro understood why *Brief Encounter* had been her mother's favourite film, watched more times than anyone in the family could count. 'So you don't disapprove?'

'Of course not. If he makes you happy then take your chance. I didn't and it's haunted me all my life. Did you really think I'd disapprove? We really don't know each other very well any more, do we?' She smiled sadly. 'Heavens! It's not as if you're with Chris now, and the girls are grown up.'

'Sometimes it doesn't feel like it. What about Lauren's idea of the flat? Do you really think it's a good idea?'

'Just testing your resolve.' Was that a wink? 'But she'll come round. You'll see. She doesn't like change. Remember when you gave her that kitten for her birthday and she wept because she thought family life as she knew it would change? A week or two later, and she wouldn't be parted from it. And everything's going to be very different indeed when those twins are born. You've always been there for her and now you might not be. She'll get used to the idea eventually.'

On her way home, Caro rewound their conversation. May had hit exactly the spot when she talked about Lauren. What kind of mother was Caro? The worst kind: so wrapped up in her own drama that she hadn't stopped to think about what her own daughter might be going through. She didn't want to replicate the emotional distance that had characterised so much of her relationship with her own mother till now. It was up to her to do something.

23

Chris had made himself as comfortable as if he still lived at Treetops. He had offered Caro a drink, produced it and one for himself and burrowed in the cupboard for crisps or nuts, then sighed audibly when he couldn't find any. 'Cupboard's bare,' he pronounced, banging the empty bowl on the table. 'What's this?' He ran a finger round the circular burn mark made when Damir had put down a frying pan.

The evening was balmy enough for them to sit outside. Caro raised an eyebrow at the navy-blue silk socks that went on show when he sat down. Gone were the hardy M&S cotton mix she had always bought him. His grey suede lace-ups were a style statement that he'd never made before. Grey check shirt and navy blue chinos completed the look. She felt quite underdressed in her leggings and loose shirt, and tucked her feet in their flipflops under the table.

'How's Georgie?'

'Not so good,' he replied, getting up to pull a weed from one of the pots on the terrace. 'I don't remember you being sick when you were pregnant.'

'That's because you were never there.' Chris had been setting up his production company at that time, bringing his own people on board, developing new projects, focusing his energies on making the success of it that he had. 'She'll get over it.' Although an infinitesimal cruel piece of her hoped that Georgie would suffer throughout the entire pregnancy, making Chris suffer too.

'I'm sure I was.' He turned his attention to the roses and had started flicking off the dead heads from Desdemona, her current favourite, with his thumb.

'Stop it,' she insisted. 'That's one of my jobs for tomorrow.'

He flicked a perfectly good rosebud into the flowerbed. 'Yes, of course, you've been away.' As he turned towards her, she thought she saw a gleam in his eye. 'I gather you had a good time.'

'Yes, I did, thanks.' She kept her voice as neutral as she could. 'So?'

'I was out this way and thought I'd drop in.' He sat down at last and lifted his glass. 'Chin chin.' An idiotic affectation he'd adopted after seeing a play set in the fifties that he thought was amusing.

'Cheers.' The wine ran down her throat, giving her courage. 'Have you talked to Lauren?'

He returned his glass to the table, crossed one leg over the other and fixed his gaze on her. And, just like she always had when being judged, she looked away. Then, she looked back again.

'Yes. Mike too. It's all about this house they want so badly and, of course, selling this place.'

Caro steeled herself. 'I should tell you that I've changed my mind. I'm not going to buy you out – or even try.' He didn't need to know anything more about her plans.

He looked surprised but relieved that she'd seen sense at last. 'It's a great idea for you to move in with Lauren and Mike – you'll be comfortable for the rest of your life. I've seen the agent's details.'

'The rest of my life!' Outrage fizzed up inside her. 'Now why would you think I'd want to do that?'

He looked as if he was going to say something else but she continued over him. 'No, I'll tell you. Because if I move in with Lauren you can shake off any residual guilt about me.'

He jerked his head away, his eyes narrowing as he absorbed what she'd said, not liking it.

'I'm right, aren't I? But I'm not going to be moving in with them.'

'It's the perfect solution for everyone,' he insisted, tapping his foot against the table leg. Tap, tap, tap.

'For everyone except me.'

'None of this is about that though, is it?' The tapping stopped. 'It's about this man you've met.'

He was impossible.

'Not at all. Although meeting him has helped clear my mind.' She wouldn't rise to the bait. Under the table she dug her nails into her palm, reminding herself to keep her temper. 'You and I have reached a certain age. Lauren and Amy have grown up and left home. I don't criticise your relationship with Georgie.' At least not to his face. 'So I don't think you've any right to comment on what I do any more. Because this is my life now. Not yours. And not Lauren's nor Amy's.' She picked up her glass again, glad to be in control of the conversation.

Chris was brushing some invisible dandruff from his shoulder. But he didn't give up that easy. 'It isn't though, is it? What you do impacts on other people i.e. our daughters. And if they're upset – and Lauren is – I have to do what I can to help them.'

Caro had to hold back the scornful laughter that threatened to burst from her. 'And what you do, doesn't? Listen to yourself.'

When the girls were young, he had always been an over-indulgent and over-protective father. Any time of the day or night, he would get in the car to take them wherever they wanted or to collect them when the last bus had gone. He vetted boyfriends, worrying about their suitability and reliability. He insisted they were brought to the house, each and every one, although Caro knew for a fact a few slipped through the net – with her help. No wonder she had wanted to keep Damir secret. He gave the girls money when they needed it. When they finally left home, he stopped all that. But here he was, back on his steed.

Caro went on. 'All I've done is meet someone, just like you

did. I'm not splitting up our marriage. I'm not threatening the stability or the happiness of my family. Any of that sort of damage has already been done. By you. Amy's cool about this. Lauren will be too. If she can come round to Georgie, I'm sure she will to Damir.'

'Damir.' He let the name roll around his tongue like a cheap wine. 'He's younger than you, I heard?' The tiniest of smirks played on his face but Caro saw it.

'Don't even go there.' She spread her left hand on the table in front of her. 'You're surely the first to agree that age is un-important.'

He had the grace to look sheepish before going back on the attack. 'I'm worried about you.'

She wanted nothing more than to knock the sudden look of concern off his face.

'I am,' he insisted. 'I know I was the one who left but I do still care, and I don't want anything bad to happen to you. I want to be sure that you're all right.'

Caro folded her arms and stared at him, willing him to re-member the hell he had put her through, their daughters' distress, her own.

Something of her contempt must have shown for he shifted uneasily, unable to meet her eye. His hand moved up and down his throat. 'I'm sorry. You know I felt so trapped here... I couldn't...'

'You explained at the time, and I don't want your apologies and justifications again. Not now. We're beyond that.' Caro moved into her stride. 'In fact, for the first time, I'm beginning to understand what it was that made you leave.'

Chris was frowning, puzzled by this new forthrightness of hers, then scratched his head, messing up his hair. 'I don't under-stand...'

But Caro cut him off. 'I'd forgotten how powerful sex can be.'

If she weren't so angry with him, she might have laughed as

his obvious confusion was replaced by the suspicion that he had just been insulted. 'What do you—'

But she had no intention of letting him get a word in until she had finished. 'Sex is...' She dropped her folded arms and searched for the right words to make her point. 'Well, it's the physical intimacy that comes with a relationship with another person...' She spelt it out as if to a child. 'I've found this out for myself, Chris... At last.' Cruel but he deserved it. It was time she had her say.

He winced.

'And now I understand why you had to walk away. We'd drifted apart and I hadn't even realised. I was too wrapped up in the girls and school, and my teaching, and worrying about your business to notice what was missing. If I'd realised, perhaps I would have done something to try to save our marriage, but you did realise and yet you didn't bother. I'm right, aren't I?'

He was staring at her, equally hurt and astonished. Then he turned away. 'Didn't you ever feel like that with me?'

'No, not in the same way. We were good together once but we were different. So what I'm saying is butt out, Chris. This is my business. I'm enjoying myself with Damir and I will do for as long as it lasts. He's shown me there's a lot still to enjoy just when I thought I was on my way towards irrelevancy! When Lauren and Mike want to talk to me, I'm here and happy to talk to them, but I'm not going to communicate with them through you.' There. A sharp pain made her look down to see a bead of blood running down her thumb from the cuticle she had sawed through with a fingernail.

'What's happened to you? You've changed. You're not the woman I married any more.'

'Well that's a good thing, isn't it?' She couldn't resist. 'You disliked that woman enough to leave her. And when you walked out of that door, you gave up any rights you might once have had over me.'

'Can I hear Fran talking?' That superior tone was inching its way back.

'Chris, please. I can think for myself. I've seen the light, that's all. Same way you did. It's just taken me longer.'

'Well!' He brushed his hands together. 'I suppose I should have expected you to find someone else in the end.'

Caro's eyes narrowed. 'Have you any idea what you sound like? As if you can hear the bottom of the barrel being scraped. If you had been even remotely interested, I could have told you that I haven't wanted anyone else. I needed time to work out what mattered to me, what I wanted. You should be pleased I've found someone who makes me happy just as you have. But, no . . .' She ran out of breath and came to a halt.

Chris was staring at her as if he didn't recognise her. He shook his head and downed the rest of his wine in one swallow before standing up. 'Enough. I've got the message – I'll tell Mike and Lauren to call you.'

'Yes. Why don't you do that? Or I'll call them myself, when I'm ready.'

An hour or so later, she was sitting with Fran. To calm herself after Chris had left, Caro had taken a quick shower and changed into her new skinny jeans and Converses that got the raised eye-brow treatment from Fran. 'Haven't seen you in anything like that before. Looks great.' Her own loose dress draped around her as she sat down. She stretched out her legs and eased off the strappy heels that Caro envied though they were not something she would ever wear.

'I've been thinking. What if you have a party? Barbecue, salads and Pimms sort of thing. Just a small one. Then everyone could meet Damir and see he's not the chancer Lauren's worried about.'

There was nothing Fran liked better than a party. Barely a week went by without her going to celebrate a client's success or a new play or film. 'That's a lovely idea but I'm not sure. I'm the only person who can change Lauren's mind about Damir. I don't think a party's the answer. Especially not with us all looking on.' If only Damir was here to discuss it too. What would he want?

Fran waved a finger back and forth at her. 'No, no. This is special. It's not so much a party for your sixty-second but more of a way of getting everyone to discover for themselves that he's not some sort of demon.' Fran kicked off her shoes so she could lie back on the sofa, feet up. 'Not that I know that, of course. I've only got your word to go on.'

In the hall, Milo started barking.

'Hang around for much longer, and you will.'

'Really?' Fran perked up just as the front door opened and shut. 'He's got a key?' she whispered, eyebrows raised.

'I didn't see the point of asking for it back.'

Milo barked again, then stopped. All they could hear was the skitter of the Labrador's claws on the wood floor and the low murmur of a man's voice.

Fran sat up, slipped her shoes back on and, to Caro's amusement, dug out a lipstick from her bag.

Caro smeared her own lips together, aware that most of her own lipstick had smudged off on her glass. She rubbed it away quickly with her thumb. 'We're in here,' she called, getting up and going towards the door, aware Fran was watching her.

Damir opened the living-room door before she reached it. Seeing him, her heart quickened the same way it did every time she'd seen him again since they'd returned from France. If anything, living apart was making her feelings for him stronger. He was carrying a bunch of red tulips, but put them on the top of the piano before hugging her to him. He was about to kiss her when he saw Fran, and stopped, taking a step back. 'You have friends. You should have said. I can come later.'

'It's only Fran.'

'Thanks very much!' Fran got to her feet, wearing her most

engaging smile, hand outstretched. 'I've heard so much about you.'

Caro stepped to one side so they could shake hands but his arm stayed around her. 'Anyway I want you to meet her. I've met your friends, now it's your turn. Fran you'll stay to supper, won't you? There's plenty.'

Fran hesitated, her head swivelling from one to the other of them. 'Really?'

'Yes,' Damir agreed. 'Why not? I'd like that.'

Caro could hear them laughing as she added the final touches to her fish curry and put on the rice. By the time she returned, they looked entirely relaxed with each other, Fran's head was thrown back as she laughed a little too loudly at something Damir had said. He was looking bemused. She rocked forward and put a hand on his arm, just a touch, before turning to Caro.

'I was asking about France. You didn't tell me about being stuck on the cable car! You must have hated that.'

Caro joined them, sitting alone in the chair by the fire. 'I was terrified but we got through, didn't we? Thanks to you.' Thanks to his memories of a life so very different from her own.

'I could have told you she's terrible with heights,' Fran confided, leaning forward, her cleavage generously displayed. 'You should have seen her when we went on the London Eye.'

'Everyone said that it was like flying,' she protested, not keen on the way this conversation was going. 'They said I wouldn't notice being off the ground. But I did!'

'She sat on the bench with her head in her hands for the full flight.' That laugh again. Her red nails on Damir's shirt sleeve. A hand brushing back her hair. Damir's eyes fixed on her, an uncertain smile on his face as if he didn't know whether or not to join in. Before he had time to make a decision, she was off again. 'Have you been to France before?'

But this was what Fran was all about, Caro reminded herself. Flirting with any man who came within touching range was her default mode. She was alive, interested, curious. Her French polished toenails glinted from her shoes. Caro curled her own untended toes in her Converses, wishing she had made more of an effort. She felt like a moth beside a butterfly. She'd been amused in the past when she'd seen Fran turn up the charm but somehow it wasn't such fun when she directed it at Damir.

The evening didn't go as well as she'd hoped. Somehow Caro managed to burn the rice. The curry was hot to the point of Saharan. The mangoes she had bought for pudding were rock hard. And all the while Fran kept chatting, laughing, almost as if Caro wasn't there. If Damir moved to get up to help Caro, Fran would stop him by asking him more questions about himself, where he came from, what he had done since the war. He seemed only too ready to answer, although he never gave away more than Caro already knew.

'Germany?' she asked when he mentioned he lived there. 'I love Berlin,' and diverted to the tale of a long weekend she had spent there. 'Do you know the Volkspark Friedichshain? We had such a good morning there.' On the opposite side of the table, she joked, she listened, she charmed. No wonder men fell for her so easily. Damir seemed to be too. And who would blame him? Caro lapsed into silence, never having felt less fun than she did beside her friend. Every now and then Damir would give her a worried smile as if he was wondering what was the matter.

Eventually, the meal was over, Caro was exhausted, upset and irritated with herself. All that Fran had done was make Damir feel welcome in the only way she knew. All Caro had done was the opposite. Fran was her best friend, for God's sake. She was no threat.

'What's the matter?' Fran hissed at her in the hall as she was leaving. 'Is something wrong?'

To say anything would sound so petty. 'Nothing.' Caro held Milo by the collar so he didn't make a break for the gate.

'He's lovely,' Fran whispered back. 'We should definitely have that party. Everyone's going to fall for him.'

'But that's not the way I want to play it.' Caro heard how ungrateful she sounded, but she couldn't stop herself.

Fran looked taken aback. 'But I thought...' She clearly took in Caro's expression. 'Never mind. Let's talk about it next week. I'll come over.' She never gave up on what she thought was a good idea. She and Lauren had that in common.

Caro kissed her cheek. 'Perhaps.'

24

In the kitchen, Damir was sitting with his elbows on the table, head in hands. Caro wanted to touch him, to explain, but instead she began to clear the table, rattling the plates and the cutlery into the dishwasher, putting the cork into the half-finished bottle of wine. She slammed shut the drawer that contained the tablemats.

As she reached across the table to pick up a side plate, his hand reached out to grasp her wrist. 'What are you doing?' He sounded puzzled.

'Tidying up.' She shook her wrist free, ashamed of how badly her insecurity was making her behave.

'Come on. Sit down.' He patted the chair at his side. 'Talk to me.'

As soon as she sat, he took both her hands in his. 'What's the matter? Have I done something wrong?'

This wasn't what she expected. 'Nothing,' she said immediately. 'Nothing at all. It's just me being stupid.'

'But something's wrong. You hardly spoke all night.' His hands squeezed hers.

'Fran can talk enough for both of us. She's great, isn't she?' She hated herself for how much she wanted him to disagree.

'She's funny. That story about the burglar in her back garden.' He laughed and Caro couldn't help smiling at the picture Fran had conjured up of her chasing the intruder with a poker until he leapt over the wall straight into the neighbour's pond. Whether exaggerated for effect or not, she had certainly kept them entertained.

'So you did like her?' Caro felt like a giddy teenager, embarrassed by her desire to hear him say he liked her more.

'Of course. I want to like your friends. She made me at home. But of course she's not you.'

How easily he could make her happy. She glanced down at her hands. 'I'm out of practice at being in love, and I guess I'm easily thrown. Can I explain?'

He nodded, curious.

'It's silly but I thought you fancied Fran and I was upset.' As she watched his face change, she immediately wished she'd kept her thoughts to herself.

'You mean I think she's beautiful?' He laughed and patted his knee. 'Come here.'

'I should finish tidying up.' She half stood.

'Leave that. We can finish it later, together.'

Still cross that she had let her insecurities get the better of her, she did as he asked and perched on his knee. 'I'm an idiot. I'm sorry.' The scent of his aftershave was undercut by the faint smell of his sweat. His arms tightened round her and he pressed his head into her shoulder before tilting his face to hers.

'You are silly. I know what you're thinking. But I don't want anyone else but you. I feel comfortable with you. I like the way you let me be me. When I talk to you, you don't judge but listen. Our time in France was the happiest I've been for ages – I didn't want that to end. We're good together. Why would I look at someone else?'

For a moment she thought he was going to add 'I love you', but the moment passed. Any disappointment was forgotten as they kissed, and her doubts went flying out of the window.

The following day, having finally cleared up the debris from the previous evening, Caro was getting ready to go to the college when the phone rang. Amy.

'I'm not phoning you to come to the shop. Although I am a bit short-handed if you wanted something to do.'

'I can't today, I'm sorry.'

'I thought you might be teaching. But I'm really phoning to see that you're OK and to ask you to call Lauren.'

'I will, but I'll have to do it later.' She snapped shut the lid of the box she kept her pencils in. 'Promise.'

'You're just as stubborn as she is! But she's been on at me, wanting me to persuade you to fall in with her master plan. It would be much more grown-up to talk to each other, so why don't you?'

'I've been putting it off because I can't bear the idea of a repeat of last time. I can't forget what she said so I've been waiting while we both cool down. I want her to understand.' But more than that, she wanted Lauren to share her happiness and to accept her choices about the way she wanted to live.

'Well don't put it off any more. You're the one who's always going on about how important family is. And ours seems to be going into freefall right now. If you don't do something about it, who will? Not Dad. Not Lauren. And no one takes any notice of me.'

Caro gave a weary laugh. 'All right. I've got the message. I'll call her.'

'When?'

'Today. Later. When she and Mike are both in. Happy?'

'Ecstatic. Now are you sure you don't want to pop down?'

'One hundred per cent. My students would lynch me.' And taking the class would clear her head, forcing her to concentrate on her pupils' work and not her own problems.

But for once she couldn't switch off. The two beginners' classes were busy, and a couple of the students did not get the hang of the early exercises at all. Caro took them back to drawing a circle, a triangle and a square then asked them to imagine the light coming from the right and to draw their 3D counterparts.

'Try not to think of it as an object but look where the light and shade falls and create the shape and tone from there.' She knew the lines off by heart, but her mind was on Lauren and how to put this mess right. How could she best explain to her daughter the change she had undergone since meeting Damir so she understood it? Over the last weeks, she had been offered the glimpse of a different path to the one she had imagined for herself, one that she would never have had the courage to entertain before.

'Flying like a bird,' he had said on the side of the mountain. 'This is your chance.' She could feel herself coming out of her shell as she thought of new things to do, places to go without being deterred by the unfamiliarity of them any longer. In the evening, she spent ages on her laptop, scrolling through travel agents, seeing what holidays they were offering. She had even taken the first step of joining the local choir by applying for an audition. And on top of that, she had Damir. But she had to be realistic. *I move on.* His words haunted her. What would she do when he dropped out of her life? Was her stupid jealousy of Fran just a symptom of her fear of losing him?

But being alone wasn't a fear of hers any more. The last couple of years had taught her that, if nothing else, she could cope with living on her own. She was shedding the skin of being a wife and mother at last and becoming herself. It was time for her to move on as well. Recognising that keeping Treetops was really nothing but a pipedream was part of that. She stared out of the window while her students got on with their work, her mind elsewhere. Accepting that she should let go of the house would help her move forward. What mattered was the memories she would take with her not the place where they had happened. She understood that now. Her sigh made the student nearest to her turn round. She smiled back at her, reassuring her she was all right. More than all right. She stood up and turned back to her class. Yes, she was ready to let go at last.

The day dragged past. The more advanced classes didn't need so much of her input as they focused on their work, concentrating on their own interpretations of what was in front of them. Standing behind her own canvas, Caro stared at its blankness, making a few desultory marks but letting her mind drift until finally it was time to go home. For once her precious art was no help to her.

Listening to Lauren's phone ring, Caro tapped on the table, covering her nervousness. She had made up her mind about what she was going to do. Just as she was beginning to feel relieved that she would only be able to leave a message, the phone was picked up.

'Lauren's phone.'

'Is that you, Mike?'

'I hope you don't know anyone else who would be answering my wife's phone!' He laughed. 'I'm afraid she's putting Danny to bed.'

'I haven't had a chance to congratulate you. So exciting.'

'But twins! God knows how we're going to cope. It's crazy enough as it is.'

'You'll manage. Danny'll be at school soon. And you'll find great help.'

'I hope. But what about the house? I know you said to Lauren you weren't keen, but we're hoping you'll change your mind.'

'That's really why I phoned.'

'Has she shown you the details? You'll love it.'

'I don't think you really want me in the way.'

He laughed. 'You won't be in the way. We'd love to have you with us. Isn't it just a great solution for all of us? I think my wife's done good.' How proud he sounded. 'They've accepted our offer.'

'You've made an offer already?' The wind that had begun to fill her sails abruptly dropped.

'We had to if we weren't going to lose it.'

'But I haven't even seen it.'

'No, but you'll love it.' So he kept saying. 'We'll have to put both houses on the market immediately if we're going to be able to move quickly enough. I'm sure they'll be snapped up. Yours is looking its best now and Chris said he wanted a quick sale.'

'Hang on, Mike. I haven't agreed to any of this.' Her grip on everything seemed to be loosening.

'But now you've had a chance to think it through, surely it's only a formality. If the problem's that you haven't seen it, that's not an issue. There's still time. Why don't I call the agent and fix a viewing for the weekend?'

Caro took a deep breath. Now or never. 'Because, however lovely it is, I can't move there with you. I did mean what I said.'

There was a brief silence. 'But of course you can.' Mike was at his most persuasive. 'You'll love being so close to Danny and the twins. You'll be so involved in them growing up.'

'I'm sorry, Mike. That's what I was phoning to say. I've decided that I'm not going to hang on to Treetops.' She heard his quiet sigh of relief at the other end of the phone. 'The place is too big for me to rattle round in for much longer.'

'Well, then, what's the problem? Lauren said she thought that's what you'd do.'

Caro suspected Chris must have sown that seed.

'I need to spread my wings. I could have at least another twenty good years ahead of me and there are things I want to do.'

'A bucket list! Or is this to do with the new man?' She had never heard Mike sound so suspicious.

'No. No, it's really not.' As she spoke she knew at last that what she was saying was the truth. 'This is something I've got to do for myself. Of course I'll be around to help when I can, just not on a daily basis. Mike, you must understand that?'

'Honestly? No, I don't, Caro. We're offering you a beautiful home, with us and the children, and you're turning that down.' Disbelief had entered his voice.

'I don't know how else to explain. I want time to myself and an adventure before I settle down into respectable grannydom.' She hoped she could make him laugh. Instead she heard Lauren say something to him in the background, then he must have passed her the phone.

'Mum, please don't do this.' Her voice was small, choked. 'If you don't come in with us, we can't make it work.'

Hearing her so upset made Caro's stomach knot. She was almost tempted to change her mind. She knew what it was like to want a house so badly nothing else would do. When she and Chris had first seen Treetops they had fallen head over heels with it. The house had been everything they had wanted in a home. As soon as they had walked through the front door, she had known it was the one. She had turned to Chris and saw immediately he felt the same. He was staring up the stairs, looking at the window that let light flood into the hallway. She sympathised with Lauren, understood her desperation. The last thing she wanted to do was puncture her own daughter's dream, but if she didn't stand up for herself now, her own dreams would be ashes too. The difference was they would find another house: she would not get another chance. She took a deep breath.

'I'm sorry. I really am. If only we could have talked it through before you went ahead and made your offer. But there will be other houses that you'll be just as happy in.'

'I hope you're right.' Lauren sounded so unforgiving. Then, when Caro failed to think of something appropriately soothing, she said, 'I'd better go. Danny's calling. Bye, Mum.'

Caro stared at the phone in her hand then put it down on the garden table. Was flying in the face of your daughters' expectations the right thing to do? Was she being selfish again? The last thing she wanted was to cause any upset. A blackbird sang in the apple tree, the plants swayed and bent in the breeze. The world went on undisturbed despite everything. And Damir would be there soon. She crossed over to the tap and switched it on to water the flowerbeds, then sat down again. She raised her shoulders and let them drop. A great weight had slipped off them and she felt light and free . . . as did her mind. Whatever happened, she had made the right decision for her and for her alone. No more being railroaded into decisions by her well-meaning daughters. No more of her ex-husband haunting her movements. She was going to take charge of her own life.

She closed her eyes and sighed, turning her face up to the evening sun, feeling its warmth on her skin. Now what? She sat there for another half hour, ruminating on what to do next. She hadn't got far by the time her phone buzzed with a text.

Something has happened. I cannot come tonight. I'm sorry. I phone you later.

A crushing sense of disappointment overtook everything else she was feeling. The anticipation of seeing him was what had propelled her through the day. He must have got delayed at the job in a brand new block of flats on the outskirts of town. But there was nothing she could do but wait till the following evening.

She tapped out a reply.

Don't worry. I'll be here. Waiting. X

After a moment, she deleted the 'Waiting'. Too needy.

Her thoughts returned to her family. She had always put her children and husband first, trying to be the best wife and mother she could. Perhaps that was at the heart of what had happened with Lauren. Caro's family was used to her putting herself second, so they expected it and took her for granted. This change in her that they didn't understand made them uncomfortable. She didn't entirely understand that either. The last thing she wanted was to fall out with Lauren, and of course she wanted to help with her grandchildren. She didn't have to be living under the same roof as them for that.

If she hadn't met Damir, none of this would have happened. She wouldn't be reaching for her independence, she would be going along with the plans that were made for her, fitting in, causing no waves. But knowing her own mind at last felt good, liberating.

A little later, Caro walked Milo over to Fran's, keen to talk through everything that had happened. She just wouldn't bring up the subject of the party.

Fran had just got home from work. 'Screening of a dreadful costume drama,' she explained. 'Two hours I won't get back. Rick was the only good thing in it.' She was always fiercely loyal to her clients even when they had under-performed. 'Go on then. Tell me what Lauren had to say for herself.'

She listened to Caro's worries, considered them. 'It'll be fine. You know what it's like looking for a house. You lose the one of your dreams and just when you think all is lost, something better comes along. You just have to keep the faith. They'll find something smaller.'

'That's what I said, but what if they don't?'

'They will.'

'And we didn't even talk about Damir at all. A bit of me's wondering whether all this is worth it.'

Fran clutched both sides of her head, pulling at her hair, her mouth open in the parody of a scream as she let out a strangled cry. 'God, give me strength. You can't turn back now.'

'But if it splits up the family...'

'How's Amy taken it?'

Caro pictured her daughter, remembering her support. 'She's fine, thinks it's great. She's got enough to think about with the business and moving in with Jason.' She told Fran about the non-existent proposal. 'Do you think everything's all right?'

'Didn't you once tell me she didn't believe in marriage? Perhaps he's waiting for the right cue that she's changed her mind and it's a long time coming. You worry too much. As for Damir. He's a decent guy. They'll like him when they make the effort. I did.'

Caro sipped her wine. 'Mmmm. I noticed.'

'What?' Fran looked mystified before understanding dawned. 'Oh, for heaven's sake. I thought you were being off the other night. You weren't jealous?! You don't think I'd do that, do you? You're my best mate.'

'Well, you did seem quite keen.'

Fran shook her head. 'You've got it bad, my friend.'

'If that's sympathy or pity, I don't want it.' Caro nudged Milo off her foot. 'He's so different from anyone else I've met. Especially from Chris who, incidentally, came over the other day.'

'Tell me in a second,' said Fran, raising her hands to stop her from going on. 'In the meantime, I guess the party's off?'

'I was hoping you'd have forgotten about that. But yes, it's off. I don't think it's the right answer.'

'You sure? Pimms. Music. Dancing.' She waved her hands in the air.

'Is that all you think about – enjoying yourself?'

'Why not?' She raised her glass, clinking it with Caro's. 'Life's short.'

The following Monday, Caro went as usual to look after Danny. Things between them, at best, civil. Lauren was waiting for her. Her black suit emphasised how pale and drawn she was. Her hair scraped back from her face added to the severity of her look. What intimidated a criminal court was enough to intimidate her mother too but Caro was determined not to let it show. Lauren's bump was noticeably larger and Caro put out her hand to touch. 'Excited?'

Lauren ran both her hands over the mound. 'Nervous, more like. Danny's just finishing breakfast. I've said goodbye to him so if I leave now he won't make a fuss. I'll see you later.'

Caro clutched the new book she'd brought for Danny. 'Lauren, let's not be like this.'

'Like what?'

'You know what I'm talking about. We can't fall out over a house.'

Lauren stared at her, her eyes unforgiving. 'We've had to withdraw the offer. It would have been so perfect. And it's not just the house. I'm worried about you.'

If she heard that again, Caro thought she might lash out. This time, she just took a breath, deciding not to re-tread old ground by asking Lauren to understand once again. 'There's no need. Really.'

'Has he moved out?'

At last.

'Ages ago.' She registered a momentary softening on Lauren's face. *And with him has gone my heart. Don't you care?* A return to safer ground. 'Have you seen anywhere else?'

'Have you any idea how difficult it is with us both working? We're going house-hunting this weekend.' Lauren's chin wobbled and to Caro's dismay her daughter's eyes welled with tears.

'What is it?' Caro remembered her conversation with May. 'This isn't like you.'

A tear ran down Lauren's face. Caro got some tissues from her bag and passed them over before putting her arms round her weeping daughter. Lauren's body gradually relaxed until eventually she had regained control of herself.

'I'm sorry, Mum. But it's all too much. How will I manage with twins? Having Danny was hard enough when we were both working, but two more!' Cue more tears. 'Suppose I can't do it.'

Caro stroked her daughter's hair, just as she had when Lauren was small, upset after not being given the part she wanted in the school play, being dumped by her first boyfriend, worried she would do less than her best in her exams. 'Of course you can do it. I don't know anyone more capable of coping than you.' Caro looked up at a framed photo of the two young sisters: Lauren, bold and fearless; Amy, happy to follow. 'It must seem a lot, but we'll all help you.'

'Will you?' Lauren looked at her through red-rimmed eyes.

'Of course. Not moving in with you doesn't mean I won't do my bit. Try and keep me away.'

'But suppose I can't do my job any more?' The thought reduced her to sobs again. 'Suppose the others think I'm not taking the job seriously enough and ask me to leave.'

Caro couldn't help laughing. 'I think a bunch of lawyers should be familiar enough with the law to know they can't do that. Look. You're not the first person to have a baby, and twins aren't a deliberate mistake, they're a blessing.'

A sniff. 'You think so?'

'Of course they are. And you're going to be the best mum in the world to them. What you'll need is some proper help, that's all. I'll be there at the start and then you'll make more permanent plans.'

'Not you?' The last hope.

'No, not me. But I'll help you find the right nursery or child minder. Danny's almost ready for nursery school and you'll find someone great to look after the twins. You won't need me although you know I'll always help out, wherever you live. That house isn't the answer to all this.'

'It would be.' Sniff.

Caro refused to get drawn in but said gently, 'No. You're seeing it as a solution to everything but there's more to it than that.'

'We wanted it so badly.'

'I know you did.'

'It would have been so perfect.'

'For you. But not for me. You and Mike need to have your own life without me tagging along in the background as a convenient babysitter. Surely you see that.' This was a difficult conversation to have but she thought she detected the slightest of nods. 'I need that too.'

'But I'd set my heart on it.'

'And I set mine on Damir.' There, she'd said it. 'Won't you at least try to get to know him.'

'But you said this wasn't about him.'

'It's not. It's about what we both want from our lives. Bricks and mortar count for nothing beside what the heart needs. Imagine life without Mike.'

'I can't.' A watery smile.

'You see? So will you try? For me?'

Her reply was uncertain. 'I'll try.'

25

The calendar showed the six months Caro had marked off were coming close to an end. She wished Damir hadn't noticed them. The dots were only meant for her. She worried that seeing them had made him feel free to do just what she had predicted. Was it a co-incidence that the heady combination of lust and love seemed to be waning? Since he moved out, they had seen far less of each other than she had hoped. He hadn't asked her over to his place, explaining that they were doing a bit of work on it and it was too much of a mess to show anyone yet. After the initial intense couple of weeks after their return from holiday, his work had kept him increasingly busy. He was working to a punishing schedule but there was something more than that going on, she was sure. He had changed. She couldn't put her finger on how exactly but something was different. Something told her that however much he had shared with her, he was still keeping something back. And she blamed herself.

'I'm working late. I have to make up the money I spent in France,' he said. But she heard a new reservation in his voice.

'I don't mind how late you get here.' She tried to sound reasonable not desperate.

'But I have to start so early. I need to sleep. The boss wants this done fast.'

But Caro was only half convinced. When they did get together, she tried to draw him out.

'Half the time we're together, I feel as though you're not really here. What is it?'

'Nothing.' But down came that shutter over his eyes, closing her out. So there was something. Even in bed, the place where they had previously shared everything, he was different. Caro could feel him holding back, unable to give himself one hundred per cent to her any more. Her worst fears were being fuelled night and day. She could only imagine that he'd met someone else.

Then, one weekend, he said he was meeting someone from 'the old days' on the Sunday afternoon. *The old days.*

'Who?' She couldn't help herself.

'Just someone from before. I'll be round later.'

'Can't I come with you?' The mystery made her more pushy than she meant to be.

When she asked again something indecipherable flashed across his eyes. 'Not this time.'

Despite herself, Caro couldn't help being reminded of Fran and the trust she had put in Ewan. What about the trust she herself had put in Chris? Was that why her suspicions were so easily aroused? She may not have expected Damir and her to last, but she had hoped. Ewan had found someone else, someone who was a better match for him. So had Chris. Had Damir done the same?

Eventually they had fallen into bed where, without the need for words, they set about making things better between them, but even then she could tell his mind was elsewhere.

'You must trust me,' Damir said at last, curving himself around her body so he fitted round her back, his knees snug in the backs of hers, stroking her left breast. 'I only want you. No one else. That's not what this is about.'

'Then tell me.' Don't push him.

'No. Please don't ask me.'

Caro rolled over so they were nose to nose on the pillows. She looked into his eyes that were as dark as night, unable to read in them anything she hadn't seen before. 'I'm really sorry. I shouldn't have gone on. You're entitled to your own life, after all. I'm being silly.'

'You are.' He ran his finger down her nose.

'It's just that I miss you. I want to be with you whenever we can be.'

'That's what I want too.' His hand moved back to her breast, stroking, circling, light as a feather.

'So when I move out of Treetops, perhaps we could find somewhere together.' His hand stopped.

She had gone too far.

'Perhaps,' he said, his hand resuming its circling again. No yes. No excitement. No commitment.

She should have waited instead of rushing things. She wouldn't mention it again.

He slid his head across the pillow and kissed her until, for an hour or two, her curiosity and her anxiety were appeased.

Amy had been grouchy all day, snapping at both Caro and the delivery man. Even the coffee ladies got the sharp end of her tongue when one of them was nudged by a customer putting on a coat and spilled coffee over a bucket of purple and pink lisianthus.

'Whatever's the matter?' Caro asked a little later. 'Mandy didn't do that on purpose. You shouldn't have bitten her head off.'

Amy looked up from putting in the final sweet peas and silver lace roses into a bunch of alliums, lisianthus, yellow dill and delphiniums. 'I'm sorry. I'll say something to her later.' She held the bunch at arm's length, eyes slightly narrowed as she weighed up the balance of the flowers.

'You've been like a bear with a sore head all day. They're all only doing their jobs as best they can.' To her horror Amy's face crumpled. 'Whatever's wrong?' She went to get a pack of tissues from her bag and handed one to Amy in exchange for the flowers. 'You and Lauren are as bad as each other.'

'It's Jason.' Amy sniffed and blew her nose again.

Caro waited for her to elaborate. She didn't want her generous, scatty, lovely daughter to be let down by a man in the same way Chris had let her down. But he had talked marriage and the last time she had seen them together, they had seemed so happy. Then she remembered Damir. You couldn't put a time on any relationship. Once one half of it decided time was up, there was nothing the other could do. Perhaps asking her if he could marry Amy had made the prospect more real and given him cold feet after all.

Amy disappeared to the back of the shop leaving Caro to serve a customer who had fortunately just come in for an orchid. No arranging required. When Caro had wrapped it and taken the money, Amy was back beside her, looking much more like herself.

'Has something happened?'

Amy nodded, her chin giving a slight wobble. 'I'm moving in with him next week. At last his flatmate's moved out. He's got the flat all ready. He's emptied half his wardrobe and even says I can use the one in the room he uses as an office too.'

'But that sounds great.' Caro was relieved. 'You're not having second thoughts?'

'No! It's not that.'

'Then what?' Caro couldn't bear to see Amy so unhappy. But gone were the days when a kiss, a sticking plaster and a biscuit would fix her daughter's problems.

'He wants us to have a baby.' She made it sound like the worst thing in the world.

Caro put her arm around her as Amy leant against her for support. 'But that's not such a terrible thing, is it?' Although her mind was racing through the few immediate problems she could think of. First of course being Bloom, Amy's pride and joy. Who would look after it? And why was Jason doing things this way round? Was this some weird test of Amy's commitment to him?

'I might want to have kids one day but not now.'

Milo lifted his head, wagged his tail once, then settled back again with a loud groan. Both women laughed.

'Well said, Milo,' said Amy, bending to pat him.

'There's never a right time.' Caro's own fears of losing her job in the TV studios, or at worst of not being able to cope with a baby, returned to her as she remembered getting pregnant for the first time. 'I was nervous too when I was pregnant with Lauren, but things worked out. They usually do.'

'But you gave up your job.'

'Not straight away,' Caro corrected her. 'Not until I'd had you. By then Dad's business was on a steadier footing and I realised how much I wanted to be around you both growing up.'

'But I don't want to do that, and I really don't want to be pregnant.' Amy's voice wobbled. 'I've got too much to do here. The business is just beginning to work and I want it to succeed. And there's so much of me in it – I can't hand it over to someone else for a year. It simply wouldn't be the same. I can't afford to either.'

What wasn't she saying? Caro sensed there was more unsaid. 'Amy, sweetheart... is that the whole story?'

Amy's gaze shifted away from her mother's face before returning. 'I don't want to have a baby at the same time as Dad,' she whispered. 'That would be just so weird.' She snipped the ends of the stalks before beginning to tie the cellophane round them.

Caro waited.

As she tied the raffia, Amy went on. 'You know all that hormone business they talk about? About how women want a baby so much it overwhelms everything else?'

Caro nodded, remembering.

'I don't have that. I'm not longing for a child.' She pulled a couple of ribbons from a drawer and began to knot them round the bouquet. 'Maybe I never will. Lauren's nervous about the twins but she wants them. That's the difference. Do you think I'm unnatural?'

'No, of course not.' She put her arm back round her daughter's shoulders. 'You're just not ready.'

'What if I never am?'

'I suspect you'll change your mind, but if you don't, you'll have Danny and the twins.'

'And what about Jason? He wants a family.'

'Have you talked to him, explained?'

'Sort of. He thinks I'm daft, and that there's never a *right* time. And maybe he's right. But I can't let this chance go. I want to work to make it succeed. Lauren's such a success story as a lawyer, I don't want to let the family down again.'

Amy had always been in Lauren's slipstream, expectations piled high on her because her sister was so successful at everything she tried. Caro put that down as the reason for Amy flunking so many of her exams. If she couldn't do as well, she might as well do spectacularly worse and forge a different furrow altogether. 'I've sometimes wondered if you felt like that.' She rubbed the top of her daughter's arm. 'Listen to me. You aren't letting the side down at all. You're just different. Dad and I don't think about you like that.'

'Other people do though.' She wrapped the string unnecessarily tightly around the bouquet. 'I know it's only a flower shop, but it's mine and I want to show you all I can do it. I've got time to have babies later. If I have them at all. Maybe I won't. But then at least their uncle or aunt will be a little bit older than them. God, I hate that whole idea. Playdates with my dad! Yeuch. I'll leave that to Lauren.' She swept the cuttings onto the floor, grabbed the hose and started filling the bag she'd made round the stems. She switched off the water and looked at Caro. 'But what if he dumps me?'

So that was what was really frightening her.

'If he loves you, he won't. He'll understand it's not the right time for you yet.'

'I really don't want to be in debt to Dad for any longer than I need to be either.'

Caro was shocked. 'In debt? But I thought he *gave* you the money to start Bloom.'

'That's what I thought, too, but he's calling in his dues now he's getting married. Or at least Georgie is. She's the one who mentioned it. Dad couldn't, of course.'

Anger zipped through Caro. 'How dare she? It's absolutely nothing to do with her.' But of course everything to do with Chris had something to do with Georgie. Especially when it came to his bank account, clearly.

'Yeah, well. It's what it is.' Amy had obviously come to terms with the situation. 'So everything's fine except for Jason. There must be something wrong with me. I should be clucking away, building a nest with him.'

Her daughter's sadness delivered a punch to Caro's gut. 'If you're not ready, you're not ready. There's plenty of time. Some women don't get that feeling until they're well into their thirties.' She smiled, remembering the unexpected force with which the desire took her over when it came. 'When it got me, I didn't get pregnant straight away. But when I did, we were ready. Listen, if Jason loves you, he'll wait. Talk to him properly.'

'I'm afraid to. What if he says he doesn't want me to move in after all?' Her eyes were welling up again.

Caro hugged her again, feeling the bones of her shoulder through her cardigan. 'I don't think he will for a moment but, if you're really worried, be so loving and desirable that he can't resist you.'

Amy pulled away, laughing through her tears. 'Yeah! Like that'll make the difference.'

'Sometimes things don't all fall into place when you want them to.'

'Like Lauren and Damir, you mean?'

Caro hadn't meant that but it was true. 'She's agreed to try and that's the best I can ask for. We've at least sorted out what the whole house thing was about. Poor thing's worked herself into

267

a state about having the twins, and the house seemed to be the answer to the problem. Now she sees that was a mistake and is going to line up the help she'll need. We all need to admit the truth to one another, then we can sort stuff out. That's all.' She couldn't admit that talking to Damir wasn't easy any more either. She couldn't begin to admit that maybe, just maybe, her oldest daughter had been right all along. Perhaps they weren't the match she had chosen to believe.

The bell over the door rang as a man and two children came in, clamouring about buying flowers for their mother. The two women broke apart and Amy went to serve them while Caro added water to another pre-arranged bouquet and put it in a bag ready for delivery.

That evening, Caro was in the garden when she heard a car pull into the driveway and the doorbell ring.

Dropping her gardening gloves on the garden table, she went through the house to see who it was. Standing on the doorstep was a well-dressed young man, sharply suited, a flop of reddish hair, clipboard in hand. Behind him were a couple in their late thirties or forties – hard to tell. The man gazed up at the exterior of the house, his attention caught by the burglar alarm, Caro presumed. The woman was half-turned away, looking around her but turned abruptly at the sound of the opening door. Like her husband – they both wore similar wedding rings – she was dressed in jeans but instead of a polo shirt she wore a patterned cotton lawn blouse, not cheap.

'Mrs Prior?'

Caro was puzzled. 'Yes. I'm sorry but am I expecting you?'

The young man gave a nervous laugh. 'Your husband said he'd tell you to expect us.'

'I'm afraid my ex –' she put heavy emphasis on the word ' – husband didn't say a thing.'

He shifted from foot to foot, blushing. 'Ah well . . . I hope this isn't inconvenient but we've...' he turned round to include the other two, 'come to look over the house.'

'To look over,' she repeated. 'And you are?'

'I'm sorry. Jim Parker from Corbett Laing estate agents.' He held out a hand. 'Your husband asked us to pop along and value the property. He said it was urgent.'

Caro noticed his bitten nails as she took the limp handshake. Although the breath had been knocked out of her, she was doing her best to appear composed. Chris hadn't said anything about getting an estate agent. She had assumed he would leave that to her. The couple were exchanging anxious glances.

'The photographer should be round later but Mr and Mrs Bradshaw happened to come in looking for exactly this type of property. I realise bringing them round before the valuation is unorthodox but I phoned your husband and he agreed it was too good an opportunity to miss. After all we valued it a couple of years ago so we have an idea of what we're talking about.' He gave the Bradshaws an ingratiating smile.

'Then you'd better come in.' She held open the door, flabber-gasted that Chris would do this without saying anything. 'Lucky I was here.'

'Oh, I have a set of keys.' Jim Parker pulled them from his pocket and dangled them between them. There was a smell of coffee on his breath.

Caro had to clench her fists to stop her anger with Chris exploding from her. How dare he put her in this position? She left the three of them downstairs in the living room, admiring the garden, *her* garden, with an appreciative Milo. Upstairs, she flung her stray underwear and spare shoes into the laundry basket, stuffed everything out of place in the bathroom cupboard and straightened the towels. She would sort it all out later. As she went back down, preparing herself to appear pleasant, another car pulled up outside. The doorbell. There was only one other person she could think of who would want to be there right then.

Caro steeled herself. If Chris was making sure she hadn't kyboshed his arrangement she would tell him exactly what she thought. And if Jim Parker and his clients overheard – she didn't give a toss. She pulled the door open with as much aggression as she could muster, ready to give him an earful, only to have to take a step back.

'Paul!'

He took a step back too, clearly alarmed by the expression on her face. 'I know you've been away and we haven't been in touch but I've been thinking about you.'

'You have?' She was immediately on the back foot.

He nodded. 'Is this a bad time?'

'It's not the best but how nice to see you.' As she recovered from her initial shock, she realised that in fact it was.

'I finished work early and was passing the end of your road but you're probably busy . . .' He turned to go back to his car.

'No, I'm not,' she said. 'Not really. Come in. The estate agent's here but we can sit in the garden.' She found herself oddly pleased to see him.

'Are you sure? I don't want to be a nuisance.'

'You're anything but.' She pulled the door back to let him in. As he came into the hall, Milo dashed out to greet him. So many people: all his Christmases come at once. In his excitement, he jumped up, almost knocking Paul off balance.

'Milo! Down! Get off him, you lump.' Caro grabbed the dog's collar and yanked him backwards before shoving him into the kitchen. 'I'm so sorry. Are you OK?'

Paul was already circling the wrist that had supported him when he reeled back against the wall. 'Fine. Nothing broken.'

There was the sound of a throat being cleared. Caro had almost forgotten about the Bradshaws who were standing in the doorway of the living room.

'Do carry on,' she said, gesturing the way to the kitchen.

Jim gave an uncertain smile and ushered his clients through

where Caro could hear them oohing and aahing over the range, then Mr Bradshaw's rather too loud suggestion that the back of the house could be extended over part of the garden, followed by Mrs Bradshaw's remark voicing her dislike of dogs being allowed in the kitchen. It was true that Milo's bedding did have a particular smell all of its own but nonetheless Caro was seething inside. She put her head round the door. 'Do be careful. I've just put flea powder all over the dog's bed. I didn't know I'd be having people looking through everything.' How dare they land on her unannounced and then criticise how she lived within her hearing? She took a step inside the kitchen, just to see their faces, her hand on Milo's collar.

'Outside,' said Paul firmly, taking her hand and leading her into the living room.

Caro's surprise at both the physical contact and his sensitivity to the situation meant she allowed herself to be removed from the confrontation zone without question and opened the living room door to the garden.

'Your garden's lovely.' He knew exactly which buttons to press.

'It's looking its best at the moment. I'm sorry about them.' She jerked her head towards the house, feeling she needed to explain. 'I'd no idea they were coming.'

'You're selling up?'

She nodded, surprised by the concern in his voice.

'Where will you go?'

She laughed. 'I don't know yet. My ex has rather sprung this on me.' She was surprised by how pleased she was to see Paul and couldn't help thinking how pleased her family would be if she had introduced him as her lover. What had Fran called him? Affable and solvent. But he would never bring her alive in the same way Damir had.

As if on cue, her phone rang and Damir's name came up. Her heart lurched. Perhaps they would meet tonight after all.

'Where are you?' Just a few words in that gravelly voice made her weak. She watched Paul walk to the end of the garden to give her privacy. He bent down over the pet graves, examining the crosses.

'At home. A friend's just called round and . . .' She was about to tell him about Chris calling in the estate agent but stopped. He didn't need to be dragged any further into her and Chris's mess. The last thing she wanted to do was make him feel she was pressuring him in any way. But the truth was she missed that easy intimacy they had achieved in the few months they had together and longed to put their relationship back on that footing.

At the end of the garden, Paul straightened up, turned and smiled at her.

Caro bent over her phone, as if she could bring Damir closer to her.

'Can we meet tomorrow?' he asked.

Her disappointment hurt. 'Not tonight, then? I haven't seen you for days.' *Don't do this,* she told herself. *Pressure drives people away.* But her desire for him meant she couldn't stop herself.

'I know. I'm sorry. But I have tomorrow afternoon off and we can meet then.'

'You'll come here?'

'Yes. About three?'

'I'll see you then.'

She said goodbye, mystified by what was happening between them. She walked down to join Paul, glancing back at the house to catch sight of Jim Parker and the Bradshaws at her bedroom window. She hated the idea of them poking into her cupboards, stabbing at the window frames, looking for rot, checking the window catches worked, finding fault of any kind. However, perhaps their arrival was a good thing, galvanising her at last. This was going to happen. The house was going to be sold and she had to find somewhere else to live: somewhere she would be happy on her own. *Let go*, she told herself. *Let go*.

26

Eventually Jim Parker and his clients had disappeared to cast a critical eye over someone else's beloved family home, leaving Caro alone with Paul.

'So what's your plan?' he asked, once she had brought out a tray with two glasses and a bottle of rather nice white burgundy that she remembered he liked.

'I honestly haven't a clue. I haven't even started looking. This has been rather sprung on me by my ex. I didn't think he'd move this fast.'

'Then your laptop is your friend. That and Rightmove. Why don't you start now? I could help.'

Why not? She wanted to feel in control of the situation not just subject to Chris's say-so. She brought out her laptop and found the site. In fact, once they started scrolling through properties for sale, she began to enjoy herself, focusing on the fact that she didn't want to move too far from her friends, her studio or from the college. 'And if I retire?'

'Then you can move again . . . to the Caribbean or Hove or anywhere you like.' He changed pages to an international agent, pulling up pictures of blue skies, villas and swimming pools. 'You're free to do whatever you want. Though I hope you won't move too far away.' He looked at her over the top of his specs.

She fixed her gaze on the screen. Fortunately she was saved by her phone. At the sight of Chris's name, her anger returned. 'I have to take this. I'll go inside for a sec.' She didn't want Paul to overhear what she might be about to say.

But Paul seemed quite relaxed, bent over her laptop still scrolling through houses. 'OK.' He didn't look up.

Caro hissed down the phone. 'What the hell are you doing? I thought I was going to handle the sale. After all, I am the one living here. How could you send someone round without warning me? What's the sudden urgency?'

'I'm sure I told you I'd talked to him.' He hadn't. 'But we want to get it on the market well before Christmas.' Someone else was talking in the background.

She could hear that she hadn't got his full attention. 'Chris!'

'I'm sorry. We've got a crisis. You don't want to know.'

'No, I don't.' She stopped. Had she really said that? Yes, and it felt good. 'What I want is to know what you're doing?'

He must have put his hand over his phone but she could hear him talking to someone else. Enraged, she hung up. Why did he always presume his time was more important than hers? She put her phone on silent, left it in the living room and went out to rejoin Paul to find him refilling their glasses.

'I've found something that might be just right.' He turned the laptop so it was facing her.

She angled the screen to see the image more clearly.

'It's in Chilworth, not far away. Change of scene but you don't have to change your friends.'

The house he'd chosen was perfect. Just the sort of place she would have dreamed of, if she'd got as far as that. Just the sort of place she could imagine her and Damir— She must stop that immediately. He'd shown he wasn't ready for that, and she hadn't mentioned it again. But this was a pretty thatched cottage like something out of a children's drawing. The front door at its centre was surrounded by a little porch overgrown with roses, with windows on either side. The front garden needed some TLC but she would have fun planting it up. She flicked through the pictures of another family's bedrooms, but nothing too small and all comfortable looking. Caro could imagine spending evenings in front of the huge inglenook fireplace in the beamed living room. The kitchen was big enough for her table. And the long back garden with a view beyond to wild countryside was a dream. There was even an outbuilding at the side that she could convert into a studio. A seed began to take root in her. 'This is my fantasy cottage,' she said. 'It's got everything. How did you know?'

'It's the sort of thing I'd like if I was starting again. Er...' He hesitated as if he wasn't sure whether he should go on and then decided he would. 'I'll come with you to see it if you like.'

'That's sweet of you but this is a decision I've got to make on my own.' She couldn't wait to show Damir.

Paul was staring at his lap. 'I know. But sometimes having someone to bounce thoughts off helps.' He was trying so hard – too hard? She appreciated that he so clearly had her best interests at heart.

'I'll call them tomorrow.'

Her rebuff had obviously hurt him so she tried to make up. 'Would you like something to eat?'

He brightened. 'I'd love that.'

They ate omelettes and salad in the garden. Caro lit candles and the garden lights as the sun disappeared. She felt herself getting pleasantly tipsy as she listened to Paul talking about the holiday he'd just spent in Cornwall with his kids. 'Gerry was home for a couple of weeks and he persuaded me to try surfing. What a disaster. They were both standing on their boards by the time we left, and begged me to stop going to lessons because it was so humiliating having me there.'

'We loved Cornwall when the girls were small. We'd go most summers, rent a cottage near St Mawes. Chris would take them swimming and crabbing. I took sailing lessons with them but didn't get it at all. When they discovered the fun of capsizing, I gave up for good!'

As they laughed, he reached over and took her hand. Caro pulled it away.

'I'm sorry about what happened before.'

'Don't be,' she said. 'We make better friends.'

'Do we?' A wistful look crossed his face. 'I'd like to try again.'

This was not what she had been expecting. Out of respect for him, she should be honest about her situation, however hard it was for her to say or him to hear.

'I'm sorry but I've met somebody else.' Not that she even knew where the relationship was going or how long it might last.

'Oh.' He jammed both hands between his knees.

'At least I think I have,' Caro said, her voice catching.

Paul looked at her in dismay. 'What have I said? I'm so sorry.' He was rubbing his hands together, pink with embarrassment.

'Nothing at all.' She ran a finger under both eyes as she regained control. 'We've been so close and now he seems to be trying to avoid me. My oldest daughter will barely mention his name. My ex is getting married and having a baby. And I've got to move house. It's a mess.' She sniffed. 'And then you were nice to me.'

'That's all?' He looked astonished, then began to smile. 'And I thought I'd offended you.'

She looked at him as the candles guttered between them, throwing shadows across their faces and, together, they began to laugh. When they finally stopped, she felt as if her cares had been lifted, rearranged and returned weighing far less than they did before.

'I'm glad you've found someone,' said Paul, pulling himself together at last. 'Although I'd have liked it to have been me.'

'It was the wrong time though, wasn't it?' said Caro, touched by his reaction and not wanting to draw any comparisons with Damir that would make him feel wanting.

'Perhaps. Friends again, then?'

'Friends,' said Caro, pleased he'd taken it so well. 'I'm seeing Damir tomorrow, so perhaps things will be clearer then.' She shivered as the night breeze caught her shoulders.

'Damir?' He frowned at the unfamiliar name.

'Bosnian.' She didn't want to explain any more than that, remembering Damir's displeasure after Paul had brought her bracelet back.

'I hope he says what you want to hear,' he said, getting up and taking his jacket off the back of the chair, obviously realising they had met.

'Me too.' Standing up, Caro realised she was more drunk than she'd thought. She staggered as they crossed the threshold of the living room. He put out an arm to steady her and somehow, despite everything, his arms were around her. 'Thanks,' she said, waiting for her head to clear but enjoying the feeling of being in someone's arms again. Then came a moment of sharp realisation. What on earth was she doing? Suppose Damir walked in and found her? That would mark the end of everything.

She extricated herself from Paul's embrace, aware of the disappointment in his expression.

'I've had too much to drink. I'm sorry.'

'I'm sorry too. But I get it.' He shrugged off the second rejection of the night. 'That's one all! Do you think we could have a cup of coffee instead and then I'll get a cab home? I'll have to come back tomorrow morning for the car.'

The next morning was grey and muggy. Caro felt as if her brain had been harvested and left to crack open under a harsh summer sun. At least it was still the college holidays so she didn't have an early start. When she eventually got up, she looked out of the window to see that Paul's car had gone. She was glad that he had been thoughtful enough not to disturb her.

She groped her way towards a shower and breakfast, then drove to the studio and prepared a couple of new canvases, stretching the fabric over each frame and pinning it in place. She sized them and painted them with gesso but she didn't have the heart or the head to do anything more, leaving her half-made paintings untouched. She considered the unfinished commission of the baby. She was pleased by the way she'd caught its quizzical expression – like a wise old man. Almost finished, just a little finessing of the background and it would be ready for its father's birthday. Then she made an appointment to see the house they had found the previous evening as well as a couple of others recommended by the same agent. She was well aware that no one could expect to find their forever home first time round. The cottage must have its own drawbacks disguised by clever photography. She would have to see others and be patient. Take a leaf from everything she'd said to Lauren. Afterwards, she called Jim Parker at Corbett Laing to make it very clear that on no account was he to bring anyone to the house without giving her due warning and certainly not before they'd accepted his completed valuation.

'And Mr Parker,' she finished off. 'It goes without saying that if you receive any offer for the house, you must tell me as well as my husband. You do understand that? It's of equal importance to both of us.'

At the other end of the phone, she heard an intake of breath. 'Of course.' He paused, and there was a rustle of paper. 'In which case, you should know that the Bradshaws won't be offering. They've found somewhere with the modern kitchen they were after and that needs less work on the secondary bedrooms.'

Not sure that she liked the satisfaction she heard in his voice, Caro terminated the conversation and hung up.

Before she had a chance to do anything more than make more coffee, the phone rang. This time it was Amy.

'I told him everything, Mum. Just like you said.'

Caro arranged her jars of paint brushes in front of her, hoping her advice hadn't been a mistake. 'And?'

'I made the effort and left the shop on time so we could have a long talk last night, and he was brilliant. He said he was proud of me for being so committed to Bloom and so determined to make it work. And he's happy to wait until I'm ready to have babies, but if I don't, he'd rather have me without them than not have me at all. He's so lovely. The only condition is that I've got to get home early at least two nights a week, and save one day a weekend just for him.'

'Can you do that?' Caro was smiling at her daughter's excitement.

'I've promised to try, but I did say there might be busy times of year when I just can't. And I did point out that there are times when he's super busy too, so we've agreed to do our very best.'

The knot of anxiety in Caro's stomach untangled itself. 'So everything's going ahead as planned?'

'Yes. I'm going to start packing up on Sunday, and Jason's going to borrow the van and drive it over for me.'

The urge to say 'Can I help?' almost got the better of her. But this was Amy's life, not hers. She should take one step back. She said instead, 'Good luck, my love. I'll be thinking of you.'

'Thanks, Mum. And – one more thing. I've saved the best for last – you'd better go hat-shopping because he's asked me to marry him!' Her excitement was infectious. 'And I said yes!'

Caro wanted to shout with joy. 'That's fantastic. I'm so, so thrilled.' She caught her breath. 'Is there a deadline for the hat?'

The rest of the conversation was when, where and what sort of celebration. When she put down the phone, Caro's elation was sky high.

So Jason had proposed at last, settling for a marriage that would allow them both space to follow their own dreams. Caro's happiness and pride in both her daughters was overwhelming. All differences aside, they had become young women who were capable of making their own way through life, with their own dreams and aspirations. If nothing else, Chris and she had somehow managed something right. Whatever happened to her, whatever their disagreements, she would always have Lauren and Amy and belong right at the heart of her expanding family.

Too excited by Amy's news and the prospect of seeing Damir,

Caro couldn't pretend to work any more so went home and, after lunch, changed out of her working jeans and shirt. She chose a dress that he'd once complimented her on, pairing it with some red espadrilles – casual but an effort made. She stuck to her usual minimal make-up, wishing she had Fran's nerve to wear poppy red lipstick during the day. As she got ready she couldn't get rid of an unsettling underlying nervousness, by this time having convinced herself that Damir was about to call time on their relationship. Despite everything he had said to her, he must have met someone else. She couldn't think of another way to explain his absences. Unless he was just running shy. Something had definitely changed things between them and she was determined to find out what.

At ten past three, Damir's van turned into her drive. She was on the doorstep as he turned off the ignition and walking towards him as he got out of the car. To her relief, the kiss they exchanged on meeting was as tender and intense as any they had shared. It made her realise once again that being with him was all she wanted. The present was what was important.

'Come in.' She led him into the house, not letting go of his hand.

Once inside, he took over the leading and they went straight upstairs to her bedroom. Caro's easy happiness made her concerns about him retreat to the back of her mind. They tumbled onto the bed, slowly undressing one another, kissing, touching, loving. She gave herself up to the sensations that thrummed through her until at last it was over and they lay side by side, slick with sweat, in a state of bliss, fingers just touching.

Eventually, Caro rolled onto her side and hoisted herself onto an elbow, running her finger along the scar on his arm. The dip of the scar was as wide as the finger she ran down it. 'Can't you tell me what's worrying you?'

He turned his head so their eyes met.

In his she saw a muddle of anxiety, sadness and desire. 'I

thought we were happy together but something's happened. I know it has,' she said.

He grasped her hand. 'Something has happened.'

She tensed. 'Can't you tell me?'

Shaking his head, he drew his lips together as he thought. 'No. It's too –' he sought the right word, looking at the ceiling as if he would find it there '– complicated.'

Caro's insides went into freefall. 'But we've shared so much. Wouldn't talking about it help?'

'I don't think so.'

His secrecy frustrated her almost beyond words. 'But then why have you come here?'

'To see you of course.' He drew her into his arms. 'And to tell you that I have to go away.'

She pulled away from him. 'Away!' This was what she had feared. 'Where to?'

'Home.' His face was full of sadness. 'There's something I have to do. I need my cash box.'

'But why?' What wasn't he telling her? What did he mean by home? Bosnia? Surely not. Having read about vendettas that continued to this day thanks to the divisions caused by the war, she was too frightened to ask if this was unfinished business. But removing the box from her safekeeping felt like a statement. As long as it was there, she could be sure he would come back. But now...

'I'm sorry, but I must go. I can't explain.'

'But...'

He stopped her from going on with a finger over her lips. But what about all the promises they had made each other, the openness they had shared. 'At the moment, I'm not the man you want.'

'Of course you are.' She was stunned that he would even say this. How could she persuade him otherwise?

'It's all too complicated.' How world weary he sounded.

'When are you going?' Her voice was small, controlled, cross, unhappy. She had pushed him too hard, driven him from her. It was her fault.

'Tomorrow.'

'Tomorrow,' she repeated in a whisper. It was like a hammer blow, hitting so hard Caro could only gasp as he held her tighter. 'When will you be back?'

'I don't know.' His hand ran down her back, his fingers following her spine. 'I have some things to sort out. And I don't know how long it will take.'

'But your work...' *And me*, she longed to say. *What about me?*

'This is more important.'

'Why can't you explain?' But why should he when she had not shared everything with him? She had to allow him his reasons too.

He pulled back from her, his face just visible in the dark. 'Remember how you wanted you and me to be a secret? This is the same.'

Caro moved towards him so her head was against his chest listening to his heart beat, her leg lying over his, her body tight against him. She had to keep calm. This was what she had always known would happen. But inside her, as the shock of his departure resonated, an inner voice was screaming, *No! Stay here with me. I never dreamed of finding someone like you.* But she knew that was the one thing she couldn't say. Not now. If ever.

27

Fran helped them both to spoonfuls of blackcurrant sorbet – 'Si made it from the ones he's grown on the allotment' – before pouring a generous shot of vodka over each. ('For the shock, darling.') They were sitting in her kitchen, having carved out a small area on the table for themselves by shunting all the junk mail and newspapers to one side. The irony of how their roles had reversed was not lost on Caro.

'I should bin them, but I need to go through them first just in case there's something in one of them that I can't live without. Like this for instance.' Fran pointed at a bright aquamarine silk camisole and earmarked the page before straightening the pile. Above their heads, the clock ticked, the second hand moving towards each new minute with a little shiver. 'So what now?'

Caro tried to spoon up the vodka with a mouthful of sorbet. Her taste buds froze in pleasure. After a minute she said, 'I don't know. Maybe Lauren was right and trusting him was the biggest mistake of my life.'

'Rubbish. Look at you. Where's the woman who let everyone take her for granted? She's gone. Look at you! You look great, you've taken charge of your life and you've discovered sex isn't just the preserve of the young.'

Caro felt herself blushing. 'I guess that's all true.'

'And you've had a great summer.'

'That's true too. I didn't really believe it would last – too good to be true – so perhaps I should just be grateful.' *But I hoped.*

I did hope. The pain of his absence was almost unbearable. She couldn't imagine how she would ever recover.

'Not grateful. You deserved it.'

'I should never have suggested we live together when I move. He backed off when I did. I should have just let things drift for a while but instead I've pushed him away by being too keen. It's over.'

'How can you be so sure?'

Caro shook her head, miserable. 'He wouldn't explain. I don't even know where he's gone. Until now, we've talked about almost anything. But not this. Either he felt trapped by me or he's got someone else. Someone younger.' She gave a resigned sigh, ignoring Fran's muttered objection. 'And he's taken his cash box with him. Why not leave the box and take the cash if he was planning to come back?'

'Because he wants it wherever he's gone?' Fran was desperate for a solution too. She threw up her hands. 'I don't know. But I've seen him with you – he didn't look as if he was about to do a runner. He obviously adores you.'

A glimmer of hope found the chink in Caro's heart. But it was soon extinguished. Damir wouldn't just leave her without a word if he were coming back. What they had must have meant more to him than that. 'But I've tried phoning and texting – nothing. Why would he cut himself off if it weren't over?' She took another spoonful of sorbet. 'How could he leave without a word of explanation after all we've been through? After we came back from France, he changed. It was fine at first but then he was more distant, as if the whole thing had got too much for him. Lauren didn't help, and that whole thing with the photos. But I'm sure there was more than that. When we were together, the sex was as good as ever but otherwise he was distracted and refused to talk. He loved me for a while – in his way – I'm sure of that. But he's scared of giving himself one hundred per cent to anyone. He told me. So he cuts and runs. That's what he does, although I tell myself to have faith.'

'Oh, faith.' Fran rolled her eyes to the ceiling. 'I had that in bucketfuls.'

Caro's spoon clattered against the bowl. 'I know you did. I'm sorry.'

'I'm over it although every now and then I do still get a pang... I don't think you ever forget that intensity of emotion. I'll never have it with Si. Don't look like that! I'm not about to go back on my word.' She waved her hand in the air. 'Nope. I'm sticking with him. We may not have the most exciting sex life but we do love each other. Will's accident made me realise how incredibly important my family is to me. Sometimes it takes something as drastic as that. You were right. I'm not going to throw everything up for some mid-life crisis affair that flatters my ego. I'm done with that. As for Damir: whatever's taken him away must be important. I don't believe he'd just run off. He's more of a man than that. Though why he hasn't explained...' She scratched her head and smiled. 'Perhaps he's a conman after all? Perhaps Lauren was right!'

Caro laughed. 'A spy, even. Whatever he is, I've decided I'm going to take on old age alone. I don't think I could bear being dumped again. Chris leaving was bad enough but this is so much worse.' This was the kind of emotional agony where there was no let up. Damir still occupied her every thought, stopping her wanting to do anything, even eat. It was only a supreme act of will that got her out of the house, trying to pretend nothing was wrong, keeping on going.

'Don't even go there. We'll age disgracefully together if at all.' Fran kicked up her leopard-print kitten heels just to show the spirit. 'Simon will just have to put up with us both.'

Caro managed a smile. 'Poor man. But I can't keep mooching about feeling sorry for myself. I need somewhere to live. I thought the property market was meant to be slow but this estate agent Chris found has brought several around already. I need to be prepared so will you come and see this house with me this weekend?'

'Why buy? Rent if everything's so up in the air.'

'I want to put my share of the equity into bricks and mortar so the girls have some sort of inheritance. I can at least do that for them – unless we spend it on my care home, of course.' She thought of May, glad that day hadn't come for her yet and that she hadn't forced her into it. 'Anyway, I'd like somewhere that's mine, so I've got it whatever happens. Home sweet home and all that.' She could imagine herself alone in her own space, coming to terms with what had happened to her that summer and with how much it had meant to her. One glorious last fling. 'And this one looks perfect. It's even got a potential studio in the garden.'

'You can't buy the first one you see. That's mad.'

'Why not? If it's the right one...'

Fran piled up the plates and took them over to the side. 'OK. I'll be there. If nothing else, you've got me to make sure you don't do anything crazy. Coffee?'

As soon as Caro walked through the front door, she knew the cottage was everything she had hoped for. The reasonable asking price reflected the need for redecoration but she could see exactly what she could do to turn it into her dream home. To her embarrassment, Fran went round poking at suspicious window frames – 'This needs replacing' – lifting up carpets – 'You could have the floors sanded' – inspecting the bedrooms – 'The mirrored cupboards are sooo past their sell-by' – and the bathroom – 'A new bath would be nice'. In short she was exactly the sort of buyer Caro resented or loathed when they came to Treetops. Any time she nudged her or gave her a look intended to shut her up, Fran just carried on undeterred, criticising whatever she thought deserved it.

'I'm sorry,' Caro said to the owner as they were shown into the back garden.

He moved his bulk to let them past, flexing a tattooed arm. On his bicep was a red heart with Gran scribbled through it.

'That's all right, love. It ain't my house. It's Gran's. She's gone into a home. That's why we want a quick sale.'

Fran gave her an irritating 'you see' sort of look and plunged off down the wild-looking garden. 'My kind of garden,' she said, disappearing behind a jutting out fence towards its end.

The man shrugged. 'It was beautiful when she could get out to look after it. I've done my best but I only get over here every now and then.'

Despite it being so untended, Caro saw a potential haven in front of her. She could immediately see the shrubs that needed attention, the intruders that needed weeding out and the herbaceous flowers to be encouraged. Her fingers itched to get going on it. To the left of the house was the perfect spot for a pergola. Further down on the right, was a spot sheltered by a laburnum next door that would provide another seating area. She was already working out how she could have a raised vegetable patch at the end, when Fran reappeared.

'Come and look at this.'

Picking her way up the overgrown herring-bone brick path, Caro caught up with her. Behind the fence was a garden shed, a compost heap and a small greenhouse.

'What do you think?' Fran's whispers were only ever suited to the stage.

Caro glanced behind her to see that the man had lost interest and returned inside. 'The garden's done it for me. South facing. I love it. Plenty of room for the grandchildren. I could even have a sandpit!'

'And you'd only be a short drive away. I could cope with that.'

'And I won't have Chris breathing down my neck about what I have or haven't done. This would be mine to do exactly what I want with.'

'And I thought you'd never give up Treetops. You were so rooted there.' They both grinned at the pun.

'Yeah, but things have changed. If there's one thing I've learned, it's never say never.'

'What about your studio?' Fran knew how much she loved that space.

'I'm going to do up that outbuilding by the house. It'll be perfect and so much easier than having to drive to the one I've got now. Just the set-up for a lady artist living on her own.'

Sceptical, Fran raised an eyebrow. 'Won't you be lonely?'

Caro smiled at her. 'There are worse things than loneliness.'

'No word from Damir I take it?'

'One text sent very late on Thursday night saying, "I'm sorry".' The memory made the ball of nausea that perpetually sat like a stone in her gut roll up towards her throat. How could he? Silence was preferable. She swallowed, angry that her emotions could hi-jack her when she least expected it. She hated being out of control like this, feeling as if each of her nerves were warring against one another. The previous day, she had to walk out of her art class when the model took up a new position that reminded her of Damir on the bed in France. The day before that, she had left the supermarket, reminded of the times they had shopped there together. His leaving, the mystery surrounding it, and the fact he hadn't been in touch properly since, had shredded her into pieces that she couldn't put together again. She had completely misjudged him. And that hurt.

'Come on.' Fran spoke gently as if she understood something of Caro's torment. 'I still sometimes think of Ewan, you know. When you've invested so much in someone, it's hard to let go. I do know what you're going through but I survived and you will too.'

Caro pulled at a piece of unruly honeysuckle that crossed their path. 'What annoys me is that I let myself get taken in. Everyone else saw what I didn't. I would never have believed that he'd do this. At least not this way.' She submitted herself to Fran's warm but silent hug.

They walked back to the house together. Fran was right. Of

course Caro would survive but her future would not be the same as Fran's. She had no Simon to catch her when she fell. Instead, she would have to pick herself up, dust herself off and start all over again. Again. Right at that moment, with her faith in her fellow man so dented, that seemed like a huge mountain to climb.

'The offer's under the asking price but I think we should take it.' Chris had adopted the brook-no-nonsense voice that he always did when he spoke to Caro these days. Though why he bothered when she hadn't put up any objections to his requests so far, she didn't know. 'Parker's done a good job, finding a buyer so quickly.'

'I suppose we should.' The sadness Caro thought she would feel when the time came to leave Treetops had been overtaken by her anticipation of moving into her new home. A new start. That's what she was going to have. She had heard nothing more from Damir. She had to accept the way things were. Their six months were over. She had torn the pages from the calendar the day before and put them in the recycling before rescuing them with a pang. But today she had put them in the fireplace, put a match to them and watched them go up in flames. Over.

Chris ran a hand over the kitchen table. 'I suppose you want this.'

A flash of Damir and her making love on the table top passed through her mind. She took hold of the back of a chair to steady herself. 'Yes, I would like it, but I don't want us to fight. Why don't you make a list of the things you want and if there's any-thing I feel strongly about I'll say.' In fact, the idea of him and Georgie eating off the table on which she had so enjoyed herself gave her a rather perverse sense of pleasure. What was the point in squabbling over what was only cargo, after all?

'I thought the nursing chair in the bedroom that came from my mother's might be useful for Georgie when the baby comes.'

Caro stared at him. Was he rubbing her nose in the fact of his new family deliberately? She decided not. He was so caught up in the adventure of his own new life that he didn't think. It was as if their shared history had been eradicated.

'No second thoughts then?'

He looked surprised that she would even ask the question. 'None at all. Did I tell you that it's a boy?'

A boy. The one thing she hadn't been able to give him. The one thing he had always wanted. A son.

'No. You must be pleased.'

His expression said it all. 'You know I always rather wanted a football team.'

'You've left it a bit late for that.' She refused to show how much she was hurting.

He laughed. 'I think we'll stop at one. Imagine. Me a father again at this age.'

She heard his underlying pride.

'We had good times though, didn't we?' Was he reassuring himself, or asking her?

'We did,' she agreed. 'When the girls were growing up.' And for the first time since he left, Caro felt a sense of resolution. This huge section of her life was over. She had detached herself at last. She felt nothing for Chris any more – not love, not hate, not jealousy, not even envy.

'And we'll always have the girls.'

'And the grandchildren.'

'And the grandchildren,' he repeated, shaking his head. 'My God. I never imagined I'd be having another child at the same time as Lauren was having one.'

'Nor did I.' But she was able to say this with a wry smile. 'At least you're not having twins.'

'Have you made up yet?'

'Superficially but not entirely.' She couldn't bear to tell either of them about Damir's disappearance just to receive another look that said I told-you-so.

'You will. Remember when we wouldn't let her go on that holiday?'

'When she said Ellie Farmer's parents were taking her and Tess to Spain and we discovered they were planning on going alone?'

'And Ellie's parents thought we had invited Ellie to do the same thing? If you hadn't been introduced to them at the school summer fair we might never have known. I'm amazed they thought they'd ever get away with it. But they were only fifteen. And even then Lauren could persuade anyone to believe whatever she wanted them to. She was furious.' Chris's face lit up with the smile she hadn't seen for so long.

'She didn't speak to us for the whole summer.' She was smiling too.

'Spent it sulking in her room. What a waste.'

And suddenly they were laughing at the memory. Together.

'You even tried to get her to learn to play golf with you.'

'No, I didn't. Really?'

'You did. I remember quite clearly. I thought she'd hit you with a club. All she wanted was to be with her friends, not us.'

'But we were right to stop her, weren't we?'

'Definitely.'

'She came round in the end. She always does when it comes to family. Be patient.'

Chris was the only person she could have this conversation with; the only person who shared these priceless memories. He was the only one who understood their girls in the same way, who cared about them as much as she did and who was interested in their futures. They might have different ways of showing their love but it would always be there, binding them. Perhaps they were adapting to a new way of being together at last.

'We didn't make such a bad fist of things, did we? I'm really proud of them.'

'Me too.' This shared pride was something that would always be there. 'And you're about to go through it all again.'

Immediately she could see she had made a mistake. His eyes narrowed as, defensive, he weighed up whether or not she was having a dig at him. He decided not.

'It'll be different this time. Georgie's been offered a big part in a West End show that'll premiere next year. She's going to go into rehearsal only months after she's had the baby.'

'Rather her than me.' Those early months with her babies had been so precious to Caro, she couldn't have imagined leaving them so soon, although she was well aware that plenty of women did.

'I know, but she's very ambitious.' Chris sounded as proud of her as he sometimes did of his daughters. 'I don't want to stand in her way, so I've decided to pull back a bit, not retire exactly but be around more to look after the baby.'

'But you love your job,' Caro protested, unable to imagine him giving himself up to fulltime childcare.

'I love the company,' he corrected her. 'And you know what? I want to be a better father this time. Work's less important to me now. And I have great people there who don't need me all the time.'

'I wish you'd felt like that when the girls were born.' Caro was suddenly furious. Why should this baby get what their girls didn't? Where was this caring soul, happy to delegate, back then? 'You were barely there for the first few years of their lives and not much better after that.'

'Don't be angry. In a way I wish I had too but setting up the company meant that you could be at home, which was where you wanted to be. I had no choice. And I should admit . . .' He held up his hand is if dealing with a heckler. 'I didn't want one then. I loved bringing it all together, making it work, but I thought you wanted that too.' He sounded confused.

She inclined her head, conceding to his version of events. 'I did. And now?'

'I'm nervous.' He looked away from her. 'What if I'm too old to be a father again?'

She was taken aback by him confiding his anxiety in her. 'It's a bit late to worry about that but I'm sure you'll be fine. The basics will all come flooding back. It's not as if you haven't changed the odd nappy. You weren't completely absent.' At that moment, she realised that she didn't envy him one bit. The sleepless nights. The tantrums. The exhaustion. The anxiety. Having children of her own was part of her history. Now she was a grandmother, she could enjoy the good bits and hand the children back, at the same time enjoying being at the centre of things where she belonged.

'Anyway, this isn't why I came round.' Always quick to hide anything that might be perceived as a weakness, he had switched back into business mode. 'So we're agreed we should accept the offer?'

'Shouldn't we try and push the price up a bit? Ask Jim if there's anyone else wanting to see it.'

'Good Lord.' Chris raised an eyebrow. 'We'll make a business woman of you yet.'

'We both need funds given we're buying again,' she pointed out. 'And don't be so bloody patronising.'

He considered her, surprised, thumb and forefinger rubbing his chin. 'True. All right. I'll tell him.'

'I can do that.' And what pleasure it would give her to keep the man on his toes.

When he stood up to go, she saw not her ex-husband, but a middle-aged man who was fighting off his years in all the ways he knew how. He hadn't asked about Damir once. He wasn't interested in what didn't touch him. 'I'll call you.'

This was the best meeting she could remember having with Chris since he'd left her. Both of them were moving into new phases in their lives, so different from those they were leaving behind. Caro was grateful, wondering whether she was as changed as he was.

28

Caro was poring over her old family photographs. Now Treetops had a buyer she meant to make a start on the big clear
out, going through the years of accumulated family belongings.
She didn't know who was buying, having decided she'd rather not
know the family that would be starting their life here, replicating
everything that Caro and her family had done over the years.
That would be too painful.

Instead, she was concentrating on moving into her new home.
Her offer had been accepted and the whole thing was going
through far more quickly than she had expected. At last she had
something immediate to take her mind off Damir and the fact a
month had passed since his one and only text. She had rung and
texted him, but her attempts had gone unanswered. In the depths
of the night when she sat up unable to sleep, she had persuaded
herself that that was all it would take. A text from her to remind
him what he was throwing away. It was almost impossible to
believe the man who had been so considerate and loving could
be so cruel. Some mornings, she could barely rouse herself, she
was so mired in grief. She had to force herself to focus on what
was happening in the present, pushing her heartache away.

Beginning in the attic, she had lugged down all the boxes that
had been up there for years and then got hi-jacked by the photo
albums. One by one, she had taken them out of the boxes and
lost herself in her family. There were old pictures from her own
childhood: blowy walks along Camber Sands with her parents;
a couple of her and her best friend Roma digging sandcastles

and damns; crabbing in Cornwall; the pony she had begged to be allowed to ride at weekends – all so long ago. Then her own family times when she, Chris, Lauren and Amy had made such a happy young family. Tens of dozens of pictures of Lauren and Amy as babies, toddlers and growing up; of her and Chris looking like people she barely recognised. Babies in Moses baskets. Sitting up for the first time. Gappy grins with missing teeth. First days at school. Family pets. School plays. Every milestone had been recorded on fading celluloid. What she saw was everything that had made her into the person she was today.

She had just opened a new album, the one that showed them on their first camping holiday in France, when she heard the front door open and shut.

'Amy? I'm up here. I've got all the old albums out. Come and see.'

She heard footsteps on the stairs as she flicked through the pictures of them setting off in Bessie, their first family car. It had taken them as far as the outskirts of Calais before they had a puncture. They had to empty the boot on the side of the road to get out the jack and the spare tyre. A snap of Chris, red-faced as he worked to loosen the wheel-nuts. Another of Lauren and Amy sitting on the back seat, kept happy with the picnic they had planned to eat in some idyllic rural setting, not by the side of a busy road. One of her loading their camping equipment back into the car, laughing.

The door pushed open.

'Look at you.' She was looking at a picture of Amy, wild curls in the wind, stroking the nose of a huge carthorse with its head bent over a five-bar gate. And there was their tent, that bloody thing Chris had insisted on buying that was so complicated to put up but that Amy insisted on having up in the garden for sleepovers.

'It's me.' Not Amy, but a voice she recognised straight away.

Caro stopped dead. 'Damir?' Her voice was barely a whisper as she swung round to check, the album snapping shut and falling to the floor.

There he stood, none other, looking down at her. 'I've still got my key,' he said, holding it out to her.

'But...' She stopped, incapable of speech, flushed with astonishment and happiness, taking in the features that she had come to know so well, and to believe she would never see again.

He knelt down beside her. 'I'm back.'

She lifted her hand to the scar on his cheek. 'What...?' But the words wouldn't come. He was kissing her and she was losing herself again, as she felt the familiar softness of his lips, the thrum of missed pleasure through her body. But then she pulled away, angry, furious that he thought he could just walk in and out of her life when he felt like it without considering her or what she might be feeling. 'What are you doing here? Why didn't you let me know you were coming? I thought you were never coming back.'

'I had to come back.'

'But you haven't rung me. You sent me one message, apologising. Then nothing. What was I meant to make of that?' For the first time, she noticed the new shadows under his eyes, the tiredness that emanated from him.

'I'm sorry.' He reached for her hand. 'It's a long story.'

'Well, I've got time.' Anger that he felt he could take up as if he had never left competed with her pleasure at seeing him and her desire for him. She stood up, pulling him to his feet. 'You can't just come back as if nothing's happened. One phone call – that would have been enough.'

His face said everything. He knew exactly how much he had hurt her.

'Let's go downstairs.' She led the way, not knowing how to be with him.

Sitting at the kitchen table, a pot of tea between them, she noticed small changes in him. He had lost weight, his face was drawn, the scar on his cheek more livid than before. She reached out for his hand. 'I can't believe you're here. I thought I'd never see you again.'

He lifted her hand to his lips. 'I wouldn't leave you.'

'But you did!' He flinched as she raised her voice. That gave her small pleasure. 'Have you any idea what it's been like? You can't imagine what I've been going through. Why didn't you even let me know you were all right? You just walked out with no explanation. You can't expect me to welcome you with open arms.' She paused. But what of him? What had happened to him? She remembered the taste of Fran's blackcurrant sorbet on her tongue and her dip of faith... *I should have known.*

'I'm sorry. I should have contacted you again but I couldn't speak to anyone.' He kissed the tips of two of her fingers. 'Not even you.' Two more. 'I should have texted but didn't know what to say. It was all too difficult. So I've come back to explain.'

'Only if you want to.' Despite everything, she found herself gripping his hand hard. This time she was not going to let go. Perhaps she didn't need his explanations. The fact he was there was enough. But the seriousness of his expression stopped her from saying more.

'I want to. I couldn't tell you before because I had to know it was true. I went to Germany to find my daughter.' He shut his eyes as if he was seeing her in his imagination, as if he couldn't quite believe what he was saying.

'Your daughter? But you never said...'

'I didn't know.' His eyes opened and looked unwavering into hers. 'Let me tell you. When we got back from France a girl contacted me saying she was my daughter.'

'But who was she?'

He smiled at her impatience. 'A girl in Germany. She told me her mother was Krista, my ex-wife.'

Caro thought her breath would stop.

'I didn't know whether to believe her, but she said things that only someone who knew Krista well would know. She knew the place where we lived together in Munich. She told me about Krista making a new life with her boyfriend. She knew a lot but none of it meant she was my daughter. I wanted it to be true.'

Caro sat quite still, a lump in her throat. Of course he wanted it to be true: even just one family member to replace all those he had lost during the war, to give new meaning to his life and hope for the future. Of course. After all, where were any of them without family?

'How did she find you?'

'Thanks to Krista, she found one of my friends who brought me to Germany in the first place. He knew I'd gone to Birmingham then London and gave her Esad's number. And then she found me.' A smile stole across his face. 'It's not hard to find someone these days, unless they want to be hidden.'

'But why didn't you tell me? I could have helped you.' She would have done anything she could towards proving the identity of this girl.

He ran his thumb back and forth over her knuckles before he spoke. 'I couldn't. If she wasn't who she said she was, that would have killed me. I so badly wanted her to be my daughter. It's all I could think about. What if she was? What if she wasn't? And I was worried you would think I was a fool for believing her.'

'I'd never have thought that.' She caught his fingers with hers.

'I didn't know what to do. Just hearing what she had to say about her mother and Ernst, the man she grew up believing was her father, brought so many bad memories back to me. I told you how hard it was to make a new start. I was not fighting in the war any more, but the war wouldn't let me go. It stayed in my head for years, not allowing anything else in with it. Krista did her best but she didn't know how to reach me. And I could not reach myself. I trusted no one in case they were taken away and I could not give Krista or any wife what they needed. But

298

gradually scars, even of the mind, heal and become less painful. It can take years.'

This time Caro didn't say anything.

'This girl knew Krista. Everything she said about her convinced me that she knew her, if nothing more.'

'But why would someone pretend to be your daughter?'

'Indeed. I have nothing to offer them.' He hung his head.

She gathered her wits. 'Aren't you forgetting something important?'

He shrugged.

'You can love her. Money isn't everything.' She squeezed his hand. 'Listen to me, Damir.'

His eyes brightened. 'You always have the right answer.'

'I don't know about that. Look at the mess I made with Lauren.'

He looked puzzled. 'That still goes on?'

She raised her eyebrows. 'No, we've just about sorted it out, but first I want to hear about you. Go on.' She poured them both more tea.

He drew himself up straight and continued. 'So this is the story Sophie told me.'

Caro gasped when he said her name at last.

'She's a beautiful girl, dark like me – not like her mother at all.' She could see how happy that made him.

'That's important. So . . . Krista was ill, lying on the sofa, and asked Sophie to get something from her bedroom. She looked in the wrong drawer first and found a box hidden at the back. She couldn't resist opening it and found two photos – old and fading like some of yours upstairs – of Krista and me. She had kept them.'

'So Krista did still love you.' Caro let go her breath.

'No, not that. Just as a memory. Sophie took them to her mother and asked who the man was in the picture. At first Krista insisted I was just a friend. But Sophie noticed her wedding ring in the picture and, more importantly that she and I looked so alike.' He paused, his eyes alight. 'Can you believe this story?'

'I can.' Caro thought of the photos of her own past that she wouldn't want to let go, just to keep that connection.

'Neither Krista nor Ernst are dark haired and they have fairer skin.' He held his arm out. 'Sophie wanted to know more about me and in the end Krista broke down.'

'But what did she say? Why didn't you know Sophie existed?'

'Be patient. You will learn everything. When Ernst came home, Sophie showed him the pictures, showing him how alike we were. He was suspicious too although, God knows, he didn't want to be. He had brought Sophie up believing he was her father. It was him who insisted they took a DNA test. That confirmed Ernst was not her father after all.'

'Poor man. He must have been devastated.' Caro wondered why Krista hadn't come clean in the first place. Could she have been so frightened of what Damir would do if he found out? 'And then?'

'After that, Krista had no choice. She had to tell them about me, about our short marriage and about how after she left me, she discovered she was pregnant. She wanted to believe that the baby was Ernst's and that's why she couldn't ever tell me. She thought if I knew there was a chance the baby was mine I would come after her – and I would have. But perhaps she was right. Perhaps I was not fit to be a father then. They were better off with someone else. She wanted the best for herself and for the baby. And she would not get that with me when I was having trouble looking after myself. When Sophie told me all this, I didn't know what to believe. It sounded as if it could be true but I had to know for myself before I could tell anyone. Even you.'

'And that's why you went away.'

'Yes. I went to Hamburg. To Krista. To find the truth.'

'You found her?' Caro's heart was hammering in her chest. She could never have dreamed up such an explanation for his absence but was beginning to understand why he had wanted to keep the reason for it to himself until he knew for certain.

'That wasn't an issue because of course Sophie told me where she was. I worried that this might all be a complicated con, dreamed up by the three of them for some reason. But why would Krista want to trick me so many years later when I have nothing to give her? My small savings wouldn't go far but of course she didn't know that. First, I spoke to her on the phone. She was crying and apologising so much, I could hardly understand what she was saying. But it all sounded possible. I wanted to believe her but at the same time I didn't. If she was telling the truth, I had missed all these years of Sophie growing up. I would have a daughter who I didn't know in the way fathers should know their daughters: in the way I would want to know her. Krista said she had been frightened of me, of what I might do . . .' He stopped, sounding ashamed.

Frightened of this kindest of men. To think the man Caro knew, who was sitting in front of her, was the same person Krista had once known: a man so traumatised by war that he couldn't control his mood swings or forge a trusting relationship with someone else. Perhaps Krista had been lucky to have Ernst to extricate her. How much Damir must have changed after mastering his experiences and coming to terms with such terrible personal loss.

'But perhaps she could tell by my voice that I'm not that man any more. She agreed that I should come to Hamburg to see her. To say everything that had to be said cannot be done over the phone. I would do another DNA test there to prove Sophie was mine.'

'If only you'd told me. You wouldn't have had to go through all this on your own.' She couldn't bear to think of him having to go through this with no one to confide in or to support him. She could have helped him, listened, comforted, reassured when it was too hard to deal with.

301

His eyes met hers and she held his gaze. 'I am used to being on my own, you know. It was just one more thing. You have given me so much but I had to do this alone.'

Her eyes stung with tears.

'Krista met me in a café. I didn't want to go to her home or to see Sophie until I had certain proof. She took me to the doctor who did the DNA test. She had explained everything to him so he understood the situation and said he would hurry the results through for us as much as he could. After that there was nothing I could do but wait. I could have come back but it was better to stay, even though I could not work there.'

'So what did you do?' She pictured him alone in a modest hotel room, eating alone, pacing the streets alone, waiting.

'I walked. There's a big lake in Hamburg, and I walked round it every day. I tried not to hope too much, not wanting to be disappointed. I thought of you, wishing you were with me. But getting in touch with you would only have made that worse. I was selfish, I know, but I was in a dark place full of memories, hopes and fears. I'm sorry. Don't cry.' He reached out and wiped the tears from her cheeks. 'This is a happy story.'

'I can't help it.' She blew her nose. 'I've missed you so much but at the same time I've tried to forget about you. I thought you'd changed your mind, that you'd never come back. That our summer was over.'

He laughed. 'But now I am. You should have had faith in me.'

'I know. Forgive me.'

'There's no need for forgiveness.' He leant across the table and kissed her. 'You could not have known. But I had to see this through. I had to know.'

'Of course.' She blew her nose.

'When the results came through they were positive. I have a daughter.'

She couldn't help her tears. 'I'm so happy for you. So, so happy.'

He laughed again. 'This is an English way of showing such happiness?'

'And you met her.' She was holding her breath as she wiped her cheeks. 'Tell me about her.'

'Yes. She's tall like me and has my black hair and dark eyes. But she's beautiful with the same smile of her mother's. She's a student in Hamburg, speaks perfect English, and is studying to be a doctor. Krista has given her a life I could never have given her. Krista and Ernst have two other children – two boys – so Sophie's part of a proper family.'

Caro heard the note of envy in his voice.

'I met Ernst too. He's a kind and warm man. He has gone through a lot over this even though Sophie says she will always think of him as her father first. How could she not?' He traced the grain of the table with his finger.

Caro stared at his hand, strong and workmanlike, yet capable of such gentleness.

'I've missed so much of her life, but it's not all Krista's fault.' He stopped her from interrupting with a shake of his head. 'No. You'll never know how difficult that time was we had together. We were young and she didn't know how to help me and I couldn't help myself for a long time. She did what she thought was best for our child. And perhaps it was. It was as hard for Ernst to find out the truth as it was for me. Imagine. Different of course, but he has decided to understand and forgives her. His family is too important to him to break it up. If he can forgive, I must do the same. After all, I have gained what he has lost.' A muscle moved at the side of his jaw.

Caro tried to imagine what it must be like not to be certain of the identity of the father of your own child but she understood Krista's driving force had been that maternal need for security. She put herself in the other woman's shoes, discovering the pregnancy, suspecting Damir might be the father but persuading herself that Ernst must be and over time managing to convince herself that he was. How shattering it must have been for her when the truth came out, and how frightening the implications.

'It was strange getting to know Sophie, seeing Krista again, hearing about their life together. I should have been in touch with you, I know. But so much was going round my head, so many memories.' He dashed the heel of his hand against his forehead. 'Even when I was alone, I was not alone. My family, friends and Krista were there with me.'

'Don't worry. It doesn't matter.' She took his hand again, imagining how such a revelation would be everything, allowing no room for anything else. 'All that matters is that you've found each other, and that you're here now.'

He rubbed his chin. 'Will you come to Germany?' The question was tentative. 'I'd like you to meet her. She wants to know as much about me as I do about her.'

'To Germany?' That was the last thing she'd been expecting.

He was grinning. 'Your face is – what do you say? – a picture. But of course Germany.'

If only she could stop crying. Instead she leant over and flung her arms around him, feeling his arms close round her. 'Of course I'll come with you. I'd love to meet her.'

29

For the next few days Caro was giddy with happiness. Hardly able to believe that Damir had come back to her, she moved through her life in a daze. Being together again had cemented something between them, giving their relationship a permanence that she had not felt before. More than that, she delighted in the change in him. It was as if he had shed a protective skin and came to her unencumbered now. He had found more than a daughter. Sophie had given new meaning to his life and as a result he had found himself. He had even pored over the details of the cottage with Caro, at one point apparently suggesting that he might move in when his lease with Esad was up. Caro said nothing but an explosion of happiness detonated inside her. Yet she was cautious, preferring to leave it until after she moved before they made any decisions. There was plenty of time for them to make up their minds about what they wanted to do, how they wanted to live. While he went back to a short contract job, Caro engineered things at work so she could take time off, finding substitute teachers to take her classes and someone to look after Milo.

May had listened keenly to Caro, thrilled to be trusted with the details of her daughter's life. But she was wary. 'Is it wise to have him back? Do you trust him?'

Caro pondered her questions. Of course they had been running round her head since Damir's return. Should she be angrier, more confrontational, more demanding of him? But then she remembered the person he was, what had made him that way

305

and what was important to her – ad the answer was clear. 'At first I was furious but I couldn't stay angry for long. I do trust him, Mum. Of course I'd have preferred him to have been open with me but he had his reasons. I can live with that.'

'You don't think you've forgiven him too easily?'

'No, I don't. I understand why he couldn't make contact. Besides, we're taking things slowly now, giving ourselves time to decide what we both want. If it doesn't last, so be it. But I'll enjoy it while it does.'

May cradled her chin in her hand. 'Happiness is in short enough supply so we should always take what's on offer. You never know what's round the corner.' She paused for effect. 'That's why I'm investigating a timeshare in Tenerife. It suited me there and I like the idea of sunshine every winter. So if this makes you happy...'

'Timeshare? You've never mentioned that before.'

'Well.' May leant on her stick. 'When I was out there, I met a very nice young man selling them... I gave him my address and he got in touch last week. A small flat's come up in the same block as Patricia's that's ideal for me. We could be out there at the same time as each other which would be ideal.'

Caro's heart sank as she sat back to listen, reining in her objections. Why should she stop her mother having a treat in her remaining years? She would ask to see the paperwork later.

There was one more thing she had to sort out before she could go anywhere, something that was more important to her than anything else.

On the train to London she couldn't help remembering her first meeting with Damir. Fate had brought them together, just when least expected. Fate married with Danny's fascination with the inside of handbags. Staring out of the window, she couldn't help but smile at the memory of his discovery of her phone and the photos of Damir. If only it hadn't caused such a lingering frostiness between her and Lauren.

Caro left Waterloo station by taxi, wanting to get to Lauren's as quickly as possible, unable to bear the long slow bus journey. Over the past weeks, Lauren seemed to be getting more used to the idea of having twins and was making plans so her work would be covered while she was off, and she would have adequate help.

Standing on the doorstep, Caro was nervous. She went through one more time what she had to say to get Lauren to come round at last. The door swung open. Lauren, very pregnant now, looked relaxed, her hair tied up messily, and holding Danny's hand.

'Gan gan!' He threw himself at Caro's legs.

She bent down and swung him up on to her hip and kissed his forehead. 'Hello, Danny.'

'Mum.' Lauren leant towards her and kissed her cheek. She smelled of her favourite floral perfume. 'I'm so glad you're here.'

'How are you?' Caro nodded towards Lauren's bump.

'Fine.' She ran her hand over it. 'Everything's fine. And at least at the moment I can still move around. I'm dreading them getting any bigger. I've seen pictures of other women pregnant with twins who look unimaginably enormous.'

As they went inside, Caro prepared to say her piece but as soon as they were in the hall, Lauren cut her short. 'Mum. I'm sorry. I don't want it to be like this between us. Mike says that he thinks we were unfair about Damir – too hasty to judge – and I know I was unreasonable about the house. I should have thought of you as much as about us. And it's true. I want you to be happy and I thought that's what I was doing but I can see how selfish I was being now.'

A weight lifted from Caro. It might have taken longer than she would have liked but this was all she had hoped for. 'Thank you. I'm sorry too. I know you'd like him if you got to know him.'

'But hasn't he disappeared?' Concern crossed Lauren's face.

'Amy told me he'd left you without any explanation. Just took off.'

Caro's heart sank. Would Lauren take her apology back when she heard Damir had returned? Caro couldn't bear the idea of battle lines being drawn again.

They went into the living room where Caro sat, picking up a cushion and clutching it to her stomach. She took a deep breath. 'It wasn't quite like that. I didn't know where he'd gone or why but he's explained everything and I understand now. I made more of the silence than I should have. I want to tell you what happened because I don't want there to be secrets between us any more. And I want you to understand.'

'And you believe his version of events?'

She took a deep breath. 'Lauren, I put up with a lot from you sometimes. I don't mind that because I know how much you've got on your plate, and I know you're only thinking of me, but . . . give me some credit. You have got to stop being so suspicious – not everyone has walked out of one of your courts. So just listen to me for a moment.'

Lauren looked resigned, but didn't say anything, rubbing the side of her stomach.

'Yes, I do believe him,' Caro said firmly. 'And I think you will when you hear the whole story.'

Lauren's face twisted with doubt but she sat down, with Danny climbing onto her lap for a minute before he took off and ran out of the room to find something more interesting.

'What then?'

'He's come back.' She felt the idiotic smile take its place on her face again. 'He came back a couple of days ago.'

Lauren was looking puzzled as she shifted position to get more comfortable. Should Caro explain everything? Yes, she must. That was why she was here. If she wanted Lauren to accept Damir sooner than she had Georgie, it was time to be completely straight with her. Was she asking too much of Lauren for her to accept his story? Even if so, Caro didn't want there to be secrets between them any more. That's what had caused these problems in the first place. She didn't want to make them worse. 'He had to go to Germany to find his daughter.'

'His daughter?' Lauren was back on the attack. 'He's married?'

'No, he's not.'

Lauren's face was at its most judgmental.

'But before you pass judgment, let me tell you the whole story.' This was the only way her daughter would ever start to understand.

'Sorry.' Lauren barely moved, except to lean forward a fraction, her hands resting on her stomach. Caro was encouraged to go on.

Lauren listened, and as Caro explained how she and Damir met, why she had kept him a secret, how she hadn't been able to believe the affair would last for long but then how things changed, how she fell in love, she could see her daughter softening. Lauren wasn't immune to the affairs of the heart and Caro made sure she spelled everything out. Eventually she talked about Damir's disappearance, the reasons for it and his return. 'So you see, I do love him,' she concluded. 'I don't want things to be difficult between us because of him any more. He and I are together.' Before Lauren could say anything, she went on. 'I can't really believe it myself. It's everything I thought I didn't want or need to happen. All I want is for you to be happy for me. This won't make any difference to you and me – that I can promise. Even Granny has given her seal of approval. You may agree with her that I've given in too easily, but that's not how I see it. There's nothing for me to forgive.' She stopped and took a breath, deciding not to share her mother's story. That could wait. Besides, it was May's to share, not hers. This was about her, Damir and her family, nothing more. She waited for Lauren's reaction. Should she go on?

Before she could, Lauren slid across the sofa and wrapped her in her arms. Danny ran in from the kitchen, clutching one of

Damir's dinosaurs, and jumped up to get in on the act. They separated so Lauren could pick him up then blew a raspberry on his cheek until he giggled. She looked at Caro who could see her previous hostility had disappeared. 'Oh, Mum. You know I didn't mean any harm. Honestly, I was only thinking of you. I didn't want anyone to take advantage of you or for you to be made unhappy again. I still don't. You deserve this after the way Dad treated you. Damir's just not quite what I imagined for you.'

'I know. You would have liked a more conventional option.' Paul popped into her mind, and she thought with relief of what was never going to be. 'Damir isn't that but give him a chance. That's all I'm asking. I know how lucky I am to have you two to care about me. But you don't need to worry. I'm old enough to make my own mistakes. But I don't think he's one of them. For as long as it lasts at least.' She hesitated, not wanting to jeopardise Lauren's mood. 'Will you come and meet him when we get back?'

'Back?' Lauren put Danny down and he ran out of the room.

'Yes, I'm going to Germany with him to meet Sophie, his daughter.'

'Wow! You really are serious, aren't you?' She pushed herself to her feet and went over to the vase of flowers on a side table to fiddle with the arrangement.

'I am. He's not Dad but I think one of him was enough, don't you?' She risked the joke and was glad to see Lauren's lips twitch. 'He's a kind man who cares about me. And I care about him.' She picked up the dinosaur Danny had dropped on the sofa and ran her fingers along its spine.

'And you trust him?'

'I do.' Was that going to be enough? 'And, as importantly, he trusts me.' Lauren would never know the torturous emotional journey Damir had made to reach that point or just how much that meant to them both.

'Then yes, of course we will.' Lauren stopped fiddling with the flowers and looked straight at her mother, all hostility gone.

The joy Caro felt was unconfined. This was more than a mere olive branch. But Lauren hadn't finished.

'By then we might even have our offer accepted on the new house. It's wonderful. Just what we wanted and near a great school for Danny. I can't wait for you to see it.'

'You've found one?' Caro should have known that something else was behind Lauren's change of heart. If her daughter's world was in place, she could always afford to be forgiving. But if that was what made the wheels of their world turn more smoothly then Caro would take it – a small price to pay. If a price at all. 'Where?'

'We saw it yesterday. Not too far from the other one. Not as big of course.' She couldn't resist.

'No granny flat?' Nor could Caro.

Lauren laughed. 'No flat. OK, that probably wasn't one of my finest ideas. I should have talked to you. But this one is much better for us. And it's got a fantastic garden. Big enough for Danny and the twins to run around at least.' She stroked her hand over her bump.

'So it's all worked out.'

'And Treetops?'

'The sale's going through, and I've found a perfect place for myself in a village not far away. You'll have to come round to see it too. I hope you'll love it.'

'Everything's changing. I've never been able to imagine you anywhere but Treetops but I'm beginning to now. Then we've got the twins, a new house and Amy and Jason getting married next year. And Dad says he's stepping back and going to be a hands-on dad.'

'I'll believe that when I see it.' Caro still couldn't put Chris and childcare in the same bracket. Although he had seemed serious about his change of role, she couldn't help wondering whether he would be able to stick to it. But if he just did more than he did with Lauren and Amy at that age, Georgie would be lucky.

They spent the rest of the morning on Lauren's laptop, examining their new houses in minute detail, looking at the areas on Google Maps and checking out all the local amenities. After lunch and a walk to the ducks with Danny so Lauren could have a rest, Caro caught the bus back to Waterloo. In this direction she was content to sit for the length of the journey, relishing the renewed closeness with her daughter, feeling that for the first time everything was possible, that she had a future in which she would not be taken for granted and through which she would find her own way.

When she got home, Damir was still at work. Only two days until Hamburg. Perhaps she should think about packing. Excited but nervous about the journey ahead, Caro pulled her suitcase down from the top of the wardrobe and opened it. Inside was a postcard of Les Gets she had never sent and a ticket stub from the télécabine des Chavannes. She took them and put them inside the box Damir had made for her that she kept on the chest of drawers. Memories.

One by one, she took from her wardrobe the clothes she might need in Germany and lay them on the bed. She held up the olive-green shirtdress that Chris had once encouraged her to buy – 'So practical and that green suits you'. She had worn it ever since but suddenly it didn't suit her any more. She put it aside for charity and pulled out the bright tops and couple of dresses that, encouraged by Fran, she had bought more recently. The brighter colours made her feel alive, good about herself.

Folding the ones she wanted and putting them in the case, she considered how far she had come in one year. At the beginning of it, she would never have imagined how much she would have changed thanks to a chance meeting on a train. She and Damir had been together for longer than six months, and who knew what the future held for them.

But for now, they were setting out on a journey together. For now. Whatever the future, she was confident she would deal with it. Meeting him had transformed her life in many ways, bringing her out of her shell and giving her confidence, leading towards a balance that hadn't existed before. He had taught her that age really was just a number and that there was still time for new experiences. He had opened her up to the possibilities there still were for her. In future, she would make her own life choices, not simply do what she felt was expected of her.

She looked at her shoes, debating which ones to take. The prospect of meeting Sophie made her nervous but that was a small thing. To Damir, his daughter meant everything and if, after all he'd been through, he was going to make a family of his own, she wanted to help him and perhaps even be part of it. Maybe he really would move on in the end – just as he once said he always did. If he did, then she would manage. She had her family, her cottage, her painting and her girls – but more than that, she had hope and optimism about the future. As importantly, she was learning to make the most of the present. It was no longer something simply to be got through but something to be relished. She picked up the red heels and dropped them in the case. Life was looking good.

The door slammed downstairs.

He was home.

Acknowledgements

So many people have helped me with this novel. First I must thank Faruk Begić. In my creation of Damir, I have drawn on some of his experiences that so he generously shared with me. The two men are by no means the same people. I also read several accounts of the Bosnian war and its aftermath. Chief among them were *The Bosnia List* by Kenan Trebinčević and Susan Shapiro (Penguin), *The War is Dead: Long Live the War* by Ed Vulliamy (Vintage), *Beseiged* by Barbara Demick and *In Harm's Way* by Martin Bell (Icon). It goes without saying that any mistakes are entirely my own.

I also want to thank my agent Clare Alexander, who always makes time to discuss even the smallest problem as well as Harriet Bourton and her fantastic team at Orion, including Clare Hey, Elaine Egan, Katie Seaman and Jennifer Breslin. Thanks are also due to Gillian Stern and Elizabeth Buchan whose input has been invaluable.

And of course to Robin and my family and friends who have all been so supportive, as always.